About the author

Patrick Lennon grew up in Cambridge and has lived
in Thailand, Italy, France and Mexico. Today he
splits his time between his young family, his writing
and running his own business. Visit his website at
www.patrick-lennon.com.

PATRICK LENNON

Corn Dolls

HODDER

Copyright © 2006 by Patrick Lennon

First published in 2006 by Hodder & Stoughton
A division of Hodder Headline

This paperback edition published in 2007

The right of Patrick Lennon to be identified as the Author
of the Work has been asserted by him in accordance with
the Copyright, Designs and Patents Act 1988.

A Hodder paperback

1

A CIP catalogue record for this title
is available from the British Library

ISBN 978-0-340-89838-3

Typeset in Plantin by Hewer Text UK Ltd, Edinburgh
Printed and bound by Mackays of Chatham Ltd, Chatham, Kent

Hodder Headline's policy is to use papers that are natural, renewable
and recyclable products and made from wood grown in sustainable
forests. The logging and manufacturing processes are expected to
conform to the environmental regulations of the country of origin.

Hodder & Stoughton Ltd
A division of Hodder Headline
338 Euston Road
London NW1 3BH

The boy was tall, with almond-shaped eyes.

In summer, his school had a tour of a hangar-shaped building named The Hall of Soviet Achievement. The young comrades saw a cosmonaut's spacesuit, a plan for new housing, and a row of farm tractors produced by the machinery factory in their city. Then the group moved on to view the statistics for wheat production.

The boy held back from the others, preferring to stay with the tractors. He had a reason. She was the leader of the Socialist Girls' Pioneers, and she was three years older than him.

The hangar was warm with the grainy heat of Russian summer, dust in the air between them. She put a finger to his lips and smiled. She loosened his collar. It was quiet, just his heart thumping. He held her against the huge rubber wheel of a Soviet tractor, and put his hands around her waist. There was the tang of the new tyre, engine oil, the clean scent of her hair.

He thought: my life will be good.

Monday Morning

Tom Fletcher loosened his tie. His neck felt damp, due partly to the summer heat. He watched the photographer take another shot, using flash despite the sunlight streaming through glass panels in the roof. The photographer stood back and turned to him.

'Is that the worst you've seen?'

Fletcher nodded. In eight years with the Cambridge police, it was the nastiest death he'd encountered. He brushed a fly away from his face.

He was standing in a large hangar-type building used as a showroom for farm machinery. In front of him was a line of yellow tape set up by the accident investigators, then a half-circle of tractors for sale. The pairs of headlamps all seemed to be watching something.

There was a different machine in the centre of the group. It was a heavy-duty mechanical shredder, designed for cutting up tree branches – really just a set of blades inside a chute that a man could fit into. A man had. A pair of legs was projecting from it, the feet twisted at unnatural angles. Fletcher noticed something puzzling.

The shoes. He studied the shoes.

The legs belonged to a young guy named Jake Skerrit, aged twenty-two and fresh out of university. Jake had worked as a management trainee for Breakman Machinery, a farm equipment dealer in the fenland north of Cambridge. The staff all agreed that Jake was a hard worker who did paperwork in the depot on Sunday nights. They added that he liked fooling around with dangerous machines. Today being Monday, his corpse had been found by the security man who unlocked the building in the morning.

The body wasn't completely shredded, because a safety system had kicked in when the blades finally reached his shoulders. So the face, wedged up against the steel intake, was still partially intact – but the blades had destroyed his arms and taken a big chunk from the side of his skull. The floor on the other side of the chute, where the machine would normally spit out its wood chips, was spattered with human debris: hair, bits of bone, two complete fingers, a shirt cuff and something that looked to Fletcher like an earlobe. Under the shredder itself, a circle of blood was in the final stage of thickening, like road tar. The flies were really gathering.

Fletcher was fascinated by Jake's shoes.

He guessed the Health and Safety people would try to prosecute, because the Breakman staff habitually left machines with keys in the ignition. Still, the death seemed like a genuine accident – one to add to the sixty other deaths involving farm machinery that happen each year in Britain. A police surgeon had attended as a formality, and a post-mortem was booked. Fletcher had other cases pending, and maybe he should have left this alone – maybe his presence should have been just another formality – but the shoes wouldn't let him.

He watched as the investigators in their white paper suits rolled up the tape, and the photographer began packing away his kit. Two morose-looking individuals came into the hangar, men known to the police as the Glum Reapers: specialised operatives from an undertaker in Cambridge. One was carrying a body bag, and the other was swinging a shovel.

Fletcher turned away, still thinking about the shoes. He glanced up at the CCTV camera bolted to the wall, perfectly placed to record the death, its red light blinking.

Breakman Machinery had closed for the day, and the staff had been interviewed and sent home, white-faced. The only employee still present was waiting in the security office, one of the simple rooms along the front of the hangar. Fletcher watched him for a second through the glass door panel.

He was a florid, overweight man in his sixties, wearing a checked sports jacket. He was sitting hunched over, with one hand caressing his bald forehead and the other hand dangling a cigarette. He was talking to himself and shaking his head. Fletcher opened the door slightly, and the man didn't notice. He was saying, repeatedly, 'Too bloody close.'

The room was small, with breeze-block walls painted white. It contained three stacking chairs, a basic desk and a steel cupboard. When Fletcher opened the door fully, there was a smell of whisky that made him wince. It was a peculiarity of his: he found the smell of alcohol painful. He sat on one of the chairs, far enough away to avoid the man's breath, and he said, 'I'm Detective Inspector Tom Fletcher of the Cambridge police. I understand you found the body.'

'Yes – I'm Ron Teversham, the security. More of a caretaker, really. I just lock up and open up.'

Two unusual things about this security man. First, he wanted to downgrade his own importance. And second, he'd been crying.

'You're very upset, Ron.'

'It's the shock of seeing it. Finding him like that, the state of him.'

'How well did you know him?'

'First-name terms. That's the job.'

'Why do you think he did it? Why start up a dangerous machine?'

Ron tried to laugh. 'Jake loved machines, that was his problem. He was always playing around with them.'

'Just now you were saying he was too bloody close.'

Ron jerked his face up. For a moment, his red eyes filled with tears again.

'To the machine. Too close to the shredder, it drags you in.'

'Tell me about him. Was he a wealthy young man?'

'Wealthy? You're joking. He had debts and stuff, loans and overdrafts.' Teversham stopped himself suddenly. 'Why are you asking? It was a bloody accident. Everyone knows, he was fooling around,'

'What kind of shoes did he wear?'

'Shoes? Just old trainers, he was skint.' Ron's eyes slid over to the hangar, where the Glum Reapers were making long scrapes that echoed around the building. 'It was an accident, right?'

'Nothing to suggest otherwise. But we'll know in a minute.'

'How will we?'

'We'll look at the CCTV.'

Teversham tried to laugh again. He turned and opened the steel cupboard. The recording system consisted of a ten-year-old VCR wired into an even older TV. The slot of the recorder gaped empty, and Teversham put his yellow fingers inside it as he said, 'There isn't always a cassette in there. Sometimes yes, sometimes no.'

'Last night?'

'No. I didn't put one in on Friday. Look, if they sack me, I'm stuffed.'

Fletcher watched him for a while, wondering if he really was that incompetent. Then he said, 'Ron, why isn't the manager *here*? There's been a death on the premises.'

'Breakman? He's away on a freebie. Caterpillar took all the dealers to Jersey to show them a new tractor. Paid for the hotel and everything, Breakman even took his wife. Can you believe that? Money to piss away and they still get free weekends.' That finally made Ron laugh: a violent sound that drowned out the scraping from the hangar. He threw his cigarette on the cement floor and opened the packet for another. 'Smoke?' He offered. 'No? Stay in shape, use the gym? You look like it. That what the birds like these days?' He lit his fag with unsteady hands. 'I've phoned the Breakmans already. First plane they can get back on is tomorrow morning.'

'What are their names?'

'He's Crispin Breakman. She's Olga. Married four months, isn't that nice?' Ron stopped himself again, and his eyes moved back to the hangar. 'Please, can I go? It was just an accident.'

Fletcher watched him a little while longer.

*

The huge machinery factory in the city of Stavropol was called the Niva Works. Between it and the workers' accommodation there was a water reservoir. In winter, when the temperature dropped to minus thirty, it froze into a block of ice that the kids could slide across. In summer they used it for swimming, and diving off the concrete walls.

The boy grew up that summer, before the winter when his life changed. He began to believe in himself. He'd kissed the leader of the Socialist Girls' Pioneers. He could swim across the reservoir and back. He could somersault off the embankment.

Once, while he was treading water getting his breath, the best friend of the leader of the Socialist Girls' Pioneers swam slowly past him. She was gymnastics champion of the Stavropol schools, and her hair trailed slick on the glare of the water. He felt her foot brush the base of his spine, and when he turned he caught the flash in her violet eyes, half-closed in the sun.

He thought, my whole life will be like this. It's going to get better and better.

He was eleven years old.

∗

Jake Skerrit's office was another white-painted space: five metres square, lit by a small window and a strip light, clean and neat. Jake's files along one wall, his desk against the other. The desk held a terminal, a framed degree certificate from Anglia Polytechnic University, and a small pile of paperwork.

The scraping noises from the hangar stopped completely. In the silence, Fletcher turned the papers over. He found invoices and schedules of machinery deliveries. He opened the drawer of the cheap desk. He found more invoices and oddments of stationery. There was a box of matches with the name of some local eating place. Then, right at the back, a small book.

Teach Yourself Russian.

Monday Afternoon

Fletcher waited in the sunshine outside the empty depot, with his suit jacket slung over one shoulder, watching the colossal fenland sky. Clouds the size of small countries were stacked in layers against the blue. In a minute, an unmarked Vectra pulled up. He folded his jacket and got in.

Detective Sergeant Sal Moresby was a few years younger than him, still in her late twenties. He'd been with her when she made her first arrest as a detective, and the memory always made him smile: the suspect, a strange little man who later became a useful informant, peering at her in admiration.

You know what, Miss Moresby. You got the face of a pre-Raphaelite beauty.

The little crook was right. She had sleek brunette hair tied back against an oval face, and brown eyes which she widened in question now, revving the engine.

'Suspicious circumstances?' She never called him *sir* – his idea.

'Puzzling circumstances. No CCTV tape for the whole weekend. The security man says he's just a caretaker, starts drinking before lunch.'

'What else?'

'The dead man's shoes.'

'His shoes?'

'They looked very, very expensive. Superb leather, hand-stitched. Plus they were brand new, I could see the logo on the sole. Then the security man told me Jake was a penniless graduate.'

'Maybe that's why he was penniless: putting fancy shoes on his credit card.'

'Maybe, but if I had a new pair of hand-stitched shoes I wouldn't wear them to work in a tractor depot on a Sunday night. I certainly wouldn't wear them to fool around with dangerous machinery.'

'You know something else unusual? I've just been to Jake Skerrit's home address. It's a big house on the edge of the village near here, a place called Thinbeach.' Sal tapped Fletcher on the arm. 'There was nobody home, but now I realise I've seen that address somewhere else today. It's the same address as the manager of the depot.'

'The same as Crispin Breakman?'

'Correct. Jake presumably lived with his boss.'

'And consequently with his boss's new wife. She's called Olga. It's puzzling.' Fletcher glanced at his watch. 'And now I need some lunch.'

'The sight of the body hasn't affected your appetite?'

'That's nature. You see death, your body says *feed*. And I found this in Jake's desk.'

He held up the box of matches, inside a plastic wallet.

> *The Bride at Thinbeach*
> *Lunch a Speciality*
> *Crab, Lobster, Eel*

He said, 'I'm buying.'

Thinbeach was on the river Cam, in the open farmland
between Cambridge and Ely, accessible only by roads
with grass sprouting through the Tarmac.

Sal drove quickly. In one field, the tower of a ruined
church stood up against the clouds, surrounded by
ripe wheat with poppies among the stalks. Fletcher put
down the window and breathed in the dusty smell of
summer in the fens. At that point the landscape
changed into an expanse of tunnels made from white
polythene stretched on frames, their translucent ridges
snaking away on either side: intensive farming for
summer fruit. There was no scent here, just the glare
of plastic in the sun.

Then they left the tunnels behind and drove through
an area of preserved fenland – a tangle of hawthorn,
willow, bulrushes and ferns – then down an incline
between two water meadows where the grass looked
fresh even in the heat. That set the tone for the village
itself.

The *Welcome To Thinbeach* sign was followed by a
sign for *Kill Your Speed* and another saying *Neighbourhood Watch*, then another sign naming a twin town in
Normandy.

Thinbeach was tiny but smart: one main street called
the Shamblings, starting with an elegant traffic-calm-

ing chicane, lined on either side with old houses built in honey-coloured stone, each with a cottage garden at the front. One had been adapted as a village shop – The Fen Deli – with a window displaying bags of ground coffee that Fletcher thought he could savour as Sal slowed down to a crawl.

The few people he noticed on the pavement looked affluent and self-assured. When he asked about The Bride, a friendly man pointed the way to the far end of the Shamblings.

The street narrowed, and the stone houses gave way to higher timber-framed buildings with black wooden ribs, the plaster between them painted deep shades of ochre. The engine echoed back from the houses on either side, until at the end Sal just managed to squeeze the car through. They came to a dead end.

It was a high grassy mound, blocking off any view, curving away on both sides to shield something beyond. On the left was a magnificent old house, part timber and part stone, set in a cottage garden, one gable built into the earth embankment itself.

To the right was a building of similar age: The Bride. It was the village pub, with a garden that appeared to run through a gap in the grass embankment to reach whatever was on the other side.

Sal turned off the engine.

'My body says *feed*, too.'

Fletcher hesitated in the doorway, but the pub didn't have that beery smell he found sickening. The place had a scrubbed wooden floor, unblemished tables, and a long brick wall holding a selection of things inside wooden frames that Sal was already studying. He stepped closer and saw they were small dolls – like children's toys – lovingly made from twisted corn stalks, dressed in scraps of bright silk, each one set inside a frame and mounted on the wall. In the middle was a printed information panel:

The Thinbeach Wedding

Thinbeach is one of the few communities in England which preserves a festival going back to ancient times.

On a summer's day each year, a corn doll, known as the Thinbeach Bride, is carried along the Shamblings to the banks of the River Cam, and there she is thrown into the water. Tradition says that the Thinbeach Bride sacrifices her own fragile body for the success of the local harvest.

This festival, known as the Thinbeach Wedding, is thought to originate from the time of the Norman invasion of the Fens in AD 1067.

Souvenir postcards are available behind the bar.

'How very quaint,' Sal said, walking to the counter.

Fletcher went over to the garden door. In passing, he caught the eye of the barmaid, a woman aged around thirty with a T-shirt saying *REBEL*. He logged her glance in his mind: it said, *I want to talk* – as clearly as the word over her chest.

Outside, he walked to the end of the garden, where it sloped down towards the gap in the mound. The walls of turf rose fifteen feet on either side, presumably some ancient defensive earthwork.

Beyond the gap, he found a wide expanse of water: oval-shaped, about three hundred metres wide, fringed with reeds. On the left bank, two tributary rivers entered, and on the right they fed into the River Cam itself as it passed in a channel of slick green water. A heron flapped away against the bright clouds. On the horizon, the towers of Ely cathedral loomed up above the fields.

'That's Thinbeach Pool,' a voice said behind him. He turned and found the barmaid collecting empty glasses, her excuse for coming out. 'You should try the crab – it was alive this morning.'

'Sounds perfect. This is where the festival thing happens?'

'The Wedding, yes.' There was still that look in her eye. 'You're the police, aren't you? We've all heard about Jake Skerrit.'

He introduced himself. She was a slim woman, with the glossy brown hair and strong jaw typical of the fens, standing in a way that showed off her hips. In the gap between her T-shirt and her jeans, a gold stud flashed in the sun. He glanced at her slogan.

'Miss Rebel?'

'I'm Debbie. Did – did Jake suffer?'

'It must have been very quick.'

Debbie sat at a table, and looked out over the water. Fletcher took a seat opposite and waited.

'Poor Jake,' she said. 'He didn't have much common sense. He used to drink in here sometimes, but he was always skint.'

'Did you ever notice his shoes?'

'His shoes? He always wore filthy trainers. He probably only had one pair.'

'You never tried it yourself?'

'What's that?'

'University.'

'I've tried a few things, Inspector. Never the weird
stuff.'

'Debbie, can you tell me more about Jake? His living
arrangements? I'm off duty.'

Debbie leaned forward, a gold necklace swinging
free, and her eyes shining.

'I don't spread rumours, Inspector.'

'Call me Tom.'

Behind her, he saw Sal emerge from the pub with
orange juices. Sal read the situation and sat at a
different table, within earshot, while Debbie began.

'Living arrangements?' She cupped her powerful
chin in her hand and narrowed her eyes. 'Crispin's
forty-five. He's a bit chubby and he's going grey.
Olga's not even twenty-five, she looks like a model.
What does that tell you?'

'Crispin was very lucky.'

'More than that, Tom. He got her by mail order.
She's a mail-order bride.'

Sal materialised at the table and leaned forward to
face Debbie. Fletcher leaned back.

'And what exactly,' Sal asked, 'is a mail-order bride?'

*

*The workers' accommodation was built in three blocks,
each block eight apartments high and twenty apartments*

wide, arranged around a square of grass crossed with pathways. The grass contained a monument to Soviet labour, and a playground with climbing frames shaped like sputniks, locomotives – and, of course, tractors.

The open side of the grass led down to the reservoir and then the Niva tractor works. In the mornings, the chimneys smoked against the sunrise as the workers filed down along the pathways.

Niva was a good place to work, a place to be proud of. It had meeting rooms with life-size pictures of President Brezhnev, plus canteens, a medical clinic, a library, and a nursery. Rising above everything were the two tractor production halls themselves, each one a square kilometre in area.

Kids grew up in the accommodation. They swung on the sputniks and raced on the grass. They attended city school 302, where the kids from Niva families felt they were special, different from the rest.

One boy knew he was special, even among the Niva kids. He'd kissed the leader of the Girls' Socialist Pioneers – and her best friend, the star gymnast, had put a pair of athletic hands around him under the glinting water of the reservoir.

His name was Ivan.

*

Debbie looked from Fletcher to Sal.

'Crispin's a nice guy, but he's got zero personality. We all thought he'd never get married, even though he's loaded. You know why Jake was lodging with him? Crispin gave him a room because he felt lonely in that

big house, he wanted some company. Anyway, back in
March, Crispin went away for three weeks. Turns out
he went to Moscow, he plucked up the nerve to go
through a marriage agency. They found him a Russian
wife and he brought her back here in April. She's
foreign but she's nice – you know what I mean?'
Debbie refocused on Fletcher. 'But you see, Jake
was still lodging in the house. A nice-looking boy,
almost her age. Only natural. Crab it is.'

Debbie gathered more glasses, the sun glinting on
her piercing. She went through to the bar, giving
Fletcher one last glance.

Sal said, 'You think Crispin really is in Jersey?'

'I checked. He's booked on the early flight back to
Stansted tomorrow.'

They spread butter on slices of warm bread. They ate
the crab, breaking open the armour, digging into the
flesh, watching gulls swoop over the surface of Thinbeach Pool and the pale lips of fish puckering the dark
water for scraps.

She said, 'Nice quiet place.'

'Yes, it is.' He looked at his phone: reception on the
civilian network was irregular, sometimes non-existent.
He threw his last scrap to a gull that grabbed it and
wheeled away. 'I just wonder what Olga thinks of it.'

Sal Moresby drove them back to Cambridge, through
the belt of old fenland around Thinbeach, where
rushes leaned under the high afternoon clouds. Sal
liked the landscape here: butterflies in the hedges, and

hawthorns close to the ground, tangled in honeysuckle. In the passenger seat, Tom Fletcher was absorbed in his own thoughts. She liked the silence. She liked Tom Fletcher as well, after two years as his sergeant.

The end of her first year, they went to make an arrest at a house near Swavesey. The man had stood in the doorway smiling at her, then reached beside the door and brought up a crossbow, aiming it at her chest. The tip of the bolt trembled for a second. Then Fletcher stepped in front of her, put his hand on the weapon and pushed it to one side.

She's with me.

She guessed that was the kind of approach that had won him a police bravery medal – something his peer group spoke about but he himself never referred to.

Now Sal drove the local road between the fields of polythene tunnels stretching out on either side, like a lunar settlement, then past the ruined church, and into the grain fields stretching away without hedges, only electricity pylons striding into the distance.

She took the car onto the Cambridge road and accelerated, the needle touching eighty. There was no rush, this was just the way she drove.

She asked, 'So it's an accidental death?'

He turned to give her his attention, and she glanced across. He had a big, honest face, with a jaw that always had a shadow, and blue eyes under his fringe – a boy's haircut. As always, he was wearing a button-down shirt and a blue suit, the jacket folded in his lap.

He said, 'Jake was twenty-two, but he lived with his boss in a village where the highlight of the year is a straw doll festival. He was learning Russian, and his boss's young wife is a mail-order bride. He was totally broke, but he wore expensive new shoes to the depot on a Sunday night. What do *you* think?'

'I think we'd better come back in the morning.'

'I think you're right.'

★

Their apartment was on the top floor of the accommodation, with a good view of the Niva Works and the plateau of Russia beyond, a green and brown mass running straight to the horizon.

During that last summer, Ivan Gorensky would sit at the table between six and seven p.m., with the smell of soup from the stove filling the air. That was the time he spent with his father.

His father was a senior engineer at the Niva tractor works, a highly skilled and respected worker. Ivan liked to ask his father questions about machines: how engines worked, how aeroplanes flew, why ships didn't sink. His father had an engineer's steel pencil, and used it to draw diagrams on scrap paper, and for Ivan the world would come down to this table, his father's explanations, the simple diagrams he was drawing. The boy felt that the world was a rational place, it could be explained and improved. Sometimes he would look at his father and just want to be like him.

That was how summer ended. Then, some mornings, there was frost on the windows.

Monday Night

Sal Moresby had a heavy case-load, and the hours spent in Thinbeach meant that she worked through until almost sunset. Off duty found her standing on the balcony of the flat she shared with her boyfriend, on the top floor of a modern building looking over the River Cam on Midsummer Common. It was a fine evening, the sun just going down, and the river still busy with skiffs and pleasure boats.

In the flat behind her, she heard the clink of glass as her boyfriend helped himself to another beer from the fridge. She glanced around. The room was darkened, just the glow of the computer screen as he flicked through sites on the Internet.

She didn't want to be here. The flat was too dark, and the balcony was too small. She wanted to be achieving something. She wanted to be out in fenland with Tom Fletcher.

Fletcher finished work just after Sal. Off duty found him standing for a moment outside Parkside police station, breathing in the dusk, the Union Jack above the University Arms Hotel rippling against the mauve sky, the lamps in the centre of Parker's Piece blurry with midges.

Beyond that was the Cambridge that was famous from guidebooks: the colleges, the churches and the punts on the Cam along the Backs – and his own apartment too, with its view of the lead and slate rooftops. Tom Fletcher turned and walked the opposite way.

There are two sides to any city.

He crossed East Road, where the homeless men were gathering outside the Methodist hostel, their faces raised to the streetlamps. He walked along Mill Road, where moths were circling the storefront lights, lads on each corner in hooded tops flicking their heads to make their gold chains rattle. In a while, he came to the road bridge over the railway yards, a place known as Electric Mile: an expanse of steel tracks under a web of overhead wires shivering and sometimes sparking in the breeze. He stopped and watched a local train roll by underneath, its connections flashing, carriage lights blinking on and off, trailing a smell of static. When it passed, the empty rail lines lay glinting in the early night, a field of steel and wires running north and south.

He walked over the bridge and turned into a system of narrow streets with low terraced houses overshadowed by the girders of the yards. Another train went past, and the vibration came up through the pavement. At the end of an alley where a steel gate led onto the tracks themselves, he found the house he wanted. He knocked on the door that he couldn't leave alone.

Tuesday Morning

Fletcher stopped shaving when the phone rang. He'd had some strange dreams: flies, a dead man's shoes, a small doll woven from straw, someone saying *She's Russian*. Then electric wires touching, and a door opening.

He answered the phone.

He finished getting dressed: a fresh blue suit, grey button-down shirt, linen tie. The percolator was bubbling, but he ignored it. His mind was racing.

He'd just had the news that an old Ford Sierra had been found crashed on the road outside Thinbeach. The driver had been thrown through the windscreen and killed. A man named Ron Teversham, security guard.

More of a caretaker, really. I just lock up and open up.

* * *

Some mornings during that last summer, Ivan would lie in the sun with his friends on the embankment above the reservoir and watch the railway lines leading out of the Niva factory. They watched the locomotives pulling flat trailers loaded with tractors come rumbling out of the works and pick up speed, clattering away from Stavropol, heading west.

'Where do you think they're going, Ivan Gorensky?'

Ivan's best friend loved thinking about the world outside Stavropol. He even knew some English: Coca Cola and Ford, hello and goodbye.

Ivan squinted into the distance, through the fumes of the locomotives.

'My father says they go all over the Soviet Republics. And there are other countries. There's Poland, and there's the German Democratic Republic. There's one called Cuba, where it's hot. Lots of countries want our tractors.'

The smoke hung against the plateau as the trailers became smaller on the plain, too far for their rattling to be heard, and then vanished.

'Where else are they going, Ivan Gorensky?'

★

The sky was perfectly blue, just a few clouds layering the horizon beyond the cathedral. The road through the fields into Thinbeach had one single bend, and this was blocked off by a patrol car, its blue lights flashing mutely in the sunshine. Behind that, the Road Traffic Accident investigators were already managing the scene, assessing angles and distances, and the sergeant gave him a concise summary. Fletcher listened, then asked, 'Suspicions?'

'No, sir. You can smell it.'

Fletcher walked down to the car. The Sierra had left the road on the bend, clipped the chevron road sign, and slammed into the base of a willow tree. Now the willow fronds were brushing across its roof as if checking for signs of life.

There weren't any. Teversham hadn't been wearing a seat belt, perhaps because of his girth. His momentum had exploded the windscreen and left his body over the crumpled bonnet, feet tangled up in the steering and his head split against the willow trunk itself, where a red smear was thickening in the light.

Fletcher leaned closer and looked at him. His thinning hair was studded with fragments of windscreen glass that reflected the patrol car lights. There was the smell of oil from the wrecked engine, but above that a reek of whisky which made him grimace.

He looked around the car: the doors dented and scratched, the back bumper full of old scars. He looked inside the glove compartment and found a hip flask that was almost empty. He opened the boot and found a long plastic box carefully lashed to the floor. He clicked open the catches and raised the lid. It contained a two-piece pool cue, engraved with the initials RT.

He walked back to the road. The willow was still scraping on the car roof behind him.

The uniformed police were beginning to clear away their equipment, discussing breakfast. The photographer was the same man as yesterday, glancing at Fletcher as he packed up his cameras.

'Must be contagious.'

Fletcher didn't answer. Just as the patrol car moved aside to let the undertaker's vehicle through, Sal Moresby drove up. She stopped the Vectra with a scrape of tyres, and got out. She was wearing baseball boots, black jeans and a khaki shirt. She'd left her hair loose, and she'd signed out an Airwave handset: a device normally used by uniformed police, like an oversized mobile phone.

The Airwave network was exclusive to emergency services, its network of masts guaranteeing perfect reception and giving encrypted access to the databases of the modern state. She showed him the screen: Ron Teversham's entry on the Police National Computer. Two convictions for drunk driving in the last ten years, and a home address in a place called Wittris – the roughest of the fenland towns.

Fletcher noticed things dropping out of the willow branches and settling on the wrecked car: small writhing insects – dozens gathering on the roof, then hundreds more on the red smear that Teversham's skull had left on the tree, until the brain fluid was a mass of squirming life.

'Airborne weevils,' Sal observed. 'They live for two days, then their bodies are food for birds. Are his shoes acceptable?'

Fletcher nodded. 'The shoes are fine. RTA guys estimate he was doing at least seventy. A sharp bend, bald tyres, reactions slowed by alcohol. Time of death to be established, probably before midnight. No indication of other vehicles being involved, no tyre marks or broken stuff on the Tarmac. So, by a tragic freak, two employees of Crispin Breakman have had fatal accidents in the last thirty-six hours.'

Sal brushed some of the insects from her sleeve. She held his gaze with her wide brown eyes, her hair framing her face.

'And we buy that, do we?'

Fletcher weighed mentally his existing workload. He took a last look at the insects writhing in the red smear on the willow trunk. He said, 'Ron didn't like the Breakman couple. Let's go and give them the news.'

Fen Lodge was the perfect home for a successful tractor dealer. It was a converted barn at the end of its own lane outside the village, with a roof of reclaimed tiles, snug little windows and black-varnished timber walls, standing in a gravel courtyard surrounded by ornate steel railings, his and hers Mercedes sparkling in the sun. It was the kind of set-up that *would* make Ron Teversham jealous.

Fletcher was in his own car today, an old Audi hatchback. He followed Sal's unmarked car onto the gravel. It was a beautiful summer morning: even the stones looked washed and tumbled.

The door opened.

'Crispin Breakman? We're the police.'

'Oh, Christ. It's about the Health and Safety?'

'Not exactly.'

Crispin looked older than forty-five, his shoulders rather stooped as he led his visitors into a large semi-dark room with bare brick walls and a fireplace stacked with logs. He raised one of the blinds, and they all sat on comfortable leather chairs.

The light emphasised that Crispin was tired and miserable. Just right for a man whose lodger has died in a shredder. He had a forgettable face, curly hair greying on top, eyes that moved around. He was wearing a tailored office suit that seemed to belong on someone

more dynamic. He said, 'We've only just got back from
Jersey –'

'On the Stansted flight. I know.'

'Right. And I've got to go into the depot now. My
wife's still resting. Jake's death has really upset her,
she's very sensitive.'

'We'd like to speak to her later,' Fletcher said. Then
he gave Crispin the news about Ron Teversham.
Crispin closed his eyes and listened. When he opened
them again, he said something that made Fletcher
reconsider his entire case-load.

'Jake and Teversham. The odd couple.'

'You mean, they were friends?'

'Right from the start, they struck up this odd sort of
friendship. But there's nothing funny about their
deaths, is there?'

'Funny?'

'Suspicious.' Crispin looked from Fletcher to Sal. 'Is
there? The Health and Safety thing's bad enough. I
can't believe the guys leave keys in the machines. I've
got my solicitor on it already.'

Sal said, 'Tell us about Jake.'

'Jake? He was such a nice, normal kid. We got him
cheap, obviously. He'd come out of uni last year, and
he was bloody desperate. He had mates with degrees
working in Pizza Hut. But he loved machinery, just
loved it. His CV came on my desk and I gave him the
office boy's job, called it management trainee. That
was before Christmas.'

'And he became friendly with Teversham?'

'They were both a bit sad and lonely. They used to

stay late at the office, chatting, or they'd go drinking together. Teversham was always looking for someone to talk to.'

'Teversham mentioned Jake was in debt,' Fletcher said.

'Up to his neck, poor sod. I reckon at least eighteen grand in student loans.'

Fletcher pictured those creamy calf-hide shoes.

'Was he a big spender?'

'Jake? No way. He had spreadsheets of how much he could spend on this or that, how much he could repay. He tried to wear a suit to work, but it was always the same one.' Crispin adjusted his own neat cuffs. 'When he started with us, he was lodging in Cambridge, could hardly afford the rent. He was a good worker, put in long hours, so in January I let him have a room here, the little granny flat downstairs. That's before I married Olga, obviously.'

'Crispin,' Sal said, 'I'm not prying, but—'

'But Olga, yeah? I know what they're saying in Thinbeach. Crispin's mail-order bride. I'm old enough to be her father.'

'I was just wondering how you met.'

Crispin seemed glad to talk about it, regarded it as a big achievement.

'Last year, I got a mailshot from an agency offering introductions to Russian women, *Steppes to Love*. I thought, why not? More and more guys are doing it. Anyway, their service was first-class. They arranged for me to fly out there and meet some prospective partners.'

'You went to Russia?'

Crispin pushed out his chest and grinned.

'Damn right. What a country. On the one hand, outside the cities, you've got the best farming land I've ever seen. The soil is like ours, the black silty stuff. On the other hand, you've got desperate poverty, crime out of control. Gangs of crooks running the place. But the agency were great. They introduced me to Olga. I knew she didn't belong there, with all that. She was like a shining light.'

'So you got married,' Fletcher said.

Crispin lit a cigarette. He was talking to himself now, not to two police officers interested in the death of a management trainee.

'We came back here in April – remember how warm it was? We had walks in the old fen. She likes taking pictures of landscapes.' Crispin suddenly put out his cigarette. 'This isn't about me and Olga. You were asking about Jake.'

In fact, Fletcher was thinking about Olga, about how jealous she could make a man. Jealous enough to kill?

'How did Olga get on with Jake?' he asked.

Crispin shrugged. 'They hardly spoke. He kept to himself in the granny flat.' His face clouded. 'What do you think happened to Jake?'

'What do *you* think? Why on earth would he start up a dangerous machine?'

'He loved machines. He was always climbing on them, fooling around. He used to sit in the yard at lunchtime and sketch them, he could really draw. He was pretty eccentric, to be honest.'

'Had anything changed recently? Had he come into money?'

'That was all he ever wanted, to come into money. But no, he was totally broke.'

'When did you last see him?'

'About midday on Friday, in the office. Then I left for Jersey. You want to check? There were two hundred people at the Caterpillar show – plus Olga.'

Fletcher nodded. 'You stayed at the St Michel hotel.' Crispin swallowed, nodded too. 'And when did you last see Ron Teversham?'

'Friday, I suppose.'

'What was his background?'

'He was with us maybe ten years. Before that, other security stuff, I think. He was cheap too, obviously. That's something else in common with Jake.'

'Tell me about the CCTV system at the depot.'

Crispin looked from Fletcher to Sal, horrified. 'It wasn't *working*, was it? It didn't record Jake?'

'It should have, that's the point. But Ron told me there isn't always a tape in it. Is that correct?'

'I think it is, yes. He was sloppy, wasn't he?'

'You're the manager.'

Crispin spread his hands to say *what can you do?*

Fletcher decided the man was dull. Not the hidden-tension-might-snap-any-minute kind of dull. Just dull. He wondered how the hell he'd built up a successful business at all.

'Thanks for your time, Mr Breakman. I'd like to see Jake's room, as a formality, and also meet your wife.'

Crispin met each request with a nod. Then he

showed them along a corridor at the back of the house, and left them at the door of the granny flat, taking a call from his solicitor on his mobile.

Fletcher looked at Sal. 'Jealous husband? Arranged the death?'

'Yeah, right. *Come to fenland and rub out my lodger. There's a thou on top if you slice up his brain.* Can you see Crispin organising that?'

He had to agree. Crispin would struggle to book contract cleaning, never mind contract killing.

He opened the door, and they both stood staring at the room. Crispin said Jake was such a nice, normal kid. Maybe this was normal for a management trainee in the agricultural machinery sector. It certainly wasn't normal for anyone else.

★

Sometimes, Ivan's mother would leave early and queue outside grocery shops. That was because rumours were spreading that the shop was getting a delivery of sausage, or soap powder, or the syrup Ivan liked. If Ivan went with her, he would stand beside her in the queue and imagine what was in the shop. In the end, it was a few tins on a shelf, or a pile of empty cartons that the other women had scuffled over. Sometimes the shop girls smiled at him.

Later, when he was an adult, Ivan Gorensky understood why it all happened like that. It was because of Vladimir Ilich Lenin.

Lenin had founded a command economy insulated against free markets: a self-perpetuating system ready to

*replace capitalism itself when the bourgeois societies col-
lapsed. Lenin got it wrong.*

*Under capitalism, goods are produced in response to
demand from consumers. Under or over production is
punished by the market and then by investors. A command
economy, by contrast, produces goods in response to a
preconceived plan. In a command economy, a gap will
inevitably appear between production and consumption.
Goods may be over-produced for years regardless of their
usefulness, and therefore have to be stockpiled or destroyed.
Other goods, such as soap powder or syrup, may be
consistently under-produced without any opportunity to
redress the balance through market forces.*

*As a man, Ivan read about all this, and remembered the
empty shelves of his childhood. He began to realise why his
life had taken the shape it had.*

*

'Crispin was right about something,' Sal observed.
'Jake really loved machines.'

The room was about fifteen metres square, painted
off-white, looking out over the garden, containing a
single bed, an easy chair and some basic furniture.

Three of the walls were completely covered from
floor to ceiling with pictures of machinery, mostly
tractors: hundreds of sheets of paper pinned and stuck
to the surfaces. There were photocopies from books,
images from tractor enthusiasts' websites and magazines – but many of the pictures were hand-drawn,
sketched neatly with careful technical detail.

Fletcher walked slowly around the room, taking it in.

The other wall had a wardrobe and a pair of shelves. The upper shelf held an old-style cassette player, then some *GQ* magazines, and a paperback of *Watership Down*.

The lower shelf held two large books. The first one was a massive English–Russian dictionary. Inside the front cover, Fletcher found more of Jake's artwork: a series of pencil sketches drawn on artist's card. They'd been sketched in this room, judging by the bed and the window with the view of the garden.

They showed a young woman arranging herself naked on the bed covers, in a series of poses which became increasingly sexual – first, leaning back smiling and letting her hair hang loose, showing off her breasts to the artist. In the next she was lying on her flank with one knee raised, showing the triangle between her legs. The third showed her from behind, kneeling on the bed, her neat buttocks raised, drawn swiftly but deftly.

Sal took the sketches.

'Careful use of shading.' A strand of hair fell across her face and she pushed it back. She looked at Fletcher. 'Drawn from life – or an active imagination?'

'Either way,' he said, 'I think we've just met Olga.' He replaced the dictionary and picked up the other book.

Gold letters on the cover announced, *The Story of The Thinbeach Wedding*, by Alain de Minching.

He turned to the first page. Sal stood close and read it too, close enough to catch her faint perfume and the scent of her hair.

When the armies of William the Conqueror reached the Cambridge fens, local resistance centred around the Isle of Ely (literally, the Island of Eels), led by Hereward The Wake (or Hereward the Watchful, in modern English). A vicious campaign was fought before the Normans subdued the Anglo-Saxons, driving the rebellious elements away into the north-western marshes. An uneasy peace ensued.

Local legend has it that the Norman commander, by the name of Chretien de Minchin, was so impressed by the Isle of Ely that he 'went native' and settled there, taking land in Thinbeach and marrying a local beauty. But a ballad sung locally until the nineteenth century tells the full story:

> *She was fine*
> *But she was faithless*
> *That nameless eely girl*
> *Faithless in the orchard*
> *With every village churl.*
> *Lord Chretien mad with jalousie*
> *Took her on his shoulders high*
> *Drowned her in the Thinbeach Pool*
> *But she will always rise again*
> *Our faithless nameless girl of eels*
> *Our faithless girl of eels.*

Whatever the reality of this little tragedy, the Domesday Book does record a Chretien de Minchin near Ely holding 'six pastures, one good orchard and a strong manor house.'

The descendants of Chretien de Minchin still live in Thinbeach today . . .

Fletcher closed the book and placed it back, thinking what a mix of interests Jake had.

They opened the wardrobe and found some cheap shirts, some tatty jeans, and a pair of grubby trainers. Fletcher turned back to the copies of *GQ* magazine on the shelf and leafed through them. One page had the corner folded down: an advert for a brand of shoes called Ungini. Shimmering Italian leather, exclusive to Bond Street. Jake must have promised himself a pair.

At the back of the wardrobe they found a cardboard box holding a few paper wallet files. Fletcher pulled it out and opened the first wallet. It contained bank letters regarding Jake Skerrit's overdraft of five grand, Visa bills which showed him making the minimum repayments on a balance of four grand, letters confirming student and personal loans of six grand. He found payslips barely covering the monthly instalments, other letters rejecting him for further credit, and some spreadsheets with Jake's desperate budgeting.

In the next folder was a padded envelope which Fletcher tipped out into his hand. Sal Moresby whistled in appreciation.

The envelope held a presentation box embossed in silver, Tiffany, Bond Street.

Inside was a simple bracelet: platinum, set with four small medium-quality diamonds, and a till receipt from Tiffany, dated just the previous weekend. Price £9,495. Paid in cash. Fletcher snapped the case shut and dropped it back in the box.

So Jake had been on a spree to London before his

death. A Tiffany bracelet – for Olga? – and Ungini shoes for himself.

'Where did he get the cash, Sal?'

'And what's in here?'

She moved over to a little filing cabinet that served as the bedside table. She pulled the top drawer out, disclosing some aspirins, a packet of Kleenex, two condoms, a plastic wrap of cannabis weed: the flotsam of Jake's relaxation.

Sal sniffed the cannabis, and grimaced. Fletcher could smell it already: the sour reek of the super-charged, schizophrenia-inducing weed called skunk. When the old hippies in the Home Office reclassified cannabis, they thought it was the same stuff that made them giggle through their beards way back in Uni. They thought everybody should have a try. They didn't know about skunk, because nobody told them.

'If he was a heavy user, there may have been psychiatric issues,' Sal said, 'which Crispin politely called eccentricity. Now, what's this?'

The drawer was stuck about two-thirds out, and when she reached under the top surface for the ob-struction she came out with a roll of money. Four thousand two hundred and forty quid, when they counted it. Used notes in fifties and twenties, crudely taped under the cabinet top.

'So his dreams came true,' Sal said.

'The Chinese say that's the worst misfortune, when your dreams come true.'

'I think there's a worse misfortune. Your dreams come true, then you get chewed up in a shredder.'

The lower drawer had a lock which she released with her penknife. Fletcher expected more cash, or more jewellery, but he found a tractor catalogue.

It was a souvenir brochure printed in 1980 to mark ten years of Breakman Machinery, the cover showing the staff assembled smiling outside the depot. Inside the front cover was a portrait photo of a tough-looking man standing by a combine harvester. Fletcher studied it. He had the feeling he'd seen this face already today, very recently.

A caption read: *Mr Billy Breakman, Founder of Breakman Machinery.*

As he looked at it, the resemblance to Crispin Breakman became obvious. But where Crispin's chubby face looked awkward and immature, this man looked capable, as if he'd fought for his achievements.

'You know, Sal, I thought Crispin couldn't have built the business by himself. This must be his father.'

'Who Crispin didn't mention. But then, why should he?' Sal took the brochure and flipped through the pages.

Fletcher ran the whole thing through his mind.

Jake had been a penniless graduate when he came to Thinbeach, so skint that Crispin had to give him a room. Then Crispin received an unsolicited mailshot and married the Russian beauty called Olga, and Jake developed an interest in – what exactly? Certainly in Olga herself. Probably in local history, and perhaps in the Breakman company too. Jake fried his brain with skunk, thought a lot, became best friends with the security guard. Then he got his hands on around fifteen grand in cash. Finally, he put on his brand new shoes and went to the depot on a Sunday night and started up a shredder. The security man drove into a willow tree. And not a single offence had been committed – except Health and Safety, drink driving and a minor drug infringement.

'Jake's given us a lot to think about, Sal. Sal?'

She was staring at the largest wall, the surface completely covered in Jake's chaotic pictures. She said, 'Can you smell something?'

He inhaled. There *was* something, a faint chemical tang like –

'Paint?'

She leaned closer to the wall and sniffed. A little crinkle went across the top of her nose. She slid her eyes over to his, then back, examining the pictures. She lifted up one of the sheets.

'There's something under here, Fletcher. There's something painted on the wall.'

She pulled away the page to reveal part of a man's head, daubed on the surface underneath. She pulled away two more sheets, and Fletcher thought he recognised the image.

'That's Billy Breakman.'

He pulled away a sheet lower down. Another face stared up at him, and the paint smell was more noticeable. In a minute they had all the sheets stacked up on the floor, and they stood back to look at the wall.

Nice, normal Jake had covered it in what could only be described as a mural. Five metres long by two metres high, it had taken a lot of work – painted in black with a medium brush on the expanse of pale emulsion. In places, he had gouged into the plaster of the wall itself to add texture. In other places, he'd added a material to the paint before it dried. Fletcher reached out and lifted a piece of the stuff away. It was clotted with black paint, but it was unmistakable.

'Straw.'

The mural seemed to show a waterfall or a flowing current, with the water forming in little eddies and whirlpools across the wall, brought into relief with the wisps of straw pressed into the paint. Inside the largest whirlpool was the name OLD BREAKMAN, with Billy's face reproduced from the catalogue, chin tilted up as if his body were just under the water. Below that were two more male faces, each surrounded by more spinning water, but these men were drawn without detail – as if Jake had no idea what they looked like, he just wanted to show that someone was there.

Fletcher took another step back and surveyed the whole bizarre thing, then raised an eyebrow at Sal.

'The two blank faces – they could be Teversham and Jake himself. What does it mean?'

She shrugged. 'Looks like a dream. Some kind of hallucinogenic art? Hard to take it seriously.'

'And yet he *is* dead. So's Teversham.' He made a decision. 'Sal, I'd like you to spend some time in Thinbeach, find out where exactly Teversham was last night, what he was doing.'

'What about our current case-load?'

'It'll have to wait, for an afternoon. Then I suggest you arrange an urgent meeting with your local informant.'

She frowned. 'He can be difficult to track down.'

'He'll jump if you tell him to. He said you were a pre-Raphaelite beauty, remember? Ask what he knows about the Breakman family, or Jake Skerrit, any rumours. I'm going to talk to Olga, then take a look at Teversham's address.' He looked around Jake's little world. 'Anything strike you as strange about this room?'

'Not really, Fletcher. Just the cash, the jewellery, the deranged mural – oh, and the naked sketches of the landlord's wife.'

'And the door isn't even locked. How long have Olga and Crispin been back? An hour or so? Crispin didn't touch the room because he's naïve and he doesn't know what's in here, and anyway he's busy with his lawyer. But Olga let us find the sketches, and everything else.'

'Why exactly would she do that?'

'Maybe she'll tell me.'

Crispin showed Fletcher through a doorway off the main room and into a huge conservatory. It was a bright space, lush with ferns and climbing plants, the humid air scented with pollen. A couple of bees droned past. Fletcher stopped to breathe in an orchid.

'Who's the gardener?'

'Mostly me.'

Fletcher inhaled, admiring the scent.

'Tell me a bit about your father.'

'Dad? He owns the company, but he's retired. I run the business day-to-day.'

'Where can I find him?'

'Portugal. He's got a golf apartment down there.'

'How long has he been there?'

'Since April.'

'April? Isn't that when Olga came here?'

'I suppose so. Look, I've got to get into the office.'

'Crispin, please lock Jake's room and don't let anyone in there. It's a mess inside. He's been drawing something on the wall, a picture of flowing water, plus your dad's face. Does that mean anything?'

Crispin shrugged. 'I told you Jake was eccentric.'

'OK. He's a tough-looking man, your dad.'

'He built the company out of nothing, out of a Nissen hut in a field. Last year we sold more farm machinery than anyone in the country.'

'And this year?'

Crispin's face tensed: the face of the boy who'd taken on too much. The tractor business, the weird lodger. The Russian wife.

At the far end of the conservatory, where the tiled floor eventually ended, Fletcher saw a woman sitting curled on a bench in the shadow of a tree fern. Her head was bowed and her hair was hiding her face.

'Olga,' Crispin said as they approached her. 'My darling, this is Inspector Fletcher.'

She glanced up. She really was a shining light.

Fletcher sat on the bench beside her, and they watched Crispin in his office suit walking away between the ferns.

'Olga,' Fletcher said. 'What's going on?'

Tuesday Afternoon

Crispin's wife didn't answer the question. She had a strong, wide-boned face under a tangle of coppery hair, and luminous grey eyes that looked at Fletcher, looked right through him, and then stared down again at the conservatory floor. She was wearing a denim dress, sitting with her bare legs curled up. Her fingernails and toenails were painted glittery mauve, and the skin of her calves was a honey colour. One knee had a tiny white scar. She was spinning a honeysuckle flower between her fingers, and Fletcher could smell the pollen.

'OK. So how's life in England, Olga?'

That made her look up with a grim smile, making her cheekbones even wider. She shook her head slowly, then pushed her hair back. She wore a heavy diamond engagement ring and a wedding ring, no other jewellery, no watch. She settled back against the bench and her dress parted on the space between her breasts. Jake's pencil sketches came flashing into Fletcher's mind as she held his look with her grey eyes.

She said, 'Life is not what I expected.'

A slightly husky accent. Fletcher thought, *Crispin must have been crazy, letting Jake stay on in the house.* He wanted to get to the question – *what the hell was Jake doing* – but that fragile honeysuckle was still turning in her hand.

'In what way?' he asked.

She looked up at the tree fern in its pot behind the bench.

'Inspector, you know how much Crispin paid for this plant? Ninety pounds, a hundred and thirty dollars. You know the salary of a good doctor in Russia? Six thousand dollars a year.'

'Some Russian people are rich, though, aren't they? At least, that's what we read in the papers.'

'Oh, yes. You know all about us, how we're all in gangs.'

'I didn't mention gangs.'

She looked at the flower in her hand, turning it more slowly. 'When I go shopping in Ely, they stare at me. I can hear them whispering.'

'They're probably jealous.'

She smiled her sad smile again, still looking down. 'I have a family at home, Inspector. I'm the oldest of the girls. My father has a workshop repairing cars. You know what his dream is?' She raised her eyes. 'He wants a house with a garden and a gate you can lock. That's his ambition.'

She was either pouring out her heart, or covering something up. Maybe, for Olga, that was the same thing.

'Olga, tell me about Jake.'

'Jake? An English eccentric, very charming. He had ambition too, you know.'

'What was that?'

'He was designing a new kind of tractor. He said it would run on solar power and vegetable oil. He wanted to take it to Brazil for testing.'

'That's a good ambition.'

'Yes, Brazilians using solar power to destroy their trees.'

'How well did you know him?'

'I know exactly what you're thinking, Inspector Fletcher. I liked him, he made me laugh. He liked *Watership Down* and so do I.'

'Were you close?'

'We were friends, OK?'

Fletcher pictured the Tiffany bracelet on her wrist. Jake had a great visual sense.

'Had he recently got hold of some money?'

'How could I possibly know?'

'Did he ever talk to you about Thinbeach, about local history?'

The honeysuckle stopped spinning, and Olga's grey eyes narrowed on it.

'Sometimes we laughed about it, this rich little village, full of people with nothing to do.'

'Did he ever talk to you about Billy Breakman, about Breakman Machinery?'

'Why?' Olga asked the honeysuckle.

'You did discuss it?'

It was humid in the conservatory, and Fletcher felt sweat gathering on the back of his neck. He could see a faint sheen in the hollow of Olga's throat.

'Did he talk to you about people Billy knows, or

knew in the past?' There was the drone of an airliner overhead. 'Olga, listen. You know I've been into Jake's room. I've seen that thing he was painting on the wall and I've seen the other stuff in there. You left it all for me to find. Why?' The buzz of a fruit fly. 'Jake died in a terrible way. Look at me, Olga. Talk to me.'

Her eyes moved around the floor. Then they lifted to his. They were the grey of broken slate, unblinking.

'Everybody has something, Inspector. Something they keep to themselves. Haven't you?'

He had to pause a moment, looking into her eyes. 'We're talking about Jake Skerrit.'

Before she dropped the flower, he saw her fingers shake.

'*Necha. Necha.* I've failed here. I've failed, and I don't even understand what I'm supposed to do.'

'Olga, what are you afraid of?'

She ground the honeysuckle under her foot, until the little flower was shredded. Its scent was still in the air.

*

By the end of the decade, the gap between production and consumption had beached the Soviet economy on an endless plateau of stagnation.

Its survival depended on importing certain materials from the West: industrial materials – in particular, metals – which a centrally-planned economy could not produce in predictable volumes. The West, of course, needed payment – but the Soviet rouble had no monetary value: its worth existing only in the minds of state planners. Forcible exports to satellite countries only brought in other streams of worthless currencies. What the Soviet Union desperately needed was a lifeline, a saline drip, of western currency. This was known, but never openly acknowledged or discussed.

As a result, the planners had established a programme known as Special Currency Initiative: a drive to generate as much hard currency as possible by increasing the export of certain high-value products. Caviar and vodka played a part, shipped to the groovy restaurants of 1970s Paris and New York.

The big opportunity, though, was machinery. The Russians began to believe there might be a capitalist appetite for their simplistic vehicles. Niva already produced a jeep named the Cossack, which sold well when exported to western Europe. Niva was instructed to prepare other machines for export, above all their farm machines. Above all, tractors.

*

Fletcher checked that Jake's room was locked, then went out to his car. Opening the front door, he found two people standing on the gravel, looking up at the house. They were a middle-aged couple: respectable, also silent. The woman wore a dark coat despite the heat, had a headscarf pulled around her face and her eyes were the red that comes from a night of crying. The man wore a faded but expensive suit, carried himself straight and looked steadily at Fletcher. Fletcher introduced himself, but he knew who they were before the man spoke.

'We're Jake's parents. We've come down from

Norwich. We've come to take his things home, from his digs.'

Fletcher pictured the insane room, the mural, Olga sitting in the conservatory crushing flowers under her feet.

'I'm sorry, that's not possible yet. If you could just wait a few days.'

The woman turned to look at him. 'He was happy here, he told us. Very happy here. He loved the tractors.'

They spoke for a few more minutes. They discussed the things that police officers discuss with bereaved relatives: the post-mortem, the inquest, the availability of counselling. Then Fletcher shook their hands. The mother's hand was frail and damp, but the father's was firm. Fletcher felt a tightening in his throat because of that. As he unlocked his car, Jake's father followed him and held him by the arm. His grip was tight but Fletcher could feel the man's hands trembling.

'She didn't see the body, but I did. They said it was an accident. Do you believe that?'

'Enquiries are just beginning. I can only ask you to be patient.'

The shaky grip tightened, then the father released Fletcher's arm.

'I'm being patient, for her.' He straightened himself up again and looked at his wife. He had creases on his face that held long shadows. There was a crease between his eyes that nothing would ever smooth out. 'Please find out. He was our only son. I thought he would live for ever.'

Fletcher drove away, feeling his hands damp on the wheel. Meeting the father of an accident victim shouldn't have this effect on him. But there was something Olga had said, and the way her eyes looked through him.

Everybody has something, Inspector. Something they keep to themselves. Haven't you?

Sal Moresby parked her car at the Fen Tiger Bite Stop. In normal weather, this was a gutted caravan lined with timber benches. In good weather, add a cable drum and a parasol flapping in the breeze. Sal tapped the dust off a plastic chair and took a seat. The serving hatch clanged shut.

She waited. On the skyline, the old Norman fortress called Giant's Hill rose above the farmland around Rampton. In a while, a battered Subaru pulled into the lay-by and growled itself silent. The door slammed. A man moulded himself into the plastic.

'Miss Moresby. May I say how you're looking more than ever very distinctly pre-Raphaelite?'

'Oh, thank you, Tony. Rossetti or Swinburne?'

'I'm thinking more Burne-Jones today. The later work.'

Tony Olland was in his thirties, freckled and snub-nosed with thin stubble across his lantern jaw. His beard and hair were gingery red – that and his name suggesting descent from the promiscuous engineers brought over from the Netherlands three hundred years ago to drain the Cambridgeshire fens. Sal knew that, in this area, a child born to a single mother was still affectionately known as *a little Dutch*.

Tony was sporting a knitted hat, and a surfer's neoprene body suit. There was no surfing in Rampton: he divided his time between Victorian art and the local criminal fraternity.

'You still have your ear to the ground, Tony?'

Tony twisted in his chair. 'What you wanting?'

'Have you heard of a tractor dealer, Breakman Machinery?'

Tony shrugged. 'Out near Thinbeach? Nothing happens out there. They got some corn dolly festival, keeps them all busy.'

'What about the Breakman family, or someone living with them named Jake Skerrit? Anything worth knowing?'

Tony shrugged again and smiled. He looked relieved: he had nothing to give.

'What about a man called Ron Teversham?'

'I'm sorry to waste your time, Miss Moresby.'

'Don't go just yet.' She wondered what other hooks would snag in his mind. 'You heard anything about a Russian girl?'

Tony's smile changed for just a moment. It didn't fade: it became brighter.

'Russians?' he said. 'Why would those men from the great plains trouble us here?'

'Who mentioned men?' Tony's throat bobbed. It looked like a sack with a rat inside. 'Tony boy, you've heard something, haven't you?'

Tony pulled his hat off and ran his hands through his ginger hair.

'Miss Moresby, I like you. But there's stuff, you know. Stuff I hear, you know, that I can't, you know.'

'You've heard something about Russians. What?'

'Could be nothing. Let me check, OK?'

'Check, then. If you can't get information, rumours are welcome. But I want it all tomorrow morning. Phone me.'

Tony's bodysuit shimmered in the sun: the neck open on a chest as pale as doll's plastic.

'And then we're settled up, Miss Moresby?'

'Don't let me down, Tony.'

Tony Olland looked up and down the lay-by. It was a hot afternoon. There were beads of sweat in his scrappy red beard.

Fletcher bought a sandwich from the Fen Deli in Thinbeach and headed for Teversham's address in Wittris. The route led north-west across the county, through fields of leeks, oilseed and wheat dotted with poppies. Sometimes there were shady folds of land tucked in beside the road: pastures with a few cows, or an orchard, or beehives. Out in the open fenland, the road crossed massive drainage channels running into the distance towards the North Sea at The Wash, their surfaces reflecting the high clouds.

Fletcher parked beside one of them and ate his sandwich, looking into the water. He tried to put Jake's parents out of his mind, and think about Olga.

Why had she come here? To get out of Russia, away from the gangs and the poverty, by marrying a man twice her age? Why not? She said she'd failed at something – was it her mail-order marriage? She'd failed, maybe, by falling for crazy Jake down in the granny flat. Now she was terrified of something, or someone. Terrified of *Crispin*?

Who else was there?

He started up again and took the turning for Wittris. From the rich farming soil of the Thinbeach area, the land changed, becoming even lower-lying, the ragged fields still blighted with stretches of old marsh, and the roadside verges scattered with litter.

Wittris prided itself on being the ugliest place in fenland: a clutter of housing into which the impoverished hamlets of the area were compressed in the 1960s. The low-inflation-high-growth British economy had skirted the resulting community like a bypass. The prominent feature of the town was a jagged row of five-storey housing blocks straddling the main road, which the council had painted a sickly yellow. They were known universally as the Wittris Teeth, for their alleged resemblance to the dental condition of the town's inhabitants.

On the other hand, at least it was on the telecom network. His hands-free rang, and he answered, watching the Wittris Teeth bared on the skyline against the late sun. The car was filled with the efficient voice of Dr Ntele, the post-mortem surgeon, her Zimbabwean accent opening the dialogue like an incision.

'You wanted a summary on Jake Skerrit's body.'

'How are you, Dr Ntele?'

'Cause of death was the brain trauma, as perhaps you guessed. A penetrating lateral injury, the carotid artery disrupted and severed. Both arms were destroyed before that event, so he may or may not have been conscious when the blades reached his head. I'm fine, thank you.'

'Anything—'

'Suspicious? From the part of him available, no. In fact, for a boy with half his head missing, he's in good shape. Minor athlete's foot. A little cannabis in the bloodstream, no alcohol. Nothing to suggest a struggle. Except—' Fletcher pulled over and reached for a pad with the engine still running. 'Some scratches between the shoulder blades and down the central area of the back.'

'Caused by?'

'It doesn't really matter. These were almost healed already, probably caused on Wednesday or Thursday last week.'

'But they suggest he'd been attacked?'

'Not exactly.' Ntele's voice had a sad smile in it, the phone closer to her mouth. 'You ask me what caused the scratching? As a surgeon I would say human fingernails. As a woman, I suspect female fingernails. You need to ask his girlfriend, not me.'

Fletcher's Audi didn't include satellite navigation among its Germanic charms, and when he entered Wittris he had no clear idea how to find Teversham's address. He slowed and cruised past a shopping arcade: a chip shop, a launderette, a Kwik Save, all with steel grilles over their windows. A toddler on the deserted pavement waved a grubby hand. At the end of the street he pulled up outside a place that made him stop and think.

It was a long single-storey building with a steep corrugated roof and a signboard running along the eaves: *The Hereward Pool Hall – Licensed – Parties Catered.*

Fletcher remembered Teversham's pool cue lovingly secured in the back of that old car, the initials carved on the base. A good place to ask the way, then.

The street beyond the pool hall petered out in unfinished cinders and banked down into a pocket of marshland. Fletcher paused in the doorway and wondered if this was a mistake: he could hear the clink of bottles and low drinkers' laughter. But when he stepped in, any smell of booze was lost in the overhead space, ventilated by open windows high in the walls.

Four pool tables stood under striplights suspended from the iron roof. They were surrounded by long benches, a juke box of the kind Fletcher hadn't seen since childhood, a silently flickering television, and a bar with a microwave in pride of place. The dozen occupants looked at him through drifting smoke without breaking off their conversations.

Fletcher studied them in return. Something came back to him, a line from the last book in Jake's room: *. . . the Normans subdued the Anglo-Saxons, driving the rebellious elements away to the north-western marshes.*

It seemed that time had stood still in Wittris. Nobody in here was black or Asian or even vaguely Latin-looking. There were certainly no Russians. The pool players were all male, dressed in jeans and out-of-date football shirts, mostly with the same slick brown hair and heavy fenland jaw as Debbie back in Thinbeach.

But where Debbie had glinted, these men looked idle and defeated. At the nearest table, a man of forty with eyes the colour of a fresh tattoo listened to Fletcher's request for directions, and leaned on his cue.

'Nice suit. You copper?'

'Yes. Where's the street?'

The man smiled. His cheeks creased into long lines, smoked dry by years of *The Hereward*.

'Well, now. A copper means a death. We've heard about Ron Teversham.'

The pool hall fell silent. A dozen pairs of inky eyes focused through the smoke. The hands that weren't holding pool cues were holding bottles.

Fletcher said, 'You knew Ron, did you?'

The player exhaled smoke and nodded. 'Ron played. Not often, but he came in.'

'Was he good?'

The man smiled. 'He thought he was. Old Ron thought he was something, because he worked up at Thinbeach. That's the old Thinbeach way.' He leaned over the table and squinted along his cue. 'That land was ours – you know that, copper?'

'What land?'

'All the farming over there, the rich land. The old Normans stole it off us. Tight shot here. Could take an angle off the back, what you think?'

'I'd go along the side, but I don't play much. And the Normans were a thousand years ago.'

The man took his shot suddenly, slamming the ball into the corner pocket, then stayed stretched over the baize. Through the gable window above him, a small bird flashed through into the hall and began circling hopelessly. The man turned his face up to watch it.

'A thousand years, is it, boy? And they ask why we don't get along.'

The bird blundered out through the window in the opposite wall, and conversation picked up again. Someone put a song on the jukebox: Bonnie Tyler. Men began leaning over the tables, sighting their shots. The man straightened up and spoke to the window with its square of late-afternoon sky.

'Past Kwik Save, take the long street across town. Turn left by the community centre.'

The directions were flawless.

Teversham had lived at the smarter end of town, where most houses were privately owned. Still, as Fletcher entered the street, the old cars and the clapboard terraced houses helped him picture Ron in his final years: the lonely security man-caretaker, approaching retirement in this corner of Wittris, one step outside the estates.

Fletcher crossed the short gravel path to Teversham's door. The house was a maisonette, badly maintained, with spiralling weeds and flaking paint. Fletcher didn't know exactly what he was looking for – but he knew Teversham was part of the Thinbeach situation. Maybe he had helped his friend Jake work out why exactly Olga was here.

Fletcher used the keys that the traffic police had taken from Teversham's body. He paused.

The cylinder had the hollow sound of a lock recently

forced, and when the door swung open, straight onto Teversham's little sitting room, he saw that someone had already been visiting.

The place had been turned upside down: the sofa with its stuffing ripped out, oddments scattered on the floor, and in the kitchenette the utensils emptied from the cupboards along with packet soups and bottles of supermarket whisky.

There was a single chair, tipped over, and a circular mark on the formica counter that puzzled Fletcher. Then he realised: Teversham had eaten alone at that place on the counter – eaten alone for so long that his plate had worn its mark into the surface.

At the back of the house, the ransacking was just as bad. Clothes strewn around the bedroom, a handful of men's magazines splayed open to the light. Plus, on the floor, a little phial of liquid. Fletcher sniffed it, and his head raced. Cheap amphetamine from the Wittris estates: Teversham's final self-indulgence.

The only other room was a small study. The desk drawers had been emptied out on the carpet, but the household files and a few letters remained untouched – including a new credit card still in its envelope.

So the burglars hadn't been kids. The front door was too cleverly unlocked, the speed, porn and plastic left unsampled. But whoever they were, they weren't looking for documents storable in paper files.

Were they looking for something physical – an object?

Fletcher stood looking down at the stuff tipped out of the drawer. It was sad old junk: a stapler, stationery, batteries, an ancient voice recorder. He pushed the recorder with his foot, then picked it up. It was the kind of thing that 1970s' executives used: a tape machine as big as your hand, designed for a full-size cassette.

It had been adapted.

The microphone had been removed and then reattached to a long wire running back into the casing. The body of the recorder itself was looped with surgical ribbon which still held a few body hairs. It was a surveillance device.

Modern listening devices fit inside a belt buckle or a pen, but Teversham had surely lacked the budget and the know-how for that stuff. Fletcher imagined him wanting to record something secretly, and resorting to what he'd seen in old films: a cassette recorder taped under the arm, the microphone somewhere under his shirt. Why? Who or what had Teversham wanted to tape?

Fletcher pressed *play*, and the spindles creaked. He opened the flap: no cassette.

Whoever ransacked the maisonette wasn't looking for this, hadn't even noticed it among the junk. Did they find the thing they really wanted?

He looked into the bathroom, found a grey carpet, grey tiles, a bathtub with a grey tideline. The searcher had been in here too, ripping the plastic panel off the bath, tipping the lid off the toilet cistern to expose the orange float hissing like a mutant fish.

He paused at the door, listening to the noise. He

turned back. The float was jammed between the sides of the tank. Fletcher reached in and pulled the sphere loose, and the water began to spurt into the unit again. He looked at the float: its two halves had been cut apart and then fixed back together with plumber's tape, making a waterproof oval slightly too big for the cistern. He shook it, and something clunked inside. He held it up. Something was definitely in there: dark inside the bright plastic. He pulled off the tape and separated the two halves, and let the object fall into his damp hand.

It was an old video cassette, scratched from years of use. It was slightly damp, but probably still workable. It had a grimy label that said it was the property of Breakman Machinery Ltd and should not be removed from the premises.

Fletcher thought – *Ron, you devious bastard. You grabbed the CCTV tape and you hid it because someone else wants to get it back. Someone else wants to see the horrible death of Jake Skerrit.*

He wanted to view it downstairs, but the burglar had smashed Teversham's VCR across the room – maybe that was the first place he looked, made him start to lose his temper when there was nothing inside. So Fletcher put the tape in a plastic wallet and walked out of the house.

In the street, he paused for a moment, considering. It was early evening by now, the air warm and still, the street deserted. His heart was beating fast.

He reached for his phone and began dialling. Just then he heard heavy steps on the stones of the path

behind him. Before he could turn, a man's voice said,
'Hello, police. Someone wants to meet you.'

*

*The Special Currency Initiative commenced. In the Niva
factory in Stavropol, the tractors' radiator covers were
retooled to show the Niva name in European lettering. USSR
took the place of CCCP. They kept the five-pointed star.*

*Working through trade missions attached to Russian
embassies in the West, agreements were made to export Niva
tractors in small numbers to Italy, Holland, Norway, Swe-
den, Denmark, Canada and Britain. The purchasers –
machinery wholesalers with farming customers – got the
tough machines at low prices. The payments joined the trickles
of hard currency keeping the Soviet Union turning over.*

*Britain – suspicious and protectionist – took the fewest
Niva tractors: barely a hundred in all. Their route ran across
the Russian plain, through Poland and over the North Sea,
wrapped in tarpaulins and with their engines coated in
protective grease, their starter batteries disconnected. In
December 1978, they arrived in Felixstowe and were loaded
onto lorries which took them to the dealers that had placed
orders. The dealers signed for them and unwrapped them,
wiping away the grease and reconnecting the batteries. They
turned the keys in the ignition. Nothing happened.*

*

Sal Moresby spent the rest of the afternoon in Thinbeach, looking for someone who'd seen Ron Teversham the night before. She made her way along the
Shamblings, as the warm afternoon sun filled the

cobbled roadway, making the cottage gardens of the
stone houses vivid with colour.

She thought again what a pleasant village this was: the
buildings perfectly maintained, everybody who answered her knock friendly and cooperative. Everybody
had heard about Teversham. Nobody had seen him.

In the Fen Deli, the shopkeeper milled a handful of
beans and made her a latte. He had a TV screen above
the counter, showing a video of fair trade in the coffee
industry: smiling Peruvians making enough to buy a
generator. He suggested a speed camera out on the
main road.

In the timbered houses leading down to the Pool, it
was the same story: no memory of Teversham. The
villagers' faces seemed to blur into one – and for a
moment Sal had the idea that they were all related.
Door-to-door enquiries always had that effect on her.
In the end, she could only find one witness to Teversham's presence: Debbie, the barmaid of The Bride.

Debbie asked, 'Tom Fletcher not here with you?'

'He's making enquiries elsewhere.'

Debbie smiled and wiped a cloth over a beer pump.
The pub was almost deserted. Over on the brick wall,
the display of little corn dolls gleamed in the light: the
coloured silk scraps taking on jewel tones, the deli-
cately woven limbs a rich amber.

'Debbie, tell me about Ron Teversham last night.'

'Poor old Ron. He sat over there in the corner, had a
whisky by himself around ten.'

'Had he been drinking already?'

'He'd always been drinking already.'

'Did he say anything?' Sal asked.

'He was mumbling to himself. I said to him, *Terrible about Jake* – because they used to come in here together, him and Jake. He just nodded. Then he upped and went over the road. I saw him from the garden. I don't *spy* on people, mind.'

'Over the road?'

'The big house there. I thought it was odd, in actual fact. Old Ron visiting someone like that.'

Sal went to the window and took a look at the superb house they'd noticed yesterday: a building behind iron railings, with a herringbone brick ground floor and timber second floor, the parts united by massive stone lintels, and by a wisteria blossoming across the walls. The whole place looked like the cover of a brochure for the hidden treasures of East Anglia.

'Who lives there, Debbie?'

'Alain de Minching.' Debbie came over to the window too.

'I know that name.' Sal thought back to Jake Skerrit's room. 'He's written a book, about the Thinbeach Wedding. There's some old ballad about—'

'*That faithless girl of eels.*' Debbie sang the line in a folky voice, drawing out the last word into two syllables. 'He's done so many things, Alain de Minching. He's a very, very clever guy.'

'He says he's descended from the Normans.'

'Just look at his house.'

The ruined church tower loomed up ahead, late sunlight slanting across the fields of polythene tunnels on either side of the road heading back to Thinbeach. Beside Fletcher, in the passenger seat of the Audi, was a man he'd never seen before today.

It was an unusual situation. Standing in the street outside Teversham's maisonette, the man had said they had an important journey to make together, to meet someone who could answer questions Fletcher might be starting to ask.

And who exactly are you?

I tell you on the way.

The man was wearing a white polo-neck sweater under a black leather jacket, and dark canvas trousers with baseball boots. He was slightly overweight, in a way that suited him. He grinned suddenly, a gold tooth shining in the sunset.

'Turn left here, my friend. Take this narrow road.'

Fletcher had already heard that accent today: the voice low in the throat, the rolling R sounds. It sounded seductive coming from Olga. From this man, it hissed and growled.

'You're Russian,' Fletcher said. 'A friend of Olga Breakman? What are you doing here?' No answer. 'Who do you want me to meet?'

The man grinned. He was in his late thirties: a big good-humoured face, creases around the eyes, a blunt nose, short hair. He looked like an ex-soldier.

'Let's just keep going.'

They followed a farm road skirting Thinbeach village and came into the area of old fenland. In a while, the narrow road began to dip, sloping down so that the brambles and rushes of the fen rose against the methylated sky. The tips of the reeds shivered in the breeze. Then the road gave way completely to a long dirt track between stunted hawthorns, and the tyres began scrabbling the loose stones. They passed a notice saying *Nature Reserve*, the first road sign for ten minutes. He slowed down, maximising the time.

'How did you enter the country?'

The Russian was enjoying the company, his eyes bright.

'Passport says I'm Latvian. I get on the ferry. Nice Latvian plumber, they wave you straight through. You need lots of plumbers in this country. Why is that, my friend?'

'So, you've got a forged Latvian passport.'

'Let's talk about something else.'

'How come your English is so good?'

'That's what they call me,' said the big man.

'What?'

'Berlitz. The school where I learned it, back home. Soon as communism was over, they come in and set up a school. I was first to sign up. I had this wonderful teacher, Samantha Smithson-Hyde. Short skirts, but wow she could drink. I bought the tapes too.'

'You really made a mess of Teversham's house, Berlitz. What were you looking for?'

'I was just waiting for you. I know all about this Teversham fellow, I guessed you'd be there some time today. But I never went in the house. If you ask me, I think some other fellows been in last night or early morning, buggered it up.'

'Who do you think that was?'

Berlitz shrugged. 'You're the police.' He had expressed absolutely no interest in the video tape lying on the back seat, as if he assumed all British detectives carry one. 'Now turn off here, go in between these damn ugly trees. Big hole here, watch out. That's it. That's my fellow. Right through.'

Fletcher edged the car between the hawthorns. Then he stopped altogether.

They were facing a massive expanse of broken debris: a huge plateau of crushed stone and concrete, stretching away to where the sun was swelling red on the horizon. At first Fletcher thought there was a mist drifting low above the ground. Then he realised that the surface was covered in the grey clock-heads of dandelions – thousands of them, flickering in the breeze.

'Where are we?'

Berlitz laughed again: he was a fundamentally happy man.

'Can't you – what's the word – deduct?'

'Deduce.'

Fletcher peered across the sea of dandelions and saw something out there – some kind of low structure rising against the mauve sky.

The Russian nodded. 'Correct. That's where we're going. But I'm thinking of your tyres, my friend. I suggest we walk.'

They got out. Berlitz straightened his jacket, and his chubbiness didn't account for the bulge under one arm. Fletcher said, 'Berlitz, I believe you're carrying a handgun.'

Berlitz looked hurt.

'But I haven't threatened you. I've been courteous. More than that, I've been genteel.'

'Show me the gun.'

Berlitz grinned. 'You really want to see?'

He unzipped his jacket and pulled out a mad-looking pistol. He held it on the palm of his hand, so there was no threat. It was very slim, with a deeply contoured plastic grip and a long flat barrel ending in a sight like a shark fin. The dark metal was burnished and scuffed.

Fletcher said, 'What's this meant to be?'

Berlitz pointed it at the ground and showed the mechanism proudly.

'It's the real thing, man. A Margolin .22. They started as Olympic target pistols when we had the Soviet Union, then people did a few little improvements. Nice and quiet. The perfect weapon for a guy like me on a trip like this – you know why?' He pulled out the magazine, flipped it over in his fingers and clicked it back. 'It's really basic. Strip it down, it looks like bits of pipe. The kind of thing a plumber got in his tool box. I don't wish to put thoughts in your head, my friend, but I think a number of these are arriving in your country right now. Plus owners.'

'You've done well, Berlitz. You've alerted me to a threat to public safety – that may count in your favour in court. So who else is here?'

Beyond him, Fletcher saw only the enormous rubble scree stretching away into the thickening light.

Sal Moresby used her Airwave handset to try Tom Fletcher's phone again. It was still unavailable. She decided to give him another thirty minutes, then start worrying.

She used the handset again to obtain a Police National Computer Profile of Alain de Minching. The computer had absolutely nothing to report.

She looked at her watch: fifteen minutes. She found it hard to imagine that Fletcher would ever get into a situation he couldn't handle.

Berlitz tucked the Margolin into a leather holster under his arm. Then he gestured towards the mound on the slope of rubble, like a friendly waiter indicating a table. They walked up the slope together, their shoes crunching the debris.

As they approached the mound, Fletcher realised it was man-made: smooth turf about three metres high, which at first glance looked ancient – some kind of neolithic burial place. Then he saw it had a modern-looking slit in its side: the entrance flanked by concrete pillars and guarded by a buckled railing.

The mound was recent: maybe an abandoned air-raid shelter. He thought the whole place might be a deserted airfield – but then, beyond the mound, he saw other structures, even larger, breaking the surface of the dandelions.

'You guessed yet?' asked Berlitz, as they walked up to the structure. 'When I was a kid, your country had the Americans pointing cruise missiles at us from places like this, and we had our ballistic missiles pointing back at you. Now we're all friends, right? We chopped up our missiles, and this place becomes a

Nature Reserve. Nice happy ending.' They were at the entrance to the mound structure, by the railings. A few concrete steps led downward. 'And this is where I stop.'

He turned and began making his way back to the car, leaving Fletcher alone.

A smoky wind blew across him. As he watched the mound, the light of a fire flickered and grew inside the walls of the slit. Then someone appeared at the foot of the steps and beckoned him inside.

When he stepped down there, Fletcher realised that the mound contained nothing but this one slit running its entire length, the walls faced in old but uncracked cement, rising to a slash of pink and grey sky overhead. Halfway along was a small fire of bleached wood. The wind over the mound drew the woodsmoke straight up, hiding the face of a man behind the flames. Fletcher could only see a powerful outline.

From behind the smoke, the man said, 'You're deep in thought there, police.'

'My name is Fletcher.'

'I know your name.'

'Olga Breakman was afraid of something. I suppose it's you. Who are you?'

A branch cracked in the fire, and the man studied it a while before answering.

'You don't know me. I'm Ivan.'

Tuesday Night

The Russian's silhouette was deadly still behind the plume of wood smoke, the firelight revealing only his shoes: military boots so highly polished they reflected the flames.

Fletcher spoke to the outline.

'Ivan, I don't know what you want here, but Berlitz is in possession of an illegal handgun. He's your accomplice.'

'He's not my accomplice. He's my roof man.'

'Your what?'

'That's the way we conduct business over in Russia. A businessman like myself, I'm known as a *krisha*, a roof for the people I protect, because I keep them safe from harm.' The smoke was still drifting around his face. 'Problems come when people don't pay for their *krisha*, don't pay for their protection. Then Berlitz and his friends make them a visit. They go up on the top floor, take chainsaws. They take the roof off, throw it down in the street. Berlitz is the best, he sings while he's doing it. He's got a voice you wouldn't believe. People come to listen to the singing, see the roof come down. In a few hours, everyone in the neighbourhood can see – this building got no roof, got no *krisha*. Nobody going to use that place ever again.'

'And if they still don't pay?'

'They always pay.'

'You're not in Russia, Ivan. You're in East Anglia. I believe you have information about the recent deaths of two local men. Let's go.'

The outline still didn't move. The light in the shelter was fading to a heavy mauve, the concrete glowing amber. Some birds flew along the strip of sky overhead.

Fletcher shook his head. He kicked at the fire, knocking a burning stick across the floor. He grabbed one end and held it up to see the man, holding it above his face. The man didn't even blink.

Like Berlitz, he was in his late thirties. He stood straight like a professional soldier still new to civilian life – and, to make the point, the polished army boots added menace to the well-cut pinstripe suit he was wearing.

His shirt was open-collared, and there was clearly a reason for that. Fletcher could see a jagged line running up the man's strong neck and underneath his chin – a huge scar from a wound that must have almost killed him. Above that, the planes of his face made him look like an old-time Soviet sculpture: slab cheekbones, deep almond-shaped eyes, hair cut short and brushed over a wide forehead.

The face angled slowly into a big grin.

'*Let's go*, he says. English humour always makes me laugh. Olga told me about you.'

'What else has Olga been telling you? About Jake Skerrit, about where and when you could find him alone?'

Fletcher threw the stick back into the fire, and the man stepped into its light.

'Jake Skerrit, the little kid in the big machine. I heard about him, about his friend the caretaker. Nothing to do with us, of course. Must be an English thing.'

'Seems to me like a Russian thing. Sounds like you've fastened onto an easy target, a local business with no defences. Is it protection money? Or are you bringing girls like Olga into the country, forcing them into marriages?'

Ivan smiled down at the fire, with the light in his almond eyes.

'I should employ you like consultant. It's true, I have such businesses. The mail-order bride business, it's the newest thing for a guy like me. But I don't like your idea – putting Russian women at the mercy of these English guys. That troubles me. I prefer that the victim is the husband. He loses everything in the divorce, the proceeds come back to me, I pay off the girl correctly, everyone is happy. Well, almost everyone. Olga's one of my girls, the best, but she's here for other reasons.'

'What reasons? Vice?'

'I must say, you take a stereotyped view of Russian businessmen. Crude stereotyping, isn't *that* an offence in this country? Mm?'

Ivan reached into his pinstripe jacket and brought out a steel flask with cups screwed on top. He poured two measures and offered one across.

'I don't drink,' Fletcher said.

'There's nothing wrong with it. Look.'

Ivan tipped back one beaker and drank it at a gulp, the scar under his neck glistening and his eyes shining in the firelight. He looked offended when Fletcher refused the other cup.

'You an alcoholic? I heard a lot of you police are.'

'I've never drunk alcohol in my life.'

Ivan looked at the extra cup in his hand. Then he downed that too, and screwed them both back on the flask.

Fletcher said, 'You're a long way from home, Ivan. If you're not murdering employees of Breakman Machinery, what are you doing here?'

'OK, police. Listen to me now, it's important. In Russia we have the idea of *delo zhezni*. You know what that means? Means critical work. It's the biggest work of your life, the turning point of your life. Not everybody gets the chance to achieve their critical work. Me, my critical work is in Thinbeach.' The sky above the slit of the mound was a violent bronze that mirrored Ivan's eyes. 'And you are obstructing it. You ask questions –'

'This is England, I'm the police.'

'Don't discuss with me.' Again the snarl under the accent. 'How deep is the water in that fen? I think three metres. You know how easy you could disappear tonight?' Another stick crackled in the fire. 'But I don't want that for you. A disappeared police attracts more police, like wasps. I just want you out of Thinbeach. You've got a report to make, OK. The English kid liked playing with big machines. He had an accident. The caretaker was a drunk, he crashed his car. Put those facts in your report. Don't come back here. Don't ever speak to Olga again.'

Above the shelter, a star blinked on in the smoke. It was going to be a beautiful night.

'Ivan, you don't understand. You're going to spend time in an English prison.'

Ivan put his head back. The firelight glistened on the ridge of the scar below his chin, and Fletcher wondered how much blood he'd lost from the wound. Ivan just laughed.

'Police, police, you think an English jail worries me? You ever heard of a place called The Cylinder? No? It's a military prison, the worst in Russia. That means the worst in the world. I spent six months there. It *is* a cylinder, see: a concrete circle, some openings at the top for light. The cells are boxes in the ground. The Cylinder is like a machine, you move from one cell to the next cell every day. The machine keeps spinning you round, won't let you rest. I've seen things happen to men in The Cylinder you wouldn't believe in your nightmares. I've seen men eat worms and be happy.'

'Is that where it happened – your neck?'

Fletcher didn't mean to get into a dialogue, but for some reason he wanted to know. The thought of that injury made him flinch. Was it pity he felt?

Ivan just lowered his head and closed his eyes for a second.

'Well,' he said. 'I've done the English thing. I've given you a fair chance. Why not take it? Just put in your report.'

Fletcher remembered the grip of Jake Skerrit's father on his arm. He said, 'We're going to meet again.'

Then he walked away from the fire, towards the steps of the entrance and up into the dusk.

Cool air. The plateau of broken stones spread out around him. Ivan called out something in Russian, and down on the plateau Berlitz stopped leaning on the Audi and ambled over to meet him. There was no sign of the gun.

'You're not leaving already?'

'I am, Berlitz.'

'Well of course, my friend. A pleasure. I hope I shall see you soon.'

Fletcher walked across the debris to his car. When he got there, he heard a sound from behind him, and turned.

Berlitz and Ivan were standing on the mound of the shelter, outlined against the mauve sky: Ivan tall and straight, Berlitz a bulkier figure in his jacket. Berlitz had one hand up in the air, the fingers quite distinct even at this distance.

The sound came again. It was a human voice, powerful and pure. It rang out across the expanse of debris, then stopped, leaving an echo which rolled away across the jagged ground. Fletcher wasn't quite sure what was happening. He saw Berlitz's fingers move again, feeling the air. Behind him, the star began to pulse in the darkening sky.

Fletcher leaned against his car. He knew he could drive away through the hedge in a few seconds if needed, but he didn't feel that was necessary.

Berlitz gestured again with his hands, and began to sing.

Fletcher didn't understand any of it, but the sound was like nothing he'd ever heard before. It began slow and deep, the clear Russian words sounding like an address to the empty landscape.

Fletcher knew that a few hundred years ago the fens were a stagnant inland sea, and the villages were harbours or just atolls in the swamps. He had an idea that if the sea ever came back to reclaim its territory, the sound would be like the voice of this Russian criminal with a gun in his jacket.

The voice stopped, and its echo hung in the dusk like smoke.

Seconds passed. The man's outline was still on the ridge next to Ivan, his hands still stretched out in front of him. A pair of geese crossed from east to west, squawking their lonely radar.

Berlitz and Ivan turned and vanished.

In a few seconds there was the rattle of a vehicle moving away on the other side of the mound. The fire inside the air-raid shelter was guttering and dying out.

He watched it for a few seconds. He let the seconds grow into minutes. He was thinking of the little house in Electric Mile. The singing made him think of that.

Then he started the car.

*

In the yards of the British machinery dealers, the Niva tractors refused to start. Their electrics sparked and shorted, and their crude suspensions looked twisted. They leaked trails of oil. The dealers studied the manuals, printed in confusing English. The tractors stayed silent, dripping oil.

The dealers spoke to each other. They contacted the Soviet trade mission in London. They refused to pay the invoices, demanded that the machines be collected and taken away. The trickle of hard currency was evaporating before it even started.

There were heated phone calls between the Soviet trade mission and the Niva Works. The trade mission wouldn't tolerate the tractors being returned. The factory management insisted that it was a misunderstanding: the dealers were reconnecting the batteries wrongly and had to be shown how to do it, or the machines were damaged in transit and needed repairs. Privately, they worried that there might really be a fault with this batch of vehicles.

Either way, the problem needed to be diagnosed and remedied urgently. It was something that only a skilled and trustworthy worker could handle.

In the meeting room at the Niva Works, under the eyes of President Brezhnev, a senior engineer was briefed.

*

Fletcher held the door pillar of Sal's car as she accelerated into a corner, the headlights full of jagged canopies of hawthorn, then the straight black channel of the road into Thinbeach past the old church, and then the bend where Ron Teversham had lost control. There was a long howl from the tyres.

They'd just met on the edge of the village and compared notes.

Tony Olland looked pretty nervous at the mention of Russians.

Frankly, Sal, I'm not surprised. But right now, we need a VCR.

The outskirts of Thinbeach appeared, the lights glinting on the twin-town sign reflecting in the dusk.

The Fen Deli had closed, but the shopkeeper came through from the flat at the back. He let them use the video behind the counter. Fletcher drew the blinds and put the tape in the slot. The place still smelled of coffee and bread rolls.

Beside him, Sal gathered her hair behind her neck with one hand and secured it with a grip. Then she leaned on the counter to watch, her eyes catching the grainy light of the pictures.

The screen was sectioned into four parts: the car park, the internal reception area, the office doorways, and the machinery hall with the shredder in front of the tractors. A clock in the corner read 6.23 p.m. They fast-forwarded, the empty spaces showing nothing but sunlight from the roof panels dimming in the machinery hall until the night lamps came on and moths began to swirl around them.

At 9.13 p.m., a slim and pleasant-looking young man walked jerkily across the car park. Sal changed to normal speed, and they picked Jake up moving across reception, the camera registering his shoes as a green smear.

The quadrant of the screen filming the machinery hall showed him standing in there for a while, glancing around as if making sure nobody else was present.

Fletcher leaned forward, wondering what kind of appalling images were coming next. But Jake turned and strolled back into the office area.

The film showed him walking along the row of doors to the spartan security office, where Fletcher had spoken to Ron Teversham on Monday morning. Jake went inside, leaving the door ajar. The time counter read 9.16 p.m.

The car park quadrant of the screen went blank. Then the reception camera did the same. Then the machinery hall. Finally, Jake Skerrit put his face around the door of Teversham's office and went back inside. The view of the office doors went dead, the screen a murky grey with just the clock counting on in the corner. They forwarded to the end of the tape.

That was it.

'So Jake Skerrit turned the cameras off. He *deliberately* turned them off.' Sal ejected the video and tapped it in her hand. 'To me, that points to a genuine accident. He didn't want his fooling recorded.'

'I might agree with you, Sal, if I hadn't found this tape inside a dead man's toilet cistern. I mean, why did Teversham take it, claim it didn't exist, and hide it so carefully?'

'Carefully?' Sal pursed her lips. 'Sounds like you found it in a few seconds. I'd say Teversham was hiding it from someone who wouldn't know how a cistern works.'

'You don't think you're over-analysing?'

'It's what I do best.' She lobbed the tape back at him.

'Anyway, we've got another visit to make tonight. Come here.'

She reached out and straightened his tie.

The gate in the railings had a wrought-iron sign – *The Blindy House* – and beyond that, a flagstone path led through shrubs to the stone-framed doorway.

'Home of Alain de Minching,' Sal commented. 'Author of the history book we found in Jake's room, and also the last person known to see Ron Teversham alive. Ron was here around ten p.m. yesterday. We know he died before midnight.'

She saw Fletcher study the house before he opened the gate, and then they walked between the shrubs. There was the smell of lavender and the river beyond the mound. The narrow windows shed a creamy light on the hanging wisteria – and close up, she noticed wild flowers growing between the wall slabs.

When she pushed the bell, a dog barked deep inside the house, and a man's voice called out to it good-humouredly. She could feel the day's heat coming from the stones, and Fletcher's silent presence beside her.

In a while the door swung open, and Sal decided that if the house looked superb, Alain de Minching matched it perfectly.

Fletcher couldn't help comparing it to Teversham's maisonette in Wittris. Teversham had a kitchenette and a few rooms. This guy shook their hands warmly and led them through an enormous stone-flagged hall where other doors led off left and right, then down a flight of steps to an archway, saying, 'Come through, come through to my *terrasse*.'

The space beyond the arch was a stone platform built on the bank of Thinbeach Pool, lit by the ground-floor windows. On either side, the mound rose against the sky, blotting out the early stars. In front, the rushes on the opposite bank were just a blur dipping in the breeze. The water was ridged with ripples lapping at a beach of silt on the edge of the platform, where a few fen lilies glowed on the sediment. There was the sound of a fish breaking the surface.

The three of them stood there for a moment, looking out across the water.

'Thinbeach used to be an island, you know, before the fens were drained,' Alain de Minching said. 'This would have been the harbour, known as the *beach*. When the Normans conquered the fens, they built a fortified manor house on the site – a *maison blindée*, hence the name Blindy House. We're standing on Norman foundations.'

Fletcher turned to look at him again. He was impressive: a lean man in his fifties, close-cropped hair, a strong-boned rather French-looking face, grey-green eyes. He was wearing loose trousers and a polo shirt with a jumper draped over the shoulders – the leisure kit of a man still confident of being in his prime. He had the easy-going charisma blended by wealth, physique and intelligence.

Sal said, 'It's beautiful. What do you do?'

Alain de Minching spread his hands. They were

elegantly manicured – but his forearms were lined with heavy dark hair.

'I invest. Usually successfully. But how can I help you tonight?'

Fletcher said, 'You can tell us about Ron Tever-sham.'

'Of course, poor Ron. Let's sit.' Alain indicated some chairs around a large teak table, where a map was spread out with cardboard markers arranged across it. A single glass of white wine held down one corner.

'No thanks.'

Alain's smile faded, and he looked out across the pool. From the house steps, there was the noise of paws clicking on stone, and two large dogs slipped through onto the terrace, statuesque hunting dogs of the type Fletcher would have called wolfhounds. The animals padded over to Alain and settled on their stomachs on either side of him, paws together, drooling a little. Alain stooped and smoothed the ears of one of them.

'Could you answer the question?' Fletcher said.

Alain straightened up and looked back at him. 'You don't understand. I blame myself, even though I'd never heard of Ron Teversham before last night. He came here about ten thirty. He was pretty drunk and quite emotional.'

'What did he want?' Sal asked.

'He was very worried about Breakman Machinery. Maybe you know that the son, Crispin, has taken over? A well-meaning chap, but not a businessman. Things are getting sloppy at the depot, apparently. Corners are being cut. There was that other terrible accident, of course, on Sunday night, which we all know about.'

'That particular victim was Jake Skerrit,' Fletcher said. 'He had a copy of your book in his room. Did you know him?'

'Never met him. Virtually every household in the village has my book, Inspector. I published it myself, and I've promoted it very thoroughly. It's the story of our community.'

'So why did Ron Teversham come to you?' Sal asked.

'People around here often do. A lot of people in the village ask for my guidance, on many subjects. This man Teversham thought I might have some influence on the founder of the company, Billy Breakman. I never knew Billy terribly well, but Ron thought I might be able to persuade him to come out of retirement. Ron said he was worried about the future of the company, but I think it was his own job that really concerned him. I got the impression that without it, he'd go under.'

Fletcher weighed it up. Teversham coming here, fuelled by drink, asking help from the lord of the manor? It was halfway plausible.

Alain turned to the table and picked up his glass of wine. 'Can't I offer you—?'

'If only,' Sal said, 'but we're on duty. Ron was drunk, and you must have known he came here by car. Did you let him drive away?'

Alain looked from her to Fletcher, and back at Sal.

'That's what I can't understand. I told you this last night.'

'You told who?'

'Oh, don't tell me you're unaware? Teversham shouldn't have been near a car in the state he was in. I wanted to stop him, but he stormed out. So I phoned the Ely police, and tried to alert them to a drunk driver in the Thinbeach area. I didn't have his license plate, of course, because he'd parked further up the Shamblings, but still I thought a patrol car or something might pick him up. I suppose I was wrong. There isn't much police cover here, is there? You're pretty overstretched. Nobody's fault but Teversham's, though I can't help blaming myself. Should I have phoned them again?'

Fletcher glanced at Sal, and she stepped up into the house to make the call that would confirm if Alain de Minching was being truthful about that call to the police. Fletcher had an idea he might be. Some things just slip through.

The night grew over Thinbeach Pool. Two cloud banks were merging together. The reeds on the opposite bank were the same blue-grey as the water. Fletcher could smell the silt below the stone platform.

In the silence, the magnificent dogs panted slightly. Alain knelt and rubbed their necks and they bucked their heads in pleasure. He whispered a few words to them – in French, Fletcher noticed. Fletcher looked at the map spread out on the table. It seemed familiar: houses, roads, rivers.

'A map of Thinbeach?' he asked.

Alain glanced up as if he'd forgotten Fletcher's presence. Then he stood and came over.

'Yes. We're preparing for the Thinbeach Wedding. It's on Saturday, of course.'

'This Saturday?'

'Yes. Up on the mound, just a few yards from where we are now, the Thinbeach Bride will be thrown into the water.' One of the cardboard markers had a drawing of a corn doll on it, the fragile limbs placed on the edge of Thinbeach Pool. 'Villagers from hundreds of years ago would recognise the festival instantly. We're very close to our past here.'

'And you're descended from the Normans, I read in your book. That seems astonishing.'

'Why? Sixty per cent of the indigenous British population live in the county where they were born. Forty per cent live in the same town. We're a static population, on the whole.' Alain took a sip of wine and glanced at the house. 'How long will your colleague be?'

'Not much longer.'

'No rush, of course. Maybe you've heard of the Cricklade Woman? She lived in Wiltshire three thousand years ago, and her skeleton was dug up in a quarry in 1999. When the archaeologists compared DNA from her bones to DNA from the nearest village, they found two families directly descended from her. Three thousand years, and they're still there. Imagine! No, my line back to Chretien de Minchin is very clear, very well documented in parish records.' He put his glass down. 'You should come to the festival on Saturday, have a taste of the past.'

'And see Chretien drowning his wife?'

De Minching smiled again, looking out over the water. He rubbed the hairs on his forearms. Under his open collar, tufts of wiry body hair were tucked together. He said, 'Chretien was rather a strong character, shall we say. He drove out those troublesome Anglo-Saxons, and peopled the village with his own descendants. That took a firm hand.'

Sal came back down and nodded at Fletcher. It was clear: de Minching really had made that call, the local police really had failed to act on it.

Fletcher said, 'Mr de Minching, I'm sorry if I was hostile.'

The man made a sweeping gesture. 'Inspector, call me Alain. Alain with an *i*, of course. Remember, I'm at your service. If there's anything about the village you need to know, just ask me.'

The dogs at his feet panted.

Fletcher said, 'Russia.'

'Pardon?'

'Are you aware of any link between Thinbeach and Russia?'

Alain looked genuinely mystified. 'Russia? Oh, I see. You mean Crispin's wife? You mean, is she the root of the trouble at the Breakman depot? Well, I've no idea.'

'I was thinking of something more far-reaching.'

Alain shook his head. 'Then I can't think of anything at all. We're pretty self-contained here, as you've probably noticed. We're still a little island, really.' He smiled suddenly. 'That's not a crime, is it?'

★

The senior engineer met two party officials across a table in the meeting room. On the table was a cardboard folder.

The two men described the problems with the tractors, and he took notes with his steel pencil.

'It could be a number of things,' he said. 'It's hard to say without seeing the machines. When are they coming back?'

The men didn't look at him, just at a point behind his shoulder. Then one of them began to explain that any dealings with western capitalist societies were bound to be problematic.

'Such societies are fickle. Their corrupt politicians strike bargains they later try to slither out of—'

'The point is,' the second man broke in, 'we can't take them back. The damn things are staying where they are. So we need you to diagnose them on-site.'

'On-site?'

'In Britain.'

There was a long silence.

'Go there personally? Myself?'

'These are unusual circumstances, which call for exceptional measures. A visa has been arranged. I think ten days will be sufficient to visit every dealer. You will travel from south to north.' He pushed the folder across the table. 'Here is your itinerary. And you needn't worry about your family, comrade engineer. During your absence, they will be looked after very carefully.'

*

When Sal left The Blindy House, she walked with Fletcher up the grass embankment, and they stood looking down at the Pool. The circle of water reflected the fenland moon, and the rushes around the bank were tinted mauve. She breathed the turf and the breeze coming across the fields.

She gave him the facts: Alain had phoned the local police station on a direct line, the call logged at 10.56 p.m. The receiving station – already two officers short and with no available cover – bounced it to another station who bounced it back. It was reclassified as non-urgent. By then Teversham's skull was split against the willow trunk. Nobody's fault but his own. Random luck.

She watched Fletcher pick up a flint from the ground and throw it into the water. He said, 'Is it random? Ivan isn't here by chance. He's here for a reason.'

Her handset buzzed. Even as she answered it, she saw lights spreading across the water: the blue pulsing of an emergency vehicle hurtling past on the main road outside Thinbeach. Before the voice on the phone gave her the news, she had an idea where it was going. The blue intersected with the ripples, lines crossing with lines.

Fen Lodge looked different at night, with the ambulance lights glittering against the windows. Inside, the big reception room was crowded with people in fluorescent jackets. They seemed to have nothing to do.

In the kitchen, Crispin Breakman sat at the table with a WPC, stirring a cup of tea. He was beyond being pale – his face was sleet grey. Fletcher listened to the story.

Crispin had stayed late at the depot, going over the Health and Safety prosecution. Olga was alone in the house. She seemed fine when he phoned her around seven. He came back at nine p.m., went around the ground floor looking for her. Then he went upstairs. There was a room she used as a study.

Fletcher nodded. He and Sal went up the staircase to a wide landing, where two big windows showed the moon hanging over the fields. The only other light came from a doorway where the photographer was standing, adjusting his camera. He glanced up and shook his head. He wasn't a young man, and the late call-out had left grey shadows under his eyes.

'This one's the worst,' he said. 'If you know what I mean.'

The study was much bigger than Fletcher expected. It was neatly done: a long workstation with a state-of-the-art Apple suite, some serious home entertainment hardware, a grand's worth of digital camera. Framed prints of landscapes. Against one wall, a gym-quality exercise unit. It was the room of a woman who took her relaxation seriously, and could buy whatever she needed to fill her time in this house.

In one corner was a day bed draped with rugs.

Olga was lying back on it, tilted to one side. One hand was curled under her face, twining some strands of coppery hair in her fingers. Her eyes were shut. Leaning closer, Fletcher could see a single line of tears across one cheek. Her lips were slightly parted, allowing a drool of vomit to coagulate in a pool on the floor, where a jumble of capsules gleamed with the colours only pharmaceutical chemists could invent. An empty vodka bottle lay on its side.

Fletcher touched the skin of her arm. It was cool now, and slightly damp.

'Why?' Sal asked. 'I don't see a suicide note. Because of Jake, because she was heartbroken?'

'No. Because she was afraid. She was terrified.'

'Of what?'

'Of the man who planted her here through a marriage agency, the man she was supposed to gather information for. She failed him, and she was terrified of what he's going to do.'

'What *is* he going to do?'

'I really don't know.'

He stood back against the workstation to let the photographer take a view of the whole room. He looked down at the few objects on the polished wood surface. They looked like a still from a Sunday supplement: the latest mobile phone in Art Deco style, a notepad computer slimmer than his own hand. He knew that all this would have to be swept by software forensics – but he had the feeling that it would all be clean, that Olga had been careful to leave no trace of her real connections.

Then he realised that she had at least left them something. Something he wanted very badly.

'Sal, do the fine hairs on the back of your neck ever stand up?'

She followed his eyes. She didn't say anything, just reached out with a Biro and lifted up the object lying among the smart, expensive stuff.

'This doesn't fit here, does it?' she said.

She was right. Among all the digital gear was an old-

time audio cassette. Battered plastic, the tape beginning to curl from the aperture. Not the sort of thing
Olga would ever need – there wasn't even a tape player
in the room. But it was exactly what someone like Ron
Teversham would use. Just the kind of cassette that
Ron would have slipped inside his clunky old voice
recorder before taping it under his hairy arm.

The flash lit up Olga's face for the last time.

Downstairs, Fletcher closed the door of Jake's room.
Sal fired up his old cassette recorder and they stood
looking at Jake's paint-and-straw mural – the image of
Billy Breakman and the two other faceless men en-
twined in swirling water – while the tape hissed into life.
At first Fletcher thought this was another dead end, like
the video of Jake in the depot, or Teversham's visit to
The Blindy House. But in a few seconds the hissing
gave way to other sounds, other noises and then voices,
that convinced him this was absolutely key.

It lasted less than three minutes. When it was over,
Fletcher went outside and asked the photographer to
take an image of the mural before he wrapped up for
the night. When he came back, Sal was staring down at
the cassette in her hand.

'The answer's yes,' she said.

He came out of his thoughts. 'Yes to what?'

'Yes, the hairs on my neck stand up. They are now.'

*

*On an evening early in January 1979, the senior engineer
came into the apartment on the top floor of the Niva*

accommodation and sat at the kitchen table. Outside, it was minus twenty-five degrees, and through the frozen condensation on the window Ivan could see only the arc lamps of the railway yard and then nothing, just the darkness of Russia.

Ivan and his mother sat at the table too. His father opened his briefcase and showed them the things he had been given: an itinerary of British farm machinery dealers, going south to north. An Aeroflot ticket to Heathrow, and a voucher for a hire car. Ivan had never imagined such things.

His father was leaving in the morning. It would take him ten days.

There was quiet in the kitchen, just the hiss of the stove and the tap of the pipes, and the rattle of a train leaving the works into the dark. Ivan looked at his mother and saw tears in her eyes.

She said, 'I don't even know where these places are.'

His father took a sheet of paper, and drew a quick outline of Britain. It seemed a funny shape to Ivan, like a man with no legs and a huge head. His father marked the points where he thought he would be day by day, so that they could follow it. There were no telephones in the Niva accommodation.

Ivan followed his parents into their bedroom and watched his mother take down a pasteboard suitcase and begin to pack it. He had to put his whole weight on the case to help her close it.

★

Sal Moresby stood on her balcony, watching a party boat move along the river, its passengers laughing under the coloured lights. She knew that barely ten miles to the north, fenland places like Thinbeach were quiet and self-contained – like little islands, as Alain de Minching put it.

Then the other images came back to her: Teversham's skull cracked open against the willow; Jake Skerrit's weird drawings at Fen Lodge, the mural of Billy Breakman in the water. The pencil sketches of Olga, Fletcher looking at them with his blue eyes; then seeing the girl dead.

Finally, that cassette in Olga's room. It made little sense to her, and Fletcher himself looked pretty mystified as he bagged it up for the early morning conference with their senior officer.

The morning. She began wondering what Tony Olland was going to tell her in the morning.

Such questions kept her there on the balcony, watching the river settle into quiet, not wanting to sleep – not wanting even to turn back the sheets and slide into bed.

There are places you can't leave, streets you can't stop walking. When Tom Fletcher opened the door in the house on Electric Mile, a moth fluttered loose and spiralled away towards the railway lights.

A single lamp showed that the downstairs room was unoccupied, the furniture neatly arranged and the bare wooden floor washed clean. At the back of the house, beyond the unlit kitchen where plates were drying on the board, a thin curtain was drawn across the open back door that led onto a small concrete yard. He stood

in the kitchen for a second and watched the flashes of a
train through the material. Then he pulled it aside and
stepped through.

She was sitting cross-legged on a mat spread out on
the concrete, her back straight against the brick wall.
She was wearing sandals, cotton trousers, an old denim
shirt, bangles on each wrist. She looked up and smiled
at him and he sat down next to her. They didn't touch
each other.

He closed his eyes. He could smell fumes from the
train, static electricity, rosemary growing from a pot.
He turned to look at her.

'Hello, Cathleen.'

She was the same age as him, barely thirty. She had
angular limbs and a face that was luminous in the dim
light. Her hair was cut short, but he remembered when
they first met it was a big jumble of brown. Her grey
eyes turned to look back at him.

'What are you thinking, Tom?'

'About when your hair was longer.'

'What are you really thinking?'

'I've seen two dead bodies today, one yesterday. A
man held my arm and said, *he was my only son*. That
got to me.'

She tilted her chin and looked at the sky. The heavy
clouds that had gathered over Thinbeach were spreading south and breaking apart, reflecting the orange
glow of the city. The wires were humming, and a siren
wailed out on the bridge, blue lights reflecting in the
upper windows.

He asked, 'How's the boy?'

Cathleen frowned. 'Something got to me today too. He asked something he hasn't asked since he was a kid.'

'What?'

'He asked who his father was.'

★

At dawn, the snow began falling in a vertical screen, hiding the smoke of the Niva Works and even the lights of the rail yard. Ivan walked with his father down the stairs of the accommodation, holding the pasteboard suitcase. It was heavy, but he carried it all the same. Some of the doors of the other apartments opened, and people watched them. Ivan liked that. He liked it as much as kissing the leader of the Girls' Pioneers, or feeling her best friend's hands on him under the water.

On the ground floor they left the stairwell, and the snow hit them. The flakes stuck in Ivan's eyes and mouth, tasting of smoke.

From a point in the snow, a black shape emerged and rolled towards them. It came closer, growing enormous. It was a Zil limousine, lent by the factory management to take the senior engineer to the airport. The driver got out and opened the boot. Ivan managed to lift the suitcase and they placed it inside and closed the lid.

From the back of the car, Ivan's father turned once and smiled, then faced ahead as the car rolled forward. In a few seconds the snow hid it like a sheet. Ivan watched until his eyes were so full of snow that he couldn't see.

Wednesday Morning

It was early, but the sun was already burning the mist off the River Cam. Tom Fletcher registered the path under his feet as he jogged along the Backs, the façades of Trinity Hall and Clare College glinting with sunlight, the slap of his feet, his lungs pumping air, the river still fresh, noise of cattle in the fields beyond. He registered it all, but his mind was running somewhere else. Not back on Electric Mile – because that part of his life was a compartment he'd sealed off – but rather, out in fenland. He was trying to put events in order, into a chain.

The chain must have started when Ivan used a marriage agency to plant Olga in Crispin's house. Was she there to harm him? Obviously not. She was there to find something out, something critically important to Ivan. What Ivan couldn't foresee was that Crispin had a lodger, and Olga became very close to Jake. She told him the reason for her presence, planting her glittery nails in his back. Something clicked in Jake's skunk-addled brain. He took it to Ron Teversham, and Ron got up to some antics, rigging himself with a voice recorder, making a tape recording so totally weird that even now Fletcher couldn't make much sense of it. Jake drew enormous pictures on his wall, and became interested in local history, in Billy Breakman. Billy, by the way, relocated to Portugal as soon as Olga arrived on the scene. Then Jake went shopping in Bond Street, and stepped too close to a shredder.

Fletcher came to a halt on King's Bridge. He could hear organ notes from King's College Chapel, distorted by the distance. He glanced at the chapel: the honey-coloured stonework set in perfect lawns, its ornate roofline against a perfect blue sky. It was the view from postcards and guidebooks: the confectionery lid of Cambridge. He knew by now that when people reached inside, the city often tasted bitter. He leaned on the parapet, the sweat cooling on his chest.

Two young women in kayaks came paddling under the bridge, the little craft cutting a clean line in the water. One of the girls glanced up and smiled, and he smiled back before the kayak took her away.

The shredder. When Teversham found the body, he hid the video tape – in a panic? Or in fear that it showed something? But it showed nothing that could possibly harm Teversham. Still, Teversham went to Alain de Minching with his worries about the Breakman company, then drove into a tree.

Maybe that's when Ivan got to hear that his enquiries in Thinbeach were going wrong. That's when he sent Berlitz out to find Fletcher, and threatened Olga with God knows what if she talked. Problem for Olga, she'd already talked. She wanted the world to know the truth, which is why she left Jake's room undisturbed, and then the cassette tape on her desk for Fletcher to find.

The reason she was planted here.

Fletcher began running again, back along the empty pavements of Trinity Lane. He took a detour and turned into the market square, where a few stallholders were unloading their gear. He stopped at a breakfast van that had a pitch in the mornings. The man in the hatch nodded in greeting and surveyed him through the smoke of the cooking. He was a mature Polish guy, with an impressive moustache and piercing eyes. Everyone called him Stan.

Stan had lived in Cambridge twenty years, working seven days a week and saving his money because he had a dream that his son would go to Cambridge University. The boy passed his A levels last year, then his driving test. Then he crashed his car on the Barton Road.

Stan pushed across a mug of tea the colour of old oak.

'A lot on your mind,' he said.

Fletcher nodded. The square was beginning to fill up: traders, street cleaners, people working early. People living their lives.

'Suppose you heard about someone, Stan. A violent man. Something makes him leave his home and travel thousands of miles to a tiny village in Cambridgeshire, where he says there's the most important thing in his life. What would that thing be?'

Stan turned some eggs over, jabbed a fork into sausages, frowning to himself. His eyes were a long way off – as far as the Barton Road, maybe. He sprinkled some pepper.

'He's looking for something he's lost. He's a violent man, but he's looking for peace.'

Before Sal Moresby joined the force, she imagined their meeting rooms as cramped and noisy, with people chewing gum and shouting acronyms. She was proved right: most were exactly like that. But the room used by Detective Superintendent Webley, Fletcher's immediate superior, was a different kind of place. Webley was a different kind of officer.

Webley's office was on the top floor, the windows shielded by the trees on Parker's Piece moving against a powder-blue morning sky. It was calm and cool, a fan humming in one corner to keep it that way. One wall was fitted out as a screen, and a digital projector was set up beside a cassette player. The chairs were pulled around a side table, but nobody was sitting on them. The table had a jug of coffee, but nobody had touched it.

Sal knew by now the way that Fletcher and Webley worked together. This morning was typical: discussing an issue, the two of them were standing quite close together, speaking in bursts, looking at each other for long stretches, considering, then starting the discussion again. It was an unusual way of working, but Fletcher and Webley's relationship was unusually close, despite the formal way that Fletcher always spoke to his superior, and Webley's often terse manner.

Webley was in her late forties, still a few years away

from possible retirement – an age when many officers look in the mirror, slow down and park. For Webley, though, the last few years had seen her demand more and more of herself and her team: everything quicker and better, wanting to finish her service on the highest possible note.

Webley was in civilian gear today: neat trousers and a sleeveless jersey showing off still well-defined arms – the result, people said, of determined hours in the gym.

Fletcher finished speaking.

Webley looked over at Sal and then back at him. Her face was lined around the eyes, otherwise smooth-toned, and her hair was still glossy, tinted a dark red-brown. She looked girlish when she smiled, but her full age when she frowned. Which was now.

She said, 'Right, then. You've got two fatal accidents, but no circumstantial evidence of criminal action. You've got a suicide, plus two illegal immigrants, one of them armed with a Soviet-era peashooter. You spent a full day out there, both of you. How *is* your case-load?'

'I think the Thinbeach situation is significant, ma'am.'

'That sums it up, Fletcher. It's a *situation*, not a case. What's on the projector?'

He activated it, and the wall flooded with the photo of Jake's black and white mural: the picture of Billy Breakman and the two other men in the swirling water. Webley studied it. The projected image caught her shoulder for a second, and she stepped back out of the beam, as if she didn't want anything this weird to touch her. Fletcher said, 'It goes with the tape.'

She looked back at him. 'Play it, then.'

Sal watched Webley's face as the hissing gave way to the sounds and then the voices. After a few seconds, she could see that Webley could sense it, could feel the importance of it. Webley's frown gave way to intense concentration as she put her fingers together, inclining her head to listen.

Before the meeting, Sal and Fletcher had already typed it out as a transcript.

> *Hissing noise: recorder not correctly wired to microphone?*
>
> *Squelching noise: microphone working, but something pressed over it?*
>
> *Suckering noise: microphone being released?*
>
> *Voice 1 (male):* Your collar too tight, Teversham?
>
> *Laughter, male voices. Sounds of glasses, cans being opened. Background music, unidentifiable.*
>
> *Voice 1:* Not this again. Put something else on.
>
> *Squelching noise.*
>
> *Different music, male voices laughing, one person clapping. Music is Paper Lace, 1973, 'Billy Don't Be A Hero'.*
>
> *Voices in unintelligible conversation, then:*
>
> *Voice 2 (male):* Oh, that old chestnut. Now there's a story.
>
> *Voice 1:* Forget it.
>
> *Voice identified by DI Fletcher as being Ron Teversham, speaking close to microphone:* You don't know, do you?
>
> *Voice 1:* Just forget it. Look at us, listening to Paper

fucking Lace. We're old guys now. Nice of you to have us, boy, but don't dig up that old shit.

Voice 3 (male): Know about what?

Laughter. After some seconds, Voice 1 laughs too.

Voice 1: Goes back a long way. Even for you, mate.

Teversham: So what does it mean?

Laughter tails off.

Voice 2: Means they were smart bastards. Clever outfit, tight-knit too.

Teversham: Who were they?

Voice 1: There were only a few of them—

Voice 2: I heard a lot of them—

Voice 1: No, just three, clever sods kept it tight. There was the little guy, Peter Charter. Little farmer he was—

Voice 2: He was nothing, he was just the driver. There was Thomas, what was his name? Big bastard, out Thinbeach way.

Voice 1: Denton his name. Thomas Denton. Haven't heard of him for years, not Peter Charter either.

Voice 2: But the big man was Breakman. Old Billy Breakman. Could give and take with any of them.

Sound of glasses and bottles breaking, laughter, music stopping. New music: Brotherhood Of Man, 1975, 'Save Your Kisses For Me'. Confused voices and noises.

Teversham: They were good, then?

Voice 2: Worked like a charm. Solved the whole problem.

Voice 1: Made a mistake, though.

Voice 2: (laughing) Yeah, but apart from that, they were clever bastards. Called themselves *(unidentifiable).*

Teversham: The what?
Voice 2: The Wake. Called themselves The
Wake.
Teversham: What does—
Suckering noise, eleven seconds.
End of tape.

Webley opened the player and looked at the pathetic
old cassette. She said, 'Not exactly professional.' She
looked at Fletcher – one of her long, thinking stares that
went on for five seconds. In the end, she said, 'Who
were the voices, anyway?'

'Old drinking buddies, ma'am. Maybe from the
security trade.'

'But why would this man Teversham record himself
in conversation?'

'He was a heavy drinker,' Fletcher replied. 'I think he
knew that unless he recorded himself, he wouldn't
remember precisely what was said. Which shows
how important this was to him, and therefore to Jake
Skerrit, therefore to Olga Breakman, therefore to the
man known as Ivan.'

'But what are they talking about? The Wake?' Webley pointed at the projected image. 'The wake of a
boat? All this swirling water?'

'Could be,' said Sal. 'But those voices were talking
about an organisation from the past, maybe a company
or agency. A team of three men, one of them being
Billy Breakman, the other two named as Thomas
Denton and Peter Charter. They're probably the blank
faces on the mural.'

'But an organisation for doing what? You asked Crispin Breakman last night, obviously?'

'He said he'd never heard of these people, or anything called The Wake.'

'He'd just found his wife dead, which might affect his memory.' Webley switched the projector off. 'Proposals, then?'

Fletcher said, 'At the bare minimum, we've got Russian criminals taking a close interest in a vulnerable community. Three people are already dead. Sal's informant is due to come back with some real information, but I think rumours are starting to spread locally that these Russians are operating in the area.'

'The informant seemed rather worried,' Sal added.

'I'm not surprised. Your two Russians would mix with the local crooks – like what?' Webley smiled. 'Like rats in a cage of hamsters.'

'And these two men with Billy Breakman,' Fletcher pointed to the places where the other heads had been on the wall. 'We need to interview them, see if they can shed more light on why Ivan is interested in Thinbeach. And Billy Breakman too, of course, even if he is in Portugal.'

'You really cannot justify going all the way to Portugal.' Webley went to the window and looked out at the trees on Parker's Piece. Without turning, she said, 'How much time do you propose to spend on this, anyway?'

'A day, two days at the most.'

'Reassign your workload for two days? Seriously?'

'I've met this Russian. He's obsessed with Thinbeach. We need an international context for him – what's his background, is he a threat—'

'Or just a fantasist? Which do you think?'

'I think he's a threat. I think he's planning something, but I don't know what.'

Webley stayed at the window for half a minute, her lean arms folded across her chest. Traffic passed, the fan whirred in the corner. Then she turned to them.

'All right. Let's see if it *is* a case. I'll network Interpol, see what's available on the Russian, check with Portuguese police on Billy Breakman's whereabouts and activity. Moresby, please check with your informant and then make a start on locating these men Charter and Denton. Fletcher, let me talk to you for a minute more.'

Tony Olland didn't phone.

In the morning sun, Sal walked the path to his front door. The house was in a 1930s' farmhand's terrace, set behind a wire fence on the edge of humid, inaccessible Rampton fen. No Subaru outside, just oil stains. After a minute of knocking, the adjacent door opened and a woman stepped out under the porch.

'Olland's gone.'

'Tony's gone? Where?'

'Got an uncle in Spalding, a cousin in Lowestoft. The Dutch do put themselves around.' Her nostrils exhaled smoke. 'Back window never locked.'

Tony was an informant, so his neighbours informed on him. Sal opened the window easily and slipped through into a dingy kitchen where a breakfast plate was unwashed on the table. Tony had left in a hurry: drawers and a wardrobe half-emptied. A collection of books on British painters was lined up on a shelf.

One was open on the sideboard, the page held down with a cider bottle. It showed a naked girl emerging from an apple tree, wrapping herself around a muscled youth, moulding her breasts against him. Edward Burne-Jones: *The Tree of Forgiveness*.

It was a nice thought, but Sal didn't think she *would* forgive Tony for this.

The bathroom cabinet was empty of razor and foam. The only clue to Tony's frame of mind was some ginger stubble cluttering the sink.

Last night, Tony had made some enquiries for her. The answers had scared him enough to make him shave his beard off and leave the area. Sal couldn't be sure exactly what he knew – but it probably involved the word *Russian*.

*

He had no brothers or sisters. In his bedroom, he had enough space to hang up the planes he made with his father, the red star painted on each wing tip. On the wall, he pinned up the outline of Britain with the towns and cities his father would be visiting.

Outside, the snow kept falling, flickering in the light from the train yard. He lay in bed and looked at the map, wondering what Britain was like. It wasn't as cold as Stavropol, his father said. People there lived in houses, not accommodations, but they had farms and needed good tractors.

Ivan closed his eyes and imagined it. He heard the trains moving out of the yards, and the rattle of the pipes, and someone singing in the apartment below. He wondered what kind of car his father would hire. He imagined his father driving through the warm fields of Britain to help the British farmers, the people coming out of their houses to welcome him and shake his hand.

He opened his eyes and looked at the first place on the map. He reached out to touch it.

КЕМБРИДЖ

The first place was called Cambridge.

*

'Yes, ma'am?'

'Coffee?'

'Police coffee? No way.'

Webley turned to him from the window. He felt her eyes settle on him, the smile in them fading.

'You're pushing this Thinbeach situation very hard. With you, there's always a reason. Something troubles you, am I right?'

'I met Jake Skerrit's parents.'

'You've met lots of bereaved parents.'

'And it always hurts. This was the worst, though.'

'Why, Fletcher?'

He hesitated. 'The father said, *I thought he would live for ever.* It was distressing, the way he said it. Thinking of his son.'

She looked at him for a while, then said, 'In the old book of coppers' sayings, what's on page one?'

'Something about loyalty?'

'That's page two. Page one says *Don't get personal*. Point taken?' He nodded, and she went on, 'How's Sal Moresby doing?'

'She's classy.'

'OK. You're a good team together. You *look* good together.'

'Are you matchmaking, ma'am? She's got a boy-friend.'

Webley laughed. 'I'm just a mother hen, you know that. How are *you* doing?'

'Ma' am?'

'Come on, we know each other well enough. Is everything OK? Nothing eating at you?'

He knew what she meant. 'My divorce has come through, if that's what you're thinking, ma'am. The force is full of divorced coppers.'

'I'm one myself.' Webley glanced out at the trees again. 'People talk about you, Fletcher. The golden boy who doesn't drink. They say you've got a secret woman tucked away.'

Fletcher's turn to smile, then feel the smile fade. 'She's not a secret woman, ma'am. She's just a very private person.'

'Well, that's good. The job and the life, they don't always mix. Wait till you're my age, Fletcher. The cliché becomes real: the police really are the only family you've got. And they still insult your coffee – it's heartbreaking really. Listen, I'm going to reallocate some of your case-load among the team, that'll be highly popular. Give me a note of priorities. First I'll call international, check out your Russian.' She picked up the phone, then stopped. 'You don't *have* to keep things to yourself, Fletcher. If you ever want to talk to someone who's been through it, I'm here. You're good. I want to keep you that way.'

When he looked behind him through the glass door, she already had the receiver cradled under her chin. She was leaning back, stretching her arms – a phone habit of hers. They were an older woman's arms – but smooth, slightly freckled. He remembered a time – just once – when she'd put her arms around him. He knew for a fact she remembered it too.

'Well, well. One half of the dream team.'

Sal was slamming her car door shut, after her fruitless visit to Rampton. She was on a short fuse already. She took her time locking the car before turning around, because she knew the voice.

DI Franks, of similar age and experience to Fletcher. Except that Franks was two inches shorter, a stone heavier, and didn't have a police medal. Those differences always seemed to irritate Franks enormously. The fact he'd obviously just picked up part of the Fletcher/Moresby case-load probably wasn't helping either.

She said, 'Are you lost, Franks? In the car park?'

He came up close to her. 'I'm lost because I'm up to my eyes in new work. And I hear such peculiar things, Moresby. You know what I hear?' His face was a foot from hers, she could see stuff between his teeth. 'I hear there's a Russian gangster who wakes up one morning, thinks, *Hm, this protection thing's going flat. Need a new outlet for my mafia skills.* He thinks, *I know, I'll pop over to East Anglia, maybe muscle in on the fruit-picking business. Anyone gets in my way, I'll stuff 'em in a fucking shredder.*' Franks slammed his own car boot and stood sweating, his face coming back close to Sal's. 'I mean, which one of you came up with that? Was it you, or Webley's perfect boy?'

Then it went quiet.

From the doorway, she heard him say, 'Shit, she hit me. The bitch really hit me.'

Sometimes when Sal wanted to think, she walked out of Parkside and turned left past the fire station, crossed the road to the sports hall and sat in the viewers' gallery of the swimming pool.

From the back row, she watched Fletcher walking up towards her, folding his jacket carefully over the seat in front, sitting down. He was holding a sheaf of notes they'd assembled together.

'Good choice of venue,' he said. 'Chlorine loosens the mind. Franks has calmed down, if you're wondering.'

She shrugged, watching a diver turn and somersault off the high board. 'A friendly slap. I'm pissed off about Tony Olland. He'll come back eventually, but his information could have been key.'

'We'll manage without little Tony.'

The diver began swimming to the side. Long arms and big hands. Fletcher's slightly stubbled face frowned down at the notes. His eyes were the blue of the chlorinated water at the deep end, where the diver was hauling himself out, water running off his legs.

'The Wake. Strange name,' Fletcher said. 'What does it suggest to you?'

'The Wake of a boat, like Webley said? That would explain the swirling water on Jake's mural. Or a wake-up call?'

'Or a party after a funeral, Sal.' She noticed his eyes follow a young woman up the steps of the diving platform, onto the top board. The girl steadied herself and prepared to make her run. 'But the funerals so far are for the people trying to understand The Wake, not for the members themselves. Billy Breakman is still alive in Portugal, and we have search data here on what appear to be the other men. Peter Charter and Thomas Denton.' The diver hit the water with a tidy splash. 'Thomas Denton,' he went on, taking the first set of notes from a plastic wallet. 'The only person of that name in the Thinbeach area is resident at an address known as Deep House, Thinbeach. Thomas has no criminal history whatever. His tax affairs are in order. He's registered proprietor of a company named Denton Landmass, property development and construction, winner of a number of awards for developments in environmentally sensitive locations. You could say he's a success.'

The female diver was clambering out now, her hair tangled around her shoulders, pulling at the edges of her costume.

Sal took the second file and said, 'And by contrast, we have the only farmer in the county named Peter

Charter, resident at Charter Farm on the Norfolk border. Registered business of dairy farming, entire herd was slaughtered as a foot and mouth precaution in 2001. Received compensation, continued trading. He *is* known to the police, but not as an offender. Persistent reports of vandalism and burglary at Charter Farm over the past few years, though it apparently stopped a few months ago.'

'Stopped?'

'Looks like the burglars just gave up.'

'We'll call on Charter first.'

'But he seems less important, Fletcher. The tape said he was a nothing, just their driver.'

'That's the best place to start in an organisation. The little guys are indiscreet, they can't wait to talk about the bigger boys. We'll pick up Thomas Denton second.' Fletcher stood and put his jacket on. 'Judging by the tape, I'd say The Wake were active a long time ago. There may be no physical evidence remaining – it just depends on getting people to talk.'

'What if they don't talk, Fletcher?'

He looked down at her, the pool light in his eyes.

'Then you smack them in the mouth.'

*

Ten days went slowly. The first day, Ivan ticked the point on the map labelled Cambridge. *The second day, he traced a line west and ticked* Warwick. *The line moved slowly north, the route his father was driving between the British tractor dealers.*

He wanted a letter or postcard, but his father had said

the post was slow over the big distances. Once, on the fifth day, he went to the Niva Works and asked if his father had phoned. The staff showed him into an office where another engineer put his hand on Ivan's shoulder.

'Your father's busy, Ivan Gorensky. He's got important work. No time to call.'

'Not even a minute?'

The man hesitated, as if he'd already asked himself the same question.

'Don't worry, young comrade. Tell your mother the same.'

In the corridor, Ivan looked back and saw the man still watching him.

Wednesday Midday

On the Ordnance map, Charter Farm was a square shadow just inside the county border, on a rising plain of land a few miles east of Wittris.

Fletcher parked up at a services near Ely, and joined Sal in the Vectra. She drove at speed along the straight roads, the pale hulk of the Cathedral dipping behind them as the Great Ouse appeared beside the road in a panorama closer to sea than earth. Until the draining of the fens, Fletcher knew, the people out here lived in huts raised on poles above the water, walking across the swamps on stilts, brewing opium from field poppies to subdue the malaria that tormented them.

A light rain clicked on the windscreen from the enormous sky. Fletcher closed his eyes for a second. He thought back to that last conversation with Webley, imagining what he really wanted to say, the way it would feel to talk to her.

Nothing eating at you?

He wanted to say: Yes, OK, something's eating at me. My wife left because she found out something about me.

What, Fletcher?

There's someone I can't let go of, someone from the past.

From the past?
From a long time ago.
But you're together now?
Not exactly.
Why can't you let her go?
Because of how it started, the way we met.
Why? What happened?

He jerked his eyes open on the border landscape: the intensive fields crossed by railway lines, lakes reflecting the white clouds. Sal was watching the road, saying nothing, her hair in an arc across her shoulder, steering with fingers just resting on the wheel. He blinked a few times, then opened his laptop and took a look at his emails. The first was from Dr Ntele.

Subject: Ron Teversham. Caucasian male aged sixty-two . . . Height/weight ratio close to clinical obesity . . . minor cataract in one eye . . . Cause of death: blunt trauma to frontal lobes. Estimated alcohol in blood at time of death: 280g per 100ml.

Three and a half times the limit.

Fletcher scanned the rest: Ron's liver was in cirrhosis. Fingernails severely bitten. No signs of injury except what would be expected from the crash.

Then, an email from the RTA investigators. *Subject: Ron Teversham. Provisional comments. A fatal RTA ascribed to driver impairment . . . excessive speed . . . illegal tyres. Vehicle had no tax disc.*

There was a final note from the mortuary: *The deceased appears to have no next of kin, or friends or associates willing to deal with the body and personal effects.*

'Poor old sod,' commented Sal.

'Watch the road, or we'll be joining him.'

'But I need my frontal lobes intact.'

He just caught her eye.

Back on the screen were some items from fenland news sites and scanned cuttings from the local press: two tragic accidents in the Thinbeach area. Photos of the Breakman depot exterior, and Teversham's crumpled Sierra. Nothing on Olga.

'Word's getting around,' he said. 'Peter Charter may have heard about the deaths. Do you think he knows Jake and Ron were researching him?'

'And if he does, is he worried? But on the other hand,' she slowed the car down to a halt in front of a cattle grid, 'news arrives slowly in a place like this.'

Beside the grid was a sign on a barbed wire fence: CHARTER FARM. STRICTLY PRIVATE. TRES-PASSERS BEWARE.

A Friesian cow with bulging udders turned to watch as the car rumbled over the grid and onto a roadway of potholes filled with bricks. The road led up a shallow incline, the car bouncing under cedar trees that let fly with crows as they passed. Then, up at the end of the track, Fletcher saw the farmhouse itself.

It was a pebble-dashed hulk boasting three chimneys. One gable wall was propped up by a timber scaffold and, behind a ragged hedgerow, there was a farmyard littered with machinery. Fletcher looked around, and found they were high enough here to see partly across the county: the yellow blocks of the Wittris Teeth were just visible over to the west. The car ploughed through a filthy puddle and entered the yard between two old tractors, each fitted with spiked arms on the front, the prongs raised into the air.

Maybe Peter Charter really was worried: Fletcher noticed razor wire strung from one tractor to the other – and at certain points in the hedge, sharpened stakes were fixed in the ground.

The car slithered across the yard, between a jumble of scrap machinery. A mist of flies rose and then settled as the engine turned off. In the quiet, there was only the calling of the rooks circling.

Beyond the house itself stood a couple of corrugated iron barns, their doors barricaded shut with lumber, and a caravan streaked with mould.

The front door of the house had its windows mostly replaced by plywood, and in answer to Fletcher's knock a man's shape appeared in the remaining cracked pane. The face studied the warrant card against the glass. Then bolts were drawn and a chain unfastened.

Later, Fletcher would go back in his mind and try to change things from then on. He shouldn't have stood there with Sal, introducing themselves in the hallway, building up to an interview. They should have dragged Peter Charter out and burned his farm to the ground.

*

Ivan sat on the stairs of the accommodation, next to the hot-water pipes. The pipes groaned, joining the other sounds: doors closing, toilets flushing, laughter, and old Viktor downstairs singing an army song.

Smells drifted up the stairwell too: golubtsy *cabbage,*

solyanka *stew, tobacco, drains, washing taking too long to dry.*

On the banister rail, the Mikhalkov family had strung up some smoked herring in the cold, on a wire hung with tin cans to alert them if the neighbours tried to take it.

Ivan saw a figure arrive on the landing below and glance up. Her violet eyes were bright in the electric light, not half closed in the glare of the water reservoir back in the summer.

She walked up and sat beside him, between the herring and the water pipes. Her thick wool coat smelled of mothballs. She looked much older than thirteen. He felt younger than eleven.

'Ivan Gorensky. Have you heard from your father?'

'He's very busy. Too busy to call.'

She nodded.

He knew that she'd heard about this situation as well. His father was a skilled engineer who should be reporting his successes at the end of each day. The silence from Britain was starting to fill the Niva factory and the whole accommodation. She glanced downstairs.

'I'm visiting my uncle Viktor. I can't stay long.'

He knew she was busy these days: spotted by an Olympic coach, she was being moved to a special training establishment for Soviet girl gymnasts. People said the coach was already giving her pills to take, stuff that would delay her growth and make her train for ten hours a day.

On the stairs, she loosened her coat. Under that was a thick felt jersey that she unbuttoned. She shivered and put her hands around his neck.

That was the first time he understood the power of

women over men. It was a force like gravity, and it terrified
him. He closed his eyes. He felt her smoothing his hair
while her uncle Viktor sang the song of Soviet rocket
battalions. She rested her face against his head and put
her arms around him, careful not to rattle the tin cans.

★

The farmhouse kitchen looked out on a pair of rusty
swings creaking in the breeze. The kitchen itself contained a bedrock of ancient family life: a corkboard
with yellowing photos, and the heights of vanished
children marked with paint on the door frame. Over
this, years had deposited layers of oily grime and the
oddments of a man living alone.

The man in question was in his fifties, wearing
overalls the colour of the mud in the yard.

Fletcher had met men like this before. He'd arrested
them for persecuting their relatives, or for beating their
friends, for bearing grudges so complex that even they
had forgotten the source. He'd found others in farmhouses like this – hanging from the ceiling or sprawled
on the floor by a shotgun with their ambitions blown
across the walls. These men were the last of the small
farmers, and they were literally dying out. It wasn't
poverty that was killing them, or Brussels, or super-
markets. It was isolation. In the worst cases, their
voices were soft and childish – because they rarely
spoke.

The man offered his visitors the best he had: mugs of
tea, and Jaffa Cakes straight from the packet among the
bits of machinery on the table. He looked at Sal for a

few seconds too long. Fletcher wondered when a woman had last set foot in the house.

'Have you been here all your life, Mr Charter?' Sal asked.

Charter grinned. 'I was born upstairs. How many people can say that? This place was like heaven when I was a kid. I thought my own would want to stay. Now one lives in Quebec and the other's in Malaga.' He pointed to two photos on the corkboard: a pair of mop-headed kids on the swings outside. 'She's a fish scientist and he's a podium dancer.'

'Mr Charter,' Fletcher asked, 'are you aware of the deaths of two men in the Thinbeach area? Names of Skerrit and Teversham.'

'No. Who are they?'

'They both worked for Breakman Machinery.'

'Breakman? Should have said. I'll always buy a machine from Breakman.'

'Have you bought a machine from them recently?'

'1986.'

'I see. Would it surprise you to know that these two men were interested in you?'

'In me? Why?'

'Have you heard of something called The Wake?'

Peter Charter broke a Jaffa Cake in half and peered at the jelly inside. The old swings in the yard creaked for a second. Fletcher waited. Charter pushed the packet over to him with a raised eyebrow. Fletcher didn't look at them. Charter held his gaze, and instead of the anxiety Fletcher had expected, the battered face broke into another grin.

'The Wake? Jesus and Joseph, The Wake.'

'What does it mean?' Sal asked.

Charter threw back his head and laughed, a sound like the noise of the rooks in the cedars. Tears in his sore eyes.

'What's funny, Mr Charter?'

'*You're* funny, you police. Years I've had trouble here, trespassing, burgling, wrecking. How many calls have I made to you? What help have I had?' He stopped laughing and threw the remains of his biscuit into the sink. 'Now one morning two of you arrive at once. And what do you want to know about? Just the bleeding *Wake*.'

'So you know what it is?' Sal asked.

'Good morning, Mr Charter. How can we help you defend your property? You didn't even bother to say it. Just, what's The Wake?'

'Mr Charter,' Fletcher said, 'do the swings still work?'

The lawn was a web of rye grass and nettles. The glassy scrape of a grasshopper sounded above the mooing of cows in the fields. Peter Charter swayed, trailing a hand-rolled smoke.

'That's what gets me, OK? The Wake was a local club, back in the seventies, for people who wanted to keep up the old history.'

'What history?' Sal asked.

'Thinbeach history. The Norman Conquest mostly. We used to dress up in costume, re-enact battles, give talks on local traditions like the Thinbeach Wedding –

you know, where the Norman commander drowned his pretty wife.'

'It was a village history club,' Fletcher said slowly. 'Were you an important member?'

'Well, yes and no. I had an old van and I used to drive people around to the re-enactments, the village fêtes and so on. They were happy days.'

'Tell me about the other members.'

'There were lots, people drifted in and out. Billy Breakman was the chairman, then Thomas Denton, he organised a lot too.'

'You just used to drive them to village fêtes? Is that all?'

Charter seemed about to speak, then he hesitated.

'Mr Charter?' Sal said. 'Anything else?'

'No, that was all. Anywhere they wanted to go, I drove.' He flipped his roll-up into the nettles. 'So you can see my point, right? I wait years, then you two turn up and ask me about this.'

'Reason we're asking, Mr Charter, is we think you may be at risk.'

'I know I'm at risk. I told you. Burgling and wrecking. Rather – no, I *was* at risk, up till April. Now the problem's sorted out.'

Sal said, 'Yes, I noticed there were no reports of any trouble here after April. What did you do, hire some security?'

'You could say that.' Charter grinned to himself. 'I got the best security going. Russian security.'

Fletcher was watching the tobacco smoke drifting from the nettles, wondering why the hell The Wake was important if it was a defunct village history society. Then the smoke stopped.

'What did you just say?'

'Russian security. Better than yours, boy.'

Fletcher ran his eyes up to the grimy first-floor windows, then around to the pastures, the old caravan and the copse on the rising ground beyond.

He said, 'I think you may be at risk, Mr Charter, from a Russian man, possibly ex-army, with—'

'A scar under his chin here? That's Ivan.' The grasshopper fell silent. Charter swung back, kicking up his heels like a boy. 'How could I be at risk from Ivan?'

'You mean you know him?'

'I mean he lives here. He's been staying here since April, him and Berlitz. He's out at the moment, else you could meet him yourself.' Charter forced the swing to a halt and looked from Fletcher to Sal. 'And *now* what's the matter?'

Back in the kitchen, Fletcher got the speech. It was the litany of falling prices, mad cow, foot and mouth. The pressure of running an old-fashioned dairy surrounded by arable superfarms fifty times the size. Peter Charter added the thankless kids who never wrote, and subsidence under the farmhouse requiring timber supports against the wall – and finally, the thing uppermost in his mind. Crime.

'You saw the flat land down there, on the west? Them yellow buildings, they call the Wittris Teeth. The kids from Wittris, they were making my life hell on earth. The thieving sods used to steal off-roaders and drive up here across the fields, help themselves to whatever was in the barns, sometimes in the house too. Wreck the place as well. They thought I had money hid away, which I don't. They called me a fucking Norman, but I'm not. Anyone they're jealous of they call a Norman.'

'Were the local police much help?'

Charter laughed. 'That's why I'm surprised to see *you*. I phone them, I'm put on hold. Or there's no cover available, or they'll take hours to get here. This year was the worst. I thought I was going mad. That's what they do, them Wittris kids. They take your life away from you. Then my luck changed. I came back in the Land Rover one afternoon, and what did I find? Three Wittris boys hanging by their feet from the timber on the gable. Spinning around, spraying puke.'

'Who did it to them?' Fletcher asked, though he already knew.

'Two Russian lads. They only cut the Wittris kids down when one of them passed out completely. Sent them home on their arses. Word must have got round after that. I've had no trouble here since.'

Fletcher was rearranging the chain in his mind. Olga had listened to Teversham's cassette tape and passed the name of Peter Charter to Ivan – and Ivan had turned up here, justified his presence, made some kind of home here. Why? Why here of all places, close to one of the men in that innocent village club, The Wake?

'So the Russians are protecting you against the Wittris kids. What do they get out of it?'

Charter was proud of his deal.

'They get lodging upstairs and use of the kitchen. They tell me what food they want and I buy it. You should taste the soup they make, it's fantastic.' He looked at Sal. 'It's nice having some life in the house.'

Sal nodded. 'I think we'd better see where they sleep.'

Charter showed them the bedrooms that had belonged to his children. There was Whacky Races wallpaper in one, and Barbie in another, both peeling. Charter tried to push the loose parts back onto the wall.

Apart from that, there was nothing childish about the rooms. They looked more like an army barracks: perfectly tidy, the lino swept and washed. Each one held only a bed, with blankets folded precisely at the foot, and on top of that a duffel bag containing shaving gear and personal oddments: chocolate, cigarettes, shoe brushes.

The bag that Fletcher assumed belonged to Berlitz also contained an old phrasebook, some parts underlined:

In the greengrocer:
I would like onions/carrots/a cabbage/some potatoes.
Socialising:
Would you like to have dinner with me? I know somewhere quiet/lively/interesting.

The other bag contained an old edition in English of Dostoevsky's *Crime and Punishment*, which fell open at a central page. Again, some words were underlined. Fletcher read:

Any man has the right to overstep legal constraints, if the achievement of his critical work demands it. Such a work may even be of benefit to humanity.

There was also a photo in a plastic wallet: a woman standing outside an apartment building. The sky was blue, with some bright clouds, and below that some plumes of smoke – maybe a factory nearby. Fletcher put it back and looked around.

It was disciplined, almost monk-like – and apart from three lines of Dostoevsky, there was absolutely no evidence of criminal intent.

'So what they are is a security firm, really,' Charter insisted, back in the kitchen. 'They're businessmen.'

'Have they ever asked you about The Wake, or about Billy Breakman or Thomas Denton?' Fletcher asked.

'No. Why should they?'

'Or about Thinbeach?'

'Never. Why?'

'Because otherwise I can't see why they're here.' Fletcher looked around the kitchen, at the old photos and the wreckage. 'What do they do all day?'

'They've got interests. They're restoring an old tractor they towed in from somewhere.'

'An old tractor?'

'They're fixing it up in the barn. Keeps them busy.'

Sal asked, 'What do they do in the evenings?'

'They have meetings.'

'About what?'

'I don't know. I can't speak Russian.'

'What kind of meetings? Political meetings?'

'More like planning meetings. Discussing things, looking at maps.'

'What kind of maps?'

'Ordnance Survey maps. But I don't pry into their business. They don't exactly socialise, least not with me.'

'So they socialise with someone?'

Charter looked out to the ragged meadow behind the house. 'They are coming back, aren't they? Christ, you don't know what it's like up here at night if you're alone. You can see the lights coming on in the Wittris Teeth, all lighting up. Without the Russians, them Wittris kids'll murder me.'

'I'll ask for a police patrol to stop by,' Sal said.

He nodded, his eyes scared.

'So who do they socialise with?' she asked.

He was called Larry, and he lived in the caravan at the top of the meadow. He'd been there for three years, labouring for Peter Charter.

Why does he live in a caravan?

Because he's a labourer. I won't have him in my house.

They could see him up there, hanging his washing to dry on a string. He saw them approaching, and took his pants down off the line.

Larry looked from one to the other.

'Police?'

'How can you tell?'

'Haircut. Suit.'

Fletcher smiled. Larry smiled too. He was a very

short and thin man aged around forty. His legs were crammed into long rubber boots, the biggest thing about him. His face was puckered with red veins. He still had some teeth. If Peter Charter was lonely, what was life like for this guy?

Fletcher said, 'You find much to do around here?'

Larry thought. 'There's fishing.'

'What about after dark?'

'There's night fishing. What you wanting?'

'Those two men living in the house.'

'They're my friends.'

They weren't two of his friends – they were all his friends.

'You talk to them much?'

'Some I do. They've been in the army. They do things people don't do no more.'

'Like what?'

'Like go out at night.'

'What, fishing?'

Larry shook his head. His eyes kept moving over to Sal. His suspicion was battling against his need to impress.

'Out in the fields. They know how to move around.'

'You ever go out there with them?'

'Once I did.' Larry caught Sal's eye. 'We walked for hours, all night it was. They sang songs and they taught me words. We drank vodka.'

'Where did you go?'

'As far as that village along there.'

'Thinbeach?'

'Don't know. Smart place. They had the maps.'

'What did they do?'

'They had binoculars. They were observing. Why?'

'Where are they now?'

'I don't know. Why?'

'Larry,' Sal said. 'Mr Charter said something about a tractor.'

Larry spat. 'Charter. That old fucker talks too much.'

'Right. So where is it?'

*

It was a Saturday, the eleventh day. When he came back from school, Ivan spent an hour looking through the kitchen window, his breath melting the film of ice until he could write his name in it. He ate a bowl of soup at two o'clock, standing at the window. At three, it began to get dark. Then he saw it: a black shape moving slowly along the road towards the accommodation. It was the Zil limousine.

His heart thumped and he wiped his breath from the window, craning his neck to see down.

The car stopped and a man climbed out. The man turned to look up at the windows – and Ivan saw it wasn't his father, but a younger man with a heavy stomach pushing out his trench coat. Even from here Ivan could see the red star in the lapel. A party official.

He felt disappointment in his throat, and set his mouth firm.

He watched the man coming onto the pathway leading across the snow-covered area between the blocks. The paths had been swept clear and they were black against the white of the snow. He was coming past the monument to labour and past the climbing frames, heading towards Ivan's block. Ivan saw he was carrying a leather satchel.

*

The barn was at the end of a deeply rutted track. It was built from corrugated iron, one single door sliding on runners, barricaded with lumber. Larry stood looking at it, shifting from foot to foot.

'They won't like this. Nobody goes in there, not even me.'

Sal said, 'Open it, Larry.'

Larry bit his lip and pulled the jumble of timber away and put his shoulder to the door. It shuddered, then rolled open. Sal was first in.

The must of an old barn hit her, and on top of that the tang of machine oil. The interior was lit by bars of sunlight coming through the doorway and gaps in the roof and walls. She could make out a concrete floor littered with junk, patterned with footprints and tyre tracks. She could hear Larry shuffling outside. She peered down to the end of the shed.

There was something in the shadows against the far wall, and Fletcher was already making his way between the bits of machinery on the floor. When she got there, she saw it was something big, shrouded in a greasy tarpaulin. Fletcher lifted up one corner and she took the other and pulled the cloth to one side, lifting it over the angles of what was underneath. Spirals of dust rose in the shafts of light as they pulled the covers clear.

It looked like something from another world. It was a

machine made from crudely pressed metal, the stamped lines showing as ribs against the bodywork. The shape was slab-sided and purposeful. The wheels were clogged with dried mud, but the engine housing had been wiped clean. At the front, where the domed engine cover projected into the light, the grille was scarred from countless impacts. Still, the Russians had restored it and brought the steel to a high polish. There was something embossed in the metal under the radiator cap. A name.

Sal put out her hand and felt the words, stamped in English into the cool metal: NIVA STAVROPOL. USSR.

Under that was a five-pointed star.

She turned to Fletcher. 'A tractor? The Russians are here because of a tractor?'

Peter Charter confirmed what he knew: that the Russians had discovered the old tractor in a field somewhere and towed it here. They treated it with more than respect, almost with awe, spending whole mornings in the barn filing and polishing.

'Which farm did it come from?' Fletcher asked.

Charter shrugged. 'Could be anywhere around here. It's an old type that was around years ago – about twenty-five years ago. You don't see them any more.' He became anxious again. 'My Ivan's coming back, isn't he?'

They stopped and parked by the cattle grid. Behind them, Charter Farm looked more isolated than ever at the end of its track. Fletcher watched the crows circling the treetops.

He said, 'You think Ivan came all this way to find an old tractor?'

'No, but I think tractors *matter* to Ivan. And where do you go to buy one – today or twenty-five years ago?'

'A dealer like Breakman Machinery,' Fletcher said. 'I can see a connection with Russia there, if Breakman ever stocked these Russian tractors. But why would Ivan establish himself here with Charter and not ask about The Wake?'

'Because he's already heard the cassette. He already knows Charter was in The Wake, and knows he wasn't important.'

Fletcher nodded. 'But then why lodge with him here at all? It's a paradox. It's as if he wants something else from Charter, but Charter isn't aware.'

Sal started the engine again and took them over the cattle grid, then stopped.

She said, 'Charter hesitated, didn't he? When you asked if he only drove them to village fêtes.'

'Yes, there was something there. Maybe he drove them to other places. Let's go and see Thomas Denton.'

'I'm just the little guy, aren't I? Just the driver.'

He was worried for a moment, then he saw she was laughing.

In the copse behind the farm, Ivan put down his binoculars and let the ferns ride up again around his face. He was starting to like the sweet peppery smell of these English ferns.

In Chechnya once, he'd stayed a day and a night like this, on his side in the undergrowth, giving covering fire for a patrol in a valley. The ferns out there had little hooks underneath and smelled like dog's breath. When he stood up, the fronds had grown and curled around his legs.

When he first came to this place, he never expected to find one of the Niva machines still here after all this time. They'd noticed it abandoned at the end of a field near Cottenham, its silhouette unmistakable against the flat horizon. When he touched it, it was like an electric shock, touching the old days again. He remembered that first embrace from the leader of the Girls' Socialist Pioneers in the Hall of Soviet Achievement, and lying on the concrete slope of the reservoir with Berlitz, watching the tractors snake away on the railway lines.

His dream was to make the tractor work again. Now that would have to wait a while, but as long as the police treated it with respect, he didn't mind. In fact, it brought them closer to him, closer to understanding him. He wanted them to understand him.

He sometimes wondered what had happened to the leader of the Girls' Socialist Pioneers. He knew exactly what had happened to her best friend.

They doped her with drugs and made a gymnast out of her, a model of Soviet youth complete with her photo in *Pravda*. She got as far as the 1982 Eastern Bloc championships, then she died in the bathroom of the Warsaw hotel room she was sharing with her coach, a man aged forty. Official cause of death was heart failure, at the age of sixteen.

In 1999, after years of searching, Ivan found a Warsaw policeman who swore he glimpsed her dead body with a lamp flex twisted around her neck. The gymnastics coach had changed his name, tried to disappear, but Ivan found him too in the end, living alone in a retirement dacha in Ukraine. Ivan spent time with him, talking about the old days. The coach confessed how age was making him claustrophobic, with night terrors. Ivan nodded slowly, reaching for the phone.

He had him locked in the cellar of the dacha and had the house bulldozed above his head, then had his men pour a layer of concrete on the floorplan. Ivan went there every day for a week, to stand on the perfectly level expanse of concrete and think about the past, about the feel of her cheek against his hair in the stairwell of the Niva accommodation.

The concrete dried and cracked slightly. There was a screaming and a knocking from somewhere underground, but on the fourth day it stopped.

Now he watched the unmarked police car disappearing along the main road.

Clever police. You did it the right way, starting with the little guy. Now you're working up the list, going to the next guy in The Wake. Problem for you is I know all about him, too. I never spoke to him, but I know him better than he knows himself, just from watching him with these binoculars of mine. You'll see what I mean.

A minute later, he raised the binoculars again to see Peter Charter emerging from the farmhouse door and clambering into one of the immobile tractors by the gateway to the yard, lowering the prongs to barricade himself in.

And good luck to you, Peter Charter. You were just a nobody, like they said, but you were still part of it, part of that thing. Everybody pays for everything they've done, sooner or later, in their own way. This is your time and this is your way.

He stood up and knocked the fern dust off his legs. Then he walked back through the copse, watching the sunlight falling in splashes across the ferns, the butterflies flickering over them, the flowers nodding in the clearings. On the other side, on the farm road, Berlitz was waiting in their Land Cruiser with the engine turning over. Smell of diesel and sweat as he climbed in, just like army days.

'Neechyo?'

'Dobro.'

Berlitz jiggled himself deep into his seat and wrapped his fingers around the wheel. He said, 'We'll be shooting, yeah?'

'Probably not. I'm just thinking it's time to let this police know a little more about why we're here.'

Ivan turned and watched the cedars slipping away behind them. In half a minute they were on the main road, heading for the next man on the list.

Mr Thomas Denton. You were part of it, too – a bigger part. And if you only knew what I have in mind for you, Mr Denton, you'd lock up your house and run.

Wednesday Afternoon

Fletcher phoned ahead to make sure Thomas Denton was going to be at home. A woman's voice answered the phone, and confirmed he would be back from an appointment around lunchtime. He thanked her and asked her name.

'Judith Denton.'

He watched the fields racing past. Then he took the Airwave handset from the glovebox and accessed the electoral roll.

Sal glanced across. 'What are you looking for?'

'Who else lives at that address. Here: Thomas Denton and Judith Denton, the only residents at Deep House.'

'She's his wife, then. Am I a good detective or what?'

Fletcher nodded. 'Brilliant. But she sounded very young.'

It was almost two p.m. when they approached Thinbeach. In the distance, the ruined church tower jutted up over fields where the grain was dipping as if big fingers were testing its weight.

Sal followed the directions of the Vectra's Satnav, onto a narrow road that skirted the plastic tunnels glinting on the edge of the village, then into an area where willow and hawthorn grew densely on either side. There were dog roses tangled in the branches, and at times the gap left by a fallen tree showed clumps of reeds sloping down to a surface of sheer black water. A sign read, *Thinbeach Fen*.

'There it is.'

Sal took a turning marked, *Deep House, Strictly Private*.

It led into the fen itself, a long curve with more banks of reeds beside the road. Fletcher realised this was a substantial property, the grounds running to a few acres in the heart of the old landscape. Then they rounded a last curve, and arrived at a clearing.

'So Thomas Denton's home is rather different from Peter Charter's,' Sal said.

The house was enormous: a cantilevered hull of wood and metal with windows reflecting the white clouds. It had clearly been designed by a visionary architect: despite its size, it fitted perfectly in the landscape, like a massive boat with its prow beached among the reeds.

Access was by a timber ramp leading up to a huge glass door – which again gave the feeling of boarding a ship. The doorway was slid half open, and when Fletcher leaned in and called *hello*, a woman's voice invited them inside.

The interior space was massive. A polished marble floor reflected the whiteness of the ceilings and the ash beams running overhead. A series of glass tables reflected the wall hangings, the bright ceramic sculptures placed in niches, a monumental piece of abstract art running the whole length of one wall. One of the tables also held the reflection of a young woman, seated perfectly still on a long leather bench, her hands folded in her lap.

Sal and Fletcher introduced themselves.

The woman smiled. She went to the stairs and called up, 'Father, the police are here.'

Sal whispered, 'I'm a *bad* detective.'

The woman came back and settled herself again. She was wearing a simple but fabulously cut linen dress. She slipped her bare legs off the bench and stretched them out on the shiny floor. She said, 'I'm Judith.'

She was around twenty-five, Fletcher guessed, and there was something unsettling about her. She had dark hair curving on either side of a face that came straight from a silent film: high-cheeked and quite pale, with lips that pursed as if she were always considering something. Her eyes, under the straight dark fringe, were a smoky green – and as for her body, he wondered if she was some kind of athlete, maybe a swimmer? Then he noticed a boxer's punch bag hanging from a beam in one corner of the room. He glanced at her hands.

He looked up and saw a man watching him from the foot of the stairs, a big man in his fifties reflected in a low glass table, taking his time unscrewing a cigar tube. He was wearing a monogrammed shirt, a Rolex, jeans and city shoes. He lit his cigar with a petrol lighter, puffing grey smoke. Finally he said, 'I'm Thomas Denton. And you're in time for a late lunch.'

'Thank you, but we're on duty.'

The man laughed. 'I'm not asking you to dance, son. I'm saying have lunch.'

Fletcher hadn't realised how hungry he was.

Denton had something already cooking over in the kitchen space beyond a long wall of ribbed glass. 'Guess what it is,' he said, with a grin, bringing the dishes to the table. Fletcher sampled it: some kind of fish, with an earthy tang.

'Freshwater fish?'

'Could be.'

Fletcher noticed Judith smiling in a shy and secret way. He noticed that Judith never looked directly at her father, and he noticed Sal watching her too. He noticed Denton's cigar smouldering in a far corner of the room.

'This must be serious, if there's two of you,' Denton said with another big grin. He flexed his wide shoulders under the silk shirt. He glanced at Sal, then back to Fletcher.

'It's about The Wake,' Fletcher said.

Denton's smile didn't change, but for a second his brown eyes moved over to the window.

'The old club?'

'Tell me about it.'

Denton raised an eyebrow. 'Hereward The Wake,' he said. 'That's why we called it The Wake, did you know that? After the local hero.' He began to nod to himself and speak more quickly, the fish untasted on his plate. 'Those were fun times. We had these historical costumes, Normans and Saxons, like the real thing. We used to tour around the villages giving re-enactments. You haven't lived till you've put on chain-mail and hefted a Norman broadsword through the air. Makes a noise like I don't know what.'

'Mr Denton—' Sal began.

'You can call me Thomas. It's OK.'

'Thomas, do you know why we're asking?'

'Like a girl sighing,' Thomas said suddenly. 'I mean, that's the noise a broadsword makes. Why *are* you asking, anyway? The Wake folded up years ago, we all got too busy.' He gestured around at the house. 'I was too busy building this.'

Judith stayed silent, her green eyes watching the trees beyond the window.

Sal said, 'Something's been happening at the Breakman depot.'

'Too right,' Thomas agreed. 'Billy handed over the business to that useless son of his. Watch Crispin wreck it inside a year. I heard his office boy got chewed up in a shredder – if that's not an omen, what is?'

'That's actually why we're asking,' Fletcher interrupted. 'The office boy was interested in The Wake. Can you think why?'

Thomas shook his head slowly. 'No. But I heard the kid was pretty weird. Except his taste in women – I heard that was distinctly international, am I right?' His confident smile came back. He went to pick up his cigar, examining the tip. 'Have you asked the other guys? My old mates in The Wake?'

'Peter Charter, yes. Billy Breakman, no. Billy was the leader, wasn't he?'

'Billy was the organiser, yes. He's a great guy, that Billy – everyone respects him. God knows how Crispin turned out the way he did. Boarding school, probably.' Thomas relit his cigar and wreathed himself in the fumes.

Sal said, 'Judith, do you know anything about all this?'

Judith's eyes moved slowly away from the window and turned to Sal. She said, 'No.'

Thomas came over to stand behind his daughter, looking down at her, one hand resting on the back of her seat, the cigar between his fingers drifting fumes. With his other hand he reached out and lifted Judith's hair from the side of her face and smoothed it back against her head.

Fletcher caught Sal's glance. Thomas said, 'Judith was born after The Wake folded up. Judith works with me.'

'What do you do, Judith?' Sal asked.

'She—'

'Judith?'

Judith moved her hair away from her father's fingers with a slight movement that seemed to be familiar to her, almost involuntary. Thomas went to the window and looked out while Judith said, 'I help my father with Denton Landmass. I have an office here, upstairs.' She paused. 'I've never heard of The Wake. I thought you were here about the other man.'

'What other man?'

'Two weeks ago, there was a man here, walking along the approach road.' Fletcher felt his own pulse pick up a beat. 'Then at the weekend, Sunday, he was here again, on the other side of the water out there.'

'Can you describe this man?' Sal asked. Thomas had turned and was staring, his cigar ash flaking onto the floor.

Judith said, 'He had something wrong under his chin, with his throat. Who is he?'

Fletcher turned to Thomas Denton. 'Thomas, someone else is interested in The Wake. There are two men in the area that we need to find, probably illegal immigrants.'

Thomas spoke to his daughter for the first time. 'You didn't tell me about this.'

'It was just a man.' She looked at Fletcher. 'Immigrants from where?'

'Russia. Does that mean anything to you, Thomas?'

Thomas Denton studied his cigar again, its glow reflected in the picture glass and the ceramic ornaments on the walls. He spoke to the tip. 'Why would a Russian be hanging around here? I've no idea.'

'Ever heard of a kind of tractor called Niva?'

'No. Sorry I can't be more help.' He lifted his eyes and smiled for the last time. 'Did you like the lunch?'

Fletcher surveyed his plate. 'What was it, Thomas?'

'Where are we, Inspector Fletcher? We're on the old Isle of Eels. You've had local eel, the best kind – caught at night. Tastes of the fen, yeah?'

*   *   *

Judith saw them out onto the ramp. Behind her in the big room, her father was watching through his mist of smoke.

Sal said, 'Judith, did the man with the scar try to speak to you at all?'

'No. I just saw him standing, watching.'

'Watching you?'

'I suppose so. Or the house.'

Sal gave her a card. 'If there's anything you want to talk about. Anything that occurs to you.'

Judith nodded.

'Judith, is your mother around?'

'She's not here any more.'

The breeze was blowing Judith's hair across her face and she smoothed it down, and for a moment Fletcher thought she was going to say something else. Then her eyes moved around to the room where her father was waiting.

'That was frigging creepy.'

They were standing under an old ash tree on the road outside the fen, and the light was making tiger stripes across her face. The air was dusty and still, and a worker bee had settled on the bark behind her, resting its wings.

Fletcher said, 'You refer to Thomas Denton's relationship with his daughter?'

'I refer to the fact he strokes her hair and she works in an upstairs room. When we get this Wake thing finished I want to look into that family some more. And by the way, he knew something more about The Wake.'

'Yes, he did. He tried to conceal it, but he made some connection. And the presence of the Russian meant something to him. Seems like the higher up The Wake we get, the more these people know.'

'I wonder what Billy Breakman could tell us?'

'Webley's onto that. Can you drop me at my car and then be back in Cambridge in twenty minutes?'

'Easy. Why?'

Judith stood on the ramp, breathing in the fen, feeling the afternoon heat coming off the house. She felt her father's presence behind her even before she smelled his cigar.

'You didn't tell me, Judith.'

'Why does it matter?'

'Why? A Russian strolling around on my property?'

She turned and faced him. They were the same height, and she felt her fingers flex.

'Who is he, father?'

'If he's who I think he is – oh, Jesus. Get inside and lock the door. I'm going to drive around the fen, see if anyone's here now. I might be a while.'

He got his Volvo off-roader from the car port under the house and took off along the roadway. Judith stood looking out over the empty courtyard until the sound of the car had gone. She smoothed her hair back beside her face.

From a clump of rushes beside the house, Ivan listened as the sound of the Volvo faded. He watched the woman at the top of the ramp go back into the house.

The breeze was moving her dark hair and pushing her dress against her flank, the way it had when he'd passed her on the road here two weeks ago. He remembered thinking then, *She's perfect.*

Only once before had he seen a woman with that beauty and that power in her body. He caught a glimpse of her profile before she closed the glass door.

He thought, *She really is perfect.*

And he was sure of his plan, seeing the police talking to her. The police hadn't seen what he'd seen, watching this house at night through infra-red binoculars. He didn't know her name, but he knew she was Denton's daughter and she was going to be part of his critical work, and he knew she would understand everything. He already felt excited about telling her.

★

Ivan put on his coat and went to the stairwell outside the apartment door. Looking down, he saw other doors opening: people watching the party man come up the stairs, his breath pluming in the cold. The man looked straight ahead, holding his leather bag.

Ivan saw him come onto the top-floor landing and check the door numbers, then knock on the neighbour's door — three sharp knocks. The door opened, and after a few words the party man stepped inside.

Ivan went back inside his apartment and sat at the kitchen table. His mother was washing clothes in the sink, soapy water steaming the window.

There was a knock on their own door: Ivan recognised the style. Ivan's mother dried her hands and went to answer. Again, some words were spoken which Ivan didn't catch.

She came back into the kitchen with the party man. He was wide enough to fill the doorway. Behind him came the woman who lived next door. She put her hands on Ivan's shoulders and held him close so he felt the roughness of her apron against his face, smelling of cigarettes and onions. The party man asked Ivan's mother to sit at the table, then he sat down too. He had a kind face, but he was very pale. His lips were stark red against the pallor.

Then he began speaking.

★

Fletcher drove straight to Fen Lodge, looking for Crispin Breakman. Nobody had anything good to say about Crispin, and his wife had just killed herself, but he was the only person in Thinbeach who had the information Fletcher needed right now. The house, though, was in mourning: the curtains were drawn, and he saw condolence flowers on the hallway table when the front door was opened by the cleaner.

She explained that Crispin was at the depot.

'The poor man can't bear to be in the house. He says he needs paperwork to distract him.'

Fletcher left her watching from behind parted curtains.

At the depot, things were superficially normal. The staff were coming and going and talking normally, or at least they tried to when Fletcher walked in. From reception, he was shown up a flight of steel stairs to Crispin's office.

The blinds were closed against the windows, but enough light came through to show dust drifting in a big room, the walls hung with photos of Billy Breakman and his staff standing proudly in front of the building, plus various trophies, maps of East Anglia, and framed adverts for fertiliser and spare parts. The window on the far wall looked down into the hangar where Jake Skerrit had died, the bright roofs of the farm vehicles just visible.

Some model tractors were lined up on Crispin's mahogany desk. Behind it, in the gloomy light, Crispin himself was in a bad way: crumpled shirt, hair unkempt, scarcely less pale than when Fletcher had last seen him in the kitchen of Fen Lodge. He was obviously trying to keep himself busy: he had some papers spread out in front of him, including some maps.

That made sense, because Alain de Minching was seated beside the desk, impeccably dressed in a linen suit, white shirt and dark tie, arranging counters on the map. He rose and shook hands formally, without explaining his presence, and Fletcher noticed in the shadows on the floor one of the superb dogs lying with paws together and eyes closed, tongue lolling in the heat.

Crispin offered coffee from a percolator: dark with a rainbowed surface, like machine oil.

He asked, 'Is this about Olga?'

Fletcher sat with some coffee. 'Not directly about

Olga. I'm sorry to intrude at such a difficult time.' He nodded at the papers on the desk. 'More preparations for the Thinbeach Wedding?'

Alain de Minching answered.

'When I heard the news about poor Olga, I thought it would help Crispin to have something to talk about. It's not easy to plan – as you know, we have to time it with the first harvest, and that's not always known in advance with great precision.'

'Why does it have to coincide with the harvest?'

Alain became enthusiastic. 'Perhaps the origin of the festival, even before Chretien de Minchin threw his wife into the Pool, was to ensure good crops, or to cast away bad luck. That might be something that goes back thousands of years, to the first agriculture. Imagine it, the way we're continuing the past.' He looked at the map and stroked the dark oval of the Pool.

Crispin cleared his throat. 'It does help, talking about something else. But if it's not Olga, what is it?'

Fletcher paused. He said, 'It's about Niva Stavropol.'

Alain de Minching looked puzzled, and Crispin frowned to himself. 'Niva? You're going back a bit now. That was a type of tractor.'

'Can you tell me what you know about it?'

Crispin leaned back and looked at the dust moving in the light across the desk.

'Niva was a works in the old Soviet Union. Back in the seventies and eighties, they exported gear to the West. I remember they made a car called the Cossack, like a little Land Rover, which you still see around sometimes. Mostly they exported farm tractors. They were pretty temperamental old things, people say. I don't think many came here – I haven't seen one for years.'

'Did Breakman Machinery ever sell them?'

'Did we sell them? I suppose we could check.'

Crispin went over to a cabinet and rifled through until he found something that Fletcher had seen before: the souvenir catalogue from 1980. Billy Breakman stared out from the inside cover as Crispin folded the page over. 'Yeah, we stocked them from '79. Funny-looking machines.'

Fletcher took the catalogue. On page seven was a photo of the type of tractor he had seen in Peter Charter's barn, and a list of prices. Niva was the cheapest tractor available.

Alain's dog licked its lips and panted.

Fletcher said, 'Crispin, please think carefully. Do you recall your father mentioning Niva at all, or these old Niva tractors, or anything to do with them?'

'No, but I was just a kid back then. I was away at school most of the time.'

'Did Jake Skerrit or Ron Teversham talk about Niva?'

'Jake loved machines in general. I don't think he ever mentioned Niva, no. Old Ron certainly didn't. Why?'

'Alain, does Niva mean anything to you?'

Alain de Minching shook his head and spread his fingers. The hair on his wrists was black under the white cuffs.

'I'm not a farmer, Inspector. Tractors are all the same to me.'

Fletcher asked his last question. 'Crispin, I'm sorry to raise a painful subject. You're being very strong. Did Olga talk about Niva at all?'

'Not Niva,' said Crispin. 'But Stavropol, obviously. She was from there, you see. Olga was from Stavropol.'

Fletcher went into a separate room and called Sal in Parkside.

'1979, Sal. That's when the tractors arrived in Thinbeach. Check 1979.'

Fletcher walked downstairs with Crispin. The guy needed a bath, and moved with a jerky energy. In reception, he said, 'Hey, come and look at this. Just been delivered.'

They went into the hangar area and stood looking at the rows of machines. Over where the shredder had stood, the cement floor had been scrubbed, but it was still a darker shade. Towering over everything was a combine harvester: a machine the size of a small house, access ladders bolted over the superstructure, its massive cylindrical cutter topped with a TV camera for the driver's forward vision. Crispin walked over and put his hand on the cutter's gleaming metal spikes.

'It's a beauty, isn't it? These combines, they're like animals that wake up for a week each year. They do their job, and they go back to sleep for fifty-one weeks.'

Above them, the driver's cab was a tinted perspex bubble, like a jet fighter.

Fletcher said, 'How are you coping, Crispin?'

'I keep asking if it's my fault.' Crispin looked up at

the machine, smoothing his messy hair. He seemed desperate to talk on another subject. 'Until you've seen one of these in action, you don't know what machinery is. This is the new high-speed drum. It cuts thirty feet wide, clean to the ground. She'll leave a plume in the air behind her for half a mile – that's grain husk, pulverised by the threshing. When the cutter's spinning, the dust makes the space around it unbreathable, plus it generates static, you can see it sparking. Imagine stepping in front of this, it's like if you stepped on the surface of that planet – is it Neptune, or Saturn? You'd be suffocated, electrocuted and crushed all at once.'

'I think that's Venus. It's good of Alain to take care of you.'

Crispin smiled again, in a different way. 'He's a good guy. You know his story, of course.'

'He says he's descended from a Norman commander.'

'A Norman commander?' Crispin chuckled, glancing up at the office window. 'Alain really believes that, he believes the whole village is descended from Chretien de Minchin. A lot of people here still believe it too. But there's another story about Alain – have you heard it?'

'I'd love to.'

'Some people say Alain's great-great-something grandfather was a horse butcher from Antwerp who sold a consignment of infected meat to Napoleon's army just before Waterloo. It's a fact that a battalion of French guards missed the battle due to dysentery.

They say the British thanked him with a bag of sovereigns and let him hide away up here. He changed his name to de Minching, bought The Blindy House and settled down. Who knows?'

'But the parish records show the family tree, don't they?'

Crispin shrugged. 'What records? Up till the war, they were kept in a trunk in the church that only the de Minchings had the key to. But then a Flying Fortress dumped a bomb in the fields, wrecked the church and everything in it.'

Fletcher looked up at the office window. 'What exactly does he do for a living? He said he invests.'

'In everything. Those polythene tunnels, they're growing strawberries in there. That's his land. He owns race horses at Newmarket and a big share in a marina development in Cambridge. It gives him time to do his Wedding stuff.' That seemed to remind Crispin of something, because he ran out of words suddenly and put his forehead against the steel. 'Oh God, I loved Olga. Last night I was thinking, was she a kind of Thinbeach Bride? The young girl who marries the older man, doesn't find happiness?'

Fletcher said, 'You didn't drown her in the Pool, Crispin.'

'No.' Crispin closed his eyes and pressed his whole face against the machine. 'I gave her everything.'

Fletcher stood on the mound overlooking Thinbeach Pool. The high clouds were reflected in its surface as a few swallows flew overhead, and the rushes along the circular bank leaned unmoving in the warm sun.

Something had happened here, he knew. Something had happened involving those Russian Niva tractors, and Breakman Machinery, and a harmless historical society called The Wake, in which people dressed up in chainmail and swung broadswords through the air. Whatever had happened back then, Ivan was now circling the local members of The Wake, Charter and Denton, trying to get close to them. Why? Why not just beat it out of them?

Or did Ivan already know what had happened?

His phone rang, and Webley came on the line. The reception failed, and he had to try twice before he got it back. Fletcher smiled, picturing Webley stretching her arms in her cool office, remembering their last conversation, remembering the version of it he'd played in his mind, wanting to talk more. But now she was in a hurry, and he found out why.

'Fletcher, listen. I can see Sal Moresby's back here doing something with records. The Portuguese police have responded – they say they have absolutely no information on Billy Breakman, except that he's listed as resident in a golfing complex called Parque da Pinta. Sounds delightful. But on the other hand, we've just had a fax from Moscow.'

'A fax?'

'A real old-fashioned fax, yes. It's got an eagle at the top and everything. From a Detective Captain Vasily Gartov, federal police organised crime department. You're going to have to read this through, but basically there are large numbers of ex-Red Army criminals in circulation over there, and a lot of them use the name Ivan.'

'Russian humour?'

'Evidently. But Captain Gartov recognises one aspect of your description: a man with a scar under his chin. There's an army ID picture here. The English in the fax isn't great, but they're saying this sounds like a notorious individual called Ivan Gorensky, formerly a Master Sergeant in the specialised brigade of the second Russian Airborne Division. The tone suggests the federal police are glad he's over here and not over there. They describe him as organised and imaginative.'

'Imaginative?'

'You know what he specialises in? Revenge. Anyone he believes has betrayed him, or even insulted him, he finds the nastiest possible way of taking revenge on them.'

'You mean, he kills them?'

That still didn't make sense – Ivan had every chance to kill both Charter and Denton. What was he waiting for?

Webley's voice was getting distorted by the reception quality. 'He doesn't necessarily kill people, no. He studies them, examines their lives, and finds the cruellest possible way of tormenting them. It's a psychological thing, maybe a Russian cultural thing, I don't know. But Gorensky finds your deepest fear, and he uses that against you. Sick stuff. Fletcher?'

Fletcher watched two swallows dipping over the Pool. He was thinking of Charter alone in his farmhouse, terrified of night coming down – and Thomas Denton stroking his daughter's hair as if he'd been doing it all his life.

'Fletcher?'

'Ma'am, I can see what Gorensky is doing here. He wants revenge for something. I just can't see what that something is. I need to bring him in—'

'Stop, Fletcher. There are words here that cause me grave concern. Words like Master Sergeant, Airborne Division, that kind of thing. They're armed criminals, need to be met with armed response.'

'They haven't committed a crime. They have not committed a crime—'

'Are you defending them? Illegal entry, illegal passports, illegal handgun. The old missile base is a nature reserve, isn't it? Did they mistreat any animals? We can add that on too. But we'll probably deport them, if they survive the arrest. Big *if*.'

Fletcher knew what she meant. The Tactical Firearms Unit of the eastern counties police was a small but highly enthusiastic team, trained by the military. In recent years, they'd earned the nickname *Glockenspiel*. Not due to any musical talent, but because of the 9mm Glock handguns they used, and the *spiel* – the stories they liked to tell about their achievements. A confrontation between armed police and the two Russians would be brief and pretty spectacular.

He said, 'Not the Glockenspiel. Ivan Gorensky's here for a reason, a grievance he's got against Thinbeach because of an event in the past. We need to find out what that event was. Shoot Ivan and we'll lose it.'

Webley paused. 'It's appropriate for you to try to identify his whereabouts. But after that, it's a firearms job.'

'As a last resort, ma'am. Not as a first option.'

Webley went quiet. Then, above the buzzing connection and the grasshoppers around him, he could hear her talking to someone else in the room. A man's voice. Sounded like a heated argument.

Then, 'We'll consult when you get back, Fletcher.'

Out in the main office, Sal Moresby was getting a headache. She knew Fletcher's reasoning was simple enough. If the old Niva tractor in Charter's barn arrived in Cambridgeshire around twenty-five years ago, something must have happened back then to make it important to Ivan. Possibly something serious enough to leave a trace in police records.

So Sal was looking for something that might fit, sifting through layers of old crimes in the villages around Thinbeach, and getting nowhere. She went back so far that she exhausted the computer database and had to go to the old microfiche machine housed in its own secure room, and start sliding rows of data through the screen by hand. There were plenty of minor offences, a few that were serious but didn't seem relevant: an arson from 1982, part of a neighbours' dispute; a strangling from 1981, result of an incestuous marriage.

Then Fletcher's call came through, emphasising 1979.

'I was just getting to that, Fletcher.'

She cranked the old tape to access the year. It was disappointingly quiet – not even a strangling, nothing to suggest an event that might tie the Russians to the area. But when she went back even further, to 1978, what she saw filling the screen amazed her.

It was a record of a crime wave in the Thinbeach area: a tide of burglaries and violent assaults on householders that were mostly, as far as the record of attempted convictions showed, committed by kids from the Wittris area.

Some things don't change, she decided: she imagined they were the parents of the Wittris kids who were making Peter Charter's life a misery today. A few names cropped up repeatedly: the same youngsters being arrested, sometimes prosecuted – usually unsuccessfully. It suggested a Wittris gang had been at work, running amok among the wealthier fenland communities.

The crime wave seemed to gather pace towards the end of 1978, and then collapse, because far fewer crimes were recorded in 1979. She stopped.

She went back a few entries.

There was something on the file under January 1979 that she couldn't read, because its details were blanked out. The blank area had been printed with the words *Refer H47*.

That meant nothing to her. She took down the obsolete files from the shelf in the microfiche room and rifled through. The files smelled musty and had steel callipers holding the pages together. In the third one, she found a list of codes used for security classification of microfiche material. The list was typed on a 1970s' daisywheel, and the codes themselves had long passed out of use. She found H47. It meant that whatever had happened on January the tenth 1979 was classified at the level of the Home Office.

Sal stopped. She thought for a minute, then heaved the callipers shut. She went out to her workstation and dialled the desk of a man in the *Cambridge Evening News* who sent her a Valentine card every year.

'Derek? It's Sal Moresby. And lovely to speak to you too. Derek, can you help me out? Can you look something up in your archive? The *Evening News* for January the tenth 1979. General interest. Anything around the Thinbeach area.'

Derek just wanted to be loved. She made a mental note to send him a Christmas card. When he phoned back, she listened for a minute, then thanked him. She went to the window and looked out at the trees on Parker's Piece. She took a cup of water from the machine and pressed it against her face.

Her phone rang again.

Judith heard a knock on the glass. It was loud and confident, echoing around the big room. She went to see.

The man was standing on the ramp. He was tall, with powerful shoulders, and he was wearing a soldier's camouflage uniform which made his body blend into the greenery around the courtyard. His face stood out, though. His honey-coloured eyes were an oval shape which she remembered from the roadway outside. His hair was neat, and she had the impression he'd just wet and combed it. His collar was open on that scar under his chin.

She went back into the room and found the policewoman's card and phoned her. The policewoman told her not to open the door. She phoned her father and heard the tyres screaming as he turned his car around.

Judith sat for half a minute, thinking. Then she went back to the door and the man was still there, waiting, with his hair smoothed down. His gaze travelled down over her dress and back up. She let her eyes run down over him in turn, and she put her hand on the door, her thumb resting on the catch. She made him wait.

Fletcher took the road to Charter Farm, thinking about how imaginative Ivan really was. The guy needed a place to hide out, middle of nowhere, easy to conceal himself, and he coincided it with an opportunity to get close to Peter Charter, the little man in The Wake he'd heard about on Teversham's cassette. Ivan liked to play on people's nightmares. Charter's nightmares came in the shape of kids from Wittris.

Sal came on the phone.

'Fletcher, I've found an event. Could be the event that connects Niva tractors to Thinbeach.'

'In police records?'

'I've been through other sources. I'm coming up to Thinbeach now because I've just had a call from Judith Denton. She's alone in Deep House and she says there's a Russian outside.'

'What does the Russian want?'

'She doesn't know.'

Fletcher turned the Audi around in the entrance to a field. If burglars were Charter's nightmare, what was Thomas Denton's?

'Is Judith afraid?' he asked.

'She didn't sound very afraid.'

'I'll be there in ten minutes. And you?'

'About twenty. I might miss the show.'

Fletcher wondered what sort of show it was going to be.

★

Ivan never remembered what was said. He didn't need to, because he remembered what he saw.

There was the party man: his pale face and his red lips moving silently, like a film with no sound. There was the red glint of the star in his lapel. There was the steam from the washing, and the smell of the neighbour woman's apron.

From the side of his vision he saw his mother bunch her hands against her face. He saw the red from the washing, against the white skin of her fingers. The red tightened so much that it became white. There was steam coming from her nails.

The party man's lips were still moving. He put out a hand and reached inside his satchel. He brought out a large brown envelope bulging with contents. He opened the flap and emptied it carefully onto the table.

Ivan felt the neighbour woman suck in her breath. He saw the things settle on the table, without hearing any sounds.

They were his father's things. He almost laughed, seeing how absurd they were without his father to use them. There was his father's wallet, and his watch, and a copper band he wore for rheumatism. The last thing was his father's steel pencil. The point was snapped off, but it only needed his father's fingers to make it draw again. Everything lay there on the table: all the pieces of his father.

The party man reached into the satchel again and brought out a dark metal casket. The casket made a shadow on the table when he placed it down. It had a label pasted on the side. It was typed in English letters which Ivan couldn't read.

The party man hesitated. He glanced at his satchel. There was still something else inside there.

Wednesday Evening

As the road straightened towards Thinbeach Fen, Fletcher saw a shape moving fast up ahead in the late sunshine: a Volvo, turning in a cloud of dust into the drive leading to Deep House.

He followed it along the curved track screened by willows and ferns, until he came onto the courtyard below the house. He found the Volvo slewed sideways with one door left open. There was no sign of any other vehicle. The only sound was the movement of the rushes, and some birds calling. The glass door at the top of the ramp was half open. When Fletcher looked inside, it wasn't immediately clear what was going on.

Berlitz was there, holding his Margolin pistol at his side, the black fin glinting on the barrel.

'Please do step inside, police.'

Once Berlitz had run the glass door shut, Fletcher found Thomas Denton facing him against the other wall, his hands curling and uncurling, his eyes sliding left and right.

Then Fletcher saw why.

The far side of the house framed a small open courtyard: high walls of glass surrounding a square of marble blocks, a bronze fountain, an acer bush as vivid as the evening clouds reflected in the other walls. Inside the courtyard, behind a glass door that had been closed for privacy, were Judith and Ivan.

They were seated on a steel bench, facing each other. They were oblivious to the others, absorbed in their own conversation. They weren't arguing, or threatening each other, Fletcher realised. It seemed that Ivan was explaining something, speaking while looking into Judith's eyes. Judith was listening and nodding and sometimes asking questions, putting up a hand when she wanted to cut in.

A dragonfly dipped down into the courtyard and hovered by the fountain, its wings an electric blue.

With that, the discussion seemed to end. Ivan stood and reached out to shake Judith's hand. He bowed his head and held it there a moment and said something. Judith nodded, still holding his hand. Ivan turned and opened the courtyard door and came through to the house.

He looked as Fletcher remembered him from the bunker, except for combat fatigues instead of pinstripe over the gleaming boots. There was the vicious scar under his chin, the slabbed angles of his face, and the almond-shaped eyes surveying the room, taking things in. If he was surprised to see the others here, he didn't show it. He studied Denton for a moment without speaking, then nodded to Fletcher, and gestured to Berlitz that they were leaving.

Denton stepped across and went to put a hand on him. Ivan turned. Berlitz cocked the Margolin with a sound like bones sliding together. Behind him, the clouds were turning sunset colour through the glass.

Denton stopped and took his hand back, but he had his eyes fixed on Ivan's eyes.

'What were you saying to my girl?'

Ivan looked back at him, expressionless. 'Ask her. She's a good listener.' He glanced at Fletcher. 'She'll tell you everything.'

Then he gestured to Berlitz again and they went through the door into the late sun, Berlitz turning in the doorway to take a last look at Denton before leaving, slipping the pistol inside his jacket. From the woods near the house came the rumble of a big engine. It revved and faded away along the driveway.

Judith came into the house and settled herself on the seating, her hair hanging either side of her face, her eyes meeting her father's. Fletcher could see specks of dust turning in the light. He could almost hear them.

Denton said, 'Who are they? How did they get in the house?'

'I don't know who they are. I let them in. He said he wanted to talk to me.'

Denton clenched his hands. 'About what?'

'Things he wanted me to know. His childhood.'

'His fucking childhood?' He jabbed a finger at Fletcher. 'His friend had a gun, did you see that? Why aren't you phoning for helicopters and things?'

'We'll pick them up. Right now, I want to know what's going on. I want to hear what he had to say. Judith?'

Judith closed her eyes a second. She settled back and

let her hands rest on her knees and began to tell Ivan's story. She started where he started, in the Hall of Soviet Achievement, with the leader of the Girls' Socialist Pioneers. Then the accommodation in Stavropol, listening to his father at the kitchen table with the snow falling on the Russian plain beyond the smoke of the Niva Works.

While she was speaking, Fletcher watched the clouds through the huge windows turning a deeper red. He was thinking of Ivan, the man with the scar under his chin, the man with a father he adored. For a moment he thought about Electric Mile.

Judith finished the story back in the kitchen in Stavropol, with a Communist Party official biting one of his red lips and glancing at his own leather satchel.

*

In the few seconds that the man hesitated, Ivan understood what was happening. His hearing came back, and he heard his mother's breathing. Then the party man reached into the satchel for the last item.

'This too,' he said. 'This was among his possessions.'

He took the thing out of the bag and placed it on the table. It lay there among his father's things. Ivan heard the chair scrape as his mother got to her feet. She pointed at it and said, 'Take it away.'

The party man looked confused. Ivan's mother began to shout, and then to scream for him to take it away. The neighbour let go of Ivan's shoulders and tried to hold her, but she was screaming with her eyes wide and spit flying from her mouth.

Ivan grabbed the thing from the table. He could feel the evil attached to it, this thing that had somehow fastened itself onto his father's body. He took it and ran out of the apartment. Other doors were opening as he ran down the stairs with the thing in his hand. Then he was outside, running across the snow past the sputnik frame and the labour monument, breath getting cold and hard in his chest. He ran out onto the frozen reservoir. The ice was hard as concrete under the snow. He ran across it, sliding and stumbling, and up the embankment on the other side.

He looked down over the railway yards and the Niva Works and breathed in the smoke from the chimneys. He stood panting, looking at the thing the party man had put on the table.

He was already thinking about the future.

*

It was quiet in the house among the reeds. Denton was still leaning silently against the wall, his eyes fixed on his daughter. Judith glanced up.

She said, 'That's where he finished.'

'What was it?' Fletcher asked. 'What was the last item in the satchel?'

'He didn't explain. He just called it *the thing*.'

'So how did his father die?'

'I asked, obviously. I don't think he even knows.' Then Judith looked past Fletcher. 'Hello, Sal.'

Sal had stepped in through the rampway door and caught the end of the story. She looked worried. Fletcher still wanted to get to Charter Farm before

the light faded, before Peter Charter succumbed to his
own fears.

They left Denton immobile against the wall, watching his daughter close her eyes again and settle back.
The sun was making the glass walls a furnace.

They took Sal's car through the woods. Dragonflies
were twitching in the shadows, Sal making no concessions to the sharp turn onto the main road, Fletcher
holding on tight as the car straightened up and began
the drive towards Charter Farm. He was thinking
about that last item on the kitchen table.

He said, 'And was that the link you found, Sal? That
Ivan's dad was a Niva engineer who came here?'

'No, I didn't know Ivan's dad was a Niva man. But
I think I know how he died, and where.'

'Tell me.'

'Hold on.'

Sal took the car over a railway crossing with a
shudder that cracked Fletcher's teeth. Charter Farm
was still a distance away, up where the sky was red-
dening.

Sal explained. She recapped on the old microfiche
records, the crime wave led by the Wittris gang that
had terrorised fenland in 1978, and the entry under
Thinbeach for January the tenth 1979 – the entry that
was secured at Home Office level.

They were approaching the fields near the farm.
Suddenly Sal braked and brought the car to a halt in
front of a bunch of ragged cows ambling across the
road between the hedges. The windscreen was filled

with the flanks of the animals, black and white stained orange in the evening light. Behind them came Larry, avoiding their look as he shut a gate behind him. Sal let the car idle, saying, 'So out of curiosity I pick up the phone to a contact at the *Evening News*, asking about January the tenth. He calls me back. He says, this is funny – funny peculiar. In the first edition of the *Evening News* for that day, there was a lot of reporting on the weather, because there was a freak chill. The temperature was down to minus nine, roads were closed by ice, the Cam was frozen on the Backs. But there was a report about Thinbeach too. A story about something found that morning in ice at the edge of the river downstream from the Pool. It was a man's body, identity not confirmed, but believed to be Russian. Cause of death believed to be drowning. The peculiar thing is that my contact also checked the later edition of the paper for the same day. The story had been removed. No reference was made to it again, ever. The body just disappeared.'

Fletcher saw in his mind the casket in Ivan's kitchen, the label typed in English.

'That helps to explain Ivan's interest in Thinbeach. His father comes here to fix tractors and ends up not just dead, but drowned. He wants to know what exactly happened. And the death itself *is* puzzling, isn't it? A temperature of minus nine sounds freezing to us – but to a Russian it must be pretty mild. And why would the man be wandering around near the river?'

'And why is the incident classified as Home Office restricted?' Sal moved off again, onto the roadway of bricks leading to the farm. 'Look, now Charter's got some official protection.'

A police car was parked by the tractor barricade – its window, reflecting the livid sky, winding down to reveal a pale young constable. He stared at them both, chewing something.

'I'm just putting in an appearance, sir,' he said, as if he sensed trouble. 'I'm off in a minute.'

'It's after dark that Charter needs protection,' said Sal. 'That's actually what I requested.'

The pale boy kept chewing. 'We'll have a car come past every hour in the night. That's a lot, around here.'

As they parked among the chickens, an upstairs window opened and Peter Charter appeared.

'It'll be dark soon,' he called down. 'And the Russians aren't back.'

An engine started. They turned to see the police car crawling slowly away towards the cedar trees.

'Who's going to look after me?'

Charter lit a hurricane lamp and hung it from the ceiling, then turned the electric light off. A rusty-looking shotgun was broken open on the window sill, plus a row of cartridges, and the fridge had been dragged against the back door. Out in the hallway there was a furniture barricade, and the stairs had been strung with razor wire as some kind of final citadel. The smell of paraffin filled the chaotic room, and Charter's features became even more gaunt as the light swung slowly over him, throwing shadows around the walls.

'Larry's up in the caravan, but he won't lift a finger to help me. He'll laugh while they crucify me.'

'Mr Charter,' Sal said, 'We're here to tell you that you're perfectly safe. And don't even think about pointing that shotgun at anyone. You'll be in serious trouble.'

Charter laughed to himself. 'But I read in the paper, I can shoot burglars. There's a new law.'

'That's a misunderstanding. You can't take the law into your own hands.'

Charter looked down at his hands: two bony working tools. Fletcher guessed they hadn't touched another human being in years. He said, 'Where did you drive them, Mr Charter? The men in The Wake.'

Charter closed his eyes. 'The village fêtes and the festivals. That's all we ever went to. The fêtes and the festivals and the Thinbeach bloody Wedding.'

He didn't change his story from that. On the way back to Thinbeach Fen, Fletcher and Sal had a good view of the low plain to the west. The Wittris Teeth were starting to shine.

They went back to Deep House to pick up Sal's car. There was no sign of human presence in the building, the door locked and only dim lights on inside. Sal proposed returning to Parkside to organise some social services support for Peter Charter. Fletcher agreed: Charter was at risk from his own fears more than the Wittris housebreakers, and neither of them wanted to see him decline further, even if he seemed to be holding information back.

'I'm going to find Alain de Minching,' Fletcher said. 'He's the leader of the community. I'm going to ask him what he knows about the Russian's death. And he should probably cancel the Thinbeach Wedding, as a precaution.'

'A precaution against what?'

'Against Ivan.'

Ivan always did what he said he was going to do. Right now, he was waiting where he said he'd be waiting, where the river curved against the edge of the abandoned American missile base.

From where he lay on his side in the grass, he could just make out that huge plateau of debris, hazy with dandelions, and the mounds of the old bunkers swelling out of the last daylight against the horizon. Beside him, the river itself was almost completely black, the water lapping against a beach scooped out from the bank: a few yards of metallic silt, where the soil was sifting into minerals. He had a long stem of English grass between his teeth. That was something he'd seen in a film: British people lounging around in summertime, chewing grass.

He looked up again.

He saw her approaching against the skyline, walking along the riverbank with her hair blowing a little in the breeze that was starting to ripple the water. He could see she was slightly cold.

He got to his feet and she saw him and walked straight up to him, along the edge of the bank, and, although he could barely see her face, he felt the energy she radiated, on the edge of the dark water.

'So how does the grass taste?' she asked him.

'Like old honey.'

'What do you think of England?'

'Strange place,' he said. 'Everyone lives in houses.'

Suddenly he flinched. Something had touched him, and he realised it was Judith – her fingers brushing the scar under his chin.

'How did it happen?' she asked.

'You ask a lot of questions, Judith.'

He sat down again on the riverbank and felt her sitting next to him. She smelled clean. Something buzzed close to their faces.

'Your father knows you're here?' he asked.

'I didn't tell him. How did it happen?'

'In Chechnya, my officer tried to kill me.'

'Why?'

Ivan took another blade of grass.

'He was sending us into a field where the partisans had a line of fire, they were cutting us down. In a while, he was sending men in and they were treading on bodies. The oldest was twenty, I think the youngest was eighteen. He changed his mind when I put a gun in his face. When we pulled back he got behind me with a bayonet, tried to cut my throat. Berlitz had to break his legs to get him off me. We finished in a military prison.'

He put his hands out and brushed the hair from beside her face, and suddenly she kissed him in a hungry way, then pulled back and he could just make out that she was smiling.

She started telling him about her life in Deep House,

her father's obsessions, his rages, the photo of her mother turned to the wall.

'I know what you're thinking,' she finished. 'Sounds like we've both been in prison.'

'But yours is more comfortable. Why do you stay with him?'

She looked out over the river. 'He's always been there. He's got a hold over me, I can't say what it is. Sometimes I want to leave him, I think of ways to hurt him, really hurt him.'

He nodded. He slipped his hands inside her dress. The tips of her breasts were warm and hard under his fingers.

'It would hurt him, wouldn't it, knowing you're here with me?'

'He'll go insane.' She laughed. 'Your hands are cold.'

'Judith, when I saw you I had a strange feeling. You look exactly like a woman I once saw years ago, in Chechnya. A famous woman. Like you got a twin sister.'

'What was she famous for?'

'I'll tell you another time. Are my hands still cold?'

'No. What was the last thing in the satchel?'

'Let your police friends find out.'

She kissed him again. 'What do you really want here?'

'Let me phrase it like this. Don't go to the Thinbeach Wedding.'

'What are you going to do?'

'Something people will talk about for a thousand years.'

Then, because he wanted to see her before the light faded completely, he opened up her dress and spread her back on the riverbank. The turf was still warm underneath her, as he ran his hands along her thighs. Her body scent and the grass made him close his eyes for a while. When he opened them, the light had almost gone. In front of him, her body was a pale outline. The only sounds were the drone of an airliner circling, the river lapping at the silted beach, and her jagged breathing. He felt her wrap her legs around his shoulders and begin pushing him down.

In the end, he found himself on his knees, sinking a little, his chest leaning against the riverbank where her thighs, spread apart for his mouth, made a pale arrow shape in the dusk, her calves hanging over the bank on either side of him and her feet digging into the silt. Another airliner flew over, its lights blinking.

She said, with a long smile in her voice, 'Do you think they can—' he felt her hands on the back of his neck '—Ivan, you think they can see us?'

He thought, *I hope so.*

From the garden of The Blindy House, Fletcher looked back along the Shamblings. The half-timbered houses huddled over the street, their eaves almost touching, lights in the windows glowing against the wooden ribs. It was humid, and the smell of the river came from over the earth mound, blending with the shrubs in the garden. Alain's dogs barked inside the house, and when Alain opened the door, his face was turned away calling to them, his profile outlined against the interior lamps. When he looked at Fletcher, his face broke into a smile as he shook hands and pulled the door wider. He was wearing his impeccable at-home clothes: linen trousers, Lacoste polo shirt with the tangle of chest hair visible, a jersey slung over his shoulders. Was he descended from a Norman commander, or a Belgian horse-butcher? Impossible to say.

'Still on duty, Inspector? Come through to the Pool again.'

Alain spoke walking across the hall towards the terrace steps. On one side, the display of corn dolls shimmered on one wall, the scraps of bright silk wrapped around their necks. On the other side, a doorway was half-open – and when Fletcher glanced in, he paused momentarily.

Alain came back from the top of the steps and pushed the door wide.

'A hobby of mine. Have a look.'

It was a large room, with a stone window giving onto the garden railings. The central space was taken up completely by a long table on trestle legs, lit by hot overhead lamps. The table was fitted out as a miniature landscape, with fields, hills and fences and a few tiny buildings carefully recreated. The landscape was peopled by hundreds of tiny figures – lead soldiers, Fletcher saw, each no bigger than his thumbnail, but immaculately painted and equipped with backpacks and muskets, squads of cavalry charging against miniature cannon. The amount of work invested in the scene was amazing.

Alain adjusted the direction of a lancer.

'Salamanca, 1812,' he explained. 'The turning point in the late Peninsular War. When you're single at my age, you find ways to fill the evenings. And I do like these Napoleonic uniforms. I like it when you come to visit me, Inspector. I want to help, you know that.'

'I know.' Fletcher surveyed the table, seeing the sabres glittering as the troops in blue scattered the troops in red, forcing them into a pincer trap. 'I think you know everything that goes on in this village, Alain, is that right?'

'Probably.'

'But when I asked you today at the depot if you'd heard of Niva, you denied it.'

Alain closed his eyes for a moment and nodded. 'I see. So you know.'

'About January the tenth, 1979? Yes – and so do you, evidently. So tell me about the Russian engineer. Then tell me why you pretended not to know.'

Alain took a breath, crouched down and looked across the table, his eyes level with the retreating red soldiers. He squinted left and right, sighting lines of musket fire.

He said, 'OK. It was a generation ago. But I remember that morning as if it were yesterday.' He stood and flexed his back and his fingers before speaking. He went on, 'It was cold. Absolutely freezing. Most people were safely indoors, so not many people knew that a body had been found on the riverbank downstream. It didn't take the police long to connect it with a hire car abandoned on the main road. They must have found Russian documents inside, you see, because later that day I was visited by a senior member of the Cambridgeshire Constabulary – a very senior member. I think you can guess what rank.'

'What did he want?'

Alain stood up and adjusted the cashmere across his shoulders. 'He wanted a promise, which I gave. I gave him my solemn word, as a descendant of Chretien de Minchin, that the villagers would never discuss the body with anyone. And we've kept our promise, those few of us who were aware of the death. Even when you asked me today, I was honour-bound not to tell you. You do understand, don't you?'

That certainly tied in with the official secrecy around the death, but Fletcher said, 'Hold on, Alain. I'm impressed by your discretion, but we seem to have missed a stage here. What I'm really asking is what happened to the man. How did he come to be dead in the river?'

Alain turned his eyes on Fletcher's, and they were genuinely troubled.

'Do you really need to know? After all this time, does it matter?'

'It's starting to matter more and more. It's time to talk.'

Alain nodded and took a last look at Salamanca. 'Can we go down to the *terrasse*, Inspector? It seems somehow wrong to discuss it here, with these men fighting their battle.'

The moon was rising, and clouds were building in the west. On the terrace, Alain stood beside Fletcher, looking out over the oval of dark water. Something broke the surface with a low splash.

'You see,' Alain said to the water, 'it was all such a terrible misunderstanding.' One of his dogs clicked over to him and settled on the edge of the platform, panting in the warmth. 'From what I can make out, this is what I believe happened. The Niva engineer had an appointment with Billy Breakman on the afternoon of the previous day, the ninth of January. Something to do with repairing tractors. But the Russian was late, hopelessly late – held up by the weather, I suppose. By the time he got to Thinbeach in the evening, the roads had iced over. We'll never know exactly what took place, but he must have lost control of his car on the main road, because it ended up half in the ditch. I suspect he suffered bad concussion in the crash. At any rate, he managed to climb out of the car and make his way through the snow into Thinbeach.'

'And what happened to him here?'

Alain paused.

'Inspector, you must remember the context. On the one hand, the country was in the middle of the Winter of Discontent. Are you even old enough to remember that?'

'It was a phase of industrial unrest.'

Alain raised his eyebrows. 'More than that, Inspector. It was an attempt by trade unions to wreck our society – how typically Anglo-Saxon, that old destructive impulse. There was chaos in the air, people were on edge. And on the other hand, in the months leading up to this, we had our own local Anglo-Saxon crisis.

The whole fenland area, including Thinbeach, had been subjected to a wave of crimes – opportunistic criminals coming across from Wittris, causing havoc.'

'I'm aware of the crime wave. It was certainly serious, but why is it relevant?'

'Because some of the crimes were appalling. Those Wittris thugs have a grudge against this village that goes back for years.'

'I think it's a thousand years, to be exact.'

'I think it is. They still call us Normans, don't they? To me, that's a compliment, not an insult – but the Wittris criminals blame us for their own idleness, their own economic failure. They hate us and they want our wealth.' Alain laughed, swatting an insect away from his face. The moon was clear of the willows now, pale and heavy above the water, but the swollen clouds were starting to feed across its surface. There was no breeze at all. 'I sometimes wonder if Chretien de Minchin was too damn tolerant. He drove out the rebels, but he let them survive in the marshes. Perhaps if Chretien had finished the job, we would have less trouble in this county today.'

'You've lost me there, Alain.'

'Just maybe, Inspector, he should have drowned them all in the Pool along with his whore of a wife.' Alain winked and smiled. 'But we're talking about the old Wittris crime wave, aren't we, yes. That winter, they began taking some sort of perverted revenge on us. In some of the farmhouses, they dragged people from their beds and kicked them down the stairs. In one house along the Shamblings, they tied up the occupants and beat them with belts, urinated on them. People here were scared of outsiders, understandably so. Any strange face could have been a burglar, an intruder—'

'Or an attacker.'

'Quite so. And because of all this, when that Russian man came walking into Thinbeach after dark, people kept their doors closed.'

'You mean, he knocked on doors for help?'

Alain raised his face to the moonlight. 'I believe he may have done. But he was a big man, apparently, all wild and dishevelled, and speaking strangely. His head injury must have made his imperfect English even more slurred.'

'Are you telling me that nobody in Thinbeach would open their door to him? An injured man, in the freezing cold?'

Alain nodded. 'They were afraid of him. They were afraid of anyone from outside. And so, tragically, I imagine he wandered off, going up onto the mound where the wind was at its worst. He was disorientated and confused. He must have stumbled down the slope into the river, where the ice was collecting. Hypothermia is a painless death, apparently. The body goes numb, and sleep descends. It was all a terrible mistake.'

Fletcher imagined that casket on the Russian kitchen table, the way Judith Denton had described it. Everything just a terrible mistake.

'But why would a senior police officer come here the next day and ask you to keep quiet about the whole thing?'

'Can't you guess? The dead man being Russian.'

Fletcher thought about it. It fitted together.

'The American missile base. It was still in use back then, the cold war was still going on.'

'Exactly, Inspector. The missile base. Some people say the Russian engineer had been briefed to make notes about it, but I think that's highly unlikely. To this day, I doubt he even knew of its existence. But just imagine the complications for our own authorities. In those days, nuclear war was a real possibility. Missile bases were the first line of defence against the Russian enemy. Then one of the enemy rolls up in a hire car and manages to drown within a few miles of the perimeter fence. It was a disastrous lapse in security. The body was taken away, I don't know where. I imagine the Soviet Embassy collaborated in keeping things quiet. It wasn't exactly a propaganda coup for them, either.'

Fletcher thought that Alain was probably right about that. It would have raised questions about their hard currency initiative, about the possible use of trade missions for spying, about how much support this unfortunate engineer had received from his own management. He could see why both the British and the Soviet authorities had quietly concealed the whole event. Ivan's father had been reduced to manageable ashes and shipped home to Stavropol. Along with—

'Alain, when the police found the body, was there something unusual about it?'

'Something unusual?'

'Was there an object found on the body that might

be counted as one of the dead man's personal effects? Something that was out of place?'

'I'm sorry, Inspector, but I didn't see the body myself. I've never heard of anything unusual about the circumstances.' He shook his head, staring into the water. 'It's a bloody awful business, isn't it? We'll always regret it, the few of us who know. We'll always feel guilty, I think. But we can't change it, you see. We can't go back and change what's happened. We just have to lay it to rest.'

Alain went to the edge of the platform and found a stick and held it up. In the cloudy moonlight, it was smooth as a length of bone. His dog moved onto its haunches, and Alain threw the stick into the water. The dog leaped in with an impact that spread across the Pool, its head forging through the ripples.

Fletcher said, 'Alain, things can't be laid to rest. I've personally met a Russian man who says he's the son of the dead engineer. He describes this as the critical work of his life. I'm not sure what he's planning, but I think you'd better cancel the Thinbeach Wedding.'

'Cancel the Wedding?' Alain stood back in astonishment. 'But it's ours, it belongs to us. If this man has a grudge, let him come into the open and talk to us. What does he think we've done?'

'He's been focusing attention on a society called The Wake.'

Alain groaned. 'The Wake? From back in the seventies? For God's sake, you mean Billy Breakman and Thomas Denton, and the other one – the little farmer?'

'The Russian seems to identify them with the death of his father.'

'The Russian thinks *what*? Oh, come on. Have you met any of them? Then you know what clowns they are. I'm a serious local historian, Inspector, but those people were just comedians – hamming it up in cheap costumes, playing around for village fêtes.' He laughed. 'Maybe your Russian has latched onto them because they represent the village at that time, in the late seventies, when his father died. But The Wake were harmless clowns – can't you see? Just harmless bloody jokers. I hope to God nobody believes they were anything else.'

Then Alain's dog burst up over the edge of the terrace, the metallic silt of the beach tangled in its coat, ears alert, the stick in its jaws dripping black water under the storm clouds. It clambered onto the platform and shook itself from nose to tail, spraying a corona of river water across the flagstones, long drops flying out into the dark.

'Cancel the Wedding, Inspector? We can't do that. This year's Bride is going to be special, the most beautiful ever. The police have to look after us. We pay our taxes. We're in your hands.'

He knelt down and whispered to the dog in French, smoothing down the fur along its muzzle, taking the stick gently from its teeth. He glanced up at Fletcher.

'Isn't he gorgeous? He's a Breton Wolfhound. They're extremely rare. Descended from the dogs the Normans bred for hunting down prisoners. The story is, they must never catch sight of human blood. It'll wake an old memory in them.' He chuckled. 'Maybe he'll protect us better than the police, him and his lovely sister. Where is your sister tonight, *mon bébé? Mm? Ou est ta jolie soeur? Mm?*'

Alain pressed his face into the dog's, kissing it again and again, whispering to it, closing his eyes and rubbing his cheek against its head.

Wednesday Night

The road back to Cambridge was slick with drizzle. The sky was full of dark vertical clouds, and at times the fields lit up with silent lightning that did nothing to lessen the closeness of the air.

Fletcher put his car window down a notch and let a few drops of spray drift in for a while. He was asking himself if that was it. If that really was what happened.

Ivan's father died in an accident; Ivan sent Olga here to find something, and together with Jake Skerrit she came up with The Wake, a bunch of harmless jokers that Ivan was now obsessed with. That would explain a few things.

He felt the cool rain wetting the side of his face as the wipers smeared the windscreen into rainbows.

It would explain a lot. For example, those voices on Ron Teversham's tape. On first listening, the men sounded as if they knew something sinister. But were they giving real information – or just taking the piss out of poor old Ron, making him believe The Wake was something it wasn't, because he was so interested? One of them even said, *Collar too tight Teversham?* – as if they knew he had that microphone under there. *Smart bastards. Clever outfit, tight-knit too* – didn't that sound like a wind-up, in fact, considering it was a village history club?

Bad things do happen. Maybe Jake Skerrit really did turn the CCTV off and lean too close to a shredder, Ron Teversham really was a drunk who panicked and grabbed the video when he found the body, then couldn't own up to it. Did Thomas Denton look jumpy today at the mention of Ivan? Maybe because he'd heard the rumours about the body in 1979, but he knew he wasn't supposed to talk about it, he was confused – two police bursting in on his weird household set-up, talking about Russians.

Was the whole thing actually a misunderstanding, born out of a political alarm over a corpse in 1979?

Over in one of the fields, a flash lit up something he'd seen before: a massive hunchbacked shape, tensing itself against the ground in the shadow of an open barn. It was one of the combine harvesters, ready for Saturday's harvest, the day of the Thinbeach Wedding.

And that was the immediate issue, Fletcher decided. Whatever the details of who did what back in 1979, Ivan and Berlitz were still out there, circling The Wake, looking for some kind of vengeance. Where would they stop? *My critical work is in Thinbeach.* The priority now was to find Ivan Gorensky before Saturday – because if Ivan hated the village, the Thinbeach Wedding would serve it to him on a plate.

Fletcher left the fields behind and came into the outskirts of Cambridge. Ahead of him, a queue of traffic was building at the junction near the science park. He slowed to a halt beside one of the futuristic domed buildings. A lightning flash made the whole mirrored surface burst into light momentarily, then return to the dark cloud.

He waited in the queue. He flicked the rear windscreen wiper. He glanced in the mirror and noticed the car behind was sitting very close on his tail: a final-model Omega, highly polished. The pride and joy of some all-night cabbie. Another ten years would see it ending up like Ron Teversham's Sierra, full of dents, lying at the side of the road.

He glanced back at the Omega again. The driver wasn't using the wipers, allowing water droplets to build up on the windscreen. The queue began to free up, and Fletcher moved forward a few metres. The Omega slowly kept pace, either obsessive about road-space or deliberately staying close to conceal its registration plate. The droplets meant that Fletcher couldn't see anything of the occupants.

Was he being followed? While he was thinking about Ivan and Berlitz – were they sitting right behind him? But nobody tails another car by sitting right behind it.

Even as he thought that, the Omega moved out from behind him and span across the road, spray flying from its tyres, taking an entry into the science park. As it disappeared into the dark between two of the land-scaped embankments, the driver killed the lights to make the rear plate unreadable.

Correct procedure now was to call for uniformed support, block the exits. Fletcher turned across the road and followed the car between the embankments.

The science park was known as Silicon Fen: a landscape of steel and glass complexes, separated by relaxation zones containing benches, fountains and lakes fringed with imported bamboo. Tonight the benches were empty, and the fountains were lit only by security lamps along the curving roadways. A few of the office buildings had lights on, with dedicated workers still visible at their workstations, but most were darkened, catching the Audi's headlamps as Fletcher moved along the ribbon road. He fully expected to see Ivan or Berlitz waiting in the shadows of a leisure area, but there was no sign of them or the car. The rain increased into a steady patter that ruffled the bamboo and made the buildings glisten. The next ribbon was empty, and the next. Beyond that, the road straightened beside a large lake that fronted the largest of the complexes – a glass hemisphere with a single translucent wall rising against the clouds, glowing in places with corporate life.

Fletcher stopped and reversed. Beside the lake was a car park, largely deserted, the rain drifting across the bay markings. At the far end was a dark Omega with its lights off, pointing nose out towards the exit road. Fletcher turned in and approached it. In the lamplight he could just make out the number plate – 03 model year. He came parallel with it and looked across.

He had time to see a man's profile, and another man in the passenger seat. After that, the car was away along the exit road, twisting out onto Milton Road. He followed it far enough to see it cross the disused rail line and turn into the maze of streets in the Arbury district. He slowed down and, not having an Airwave set, called the number plate into Parkside for a PNC check.

'I'll call you back in a minute, sir.'

'No need. I'll pick it up myself.'

He was wondering if this was yet another misunder-standing – if the car was just a random stolen vehicle with a driver who panicked easily. Because the men he'd seen inside weren't Ivan or Berlitz. They were English-looking, with tough faces and cropped hair. It was hard to say, but he estimated they were aged in their fifties.

Detective Superintendent Webley watched Tom Fletcher reading the memo from the Home Office. At ten p.m., his suit still looked neat, his tie straight under the button-down collar. She saw him frown and read the memo through again. Sitting beside him at the conference table, Sal Moresby also looked unhappy. She'd already seen it.

Fletcher passed it back across the table and looked at Sal, then at Webley herself. Blue eyes.

He said, 'They made a body disappear.'

'So it seems.'

The memo was brief, but carefully worded. It con-firmed that the body of a Russian national had been repatriated to the then Soviet Union in January 1979, on compassionate grounds. There was no mention of drowning or cremation, or of any request for silence from the local community, or any object found on the body.

Sal said, 'You think this sort of cover-up was com-mon back then?'

'Not common, but it was certainly manageable,'

Webley replied. 'I was just starting in the job those days myself – not around here, but over in the Essex force. The world was different.' She wondered if these two young people could imagine the difference – how everything in policing had been black and white. Even the grey areas were black and white. She smiled suddenly. 'For example, you know where I'm going tomorrow? A two-day seminar on holistic policing. You see, you two aren't even laughing. In 1979, that would have been hilarious.' She picked up the memo and placed it in a desk drawer. 'Frankly, I'm surprised we've got this much out of them, but it does seem to support Alain de Minching's account, as you've described it, Fletcher. So all in all, what exactly *is* your view now?'

She watched Fletcher tilt his head back and look at the ceiling. She noticed Sal watching him too.

He said, 'It does seem possible, ma'am, that the whole thing is a bizarre misunderstanding. Ivan's father dies, Ivan becomes obsessed, does the investigative thing using Olga. It goes wrong when she gets involved with Jake. There are things we can't explain yet, such as who turned over Ron Teversham's house and where Jake Skerrit got hold of that cash. On the other hand, though, I've got to admit we haven't found anything circumstantial that's suspicious about their deaths. We can come back to that. I think the priority now is to detain Ivan Gorensky before he widens his interest from The Wake to the whole village. Which could be on Saturday.' He picked up the fax from the Russian police and looked at the photo again. 'This is him, no doubt at all.'

Webley looked at Sal. Sal said, 'Simple. We instruct Alain to cancel the Thinbeach Wedding. Public safety.'

Fletcher shook his head. 'We could, but I've had second thoughts about that. I think it would provoke Ivan into an attack. The village is always going to be there as a target, Wedding or no Wedding. He's probably planning some sort of weird psychological revenge – but at the moment, at least he's proceeding quite methodically. As long as he behaves like that, he can be located and contained.'

Webley nodded. 'Interesting. When I called you today, I was having exactly that debate in this office. It's been discussed at Commander level and above. At first, the option of – shall we say – neutralising the Russians by using our armed colleagues was the preferred approach. Obvious problem: we don't know where the Russians are right now. And then a second view emerged. More of a management view.'

Fletcher and Sal both looked up.

Webley explained. '*The role of the modern police service is to manage crime, and also public perception of crime.* I'm quoting someone above Commander level there. You see, public perception of crime in Cambridgeshire is actually quite positive. In the Home Office Crime Survey, we came high in the league tables under headings such as *Do you feel safe? Do you feel the police are in control?* and so on. At the highest management level, those are important results. *It means the brand values around the police are virtuous* – I'm quoting again there. The management's feeling is that a firefight with the Russian mafia would damage that perception. Firefights with armed robbers would be OK, or with hostage-takers, terrorists, those kinds of people. That makes our brand look strong. But not, please, with Russian ex-army mobsters. Whatever the outcome, the public would ask questions such as, *How did these Russians get in here? How many more are there? Am I safe?* Our brand value would be undermined.' She paused, the fan whirring in the silence. 'Finally, and most importantly, there's the whole question of this episode from 1979, which no doubt the Home Office would prefer to remain in the past. *And it's important for a modern police service to be in tune with the Home Office.* That's the last quote for you tonight.'

Fletcher was looking back at her steadily. 'So what with the league tables, the brand values and the Home Office, no shooting.'

'In your own words, only as a last resort. You wanted it this way, now you've got it – probably for different reasons than you expected. But you need to find these Russians before they start causing havoc in our rural community. You've got some kind of rapport with Gorensky, exploit that. If he'll listen, tell him his father's death was accidental. Tell him the Glockenspiel are queuing up to have a crack at him. Bring him in on immigration charges. Then we'll send him home quietly.'

Sal said, 'Just like we sent his dad home, really.'

Webley had to smile. These two had a major piece of work to do now, and she had to ask herself if they were capable of it. She thought back to when she was Sal's age – going too fast, punching men who annoyed her.

Sal was strong enough. It was Fletcher that she wanted to know more about. For all his high-flying and his bravery medal, there was something else there, she sensed it. Something hidden about him. She wished he would talk more, so that she could hear it all.

Damn, that bravery medal. I remember when it happened. I was so proud of the boy, I put my arms around him and held him close. I was so damn proud of Tom Fletcher. Was that a mistake?

She glanced up. He was looking back at her.

She said, 'Go and do it, then. Find the Russians before Saturday.'

After a final discussion with Sal, Fletcher walked along the row of offices. Most were empty, the strip blinds throwing bars of streetlight across the desks, hardware diodes glowing in the dark. DI Franks was asleep in his chair, a pizza box on his desk.

Fletcher went into the control room and felt the tension that didn't stop for the night: the plasma screens full of incidents, flickering as the city rolled around to get to sleep.

A sweating PC handed him a single line of print: the result of his call-in on the dark Omega. The plate was false. Patrol cars had already been briefed to watch for it, but none had reported a sighting. Fletcher threw the print in the bin.

'Call me if they find it. I'll be at home.'

Fletcher used a parking space in All Saints' College: a gesture of thanks for his work two years beforehand in tracking down the bursar's missing son. Fletcher knew that, in Cambridge, eight square metres of Tarmac was the highest reward on this earth. He valued it. He valued the key in the padlock across the parking space, the sound of it swaying as he walked away.

The rain had slackened into a greasy mist, and he felt the coolness on his face as he turned into Green Street with his keys in his hand. The pavements were slick with water from the drainpipes, and the shop windows were filmed with damp, distorting the light they threw on the street. He reached his door.

In the aftermath of his divorce, he'd abandoned the idea of buying another house, at least for the time being. On impulse, he'd taken a lease on this place: an oddly-shaped apartment that had once been the caretaker's flat of an independent department store. He pushed the stair light and began to climb to the top storey. Although the store had been closed for years, that old caretaker had left his presence: there was still the aroma of wax ingrained in the wooden stairs.

The light clicked off before he reached the top, but the stairwell wasn't completely dark: the big moon glowed through the rain-streaked cupola in the roof as he came onto the top landing. He reached for his front-door key, wondering when he'd get sick of that wax smell. He stopped. There was the wax, and below that something else.

A smell of damp clothes and cigarettes. He turned around.

The boy was standing in the shadowy part of the landing. He stepped out and the mottled light from the cupola fell across his face. He said, 'Hey, Tom. I've been watching the rain.'

Fletcher looked at him. He wore trainers, loose jeans and an old army coat flecked with rainwater. He had red-brown hair, dark with rain, wide grey eyes, freckles on his pallor. Good-looking.

Under that, Fletcher saw what he always saw – something that made him turn his eyes away for a moment. He said, 'Luke, mate. Does your mother know you're here?'

'She's working. Why do some raindrops move faster than others?'

He unlocked the door to his flat. 'I think it's called surface tension. What's going on?'

'Something's happening. Let me in.'

Fletcher watched him as he went into the hallway. He had the angular body and in-built grace of his mother. Just the questions he asked sometimes were hard to answer. Maybe that was normal. Luke, Cathleen's son, was fifteen years old.

The layout of Fletcher's flat was illogical, because the hallway was bigger than any of the other rooms. They crossed it and went into the living space. He threw Luke a towel, and the kid looked at it as if the idea of drying his hair was totally alien. Fletcher phoned Cathleen, told her Luke was there, promising to drive him straight home.

'Why's he here? I don't know. I'm sure he'll tell me now.'

He put the phone down.

Luke said, 'Someone's following me. They're out there now.'

Fletcher opened the window and looked out: the street was empty, the pavements glinting grey and orange.

'Why do you think that?'

'A car was outside the house tonight. Someone in it took a photo of mum as she was going out. She didn't see, but I did. Then the phone rang twice, and nobody answered. I thought, I'll go in and see Tom. Then when I was walking into town I saw the same car was following me.'

'What kind of car?'

'Omega, dark blue metallic. Here's the number.'

Fletcher glanced at the scribbled note. He already knew the plate was false. He said, 'Did you see who was in it?'

'Two old men.'

'Old? More like, in their fifties?'

'Yeah, old. What's the matter? I wanted to do the right thing, coming to find you. Mum says you'll look out for us.'

'Your mum says that?'

'All the time, she says that.' Fletcher closed the window and drew the blind. Luke asked, 'So who are the men in the car?'

'I don't know. Come on, I'm taking you home.'

Fletcher watched the mirror. Nothing following.

Luke had the window part-open and was looking out at the last of the rain. He said, 'I don't think it's surface tension. It's the amount of water in a drop. Some are very slightly bigger than others.'

'How's school, Luke?'

The boy turned his face to Fletcher. Fletcher could guess the answer. Luke didn't like school, it stopped him concentrating on things he was interested in. Like raindrops.

Fletcher stood beside Cathleen in her little kitchen, the door open. Rain was dripping from the electric cables in the rail yards, and when a train passed they released spirals of vapour that drifted away in the breeze, lit by the car lights from the bridge.

Luke's army jacket was hanging in the doorway.

Fletcher had checked with the station twice to see if the dark Omega had been sighted, but it seemed to have vanished into the streets of Cambridge.

'So who are they?' she asked.

'Not your normal perverts. They were following me tonight. I think maybe they've followed me coming here before. It's someone who's interested in me and you and Luke.'

He didn't add what he was thinking: why follow people, and not care if those people notice it? Almost as if they *wanted* Fletcher and Luke to see them.

She looked back at him in silence. He could see Luke's face in hers, in the eyes and the pallor, the shape of the cheekbones.

'Someone interested in us? Who would that be?'

He let the question go unanswered, because he had no idea. For fifteen years he'd had two parts to his life.

His obvious side, school and then college and the job and the marriage, until that ended. All the time there was this other side: keeping in touch with Cathleen, watching Luke grow up as he visited once or twice a week. He and Cathleen were friends now, nothing else, he told himself. But back then something had happened, something that tied him to Cathleen and Luke and wouldn't let him go. Now someone was trying to bring those two sides of his life together.

She said, 'If they find out, Tom. If Luke finds out, through them.' She didn't finish the sentence.

He said, 'They won't find out. I won't let them.'

Cathleen smiled, but the shadow didn't leave her eyes.

'That's why he likes you, Tom Fletcher. You're such a bloody hero.'

He managed to smile back, despite what was going through his mind. He said, ' "Billy Don't Be a Hero". I had to listen to that yesterday, in the line of duty. That and "Save Your Kisses For Me".'

She closed the back door and locked it.

'That must have been hell.'

'It was. What kind of men sit around listening to Paper Lace and Brotherhood of Man?'

'What kind of men? Probably policemen.'

'Thanks.'

'Any time.'

She drew the bolts across and rammed them shut.

When Sal Moresby got home, her flat seemed empty. The table in the main room held a couple of beer cans, and in the kitchen she found an empty wine bottle beside the bin.

She looked into the bedroom and heard the sound of her boyfriend's breathing, and saw his shape in the dim light. She realised she'd hardly spoken to him all week, and then realised she didn't miss it.

She took a long lukewarm shower and washed the Cambridge rain out of her hair. She was thinking about Fletcher and Webley, that weird link between them. The way Webley was looking at him tonight. Caring about him.

That happens after a while, everybody says. You start to have more in common with colleagues than with anyone else. The police become your family.

She grinned to herself, with her face up to the water: she wasn't there yet.

She got into bed naked. The sheets felt crumpled and hot, when she wanted them cool. She twisted sideways to avoid his body, his breath. She closed her eyes.

Driving home along Mill Road, Fletcher checked in the mirror again and watched in the side streets for the Omega, but there was nothing there. The streets were largely empty – still damp, but the breeze that had sprung up after the rain was giving way to warmer, muggier air.

Fletcher was thinking about Cathleen bolting her back door. *What kind of men?*

He swung left into Gonville Place, past the swimming pool glowing in its security lighting. Parker's

Piece was a big plane of mauve. Outside the Scott Polar Institute, the bronze statue of a man with outstretched arms raised his face to the plates of cloud fragmenting overhead.

Fletcher didn't see him.

He was seeing that old battered cassette, hearing again the sweaty microphone, the clink of glasses, the slurred voices. The recording was so short, he'd been right through it in his mind by the time he got into Trumpington Street, and he started recalling it over again. Then, outside the Fitzwilliam Museum, under the eyes of the stone lions watching the water in the gutters, it clicked and stopped on one place.

In the end, Sal fell into a summer sleep: the kind where daylight is always present and something is there at the edge of the mind, coming closer. When she woke before dawn, it vanished.

She turned on her back and tried to sleep again. Her boyfriend stirred and she felt him running a palm across her, probing the line of her ribs into her navel.

She cursed and pushed his hand away and stood up. She went out to the balcony still naked, sliding the door behind her. The night was still warm. She felt the rainwater on the floor between her toes, and the cool of the railing against her hands and thighs as she leaned on it in the dark, letting the warm damp breeze move over her. A few patters of rain touched her breasts. The eastern stretch of the sky was light in one corner, filled with heavy, slow-moving clouds, the river below completely static.

The railing in her hands felt like the bars of a cage. She closed her eyes and wondered how much longer she could live here.

When her mobile rang, she ducked back inside and grabbed it from her bag on the table. She spoke looking at the prints her wet feet had made across the floor tiles, at her naked outline in the glass door with the rolling clouds outside.

'Fletcher? Where are you? You know what time it is?'

'Sorry, Sal. I wanted to leave a message. I'm in Parkside. I'm looking at Ron Teversham's police record.'

'I showed *you* that, remember? A couple of DD convictions. So what?'

'Not his police *record*, his *police* record.'

She stretched.

'It's before dawn, Fletcher, and you're not making much—'

'His *police* record in the sense of his *personnel* record. Shows he joined in 1970, aged twenty-five. Probationer, then constable.'

'Ron Teversham was in the job?'

'Until he was dismissed in 1981 with loss of all pension, still a constable. Some kind of scandal over confiscated drugs. So long ago, it's only on the paper records, not the databases.'

'Where was he stationed?'

'Guess. He lived there till he died.'

'You mean, Wittris? But the police station there—'

'Closed down in 1993. It's a part-time rural office

now. But are you thinking what I'm thinking? About his little drinks party?'

She suddenly wanted something around her.

'Those men on the tape were policemen?'

'Retired or ex-policemen, I'd guess. Constables from back then. Teversham laid on drinks for them, tried to find out more about whatever Olga was here to research. One of them said, *That old chestnut*, remember? It was something Teversham had asked about, something they associated with The Wake. They knew all about it. And they said something else – remember?'

Sal took her raincoat off the rack and pulled it over her shoulders. 'Something about *clever and smart, tight-knit?*'

'After that.'

There was a click from Fletcher's end, and the tape creaked into life again. The voice rose over the laughter and the music.

Worked like a charm. Solved the whole problem.

Fletcher clicked it off and said, 'What problem needed solving back in 1978?'

She ran her damp toe along the floor. 'The Fenland crime wave, the gang of kids from Wittris? That was the big problem.'

'And the crime wave stopped, didn't it? You know what else I've been thinking about?'

'Actually, no.' She could see the corner of the bed through the doorway.

'That gang from Wittris. The way it just stopped being active at the end of 1978. I'm wondering why it stopped. I'm thinking those old coppers weren't taking the piss out of Teversham at all. They were talking about something they'd heard about back in the seventies, connecting The Wake with the Wittris gang.'

Sal reached over and closed the bedroom door. 'Great. So we need to locate every ex-copper in Cambridgeshire who was serving around 1978. That must be—'

'About six hundred people. Males only, constables and sergeants, three hundred and thirty-nine. Not really practical before Saturday. So we'll pick up the men we know about, in The Wake. Because I've changed my mind again. I don't think The Wake were jokers after all. I think Peter Charter and Thomas Denton need to come in for questioning tomorrow—'

'Today. But we're tracking down Ivan Gorensky, right?'

'This comes first. I don't like facing someone who knows more than me, especially a Russian with a grudge. And I think Ivan's a step ahead of us – he's already made this connection. He knows more about his father's death than we do.'

When Sal ended the call, she realised she was still standing there naked under her raincoat. Beyond her monochrome reflection in the window, the sky in the east was coloured a faint red. She had the feeling this was going to be a long day.

She didn't know that nightfall would find her a thousand miles away, sleeping alone under cool sheets in the valleys of Portugal.

Thursday Morning

There were no cars with false plates behind Fletcher at seven thirty a.m., as he gunned his Audi along the Ely Road and on towards the Norfolk border. He wanted Peter Charter sitting in an interview room by nine, and the traffic was light enough to make that possible. The road was glossy and clear, the sun glinting off the Great Ouse under a blue sky that seemed even bluer on the horizon, where the river met the North Sea.

Sometimes, rabbits went flashing across into the roadside poppies, or the shadows of sparrow hawks flickered on the Tarmac, waiting.

Things looked normal from the track leading to the farmyard. Getting closer, Fletcher noticed the tractors by the gateway had their prongs still lowered, blocking the entrance. He made his way on foot under the razor wire and onto the mud, scattering the chickens. He could hear the distressed lowing of Charter's cattle from a shed beyond the house. The front door was locked, and through the glass he could see the furniture still pushed against it.

He shouted Charter's name, and the words echoed across the yard with the cow noises. Around the back of the house, he found the fridge still jammed against the door. He smashed a side window and clambered through.

The kitchen was almost as they'd left it the previous night, except that the table had been cleared of junk. One single place had been set. Around the table, at each empty chair, were the photographs of Charter's family.

Fletcher unhooked the razor wire from the stairs, the boards creaking under him. He checked in the Russians' bedrooms: nothing was touched. He looked into the main bedroom, where the sun was streaming in through an open window.

The old shotgun was lying on the floor. Fletcher didn't touch it, the hammers being still cocked. The rusty mechanism had seized up at the final moment: the last of the many things that had let Peter Charter down.

Instead, he'd used a length of nylon rope. He was hanging from a beam, his boots describing an ellipse in the morning breeze. He obviously knew what he was doing: the knot had broken his neck.

On the dressing table, next to the wedding photo, Fletcher found a letter in a sealed envelope. He expected this to be for the children or the wife, or even the solicitor. He turned it over. It was addressed in shaky ballpoint: *To Ivan Gorensky, Businessman.*

He opened it.

Dear Ivan,
  I don't know why you wanted to leave me. I curse you for it but I forgive you too, because in these last

*months you brought me peace and that's something a
man can't put a price on. I still wish you the best in
your life. I wish I knew your mother and father to tell
them what a help you been to me. I won't say what a
friend, because we didn't socialise did we. But I wrote to
Barclays in Ely today and put £7,654 aside for you.
You'll need two forms of identification. Count the
money, don't let those sods con you. For Berlitz there's a
dictionary paid for in Smiths, the biggest bastard they
had. Wittris will burn in hell and so will all Cambridge
police.*

> *Your landlord,*
> *Peter Charter*

£7,654. The only way Peter Charter could show his
love.

Fletcher folded the note away.

Ivan was a disturbed individual, a man brutalised by
whatever he had seen and been part of. But he was also
a man of weird insight, a man who carefully researched
those he had a grudge against, before taking his
revenge.

So what was he planning for Thomas Denton?

Judith woke with a start in Deep House. Her bedroom
had a view of the rushes moving in the sunlight, still
damp from the night's rain. The glass gave back her
own reflection too: the curve of her legs, reclining in the
landscape.

She lay for a while, watching the rushes, thinking
about Ivan. Ivan smelled of engine oil, but his hands

were perfectly clean. Their grip had left bruises on the backs of her thighs. She knew he was capable of violence, he'd seen and done things in the army, but on the riverbank last night he'd held her breasts with those clean hands, put his lips against her ribs and kissed her heart while it slowed down.

She wondered who that famous woman was in Chechnya, the woman she resembled.

She put on some exercise clothes and leaned her ear against the door, listened, heard nothing. She unlocked it and stepped through into the corridor, where things were bad. She had to step carefully through the debris to the open gallery that looked down on the living space. Down there, things were worse.

The abstract pictures had been torn from the walls, the glass tables smashed apart and their fragments strewn across the slate floor. The bisque porcelain lighting, the primitive clay sculptures, the Milanese leather seating – all demolished by a berserk energy.

Last night, she'd lain awake with her door locked and her window open on the fen where the rain was pattering, listening to this wave of destruction move around the house: her father running out of control because he guessed where she'd been.

The wave had smashed around the lower space, coursed along the corridor to her room and broken there, stopping outside the door he could have kicked down if he'd wanted to, subsiding into a desperate sobbing. She'd fallen asleep smiling.

Was he in the house now? She breathed the air for his cigar smoke, found just the pollen of the fen. In the courtyard, the willows were static beside the drive. The Volvo was gone.

She put on her practice mitts and began to beat the punch bag hanging in the corner, relishing each impact against her knuckles, the cool sweat on her back.

She began thinking of Ivan again. She had no idea where he was today. She had a phone number which he'd made her memorise, not write down. She knew that her father would be out there on the cracked Tarmac of the fenland roads, searching. Between punches, she wondered if her father was going to find him.

The sloping meadow behind the house released tiny insects as Fletcher strode across it: primitive creatures with jagged wings. The cows were making agonised snorts that echoed across the landscape. Up at the caravan, where the sun was drying the earth under the washing line, he found Larry sitting back in a deck-chair, boots stretched out in front of him and hands behind his head, a canvas hat over his eyes. A four-pack of Special Brew was cooling in a pail of river water, two cans open. It was a hot morning.

'Get up, Larry. Cows need milking.'

Larry lifted the hat and squinted at Fletcher, a big snaggly smile on his veined face. 'Nice suit again.'

Fletcher tipped the bucket over him, the water gushing over his head into the mud – from the bottom of the bucket a silt creature with claws taking a grab at Larry's hair and losing grip.

Larry clambered to his feet and wiped the hat over his face, his sleeve in his eyes.

Fletcher said, 'Peter Charter's dead. What did you hear last night? Wittris kids coming by the house?'

'The Wittris? They too scared of the Russians still.' Larry walked over to the caravan, dried his hands and face and checked his tobacco tin. He lit a roll-up and smiled down at the house. Long strands of hair twisted around his face. The thing alive in the bucket was dying in the sunshine. 'He's really dead then?'

'You'll be giving a statement, if you were on the property.'

'You want a statement? A six-day week, he paid me two hundred pound cash. He took ten pound off, says for wear and tear on the caravan. Wouldn't let me wash in the house. But some nights he came up here in the dark, just in his pants. Those weeks he let me off the wear and tear.' Larry took a long drag, watching the house. 'Last night, top windows are open. I hear him screaming like a girl. Goes quiet, there's a snap and a creaking. I say to myself, *Larry boy, that's something with a weight on it.*'

'You didn't go down to check?'

'Why?' Larry grinned again. 'I see a police car comes past every hour, on the hour. Waits outside the yard a minute, then fucks off. They're the professionals, right? They don't worry, I don't worry.'

One of the cows screamed, a long note that set the others off. Fletcher didn't know whether to arrest the guy or send him to work. He said, 'Or maybe I'm wrong, Larry. Maybe it wasn't suicide. Charter had information that your Russian friends want to keep hidden. You yourself had reason to wish him harm.

You could have forged Charter's handwriting on a suicide note.'

Larry nodded. 'Lovely thinking, copper. Just one little problem.' He spotted the writhing crustacean and crushed it with his heel. 'I can't fucking read or write.'

The last person to arrive at the farmyard was a young guy in a 60s' VW Beetle. Fletcher watched him peer at the mud, park outside and make his way carefully across, looking at the photographer's car, the undertaker's van, the forensic people packing things away, the patrol car with Larry snoring in the back, his milking completed.

The kid came up to Fletcher and flashed a laminated card with the insignia of Cambridgeshire Social Services.

'I think someone needs our support.'

The photographer was standing in the doorway, reviewing the images on his camera. He still looked tired. Without looking up, he said, 'I think he's had enough support for now, boy.'

'Dairy cows *and* a hanging. You get all the glamour, Fletcher.'

'The next glamorous one's all yours, Sal. I can't even decide what to charge Larry with. Ignoring a suicide?'

'A legal debate I wish we had time for.'

They were standing by the cattle grid outside the farm, the raised hatchback of Sal's car shielding them from the sun. Up in the boughs of the cedars, the crows were motionless in the heat. Sal was arranging some A4 pages from plastic folders across the car's rear shelf. She went on, 'The clock's rather ticking on our search for Ivan now, isn't it? No tips whatever from the software forensics on Olga's room, by the way.'

'I've been thinking about that. I think there's another young woman who might be in touch with him. Remember Judith Denton, the way they were talking together? When we get to Deep House we'll speak to her too. Now, what have you got?'

Sal stood back and tied her hair behind her neck and let it fall. She was wearing tailored cotton trousers and a sleeveless top, and he noticed the small inoculation mark among the freckles on her bicep. Her eyes moved around to his. She said, 'Two hours' research on the Wittris crime wave of 1978. A spasm of lawlessness and violence that shocked the county. You don't remember it?'

'I was three. You were—?'

'Just being conceived.' She indicated some of the sheets in front of them: prints of old newspaper cuttings.

'Your friend in the *Evening News*?'

'My friend Derek. You see, Fletcher, the police database doesn't give a feel for how scared people were back then. I should say: certain people. Because the crime wave wasn't random. It was carefully focused on one type of victim. The wealthy.'

The cuttings showed old photographs with crude pixillations, pictures of prosperous-looking houses. The headlines underneath told what had happened there:

House and stables ransacked,
horses stampeded, luxury car burned

Antiques stolen, couple beaten with cosh

THEY LOCK THE DOORS AND PRAY –
we report from the villages under siege

'Nasty stuff,' Fletcher agreed. 'But nothing here refers
to Thinbeach, or The Wake.'

'We know that a few similar crimes were committed
in Thinbeach. This just gives you a flavour of the
atmosphere at the time. As for The Wake – true, that's
not mentioned at all. Why should it be? It was a local
history club. But there is another organisation referred
to quite frequently.'

'Which is?' He glanced at her, and found she'd put
on grey sunglasses that made her eyes difficult to read.
He put on his own, because the glare even through the
raised hatch was quite intense now.

On the shelf, Sal placed three photographs, the kind
that used to be called mugshots. A horsefly landed on
one for a moment, then buzzed away towards the cattle
chomping silently in the pasture. The photos were of
three Caucasian males, probably still in their teens.
They had big lantern jaws, greasy black hair mopped
over their eyes, hooped rings in their ears, and scowls.
Below them she placed another press cutting:

They call themselves The Lovely Brigade
Obscene graffiti explained

Rumours are sweeping fenland that the gang responsible for terrorising property-owners have named

themselves The Lovely Brigade, in imitation of the Italian terrorist group the Red Brigades. Graffiti daubed near the site of the latest break-in reads 'Lovely Brigade – we steal from the rich and we **** them up.'

'The Red Brigades?' Fletcher said. 'They were the kill-the-rich terror movement, right? But The Lovely Brigade?' He studied their faces. 'They don't look very lovely.'

Apart from the pixillation, the lads could have been from centuries ago: grimy and resentful, slightly underfed.

Sal rubbed her shoulder thoughtfully, over the pucker of that old vaccination. She said, 'Back in the records, you see, there was a set of names that kept coming up again and again. Generally they were names of lads arrested but not successfully prose-cuted, or convicted of trivial offences compared to what the police and the village folk believed they'd really done.'

'These three names?' Fletcher looked at the captions to the photos: *Terry Swilter, age 19*; *Shane 'Flame' Gaffy, age 17*; *Paddy Legsey, age 16*.

'Yes, they were the ringleaders.'

'But why *Lovely*?'

'Because they all came from the same street. A nice name: Lovely Street. Now guess where Lovely Street is.'

He looked at her over the top of his sunglasses. 'Wittris?'

'The fine town where Ron Teversham was a constable until his dismissal. In fact, I'd guess he was there in 1978 while all this was going on.'

A few of the crows lifted off from the cedars with a shriek, and a grasshopper began to chirp nearby. Then an airliner executed a curve overhead, its engines wailing.

Fletcher said, 'So the Lovely Brigade stopped causing havoc around the time that Ivan's father drowned in the river. That's interesting. These boys would be in their forties now. If they're not in prison, maybe they're still local.'

Sal stacked the files, reached up and shut the hatchback with a clunk.

'Probably. They're not going anywhere, because they're dead.'

'Dead?'

'You remember how the fenland crime wave stopped so suddenly at the end of 1978? It stopped because the Lovely Brigade became careless. You want to see what happened?'

'Yes. In the car, with the air conditioning on.'

Sal watched the last of the scene of death vehicles rumbling back over the cattle grid and turning onto the main road. The Tarmac up there was already shimmering in the heat, and her dashboard read 32 degrees.

In the blast of cool air, Sal passed across the summary Coroner's reports she'd located. Like the old police records, they were held on microfiche, and she'd had to be very persuasive with a clerk at the county archive to get them scanned and emailed this quickly. The way Fletcher didn't say anything, she could see he was impressed.

She glanced at him and was sure he'd been glancing at her. Maybe at the effect all the cold air was having. She watched his eyes for a second. She knew what they were reading. A one-page summary of each fatality.

Terry Swilter met his death on the 30th of November 1978. Swilter had a string of juvenile convictions for breaking and entering and assault, but he'd learned to give himself alibis. Victims of the crime wave reported a male of his height, but the person always wore a balaclava and gloves, and Swilter was never convicted of a Lovely Brigade offence. Then, on the night of the 30th, he climbed onto the roof of a stable block at a minor stately home on the Cambridgeshire/Suffolk border. The house was famous locally for a collection of silverware which Terry must have fancied. He didn't know that behind the stables, the building had a small electricity substation: two high-voltage wires running down from nearby power lines into ceramic blocks. Terry Swilter fell from the roof straight onto the cables, and the resulting flash closed down the supply across three villages.

The monochrome scene of death photo that the clerk had scanned showed what was left of him: a husk with clothes burned away and skin charred into jagged flakes, fingers like black twigs reaching out for the balance that had finally failed him.

His friend Shane 'Flame' Gaffy left school at fifteen and made a career in TDA: taking and driving away cars. They called him 'Flame' because when he finished shredding the tyres on the fenland roads, he liked to drive them back to their owners and torch them in full view of their houses. A week after Terry Swilter's demise, he stole a Jaguar from a weekend cottage near Ely and tried to burn it in the cover of a nearby drainage culvert. He made a mess of it. The blowback from the petrol tank caught him across the face, and although he was found alive, the burns external to his skin and internal to his lungs meant he never regained consciousness, before dying in Addenbrooke's hospital. His still-living body was absent from the scene photo, but the skeleton of the car was pictured, licked clean by the fire.

'And the third one, named Paddy Legsey?' Fletcher turned to her.

'He had a history of juvenile burglary, like Terry Swilter, but I can't see anything in the records about his death. But he's just like the others, he disappeared completely from police data after the end of 1978. Maybe he saw sense.'

'Maybe he moved away. What about press cuttings – your friend let you down?'

'Derek never lets me down.'

She passed him the final cuttings. The aircon was humming away, but otherwise it was quiet in the car. She watched his eyes flicking over the grainy press photos. Two photos. The first was taken the morning after the high-voltage death of Terry Swilter: a crowd of onlookers hanging around the gates of the stately home.

Break-in youth electrocuted

The second was the extinguished wreck of Shane Gaffy's stolen Jaguar, again with a few people standing nearby, beyond the police tape.

Youth dies in car blaze

His eyes moved to her, then back to the photo.

He said, 'You already know, don't you?'

'Know what, Fletcher?'

'You do, you're just testing me.'

'What?' She grabbed the photos back and examined them. It took a few seconds before she realised what he meant.

She said, 'Holy cow. It's *him*.'

Fletcher said, 'Let's get to the Dentons. Then, you want glamour? Book yourself on the next flight to Lisbon.'

She nodded, still studying the pictures. Each crowd of onlookers was wrapped up against the December cold. They were peering at the iron gates and the destroyed car with grim curiosity. One man among them had a different expression: his big face was completely blank. It was a tough, capable face: a man in his prime who'd just put his own portrait inside a souvenir machinery brochure for the forthcoming year of 1979. A man who'd just taken delivery of a batch of problematic Niva tractors. It was Billy Breakman.

Thursday Afternoon

Judith Denton saw the police inspector approach her through the reeds, to where her punch bag was hanging from a willow tree. She liked working around it at this time of day, the sky deep blue with the afternoon. She gave the bag a last strike and let the impact die out. She turned to him.

The policeman looked preoccupied: his pleasant, wide-boned face was frowning. Maybe he already knew why the house was in that state. He studied the punch bag. She quite liked the way he didn't look at her body.

He said, 'Judith, your father's not under arrest, but he's coming back to Parkside station to answer some questions.'

She felt her heart thump. She put out a hand and stilled the bag.

'Questions about what?'

'What do you think?'

She closed her eyes, saw shapes moving behind them. When she looked up again, he was staring at her.

'What, Judith? It's about 1978. Is there something else we should ask him about?'

'No,' she lied.

'Judith, I think you might know where Ivan is.'

'No, I don't.' That wasn't a lie.

'But you can get in touch with him?'

She shook her head, seeing the digits of Ivan's phone number. She wanted more than anything to dig her nails into the muscle of his neck again.

Fletcher said, 'I could arrest *you*, Judith, for obstructing an enquiry. You could be in the cell next to your father.'

'We have adjacent rooms anyway.'

She felt his blue eyes on her, unblinking.

'Let's say I believe you. Let's also say I want to discuss something with Ivan, there's something he needs to know. Let's say he can meet me on safe ground, maybe at the old missile base. Let me know what time.' She made no reply, just punched the bag with an impact that made a couple of moorhens scramble from the edge of the water. 'Ivan's exploiting you, Judith. He's using you to torment your father.'

She ignored him, but the thought stuck inside her. *Is that true?* She saw Fletcher start to leave, then turn back.

He said, 'You have to realise that he's a very dangerous man. He's violent and he manipulates people.'

Judith looked over at the house.

'Who exactly do you mean?'

'My client is prepared to assist you now.'

Fletcher said nothing, just as Thomas Denton had said nothing when they picked him up, nothing when he glanced back and saw Judith watching them leave, nothing all the way back from Deep House, except to ask for his solicitor.

'Inspector? I said my client is ready.'

The solicitor was an expensive man from Newmarket with a suntan and a signet ring. Sitting next to him, Denton's eyes glinted under the strip light of the interview room.

The solicitor looked from Fletcher to Sal Moresby. Sal didn't even look up, scrutinising a sheet that Fletcher knew was a flight booking for the 18.30 Stansted to Lisbon, plus the address of Billy Breakman's golf complex. The solicitor scowled.

'If there are no questions, Inspector, we'll leave.'

'You're free to go at any time, Thomas. You can just walk out.'

Denton's eyes narrowed. It was hot in the interview room, but he kept his leather jacket on, his big hands curled on the table.

'That's it, Inspector. My client and I are leaving. A formal complaint will be made about this.' The solicitor made to stand up. Thomas Denton seated him again with one of his hands. Then Thomas adjusted the Rolex under his cuff.

'Come out with it,' he said, without intonation.

'OK, Thomas,' Fletcher responded. 'It's about things that happened a long time ago.'

Denton glanced at his solicitor, who looked down at his pad.

'Things that nobody really seems to understand, even today. But people can't escape the consequences of the past.'

'All very profound, but is there a question for my client?'

'Yes.'

Denton looked Fletcher in the eye, and for the first time, Fletcher realised he was worried.

'The Wake.'

The solicitor frowned, but Fletcher was watching Denton. He didn't like what he saw. Denton lifted his chin and the sheen of fear left his eyes. He was a man unexpectedly on safer ground. That thought lodged itself in Fletcher's mind like a formal complaint.

Denton said, 'The Wake? I told you, when I cooked you lunch. We were a local historical society, dressing up in costumes. You got me all the way in here to ask about this again?'

'You've *already* questioned my client? That's concerning.'

'I frigging cooked him lunch.'

'What's concerning,' Fletcher said, 'is that we've got a Russian psychopath at large who identifies The Wake with the death of his father in January 1979. Now, Russian psychopaths generally speaking are quite erratic people, Thomas. They drink anti-freeze, they're prone to mood changes, that kind of thing. But this particular Russian psychopath is highly focused. He's perfectly clear in his own mind that The Wake is relevant to the death of his father. Why would he think that?'

'Because he's deranged. His friend had a gun and you did nothing. They're both fucking insane.'

'Are they? Or is there something about The Wake that I don't know?'

Denton returned his gaze, that trace of fear still gone from his eyes. It was being replaced by something else almost impossible to feign or conceal: puzzlement. Thomas said, 'Why are you chasing this?'

'Why? You have to realise, Thomas, that Ivan is working his way up the organisation. Peter Charter's just committed suicide, did you know that?' Denton didn't blink, didn't move a muscle. 'You're next on the list, Thomas.'

'Inspector, it sounds as if my client needs police protection, not police harassment.'

Sal looked up for the first time. 'Maybe he does. What does he remember about the Lovely Brigade?'

The solicitor looked confused, but Denton adjusted his cuffs again and settled himself square in his seat. 'Just what anyone my age would remember. Bunch of thieving kids, thought they were heroes.'

'They were a problem, weren't they?'

'You could say that.'

'Then the problem was solved. Did The Wake have anything to do with solving it?'

'I don't know what you're talking about.'

Sal placed on the table the press photos of the crowds around the gates and the burned-out Jag, and explained for the recording what she was doing. Denton glanced at them.

'So?'

'Billy Breakman was a friend of yours, wasn't he? In The Wake?'

'What's Billy got to do with this?'

'What was he doing in these pictures, Thomas? At the places where Terry Swilter and Shane Gaffy died?'

Thomas looked at the photos again, taking his time now. He didn't seem at all stressed or nervous. He said, 'I've no idea. Why don't you ask him?'

'Maybe I will. I believe this interview is over.'

Rather abrupt, but Fletcher appreciated the way she tried to end it on an assertive note. Still, the interview had gone the opposite way to what he expected. Thomas Denton had entered the building a worried man and was leaving it less worried. It wasn't meant to work that way.

Sal Moresby escorted Thomas Denton onto the exit ramp. The solicitor went on ahead for his vehicle while Thomas stopped and lit a cigar.

Sal said, 'Do you want to talk, Thomas? That's the only reason anyone waits here.'

'My lawyer's an asthmatic, I can't smoke in his car.'

'Sure.'

The sun was slanting in between the concrete slabs of the car park tiers, midges and dust and Denton's cigar smoke spinning in the light.

'What does that Russian think he can do to me, anyway?'

'What's the worst he could do?'

Thomas didn't reply, just watched his own smoke.

Sal said, 'Families are dangerous places, Thomas. Half of all murder victims are killed by a relative. That's nationally. In Cambridgeshire it's probably two thirds. You thought it was Judith, didn't you?'

'What was?'

'The reason we brought you in. That's why you clammed up, called your brief. You were pissing yourself.' On the top of the car park, a Mercedes appeared, taking the ramp downward. 'You thought we were going to uncover your relationship with your daughter, whatever's been going on in Deep House all these years. Then you realised it was just The Wake and the Lovely Brigade, and you didn't care. Why not?'

'My lawyer's in that car.'

The Mercedes came onto the middle ramp and turned down.

'Lawyers can't help you, Thomas. When I'm finished with your old pal Billy, you know what I'm going to do? I'm going to dissect your entire life, starting when Judith was a girl.'

'Judith—'

He stopped as the Mercedes came onto ground level and rolled towards them, the solicitor putting the window down.

'What, Thomas? Judith won't press charges? I'll encourage her. Prison will do terrible things to you, Thomas. Dreadful, humiliating things.'

The solicitor leaned out. 'Don't talk to my client unless I'm present, please.'

Sal slapped her forehead, then leaned close to Denton's ear. 'But I'm a fool, aren't I? Prison won't punish you, will it?' He leaned back and blinked at her through his smoke. She whispered, 'Prison won't punish you, Thomas. Because the Russian's going to do it first.'

★   ★   ★

Leaning against the window of his office space, Fletcher watched the car leave. Whatever Sal had just said made Thomas throw his cigar in a shower of sparks against the wall and slam the Mercedes' door behind him.

Fletcher guessed it was something about Judith, but he was still thinking back to the other side of the interview. The way Thomas became so self-assured. The way he said, *Why are you chasing this?*

Interesting remark. Not, *What's this about?* or *Why are you asking me?* Just *Why are you chasing this?* As if he was puzzled to find that Fletcher was pursuing the enquiry, but it didn't really matter anyway.

Fletcher began to fill out an MG form, the Home Office spreadsheet following any interview on police premises. He detailed Thomas Denton's ethnic origin; whether he had taken any medication; whether he had asked to pray, fast or meditate; whether counselling had been offered.

Fletcher stopped. He picked up the phone and called the county archive office. The clerk had a nasal voice, said he had a lot of files to pull out before five p.m. A whole chuffing stack. Fletcher closed his eyes. Said he knew for a fact that Sal Moresby would appreciate some help.

Sal went home to grab her passport. The deserted flat was baking hot, despite the curtains drawn across the balcony window. In the half-dark, she pushed some overnight gear into a roller case and was out in five minutes. It felt good, leaving on her own with her own stuff.

She found Fletcher in the gallery of the swimming pool. It was humid and noisy. A trio of divers was waiting in line for the high board. One of them took his run and lifted off, turning and spinning before socketing into the water.

Fletcher was staring up at the roof with his hands clasped behind his neck. His collar was open, the pool colours spangling on his throat. He had a series of printed sheets on the seat beside him.

He said, 'You owe the archive clerk a drink. Sorry.'

'Cider's cheap.' She sat down. 'You asked him for the complete files?'

'Every page of the coroner's reports.'

'Annoyed by Thomas Denton?'

'Puzzled, but ultimately Denton isn't the key. Billy Breakman's the key. He was the member of The Wake that Jake Skerrit knew by sight and by name. He was the one recognisable face in Jake's crazy mural, remember? And Billy is definitely there in those photos. Your interview with Billy is critical.'

Her eyes followed where he was looking: the contours of the ceiling, slick with moisture.

'Why don't you come too, Fletcher?'

She took the piece of paper he showed her. It was a switchboard message slip: timed today at 15.23, anonymous female caller, number withheld. Message: *SUNSET*.

'That's my time to meet Ivan.'

When she'd gone, Fletcher sat there a while longer. *Why are you chasing this?*

He checked that nobody was sitting nearby, then picked up the material that the clerk had mailed across: the complete files from 1978, recording the accidental deaths of Terry Swilter and Shane 'Flame' Gaffy. He took the Swilter file first.

There was the scene of death photo: Terry's corpse charred on the substation cables at the stately home. Part of the house was visible in the background, an impressive Georgian roofline. What was it called? Fletcher checked in the notes.

Ulsingham Hall.

The name seemed familiar.

He looked through the pages of the pathologist's report. In the fall onto the cables, Terry Swilter's left leg and right arm had been broken and three vertebrae fractured, leaving him (the coroner assumed) unable to drag himself clear as the national grid exploded around him. Cause of death was ascribed to multiple burns. Fletcher closed the file. The guy had roasted alive and fully conscious.

He opened the other file: Shane Gaffy. Shane had inhaled so much burning petrol from the exploding Jaguar that his skin, airway and lungs had suffered severe burns, and his shocked body had closed itself down within seconds into the unconsciousness from which (the coroner concluded) the boy had never recovered.

The verdict on the two youths was the same: misadventure. And not *only* the verdict. Fletcher noticed that the coroner at Shane Gaffy's inquest was the same as for Terry Swilter.

Fletcher recognised the coroner's name. The man no longer chaired inquests, because he was now Vice Chancellor of possibly the most prestigious Cambridge college. He'd recently been in the news, pushing the University's proposals for a new animal laboratory.

Yes, the files were similar. They even felt similar. The print-outs were both the same thickness, about twelve pages. The originals were both typed on an extinct 1970s' typewriter, and looked pretty dog-eared.

Fletcher looked through them again. He noticed another similarity. In both cases, the name of the investigating police officer was the same: a detective sergeant. Fletcher recognised that name too. It was the name of the current Assistant Chief Constable of the police service in a neighbouring county. If it *was* the same man, his thoroughness had obviously paid off in the long climb to seniority.

There was one final similarity. A coroner's report contains at least six scene of death photographs, taken from different angles, to record the context of the fatality. These files, however, contained just one single photo.

Fletcher watched the divers making their way up the ladder to the high board, dripping water, staying close.

He looked back at the report on Terry Swilter. The name of that stately home: Ulsingham Hall. He felt uneasy in his stomach. Maybe it was the tropical warmth in the gallery. Or maybe he was thinking about coroners, and ambitious detective sergeants, and the kind of people who live in places like Ulsingham Hall.

People like that climb their ladders right to the top. Then they stay up there, on the top board, looking good.

Webley's seminar ended slightly after five p.m. By then, she'd had enough. The room in the Guildhall was stifling, and the jugs of tepid water did nothing to refresh anyone. She managed to leave while the various delegates were starting to mill around, networking, sniffing each other like mutts. Despite the heat, she was looking forward to walking across town in civilian clothes, through the bustle of late-afternoon Cambridge, back to her office in Parkside. Then after that, some time in the gym, thinking.

She came out of the foyer onto the glare of the Guildhall steps. She paused when she saw Tom Fletcher standing on the pavement, evidently waiting for her. She walked down to meet him. Apart from the missing tie, he looked as calm as ever, but also as if he needed to talk.

She said, 'Police escort?'

'Good seminar?'

She looked around, enjoying the sunlight.

'The role of the police in a holistic approach to crime prevention. You see, we're one of an interlocking series of organisations that militate to combat and pre-empt crime. We work alongside the social services, the health services, immigration, private security providers, even the criminal community itself.'

'Sounds admirable. We really need to discuss this Thinbeach situation.'

'Holistic policing, Fletcher, implies total respect for all segments of the community – regardless of race, gender, religion, sexual orientation, or physical or mental disability. Incidentally, I hope your demented Russian bastard is in the cells by now?'

He looked at her, and she sensed real trouble in him. For a moment, she wondered again if he was the right person for this. She said, 'You really do want to talk, don't you?'

King's College chapel murmured with the voices of the last tourists: soft waves on pebbles. Above that, the organ notes followed their course perfectly – only the glimpse of the organist's face in his mirror showing that the sound was created by human activity.

Webley listened to Fletcher while the *Prelude To Parsifal* gave way to the voices again, and then Bach's *Heiliger Geist* began.

They were sitting close to the organ, but still with a view of the stained-glass windows starting to burn with colour in the mature light. Nobody else was within earshot.

She listened while Fletcher expressed his concerns succinctly. He outlined the connecting link between the deaths of the Lovely Brigade and the death of the Russian engineer: Billy Breakman, hence Sal Moresby's visit to Portugal. He explained that there was something unusual about the files on the deaths of the Lovely Brigade. He highlighted the current roles of the then coroner and investigating officer. He pointed out the missing photographs.

She said, 'Sure the clerk sent you all the photos?'

'I checked. He swears those are the only ones in the files.'

'It's certainly an oddity. It's peculiar.'

'There's another dimension. One of the Wittris boys died in a place called Ulsingham Hall. Recognise the name?'

She nodded.

Ulsingham Hall was the home of the Ruddick-Spencer family. An obscure species of country barristers until the current owner, Jonathan Ruddick-Spencer, changed his name to Jon Ruddick in 1997 and became an unelected but influential Home Office adviser with a fresh view on sentencing policy. He was rounding off his career now as Lord Ruddick: unelected, influential Home Office advisor on crime reduction strategy.

The organist broke off suddenly, then restarted.

She said, 'OK, that needs to be handled sensitively. But I thought we agreed the priority was stopping this Russian criminal.'

'I'm meeting him tonight. I think he's a step ahead of me. He's astute.'

The air around them was breaking up into a spectrum of blue and red. She sighed. She put her hand on his arm. She could feel his skin, feel the warm muscle. It was the way she remembered it, that time she held him close – except that back then, he was freezing cold, shivering, needing someone to keep him warm. She'd given him that, for a few minutes. Nobody else had seen. Now she said, 'Fletcher, listen to me. All through this, I've had the feeling that there's something else affecting you. The way you talked about Jake Skerrit's parents. The way you're starting to regard Ivan Gorensky. You said you wanted to talk. I don't really think it's about Lord Ruddick, is it?'

He looked back at her. For a second she felt a concern for him that made her touch his face. It occurred to her that he was young enough to be her son.

He said, 'It's hard to explain.'

'Try me.'

Some specks of dust moved between them, tinted red and blue.

'I really want to. But I can't. Ma'am.'

Webley held his face for a moment longer. She felt so sorry for him. She said, 'Look, I trust you.' She let her hand fall from his cheek, and adjusted his collar. 'Just bring this whole thing to a conclusion.'

She watched him leaving the chapel as the *Heiliger Geist* lifted to its central motif. She shook her head, thinking back.

I held him. I gave him my body warmth. I hoped he wouldn't die. Then for what he'd done, I got him his bloody medal, put my stamp on him.

Now here she was, asking what the hell was really going on in Tom Fletcher's mind. She glanced up and saw the eyes of the organist watching her in the mirror.

*

Tom Fletcher heard her leaving before he saw her go. He heard the door open and he waited for it to close, but it didn't. He went downstairs and saw her walking away

*along Alpha Road, pulling a suitcase on wheels. He went
out and caught up with her.*

*She looked around at him and kept going. It was early
and cold, the Cam at the end of the street filmed with mist.
He walked beside her as she crossed Chesterton Road and
along the river towards the footbridge across the weir. She
didn't speak. The suitcase made a clicking sound above the
traffic and the noise of the water going into the weir.*

'When will you be back?'

She didn't answer.

*At the footbridge, she said, 'Don't come any further.'
The Cam behind her was rushing through the sluice gates,
the green water turning white as it fell through the mist.
She took his face in her hand and smiled at him. He was as
tall as her, now he was fifteen. Then she turned and hoisted
the suitcase onto the bridge and walked away. In a while
the river was louder than the noise of the wheels.*

*He went back to the house and went into the kitchen and
sat at the table with his father. There was condensation on
the windows and the vapour was beginning to drip. His
father had a bottle of beer already open, the metal cap lying
on the table.*

*His father said, 'She'll be back. It's just a holiday. She's
just going on a holiday.'*

*Then he winked, the creases around his eye sharp like
the edges of the beer cap.*

*Tom Fletcher didn't see her again. His mother walked
across the weir and disappeared from his life.*

Thursday Evening

The river beyond the fields glinted in the last of the sunset. Fletcher found the gap in the hedge, and the Audi wallowed through onto the escarpment of debris around the old American missile base.

He stopped the car, took his steel torch from the glovebox and climbed out. The expanse of dandelions stretched away. His feet clicked and slid on the escarpment, setting off drifts of clockheads. Up ahead, the mound structures loomed out of the shimmer. Reaching the first one, where he'd met Ivan, he climbed its side and looked into the slit that ran across it. It was empty, except for some blackened firewood. From up there, he saw the other mounds stretching out across the base, all pointing east-west. The only life was an arrow of geese flying low. He waited a while. Sunset gave way to dusk, and a single star flickered overhead.

He walked down and came onto a cracked Tarmac road that ran towards the other mounds. Some of these other structures were huge: more than air-raid shelters, they must have been the silos for parking the old American missiles. He counted a dozen of them, in a staggered line across the plateau.

For a second he hesitated. Then felt the trust that

was placed in him: Webley's hand on his arm in the chapel, and for that single moment her fingers against his face.

He smelled the clean smell of grass growing on concrete.

Thursday Night

Ivan put down his nightsight binoculars for a moment, and looked up at the star pulsing over the fen. He wanted the other stars to come out: the stars he'd seen last night above Judith, with the silt under his knees. Her taste was still metallic on his tongue.

When he focused again, he saw the policeman walking cautiously along the road towards his position, coming to the first of the old silos that Ivan knew consisted of four metres of concrete under two metres of packed earth. He saw the policeman produce a flashlight and shine it into the entrance.

He'd seen men doing that before. Men trying to check a partisan bunker, going inside when they should have called for help. Men aged eighteen, with nine weeks' basic training before they were sent to Chechnya.

Policeman Fletcher told Judith he has something to tell me. He doesn't know what I've got ready for him.

Fletcher stepped inside. The mouth of the first mound was enormous: a dark space high as a house, framed by a concrete lip which gleamed under the torchlight.

The interior was a vaulted space with a roof of

concrete ribs, each as wide as a car. It was completely empty: no fixtures, nothing man-made except the concrete. No people, either.

Ivan watched him come out of the first silo and walk along the Tarmac towards the second one: a figure in the pink light of infra-red, casting a thin shadow in the moonlight.

Then the figure re-emerged, and went up to the third silo. This was the largest one: a colossal shape in the centre of the herd of other shapes. He watched the policeman's torch cross the flanks of it for a second, tracing its dimensions. Then he saw him enter.

He packed away his binoculars, gestured to Berlitz to follow, and they got to their feet. Berlitz stretched his arms, curling his fingers and moving his neck.

'*Gotovy?*'

'*Prestupay.*'

They walked down from the mound they were lying on, and continued walking along the central roadway towards the giant silo.

It would start now.

The silo was sealed with a wall of corrugated iron, leaving a single door which swung in on the blackness inside. Fletcher stepped through, sweeping his torch around. More concrete ribs, three storeys high. Dust on the floor, damp on the walls. He watched his own breath drifting, despite the warmth of the evening outside.

'Those Yankees liked concrete, my friend.'

Fletcher turned. Berlitz was standing behind him, looking up at the massive ceiling. Fletcher shone the torch over him: same baseball boots, canvas trousers, bare-chested tonight under the leather jacket. He looked fit, slightly tanned, eyes glinting in the torch-light.

Fletcher said, 'Where's Ivan?'

'Outside. And I think he's got a proposal for you.'

As Sal was checking in amid the chaos of Stansted Airport, her civilian phone rang. She answered it, fumbling for her passport.

'Yeah?'

There was a sound like seagulls. No: they really *were* seagulls.

'Miss Moresby?'

'Tony Olland, is that you?' She could picture his nasty red informant's stubble moving over the mouth-piece. 'Where the fuck are you?'

'Lowestoft.'

'I see.' She took her boarding card and began walking to the gate. 'And how does it feel?'

'It's a bit dull. It smells of fish.'

'I mean, how does it feel letting me down? Scuttling off like a rodent—'

'I'm sorry—'

'—because you were scared of a couple of Russians.'

Tony Olland began slurring over the seagulls.

'It wasn't the Russians. It was the others. I'm worried about you.'

'You're half-pissed, Tony.'

'There's talk, Miss Moresby. The fens is talking.'

'About what?' The Lisbon aircraft was visible through the glass wall of the lounge, people beginning to board. 'About what, Tony?'

'That village, Miss Moresby. The stories about that crazy village. Just be careful, OK?'

Then Tony Olland disappeared back into the emptiness of the Suffolk coast.

Outside the silo, the moon had risen on the edge of the fen, and the Tarmac path was a mauve ribbon among the shapes of the other mounds. Berlitz pointed up at the one they had just exited.

'That way, my friend.'

Fletcher began to climb the turf slope, feeling the night breeze drying a sweat on his face. Halfway up, he glanced back and saw no trace of Berlitz down on the ground. Then, at the top, he found himself on the concrete lintel of the silo entrance, the sheer drop going down into shadows.

Off to the right was the black of the fen, then the lights of Thinbeach, and on the horizon the pale outline of the cathedral in the moonlight. Here on the plateau, the other silos were dark hulks against the grey surface, and a few clouds sailing in front of the moon threw shadows that made it seem the mounds themselves were in motion.

Ivan was standing on the edge too, looking out over the landscape, with the clouds above him streaming light and dark. He was back in his pinstripe suit, the ridged tissue of his throat gleaming as he broke into a smile.

'A police asks to meet me, I must be important.'

'Peter Charter is dead. Judith Denton is a vulnerable and confused person. You're causing problems, Ivan.'

'Have I broken a law? Apart from the gun, the passport?'

'That depends what you're planning for Thinbeach.'

Ivan nodded. 'Planning is the word. For most of my life now, I've been carrying a map of Thinbeach here in my head, studying it. I told you I was in The Cylinder, remember? Even in there I misbehaved. I spent a month in the punishment cell, a box the size of a cupboard, light from a slit three metres above. Not many men survive that. I did, because all that time I saw the map of Thinbeach in my mind, I walked the streets, I could smell the air, see the people how I imagined them to be. I took my time and I decided how things would be when I could really come here.'

'Listen to me, Ivan. You have to understand this and start to accept it. Your grudge against The Wake and Thinbeach is pointless, it's just a symbol for your obsession. I know how your father died: he crashed his car and walked away, but he froze to death in Thinbeach Pool. It was a tragic accident.'

'He fell in the river? My father? I don't believe that, and inside your mind you don't believe it either. I can see it.'

Fletcher paused. He thought about Alain de Minching's account of that night, the doors closed against the injured man, the terrible misunderstanding. That terse, evasive memo from the Home Office. But he said, 'It's over, Ivan. This place will be flooded with police in an hour.'

'That would be a mistake. If you take me in, or if you try to stop the Wedding or fill it with your police, I promise you things really begin happening. You think I only got Berlitz to help me? I've planned this too well. Every day I make a phone call to a certain number, a British number. Every day. I say, not yet, wait. The day I don't make that call, more Russians arrive and they start bad things with the people of Thinbeach. And besides – I've got a proposal for you.'

Ivan squinted up at the clouds, and their shadows moved in his face for a second. Then he held out his hand, and when Fletcher looked down at it in the moonlight, his heart thudded cold.

Ivan was holding out a little shape. It was black and twisted, with fraying edges and broken limbs, and it took Fletcher a second to make out what it was. Then he began to picture where he'd seen it before. It was in the Thinbeach pub, and in the hallway of Alain de Minching's house. Those examples had been lovingly crafted, gracefully proportioned and finished with scraps of rich silk. This one was a vicious cousin. It was a Thinbeach corn doll, a miniature Thinbeach Bride – naked, with its straw frayed to sharp edges. It had kinked limbs, splintered fingers clawing the air, and a face with no eyes but a mouth stitched from thread, grinning up at the moon.

Fletcher looked at it, then at Ivan, and saw the last of the cloud shadows leaving. Clear moonlight began flooding across the land below the silo.

'What's this, Ivan?'

'You know what it is. It's a corn doll. The man with the red star in his lapel put it on our kitchen table beside my father's ashes.'

'You're saying a corn doll was found on his body?'

'Your police counted it among his possessions. But my mother and me, we felt the evil coming from it. We knew someone put it there for a reason. When I took it and ran out on the reservoir, I stood there for a long time until people came to find me. I promised myself to find out what happened. I swore it to myself again and again. You know what I hate the most? It was me not knowing. Me looking at the map every day and marking off the places I thought he was visiting. He only made it to the first place, Cambridge. After that he was dead. And someone here put this thing on his body.'

Fletcher realised that Ivan wasn't talking to him any more, just to himself: making the promise he'd been making since 1979, even in a military punishment cell, getting it stuck in his mind so badly that nothing could shift it now.

'Ivan,' he said. 'I can't explain the corn doll. I don't know why it was found on your father's body, but you can't be sure that anyone in Thinbeach was responsible for his death.'

Ivan stood looking out over the fen. The breeze was ruffling his suit a little, pulling at the lapels. The moon was slipping over to the west, where a jetliner was crossing, its lights brighter than the stars. Ivan said, 'I thought Olga would find out for me, but she failed.'

Fletcher thought back to the voices on Teversham's

tape. Teversham asking *What does it mean?* The old copper saying, *That old chestnut . . . worked like a charm.* That's what Teversham was asking, because that's what Jake wanted to know. What does a corn doll *mean* in Thinbeach? Why would anyone place it on a dead man's body?

'Olga betrayed my critical work. You can finish it.'

Fletcher saw what Ivan's proposal was.

'You're saying you want me to uncover the exact circumstances of your father's death.'

'You're the only one who can do it. And in return, nothing happens at the Thinbeach Wedding.'

'What makes you think I would agree to this?'

'Why? Reason one, because you're afraid of what I'll do at the Wedding. You know I won't touch the people with my hands, but you know I'll do something terrible. I'll do the one thing they fear the most. Think of Charter, think of Denton, multiply it a hundred times. And reason two – that's easy. Because you want to find out what this corn doll means.'

Then Ivan turned his almond eyes on him. Fletcher thought of all the things those eyes must have seen – the bodies, the walls of the punishment cell, Ivan's own victims taking their last breaths.

Ivan said, 'And reason three, what is three? A reason I think is inside you, the reason you've come this far at all.' He put the corn doll away inside his jacket, buttoning it carefully, smoothing the material down. 'I'm a pure man, police. Sometimes I think I'm a kind of holy man.'

'If a crime was committed against your father, I'll find out what it was.'

'You agree. Thank you.'

'But this is still the UK, Ivan, even out here. I'll find what happened to your dad, and then I'll deport you. Meanwhile, stay away from Judith Denton.'

'Judith.' Ivan rubbed his chin again and smiled. 'She reminds me of a woman very famous in Chechnya. You heard of the Angel of Izny?'

'What's Izny?'

'A region where we lost a lot of men. The Angel was a beautiful woman, one of the partisan fighters. She used to just appear out of the crowd or out of the trees, and kill one of our troops, then disappear again. Nobody got a good look at her face. She became like a legend. Some of the boys got tattoos saying *Schadet, anyel.* Means, *Spare me, angel.* Then one time, my unit was positioned along the edge of a maize field. I saw a movement in the maize, going along towards my man on the flank. Suddenly she came out of the corn, this beautiful woman in black, those long black robes they wear, face really was like an angel. He couldn't move, just knelt looking up at her. He was a kid, a conscript from school. He knew the Angel had found him. She shot him in the face. That's how we caught her.'

'What happened to her?'

'The boys gave her a good burial. Needed three separate graves, but it was a good burial. And Judith, she's beautiful like that. She's perfect, isn't she?' Ivan smiled. 'You're crafty, you got me talking too much. That's a police technique, right? You only got tomor-

row, police. Don't waste any time. I know The Wake
were involved, but I think there's more to this, more
than just the three men we know about. Tell me who
else was in it, what they did, why they put the corn doll
on my father. Or all of Thinbeach pays the price, every
one of them.'

Ivan turned to go. Fletcher watched him walk away
down the side of the silo and onto the plateau of
dandelions, leaving a trail of them behind him until
he disappeared into the dark.

Fletcher waited until there was no point in going
after him, even if he changed his mind. It was a slim
risk, because he almost never changed his mind.

On the plane to Lisbon, Sal Moresby was next to a
man who smelled of Kouros and sold high-quality
timeshare. He said, 'I can show you round. No pressure. We're a professional company.'

She closed her eyes – letting the sounds of the
aircraft, the voices of the passengers, the yelps of
the children, flow around her in a slipstream. Her
annoyance at Tony Olland's idiotic rambling faded
over the English Channel. Somewhere over the Bay of
Biscay, she dozed for a few minutes, and in her half-
sleep she glimpsed something that her conscious mind
hadn't registered.

She woke. She couldn't get back to it. She bought a
Bloody Mary, and watched the coast of Portugal
swelling like a bruise in the dark sea below the plane.
The timeshare man offered his card. She said, 'Can't
you see I'm thinking?'

By the time she collected a hire car, it was late at night. She asked the clerk to recommend a hotel. He said, 'A lady such as you, must sleep somewhere beautiful.'

'Somewhere quiet will do fine.'

Fletcher stopped at Electric Mile and found Cathleen sitting in the heat of her downstairs room, her legs drawn up on the sofa, wide eyes looking at him over her knees. From the yard, the sound of Luke throwing a basketball was drowned out for a second by a train.

'Is Luke worried?' he asked.

'He trusts you to keep those men away.' She closed her eyes. 'If he finds out, Tom. I don't know what it'll do to him. It'll kill him.'

'I told you, he won't find out.'

'And you too, Tom. It'll kill you too, won't it?'

It was a hot night, the city centre peopled by thin shadows, the college buildings hushed. Fletcher pulled up by his slot at All Saints and stood watching the padlock dangling from the chain. He was asking himself about Ivan and Ivan's father. What would Ivan do, how far would he go, to have the chance of speaking to his father again?

He started the car again and headed along Sidney Street.

He put the windows down and breathed in Cambridge. The smell was old stone, perfume, cooking and drains, the tang of the river when he crossed Magdalene Bridge. In a while there was the scent of grass as he drove west along the Madingley Road. He crossed the M11 motorway, lines of headlights blurring under the flyover.

He turned into an area of woodland where the motorway was just a droning echo. The woods were mostly conifer, the trees fresh and green but the ground around them dry and littered with brown needles as the headlights swept past.

He passed a sign: Wilber Court, Residential Care.

The building was a red-brick oblong, with window boxes visible in the glow from some of the curtained windows. He parked and sat for a while looking up at the windows. A few had lamps shining between drawn curtains. Then he walked over to the main door and pushed the night bell.

Inside, there was a reception desk with a nurse reading a Czech newspaper. Eyes the colour of broken green glass turned up to him.

He said, 'I'm looking for Mr Fletcher.'

She hesitated.

He said, 'He's my father.'

*

Tom Fletcher heard the street door opening, but not closing. It was late, and the streetlamps were spreading orange light into the darkened lounge, car headlights fingering through the curtains and across the walls, the television showing news footage of tanks rolling between sand dunes.

He went to the doorway. He could see from there to the front of the house. The open door was letting streetlight spill in, and a current of cold air smelling of the river.

Tom went to the front door. He found his father sitting on the doorstep, leaning on the door itself, looking out into the street. His keys were swinging in the lock. A car passed and sent its lights over him briefly. He had a cut on his face that was dried, and newer blood under his lip. He smelled of beer and pavements, and wherever he'd been in the last forty-eight hours. He said to the street, 'I've lost my winter coat. That sounds like an animal, doesn't it? Losing its winter coat.'

Tom said, 'They're coming tomorrow.'

'Who?'

'They said you weren't capable.'

'I am capable. Who?'

'You can come and visit me.'

'Visit you where?'

Tom Fletcher took his father upstairs and pulled his shoes off. His father stretched out on the bed and said something to himself, the streetlight across him. Tom Fletcher watched him for ten minutes, the heating clicking and tapping in its pipes.

That was the last night Tom Fletcher spent in the same building as his father.

*

Fletcher stood looking down through the conifers. There was a path leading through them, trodden with brown needles.

He began to walk, breathing the smell of the needles, hearing the crunch of twigs under his shoes and the motorway muffled through the plantation. The trees were planted in perfect rows, and there was a light at the end of the path that kept him walking straight. After a few minutes he reached the end of the trees. In the empty field beyond, a small fire was taking hold, lit in a circle of earth. He guessed the flames were burning conifer branches, because oily smoke was drifting in the still air.

He stopped a few yards away, still just among the trees. In the firelight, he saw a man standing with his hands in his pockets. He was slightly hunched, his head pushed forward on his neck. The flames settled down and showed him in profile: a tangled head of hair on a face that was scarcely visible. Suddenly the man turned to look at the pathway, and the flames lit him up.

The face was creased with lines that gathered the firelight. There was a deep scowl furrowed between the eyebrows, and the eyes reflected a flash of green.

Fletcher kept in the shadow of the trees, unsure if the man could see him. A cold breeze blew down the track between the conifers, making the fire shudder. The man threw on another shred of pine branch.

Fletcher backed away, moving slowly so that he wouldn't be noticed. Then he turned and walked back along the path until the lights of Wilber Court shone down along the row of trees. He got back into his car and sat for a minute, looking up at the windows. He could still smell the smoke of the conifer branches clinging to him. He turned the engine on and flicked through the radio stations. He wanted anything that would help, anything from outside himself. In the end he turned to the plug-in MP3, choosing the first track.

From the age of fifteen, Fletcher had lived with his

uncle, a career army officer. His uncle brought him things back from his tours of duty. One time he came back from Belize, the British enclave in the jungles of central America, with a vinyl record cut by a teenage sax player who made this one thing and then died in a dispute with local police. Fletcher had it on digital now: the crackles and hisses of the vinyl like the sounds of the jungle itself under the tenor solo.

He turned it up loud. He knew he was going to drive the three miles back into Cambridge, to sleep in his rented flat. Three miles that set him apart from his father. He kept the track on while the song swayed around for long minutes. The road was empty up ahead, just one pair of headlights behind, not getting closer.

Fletcher swung into Northampton Street, then Magdalene Street, with the windows down, letting the dead sax man wail his lullaby to the hot empty streets of Cambridge.

Those headlights behind him were closer now, and as he slowed at the bridge he recognised the angles of a late-model Omega. He slammed the brakes and stopped in the middle of the street with a snarling echo. He breathed tyre smell, keeping his eyes on the mirror. The Omega had stopped just as sharply, twenty metres back, staying out of the streetlight. There was no rain tonight to blur the windscreen. The false plates were unchanged. Fletcher snapped the music off, and in the quiet he heard the Omega's engine running. Moths swirled around it, clunking into the headlamps.

He got out, leaving the Audi's door open, and began walking towards the other car, reaching into his pocket for his warrant card, pointing one finger at the driver's position even though there was no eye contact.

He shouted, 'Who are you?'

Coming closer, he could see two men in outline through the windscreen. The same men as last time? He stepped onto the pavement and approached the car. He came level with the passenger window and saw the man with neatly-cut grey hair, his lined face tinted orange-green by the dials. The man looked through the glass at him and suddenly grinned, then broke into a silent laugh. The driver leaned forward and looked over at Fletcher. He was smiling too, and he mouthed a few words before he drove off, accelerating with enough force to push the passenger back into his seat. There was a rush of heated air and a smell of exhaust before the Omega hit the open door of the Audi.

There was an explosion of glass. Fletcher saw the ripped door flip up over the Omega's bonnet and land in the street, scattering flakes of safety plex – then spin around, trailing its severed wires. Before it stopped, the other car was gone, not even its tail lights visible over the bridge.

Fletcher ran across the shattered glass, climbed into the Audi and turned the keys. The ignition fizzed with a short circuit, the fuses blown.

A few people were gathering on the pavement, pointing at the car with no door. A student stood swaying on his heels, shaking his head slowly.

'Lucky you weren't standing there. I mean, lucky.'

Fletcher got out. He kicked the wrecked door hard enough to turn it away across the road.

That wasn't lucky. Those men had absolutely no reason to stop where they did, except to let Fletcher know that they were getting close to him. They knew where Cathleen and Luke lived, and now they knew where his father was. The more he learned about Thinbeach, the more they learned about him.

And the driver had said something to him. Fletcher wasn't sure, but he thought the words were: *We know*.

There was something in the air, hard to escape. Fletcher smelled his own shirt. Conifer smoke.

Friday Morning

The hotel that the clerk recommended for Sal turned out to be both quiet and beautiful. It was a little place in a valley north of Lisbon. Cool floors, geraniums, shutters on the windows. A big bed. She found a message on her phone from Fletcher, saying the object on the dead Russian was a Thinbeach corn doll. She stretched out on clean sheets and closed her eyes again, pushing her face into the pillow. The silence was intoxicating.

A corn doll? For God's sake. Is that what Tony Olland was trying to say? The stories about that crazy village. The old stories about the Thinbeach bride.

She fell asleep quickly.

Towards dawn, she found herself a thousand years ago. She was in a different bed, in flax sheets, sprawled beside her husband. He was twice her age, his cropped Norman head glistening damp and his open mouth reeking of wine as he mumbled his own stupid language in his sleep.

She stood up, and she was naked. The room was cool after the sweat of the bed. She went to the doorway of The Blindy House, feeling the stone under her feet. The door was open, and instead of the Shamblings there was an orchard outside, stretching away across the island towards the new Norman church where the village women had drugged her with poppies before her wedding.

The apple trees were heavy with fruit against the dawn sky. Everything was blue and grey. The grass was wet between her toes, and the bark of the trees buffed her skin as she brushed between them.

One tree had a ladder pegged to it with wooden spikes. She climbed it and felt the apples parting around her, leaving their damp tangling in her long hair and glistening on her breasts. She felt her nipples running with thick apple dew. Some apples fell and rolled into her thighs, sudden and wet. They bounced on the turf and rolled away, spinning dew.

She reached the crown of the tree.

Her village boy was already there, leaning on a bough and watching her with a shine in his blue eyes. She said his name in their own language, then she got a grip with her toes on the branches underfoot. The boy's hair was wet, and cool drops spattered against her when he took her wrists and wrapped them around the tree trunk. She felt her own pulse against his thumbs as he held her so she wouldn't slip.

Then a branch snapped in half. She was being dragged down from the tree, the pegs ripping long lines on her skin, her husband hoisting her onto his shoulders, carrying her back through the orchard, slamming her against the apples, chanting something in Norman.

In a moment he had her by the bank of the Pool and she was flying through the air. Dew went trailing from her fingernails. She saw the landscape pitching over, the corn fields and the orchard upside down, before the black gloss slapped her face.

The water was cold, and the silt stung her eyes when she went under. Her ears hushed, just their blood thumping. She felt river weed, and the eels puckering her lids and sliding between her limbs.

She came up in the light just once. She shook her head, gasping, and saw her husband standing on the edge, smeared with sweat and dew, watching her drown, his hands on his furry hips. She spat out a curse on him and all his bastard sons: a long tangled curse that took the last of her breath. Then she saw the village turn one last time before the eels coiled around her thighs and pulled her back down into the dark.

Sal Moresby woke with the light of Portugal slanting through the blinds. She lay there for a while, getting her breath back, watching the dust moving slowly across the room. When she stood up, the tiles felt cool under her feet.

She ran a long shower, watching her toes in the warm water.

Checking out, she asked how to get to the golf complex called Parque da Pinta. The man explained and gave her a one-sheet map. Then he said, *May your day be a good one.*

She liked Portugal. The road was smooth and lined with eucalyptus and pines, stone walls giving onto fields, ash leaves in drifts against fences, and then up on the hills above the valleys a few houses with red roofs bright against the scrub. She drove slowly – by her standards – planning her conversation with Billy Breakman. She pictured that tough, confident face from the brochure photograph – and the same face painted by Jake Skerrit on his bedroom wall, surrounded by wisps of straw; and the face in the news cuttings, staring blankly.

She pulled over for a minute to check the map. There was a roadside shrine, a Madonna in a glass box. An old woman leaving flowers said, *May your day be a good one.*

She took a route out of the valley and into a landscape of wooded hills. In another twenty kilometres she picked up the signs for Parque da Pinta, and just before nine a.m. she arrived.

The complex had a gated entrance designed to impress: a semicircle of flagstones, inlaid with the word *Pinta* in coloured glass catching the sun. The same word was embroidered on the pocket of a bored security man as he leaned into her window, smelling of cigarettes, asking who she wanted to see. When she told him, he raised his eyebrows and studied her warrant card, looking at her differently. Then he made the wrought-iron gates roll open, and waved her through.

She saw the gates rolling shut again in the mirror, before the road took her between a row of eucalyptus and a slope of lawns with sprinklers making rainbows in the sunlight, spreading down towards a golf course between the low hills. Bright figures stood against the greens and the bunkers. Then the complex itself came into view: a semicircle of apartments with domed roofs rising against the blue sky.

Inside the reception lobby, when her eyes had adjusted to the shade, she found a mahogany counter unstaffed. She asked two passing men in golfing clothes if they knew which was Billy Breakman's apartment. They glanced at each other and looked her over, and she had to ask again in a sharper tone before one of them answered.

It was on the top floor, at the end of a cool corridor, the marble on the floor being polished by a woman who stared when she saw Sal approaching Breakman's door, before stooping again over her cloth. It seemed that everybody here was slightly afraid of Billy Breakman.

She rang the bell, waited and rang again. Hearing it chime inside, Sal had the feeling that someone was observing her – not the cleaner, but someone she could hear moving behind the spyhole in the door. Then the door opened a few centimetres, held by a chain.

'What do you want?'

The voice was deep and hostile. She couldn't see the man properly, because the light was behind him.

'I'm looking for Mr Breakman.'

She held out her warrant card. After a few seconds the door closed and the chain clanged free, leaving her to open the door herself. Stepping inside, she found things were very different to what she expected.

The apartment looked as if someone was living under siege. It was dusty, strewn with newspapers, files and books, a jumble of mail-order packaging near the door. There was a smell from the kitchen area,

where she could see pans jumbled in the sink and an
overflowing bin attracting flies.

Billy Breakman had his back to her. He was closing a
slatted blind, sending spears of light across the mayhem. Then he turned and asked again what she
wanted, and she needed a few seconds to take in his
appearance.

This wasn't the apartment she expected, and this
wasn't the man she expected either. He was the man
from the photos, without a doubt: the same height and
the strong face still recognisable after a generation. But
something had changed him: he stood with rounded
shoulders, watching her with eyes sunk deep in shadows,
a week's growth of beard patterned with grey. He was
wearing creased golfing clothes and grimy slippers.

She asked him what plans he had to return to
Thinbeach.

'None. I live here now.'

'You know about Olga, your son's wife?'

Billy Breakman nodded. 'I knew she'd bring him
sadness. Why would any girl marry a man twice her
age?' For a second, Sal saw apple trees, a ladder of
wooden spikes. Billy stood watching her from the
window. 'No, I'm staying here. I'm safe here.'

'Are you afraid of something, Mr Breakman?'

'You still haven't told me what you want.'

'Mr Breakman, something is happening in Thinbeach. The events of January 1979 are becoming very
important to a lot of people, including me.'

Breakman took the cord of the blind in one hand and
began winding it between his fingers, making a little

cat's cradle. Then he shook it loose and began again without looking at it. That must have taken a lot of practice.

'Look,' he said suddenly, 'why don't you drive down to Lisbon? I'll get you a table at Verdi's, the best restaurant. I still have contacts.'

'I need you to tell me about The Wake. I believe you were the leader.'

Billy's hollow eyes closed for a while. He said, 'Was I the leader? Maybe I was, yes.'

'Why did you visit the places where the Lovely Brigade died? I've seen photographs of you at the scenes.'

Billy's eyes flashed open. 'The Lovely Brigade. They were kids, weren't they?'

'They were teenagers. Why were you there?'

Billy shook his head. 'I don't know. I can't explain.'

'You must have had a reason.'

'I just went to look.'

'I see. In 1979, a Russian engineer who had an appointment with you drowned in the river. Can you give me any information about the circumstances?'

From outside, she could hear the lawn sprinklers hissing and spluttering. Breakman peered out through the blinds, the bars of light across his face, his fingers still twining distractedly.

'How much?'

'I'm sorry?'

'How much do you want?'

Breakman snapped the blind suddenly and the room

became darker, thin bars of light striping across him. She knew he was frightened – not of her, but of whatever kept him alone here in this pit.

'If I pay you, will it be the last I hear of it? But you people always say that, don't you? It never ends.'

'Has someone been blackmailing you?'

Asking the question, she knew it was a fact. She pictured the wad of money in Jake Skerrit's room, and the Tiffany bracelet for Olga.

The sprinklers hissed.

'It's beautiful here, isn't it?' Breakman said. 'And it's private. It should be perfect, but the other residents stare at me in the corridor. The cleaners call me a *porcalhao*, they think I can't speak Portuguese.'

'Let's stay on the subject. Who's been blackmailing you? Was it Jake Skerrit?'

'So you're not asking for money?'

'Obviously not. Whatever happened in 1979 will have to come into the open. Once it's known, nobody can threaten you.'

'Are you quite sure about that?'

'Tell me what happened. Is it something on your conscience? Something that troubles you?' Breakman closed his eyes and made a movement that could have been a nod. 'Is that why you won't go back to Thinbeach?'

Breakman opened his eyes on her – reddened and damp. He wiped his mouth with the back of his hand, but said nothing.

'Mr Breakman. Something was found on the Russian's body. An object. Do you know what it was?'

Breakman shook his head. The apartment was silent again, apart from the sprinklers.

'It was a little corn doll, Mr Breakman. Why would that have happened? What does the doll mean in Thinbeach? Does it symbolise something?' Breakman stayed silent, his fingers coiling and uncoiling the cord, his face set in a scowl. Sal went to her next step. 'You have to understand that the death of the Russian is becoming critically important. His son has come back to Thinbeach.'

'*His son?*'

'Yes, and he's got a grudge. He's an expert in psychological torment. Peter Charter is dead and Thomas Denton may be next. And the Thinbeach Wedding is on Saturday.'

'The Wedding?' Breakman began to laugh, a line of spit running down his chin. Dust scattered from the blind as he wrapped his arms around himself, shaking his head at the joke. Suddenly he stopped and wiped his mouth, turning his eyes on Sal. 'She'll fight back, though. She always does.'

'Who?'

'The Bride, of course. The bloody Thinbeach Bride.'

'But the Thinbeach Bride is an effigy, a little corn doll.'

'A little corn doll? Have you ever seen her? She's so strong, she could knock a man over. One of her hands could wrap around your waist, Sergeant.'

'She's not real, Mr Breakman.'

'Oh yes, she's real. The Bride is real. She's the root of it all.'

'The root of what?'

'The Bride's the one that talked me into it in the first place. She whispered and she seduced me until I took part.'

Breakman stopped himself. Sal waited for more, but nothing came.

'That's interesting. Took part in what?'

Breakman just stood rocking on his feet.

Sal looked around the apartment. The corners of the room held drifts of rubbish: empty microwave packets, wine bottles, gin bottles. She wondered if Breakman really knew something – whether he'd really taken part in something that tortured his conscience – or whether those bottles had been full earlier on that morning.

'Mr Breakman, have you thought of getting some help?'

'The cleaners won't come in here.'

'I mean, psychiatric help. I think you would benefit. I think there's something terrible on your conscience that's been brewing inside you for more than twenty-five years, and now it's spilling over because Jake Skerrit figured it out. So what exactly did you take part in? Was it something criminal? Did it involve The Wake?'

'Oh, I see. I get it now.' Breakman nodded. 'You don't know, do you? You've got absolutely no idea. Christ alive, you've got no idea at all. Now I've changed my mind, Sergeant Moresby. Don't go to Lisbon – you wouldn't like Verdi's anyway. Get on the plane and get back to Thinbeach and talk to that woman, the Thinbeach Bride.'

'Corn dolls don't talk, Mr Breakman.'

Sal stood up, brushing the dust from her trousers,
turning to the door. Maybe there was a charity for
people like this: expatriate alcoholic machinery dealers.

'I'm asking you once more, Mr Breakman. Perhaps
your conscience will be easier if you tell someone.
What happened?'

Billy Breakman reached down to a gin bottle and
shook it. He kept his lips pressed together. The discussion was at a close.

'Goodbye, Mr Breakman. Make peace with the
cleaners. May your day be a good one.'

As she turned, Breakman called out to her in a
clearer, stronger voice.

'The Bride's the woman to talk to, Sergeant, if you
want to know what happened back then. She's the
spirit of Thinbeach – you realise that? The Bride is all
the women trapped with the men they detest. Chretien
de Minchin's young wife, and Olga stuck with Crispin,
and Judith Denton stuck with Thomas in that bloody
house in the fen. It turns them strange after a while.
Makes them cruel, capable of anything. That's who the
Bride is. She's blind and dumb and every year the men
try to drown her and she sinks, but she *lives* down
there, under the water. She's alive under there, and she
comes reaching for me, I can see her face when I look in
the sink. She'll live for ever. She just won't die. She just
won't fucking die.'

Sal closed the door behind her.

She knocked on the door of an office behind the
reception area. The manager of the complex was a

bored guy in his thirties. Crucifix around his neck, neat moustache. His English was excellent. He smoked heavily.

He wiped some ash off his desk and looked at her warrant card and shook his head sympathetically at the mention of Mr Breakman. His opinion was that Billy used to be a fine man, a gentleman. Now he was breaking many conventions – both as a resident of the complex, and indeed as an Englishman.

'When did it all start?'

'Quite recently, in about April. He suddenly did that.' The manager snapped his fingers to demonstrate the breakdown. 'He had a visitor.'

'Can you describe the visitor?'

'Young English man, early twenties. Very poorly dressed. He was up there for an hour with Breakman, came down looking pleased. Breakman was never the same after that.'

So it was true. Jake had taken the plane to Lisbon to confront Billy with what he knew about the Thinbeach Bride. He'd gone away with pockets full of used notes, or a money order to cash in Ely.

Sal declined the offer of a Marlboro. She watched the manager tipping more ash. The desk held nothing but an instruction manual for a lawn sprinkler.

She said, 'If you have time to spare, would you like to assist the British police?'

The manager moved his eyes across her and then across the sprinkler manual. He flicked some ash.

'Assist you like how?'

★ ★ ★

Fletcher stopped at the breakfast van in the Market Square, under the smoke from Stan's cooking. It was before seven a.m., but already warm. Stan pushed across a mug and turned some bacon. He said, 'I hear a problem with your car.'

'It's better with no door. Keeps it cool.'

Stan nodded. 'And what's happened with your friend?'

'My friend?'

'The man comes here from another country, comes looking for peace.'

'He's not a friend of mine, Stan.'

Stan raised his eyes to Fletcher's, then looked down again.

'Must be my mistake. It was the way you talked about him.'

★

They took him there in a taxi. A Granada, cloth seats, smelling of fast food and smoke. The driver glancing at him once in the mirror, then just watching the road ahead. The social worker woman beside him on the back seat, looking out of the window.

She said, 'This is just for a week, OK? After that, your uncle's family are back from Germany, and you go to them, OK?'

They turned into the street. Blissey Avenue. Conifer hedges in the gardens, a red postbox, ice in the puddles. The last of the suburbs before the empty grey fields.

'They're an experienced foster family. The Hartnells, Edmund and Maria. They'll make you very welcome.'

The driver pulled up outside number thirty-four.

'There are other kids there. Young people, I mean. Young people they're looking after, like you. You'll get on well.'

From the window, Tom Fletcher watched the taxi disappear at the end of the avenue. Then he turned and looked at the room. A single bed, some posters. A pine chest of drawers, some scratches. An iron radiator clicking with heat. The door opened slowly.

A man wearing corduroy trousers, a cardigan over a T-shirt. In his forties, receding. Around his neck, a pair of glasses on a cord strung with wooden beads. Fingers turning one of the beads. Fingernails that needed cutting.

'Hello Tom. I'm Edmund. Welcome to the family.'

*

Fletcher showered and put on fresh clothes: a light-weight suit, linen shirt and tie. At Parkside, he checked what progress there was on a damaged Omega wanted for FTS – Failed To Stop. Absolutely none. He signed out an Airwave handset and an unmarked police car, twirling the key on his finger while he dialled Webley's mobile. Caught her on the way to the seminar.

'Holistic policing can wait, Fletcher. Tell me.'

It turned into a long call: the corn doll on the Russian's body, Ivan's threat to torment Thinbeach unless the circumstances of the death were made clear. When he finished, Webley herself was quiet for a while. He thought he could hear the sound of her breathing as they shared the silence. Then,

'Torment them how?'

'I don't know, ma'am. Something sick. Something

that'll completely traumatise them. Think what he did to Peter Charter, what he's trying to do to Judith Denton. It's vicious. The catch is, cancelling the Wedding or flooding the area with police will make things worse in the long run. We can't permanently evacuate a whole village.'

Another silence.

'The management are behind you, Fletcher. You know that. But you've got something like twenty-four hours left. How exactly do you propose to stop him?'

'There's one sure way. I'm going to find out how his father died.'

Fletcher listened to Sal on his desk phone, watching the trees on Parker's Piece through the window. She was miles away from all this, speaking from the gardens of Parque da Pinta.

She said, 'Two things. First, Breakman's either a brilliant actor, or he's had a real breakdown. He couldn't explain why he was at the Lovely Brigade scenes. He just said, *They were kids, weren't they?* As if he felt sorry for them. But then he told me he'd taken part in something, something involving a corn doll like the Thinbeach Bride.'

'Taken part in what?'

'It was hard to understand – he was pissed. But he's terrified of the Bride, the corn doll, whatever it is. The fact is that Jake Skerrit flew out here to blackmail Billy over something from the past, maybe the Russian engineer. There's something really terrible on Billy Breakman's conscience.'

'Is that the second thing?'

'No, this is the second thing. You see, the management here keep tabs on all the residents. They open people's mail and listen in to their phone calls. And they've got a whole file on Billy Breakman, trying to get him evicted for bad behaviour. The manager showed me a log of his outgoing calls. One phone number kept appearing, because Breakman's been making the call two or three times a day – including today, just after I left him. International, a Cambridge number.'

'What number?'

'Wait. The call was still in progress – the manager let me listen in on his switchboard. Breakman was ranting until someone else cut in and told him to shut up. I recognised the other voice.'

'Yes?'

'Helpful guy, lots of body hair. Descended from the Normans.' Fletcher watched the trees. They were utterly still. 'Fletcher?'

'Alain de Minching? Are you sure?'

'Alain with an *i*. It was his voice and his number.'

'What exactly did he say?'

'Are you ready for this? Alain said, *She'll deal with them too*. Then he hung up – maybe he heard something different about the phone line.'

'*She'll deal with them too?* Who is *she*?'

'The Bride, Fletcher. The corn doll thing. And who is *them*?'

'The Russians,' he said.

'Or us.'

*   *   *

Fletcher held the phone for a while. The offices were busy now, phones ringing and people talking, eating takeaway breakfast, but Fletcher didn't hear them.

He thought of Jake and Teversham in the long winter nights, complaining about lack of money. Then Olga arriving, letting slip to Jake that she was here to find out what a corn doll means when it's found on the body of a drowned man. Teversham inviting his old police friends around, asking *them* what it meant. Jake flying to Lisbon to tell Billy Breakman that he knew.

Then Jake turning the CCTV off – why? Not because he planned to fool around with machines, but because he was meeting someone. Jake being chewed up in the shredder – the side of his head sliced away. Teversham grabbing the video tape in a panic. Teversham visiting Alain de Minching, setting off home on his bald tyres, another accident statistic.

She'll deal with them too.

Meaning the Bride had *already* dealt with someone or some people. She'd already dealt with Jake and Teversham.

Out on the Piece, a breeze just lifted the branches of the trees. Fletcher was already gone, taking his unmarked car onto the long straight road towards Thinbeach.

At the front door of The Blindy House, Fletcher listened to the bell ringing inside. No answer, no barking of dogs. He looked through the nearest window: just the empty hallway.

He walked around the side, where the gable wall was

sunk into the earth embankment. There was one other window here, looking into Alain de Minching's wargames room: the huge table laid out with a new battle, more painted soldiers in combat. Fletcher started back to the garden, then stopped and turned again.

It was a medieval battle: knights charging across a plain, trampling a line of longbow archers. It looked like the battle of Agincourt. But Agincourt didn't happen like this – the bowmen demolished the knights, didn't they? What was Alain's other wargame – the battle of Salamanca? Fletcher suspected that if he checked it out, history would say the red jackets won – they weren't scattered by the blues.

When he got back to the gate, he found Debbie, the barmaid, watching him from the garden of the Bride. She came over, smiling.

'Alain's not in there,' she said. 'You want some breakfast, Tom? Something hot?'

'No thanks, Debbie. You know where he is?'

'It's the day before the Wedding, Tom. Alain always goes for a hike with the dogs, down the river to Ely. He says that's how the de Minchings have always got ready for the big day. And that's not all. Between you and me—' she stood a little closer '—he shaves his chest too.'

'He does *what*?'

'It's another tradition. They say when old Chretien's wife was drowning, she put a curse on the de Minchin family. That all the men would grow fur on their bodies, like dogs.' She winked. 'Norman soldiers had to shave themselves, did you know that? So the chainmail wouldn't catch in the hairs. And Alain still does it for the Wedding. Bless.'

'You know everything, Debbie. Does Alain have a car?'

'Mm, big Citroën from the old days, looks like a fish. You sure about breakfast, Tom? We could make it quick.'

'You're very kind, Debbie. I'm in a hurry. Where does he keep the Citroën?'

The garage was at the other end of the Shamblings, in a row behind the stone houses. The door was locked, but with some help it swung open and sunlight flooded in. The Citroën was an old DS from the sixties, black, beautifully preserved. It was nose-in, and Fletcher had to squeeze against the wall to get around. Debbie was right: it was a huge metallic fish. Right down at the front, where the bumper curved under the nose, there was a single dent that had been cleaned to remove traces of whatever it had hit.

Was that how Ron Teversham died? Did Alain get him even drunker than he already was, then make that call to the police, guessing correctly that it wouldn't be followed up? Not much of a gamble, with police cover as tight as it was in fenland. Did he follow Teversham in this Citroën, then just nudge the Ford to make him lose what control he had?

Fletcher closed the garage door.

An overheard phone call in Portugal and a dented bumper in Thinbeach would never make it into court as evidence, but it gave him a picture of how the Bride was dealing with people who tried to get close to her. Those people were having accidents – accidents carefully staged, the way battles could be staged to change what really happened.

Why?

What was the secret?

What did Alain know about The Wake, the men he described as clowns and jokers? Why was Billy phoning him for reassurance? And how could any of this explain the question that had to be answered today – why did an innocent Russian engineer die with a corn doll on his body?

Fletcher went back to his car. It was a small 4×4 Nissan, metallic green, no air conditioning. He got out the files on the deaths of Terry Swilter and Shane Gaffy. He loosened his tie. He read through each file again, going back over the copy of each dog-eared page.

When he finished, he sat watching a harvester moving into position in a grain field, shimmering in the heat against the polythene tunnels beyond. He took his tie off completely.

There was one further similarity between the two files, one that wasn't immediately obvious. Each coroner's report had the usual who's who sheet, detailing all the personnel involved at the scene and afterwards. In the traditional fashion, this went from top to bottom in order of some perceived social ranking. At the top of the page was the coroner himself; then the doctor who had examined Terry Swilter's corpse at Ulsingham Hall; the others who tried to save Shane Gaffy in the burns unit at Addenbrooke's, and the post-mortem pathologist. Lower down was the investigating officer, then the photographer whose evidence had disappeared, then the firefighters. Right at the foot of the page was the name of the police officer who was first on the scene, the one responsible for preserving the site intact. On both reports, that name had been torn away, leaving a blank triangle in the lower right corner. The pages weren't dog-eared – they were deliberately mutilated.

Of course. The first officer on the scene had concealed his involvement. He was the bent copper from Wittris.

Ron Teversham.

★

In Blissey Avenue, they ate in a room with a big window showing the garden. Frost on the grass, bare trees, a children's slide, a swing with the seat twisted up off the ground. Winter dusk, the moon a big thumbprint in the sky.

Edmund Hartnell and his wife Maria sat at opposite ends of the table. Between them, Tom plus two boys younger than him, brothers. A fourth place was set, but empty.

Maria and the boys were eating soup, sliced bread, ham from a packet. Edmund Hartnell was stirring his soup, his eyes moving around the table, onto the empty place.

The first Tom Fletcher saw of her was through the doorway: just one eye visible, bright against the dark hall, coppery hair over her shoulders. A woollen dress the same colour as her eyes. She slipped into the room, slipped into her chair, glanced once at Tom, then down at the soup Maria passed her.

Edmund watched her, stirring his soup. In a while, he said, 'Cathleen.'

She raised her face to him.

'Cathleen, this is Tom.'

She looked at Tom again.

The way the house had been adapted, there was a metal fire escape leading off a landing on the third floor. The door had a key permanently in the lock. Tom Fletcher stood on the fire escape in the dark, watching the moon on the roofs of the other houses, feeling the cold breeze. There were sounds below him: pipes groaning, something moving around in water.

The door behind him opened and light spilled through onto the fire escape. She stood next to him, her profile clear against the roofs. She was wearing an old raincoat too big for her.

He said, 'What's that noise downstairs?'

'It's Edmund, he's in his bath.'

'How long have you been here?'

'A year,' she said. The breeze was blowing her hair, moving the big sleeves of her coat.

'I'm only here for a week. Then I'm going to my uncle.'

She nodded.

He said, 'How long will you stay?'

'I don't know.'

She rested her hand on her stomach.

Friday Midday

This time, Ivan wasn't waiting.

He was striding along the raised bank of the tributary river that fed into Thinbeach Pool. This was classic English countryside: pylons across the fields, a main road in the distance, the sky diced up by vapour trails, a wartime pillbox sinking in the riverbank. He climbed up on the pillbox to see if he could find her.

He saw that parallel to the river was a series of oxbow lakes: curves of the original river left behind as it straightened its course. One of these was completely dry, leaving a bowl of mineral silt glittering under the edge of a cornfield studded with poppies. He jumped down and walked towards it across the springy ground.

She was lying on the concave silt with the corn above her, where she couldn't be seen from the surrounding fields. She'd make a good infantry soldier, he thought. He was going to tell her that, as he jumped down and landed in front of her, spreading his hands wide.

She got to her feet. She was wearing another of her dresses, and he saw a long burst of her thigh and the curve between her breasts, corn-coloured skin.

She hit him in the face, hard, with a clenched fist that stunned him. He tasted blood on his tongue. He swore long Red Army curses and stooped to spit into the silt, shaking his head. Then he felt her grab his hair and yank his face down close to hers, and he thought, *She really is perfect.*

Her voice was more like a hiss.

'You're just using me. That policeman told me. You're using me against my father.'

He had to twist his head to keep her from tearing his scalp off.

'Judith, who's using who?'

She let his hair go and he pulled himself up and looked at her, getting his breath back, wiping the blood from his chin. She looked away for a moment.

He laughed and flipped her over on her back. As she landed, she sent a spray of silt across the little beach, but he noticed she knew how to fall, like a real fighter. She clambered to her feet. She was breathing hard, her hair tangled across her face.

He said, 'I've got work to do here. You could be part of it.'

She already had her hands on him, pushing him down onto the metallic silt. He didn't fight back. She straddled him, with her hair falling in her eyes. He ran his hands up under her dress. She began to unbutton his tunic, then stopped, looking at his tattoos. She finished unbuttoning and ran her hands across them.

'What do they mean?'

'That one you're touching is Red Army, Petrov Division. The one underneath means we were in Chechnya in 1994.'

Her fingertips were moving across his chest, feeling

the muscles, pushing his tunic further back to see the tattoos on his shoulders, fascinated.

'What's this?'

'The Cylinder. Done with ballpoint and beetroot.' She took a handful of the glittering silt and rubbed it on the tattoo. He held her hand. 'You can't rub it out.'

She took the shining dust left on her fingers and made stripes on her face and his, glinting in the sun. She grinned and swung her hair, making the warpaint flash.

She took the rest of his uniform off, laughing when she pulled the heavy boots. He unbuttoned her dress and slipped everything off. She pinned him down against the bank and mounted him, getting a grip in the corn stalks above his head. They made a shivery noise, as if a storm was getting near, and released a fine dust. He knew she was looking at his tattoos all the time. He closed his eyes on the corn and the poppies. He opened his eyes and there was just her smile. He reached for her hair and began to ask her something.

She hit him one last time, a heavy slap across his face while he was still inside her.

He laughed and rolled her over on her belly and rubbed her in the sediment, even though she yelped and protested. He put a leg across her flank and reached up and tore off a poppy and tucked it behind her ear. It looked great, the red flower against her shiny dark hair, her shoulders flecked with the silt, catching the sun. He leaned down and kissed the back of her neck as he asked his question.

'You want to join my work, Judith?'

She twisted him off her. 'And do what?'

He explained. She listened, sprawled on the silt, watching the sky, twisting a corn stalk in and out between her fingers.

In the end she said, 'Yes. I'd like to do that.'

Fletcher drove back to Cambridge, the windows down to let the air blast through. He had his eyes on the road but his mind elsewhere. Thinking about Ron Teversham.

Teversham must have been first on the scenes, and he'd wanted that fact kept out of the records. He must have bribed a filing clerk to tear off the corner of each page. Why go to that trouble?

Because Teversham *saw* something at those scenes of death. He saw something that stuck in his mind. It stayed with him, even after he left the force. And earlier this year, when Jake Skerrit came to him with Olga's story, Teversham remembered what it was, clear enough to make it worth pulling his police buddies together again for a drink.

Then whatever he'd seen died with him in the wreck of his Sierra, with insects feeding on his brain fluid as if even they wanted to know as well.

What was it? Would it be recorded in the missing photographs, the ones that had disappeared from the county archive?

Fletcher broke off his chain of thought as he came into Cambridge. What he needed now was someone who'd been around in those days, someone who might have rubbed shoulders with Teversham in the Cambridgeshire force, who might have heard rumours about what those scenes contained, what those photographs showed. He needed someone he could trust.

Instead of heading to Parkside, he swung west on the ring road and called directory enquiries for a number. It came back on a crackly satellite from India. Fletcher dialled. The phone rang out.

He listened, thinking of his flat. Under the window with the view of rooftops, there was a desk drawer holding various things. Envelopes, a penknife, some stamps. At the back of the drawer was a slim leather box about the size of a cigarette packet: red leather embossed with the royal seal. Fletcher hadn't opened that box for years, not since he'd been awarded it by the Chief Constable in an awkward ceremony on the top floor. It was a thin disc on a ribbon: the police service medal for outstanding conduct on duty. It meant there was at least one old Cambridge copper he could trust. Meaning, one who owed him something.

He dialled again.

After many rings, a young woman's voice purred an answer.

'The Washpit at Girton. Lunch booking?'

'I need to speak to Stephen, please.'

'Stephen's in creative mode. Lunch starts twelve-thirty.'

'Just tell Stephen it's Tom Fletcher. Tell him I want to hear about the old days again.'

The person he remembered was named Stephen Jenks: a lean, steely-haired Detective Sergeant who had held the same rank for twenty years and taken Detective Constable Fletcher under his wing in a rough way at Parkside. Fletcher liked his blunt attitude and the endless stories about policing back in the early days.

Colleagues felt sorry for Jenks, destined to retire on a sergeant's pension – but Jenks was luckier than that. He was lucky enough to develop a heart condition as a result of prolonged immersion in freezing water while on duty. The compensation and early retirement allowed him to buy his dream: a share in a tatty pub in the village of Girton. After three years, the Washpit had become a destination restaurant: conveniently off the M11 for the weekenders, near enough to Cambridge for the dons and the expense accounts.

It was so successful that it had an unobtrusive sign which Fletcher almost missed. He doubled back in the village and parked in the courtyard.

A feline girl dressed in black opened the oak door and showed him past empty tables to Stephen's office. As they arrived, she brushed against him and he caught a flash of her grey eyes.

'I thought this was about the old days, Fletcher.'

Stephen's voice hadn't changed, but when Fletcher stepped through, he saw that the man had put on weight.

He was wearing a chef's tunic with a cravat. The old Stephen still existed in the unblinking eye contact, but success had built up on the belly pressed against the desk where he was sampling a selection of dishes.

Fletcher took a seat. 'You've done well for yourself.'

'Calf liver,' Stephen replied, swallowing. 'Drink?'

'Just some water.'

'No change there.' He lobbed Fletcher a small bottle of mineral water. 'I assume this isn't purely social.'

'What have you heard?'

'I've heard Fletcher's fighting the cold war again, all by himself. That true?'

Fletcher took a swig of water and studied the plates on the desk. 'I don't know if the cold war's over, Stephen. The celebrations may have been premature. What's that one there?'

'Buffalo mozzarella,' Stephen said. 'Fifty years I lived on egg and chips. Now this.' He sampled and pushed it away, turning his stare on Fletcher. There was silence for a second. 'Enough sampling. You've got problems, haven't you?'

'Yes, Stephen. You remember the reservoir?'

'That's what this is about? Jesus.'

Fletcher knew what he was remembering. Fletcher's first winter in the plainclothes job. Stephen Jenks taking him to record an illegal dog fight on the bank of the reservoir, east of this same village. Both of them lying flat on the frozen grass, aiming their camcorder. Stephen trying to get a better shot, testing the ice on the edge of the water, going through with a sound like one of the dogs losing the fight. Fletcher plunging in, going under twice until he found Jenks, catching him by the hand, dragging him out and lifting him clear. The dog fight vanishing like a shower of ragged sparks.

Then, the thing nobody had seen. Webley driving out from Parkside, thinking she'd just lost two staff to hypothermia. Webley finding Tom Fletcher in the back of a police van, all the medical attention on Jenks over in the ambulance. Webley with her arms around Fletcher, holding him close.

I'm so proud of you.

Holding him while he shivered. It went on for two minutes, then she let him go. He remembered the feel of her arms. Her fingers melting the ice in his hair.

Now he blinked. Jenks' eyes were the colour of frost.

'What you wanting, Fletcher?'

'When did you join the Cambridge force?'

'1976.' Stephen grinned suddenly. 'Now *that* was a different world. But you don't want to hear my stories, do you?'

'Not now. Ever heard of Ron Teversham? A PC from Wittris?'

'Heard of Teversham, never met him. There but for the grace of God.'

'Right.'

Fletcher took out the two coroner's pictures of the death scenes of the Lovely Brigade. Jenks picked them up and studied them for a while, reading the names and dates printed under each one. Then he pushed them away. He wiped his fingers clean.

'Digging up the past, boy? Why?'

'You know who the victims were?'

'Victims?' Jenks threw his napkin away. 'If I remember, they did it to themselves. The glorious Lovely Brigade, right? Nobody shed any tears, Fletcher. Don't tell me you are now.'

'I just want to know one thing. There are only these

photos in the files. I want to know what happened to
the others.'

Jenks looked around his study at the pictures of him
shaking hands with television actors, table mats signed
by minor politicians.

'I can't help you, Fletcher. I don't know. This time
next year, if it all goes well, you know what I'll be? I'll
be a TV chef.'

Fletcher leaned forward and put his hand on Stephen's heavy chest. 'That's OK. Stephen Jenks the TV
chef. Now I'm going to look out of that window for a
second. While I'm doing that, you think about Stephen
Jenks under the ice on Girton reservoir, the Stephen
Jenks who grabbed my hand. Then you'll tell me.'

The view out of the window was sky, trees unmoving, glare off parked cars. When he looked back, Jenks
was staring down at the table.

'I don't know where the photos are, Fletcher. How
can I? I wasn't even there.'

'But?'

'There's something called the Doomsday Book.'

'For Christ's sake, the what?'

Jenks adjusted his tunic and cravat, keeping his eyes
on the plates. 'I've never seen it myself, OK? But it
exists.' He raised his eyes to Fletcher's. 'There are
people, you know, who like seeing pictures of accidents, murders. Dead bodies. Call it curiosity or whatever. These days there are websites with that stuff,
right? A lot of the pictures are taken by coppers. Back
in those days, there were coppers used to take snaps
and pass them around in a book. I mean it really was a

book, a big leather album. The kind of photos you're looking for, they might have ended up in there.'

'Where is this book now?'

'Last I heard, which was years ago, somebody was keeping it.' He glanced at the phone. 'You want me to call them?'

'Who is it?'

'I think it's someone you know.'

'Pick up the phone, Stephen.'

Out in the restaurant, the staff were getting ready for lunchtime. Almost twelve-thirty, and the death of the Russian engineer was still a long way from being explained. Fletcher felt grey eyes follow him to the door.

He started his car.

Friday Afternoon

From the plane, Sal watched the farmland sliding under her for yet another time. Ninety minutes late in taking off, then half an hour stacking up to land, and the day was disappearing fast. No timeshare man next to her this time; just a Portuguese nun fingering her crucifix every time the plane made its turn over the fields.

The landscape down there was enough to scare anyone: the electric yellow of oilseed, then tilled fields like congealed blood, the drainage channels between them glinting razor-bright in the sun. Welcome home.

She saw it all tilt for the last time as they finally made their descent. She saw the plane's own shadow rushing across the fields. She closed her eyes, a moment's dizziness after all the turning. She thought she saw it again then: the thing she'd glimpsed the night before in the dusk over Portugal. Something that didn't fit. She opened her eyes as the plane lurched down towards the flat land. She heard the nun begin whispering to herself, whispering the same phrase over and over.

It hit Sal then. It wasn't something she'd seen, but something she'd *heard*. A phrase, a form of words.

The plane touched down with a thump.
What was it? Who said it?

Some Cambridge summer afternoons are hot and still.
The smell of cut grass, the click of cameras.

Fletcher drove across Magdalene Bridge. Glass
crystals from his shattered car door were still glinting
beside the kerb. His Audi was in a repair shop already.
He knew that Cathleen was right. If his past came out
into the open, it would be the kind of impact – for him
and for Luke – that could never be repaired.

He showed his warrant card and parked in a visitor's
space at Shire Hall, the county headquarters. Instead
of entering the building, he walked across the car park
and began to climb the highest point in the city: a flat-
topped hill rising above the river. This was Castle
Mound: the stump of the fortress built by the Normans
when they occupied the marshland along the old river
Granta, constructing something the locals had never
seen or imagined: a stone castle.

Climbing up, he thought about it for the first time.
The Wittris people resented the distant past – but
wasn't *this* the same thing? For a thousand years,
Castle Mound had passed from one generation of
rulers to the next, until today's county management
could lean out of their windows and touch the Norman
fort. The message for a thousand years was the same:
the high ground is ours.

He climbed the modern steps and stood looking
across Cambridge, sweat between his shoulders, waiting. In the haze, he could see the colleges in their lawns,

the Cam in its manicured channel, the chimneys of Addenbrooke's hospital just visible before the swell of the Gog Magog hills. He waited into the mid-afternoon. When he heard laboured breathing coming up the incline, he turned, not knowing who to expect.

He said, 'You.'

'Surprised? Why?'

'Because you seem so professional.'

The photographer smiled and slumped down to sit on the grass, getting back his breath. The last time Fletcher had seen him was at Charter farm, leaning in the doorway. Now he was resting something bulky on his knees, something wrapped in a carrier bag.

'I am professional, Fletcher.' The photographer wiped his face with a Kleenex. 'I've always respected you. I wondered about it, what was happening all this week. I saw you getting deeper. Now you're very deep, aren't you?'

'Apparently. Did *you* take the photos of the Lovely Brigade deaths?'

'No. But they're in this book.'

'How did you get hold of it?'

'When things changed, in the eighties, people didn't want to look at this stuff any more. I bought it off a sergeant, in fact, for a small sum. I knew the things in here would be important. Will you do something for me? When you've finished with it, keep it or destroy it, whichever you want. I don't want it back.'

Fletcher placed the Doomsday Book in the boot of the Nissan. It was surprisingly heavy. He was trying to think where he could go to examine it. Not here. He wanted somewhere private, cool, shady. Somewhere with a breeze.

He looked back and saw the photographer still watching him from the mound.

*

Tom Fletcher lay on the bed at midnight, still dressed. The house was quiet except for the pipes cooling down. He was thinking of the noise of the weir, his mother's suitcase clicking across the footbridge.

He closed his eyes.

There was a noise from the landing below. A board creaking, then silence. Tom swung his legs off the bed and stood up: no creak. He went to the door and out onto the landing, looked down to the floor below. The space was lit by an orange streetlamp through side windows. Edmund Hartnell was standing in the glow, wearing a black dressing gown, his hair combed back off his high forehead. He still had his glasses around his neck, the wooden beads dull orange. He raised a hand and fingered one of the beads for a while. Then he crossed the landing and opened a door on the other side and closed it behind him.

*

Fletcher took the Doomsday Book to Grantchester. Parked on the edge of a field and walked down to where the river curved under a clump of willows. A few cattle were grazing in the meadows, and the river was empty except for some distant punts. The water was glassy dark.

He climbed up on the trunk of a fallen willow tree and sat against an upright branch, shaded by the other trees. There was a breeze off the river that made the tips of the leaves tremble. He opened the bag.

The Doomsday Book was a hefty thing. It was a photo album: red leather covers embossed with the word *Memories* in flowing script. The edges were black with years of fingermarks – clearly a book that had been cherished. He opened the pages.

The photos were clumsily taken with Polaroids and Instamatics, glued under Cellophane that crackled as he turned. He found men and women, suicides, car crash victims, a shopkeeper stabbed and crumpled in a pile of tins, a female student in a pool of blood, a farm worker gored by a bull. The photos had scribbled captions of gallows humour:

Looks like he got the point.

She was really cut up about it.

This went on until the succession of bodies and their grim titles blurred into a single grotesque joke.

The pages dealing with Terry Swilter and Shane Gaffy were different. They had been taken professionally, well composed and lit.

The inquest photo of Terry Swilter's corpse at Ulsingham Hall was here: the charred fingers clawing at the power lines. But as Fletcher turned over, he found the images missing from the coroner's report: general shots of the site where the body was found, various undertaker's staff and electricity board workers milling about waiting to pick up the pieces, a police officer, back turned to the camera. The shots were mostly of the stable block Swilter had fallen from. The drop was about fifteen feet, enough to stun and immobilise him but probably leave him conscious. Fletcher stopped and turned back a page.

One photo of the stables had been taken from the window of the main building, an elevation showing the roof Terry Swilter had fallen from. The roof was shallow and presumably north-facing, because it had a cover of ugly winter moss running from the eaves to the apex. It looked sticky and damp. Anyone climbing on it would leave gouges and footprints in the stuff. It was completely undisturbed.

Fletcher took the photo out of its sleeve and studied it in the shadows of the willow leaves. Whatever way the lad came to land on the substation, it wasn't from falling off the roof. That was an obvious and crucial point that should have been highlighted in police evidence. Even if omitted, any coroner would have asked for it.

He turned back to the shot of Swilter's corpse, and took that from its cover too. It *seemed* exactly like the one in the official file. He held it out of the shadow of the tree, into the sunlight, then back again. There was one big difference. There was something else there.

He flipped over to the pages of Shane Gaffy. Again, the existing coroner's photo was included, but also a wider view of the scene of death missing from the records. It showed that the Jag had been torched in a culvert overhung with a canopy of hawthorn. In the inquest shot, this wasn't apparent, but here it was obvious that the canopy had turned the enclosed space into a furnace, the overhead branches catching the exploding petrol and concentrating the fire downward before they burned away. Only an idiot would fire up a car in a place like that – and Gaffy was an experienced torch.

The next page had another photo that wasn't in the coroner's inquest file. It wasn't a professional shot, because they were only taken after the unconscious Gaffy had been stretchered away. This one looked hastily snapped, maybe by PC Ron Teversham himself, first to arrive on the scene and wanting to record something juicy for the scrapbook.

It showed Shane Gaffy's unconscious body on the ground after he'd managed to drag himself clear: his face savagely burned, the hair scorched away, teeth fixed in the gasp that had only sucked more burning fuel into his lungs.

He put this photo next to the one of Terry Swilter. They had one thing in common.

On each body, on the chest, an object had been carefully placed. A small shape, not noticeable at first, but one that began to demand attention. A grotesque little figure with long limbs and reaching hands: the nightmare sister of the beautiful ones on display in their wooden cases in Thinbeach. A little corn doll, a little Thinbeach Bride. The same as the one found on Ivan Gorensky's father.

A passing leisure cruiser was chugging away from Cambridge, sending a wash onto the bank. A woman on deck turned to look curiously at Fletcher: a man in a suit holding a big leather book on the trunk of an old tree. Fletcher ignored her.

The little corn doll certainly meant something. It meant death. It meant the marauding thugs of the Lovely Brigade had been thrown onto electric cables or doused with petrol and set alight. It meant corn dolls had been placed on their charred bodies, the dolls removed by the police before the photographs were taken, the scenes carefully staged by people who delighted in falsifying reality, the cases superficially investigated, closed and filed away.

But why these kids *and* the Russian engineer?

Fletcher flipped backwards and forwards through the Doomsday Book, trying to see if any other bodies had corn dolls placed on them. None did: the other corpses seemed to have met with genuine accidents or violent deaths unconnected with the Thinbeach Bride.

Except one.

Inside the back cover, another grainy photograph, another copper's Polaroid.

It showed the sprawled body of a boy, much younger than Gaffy or Swilter, barely a youth. He wasn't burned but he was clearly dead, face up against a background of stone slabs glinting with frost. He was a good-looking lad, with a fenland jaw and a ring in each ear, and someone was examining his head with gloved hands. He was wearing a boiler suit, and there was something tucked into his pocket over the heart.

Another Thinbeach Bride. The same limbs and hands, long claws from corn spines, but she was different somehow. Fletcher realised she was placed face downward, as if listening to the boy's ribcage to make sure his heart had stopped. Her little face was turned to the camera, and she had no eyes, of course, but her ragged little mouth was blurred in a smile, like a lover.

The scrawled caption read, *She got him then, that girl of eels.*

Fletcher tucked all three photos into his jacket pocket. Then he looked up at the sky. Beyond the willow canopy, it was brilliant blue. Close to his face, the fronds were flickering in the breeze with a whispering noise that should have been soothing. Right now it sounded like the shaking of ashes in the wind. A fly buzzed past his face, then another, and—

'You be there all day boy?'

He looked down. A boy of twelve or thirteen, galoshes planted in the silt, a fibreglass rod in one hand, a joint between his teeth. Big tub of maggot bait dragging in the water, flies spinning around it.

'Only that's where I fish if I get the fuckin' chance.'

Fletcher put the leather album back in the plastic bag and smoothed it down.

The maggots in the tub were like a single organism, working together, moving over and under each other.

'Not in school, boy?'

He kneeled down and held his warrant card under the kid's nose. The kid blinked and flicked skunk ash into the water. Like many kids, he had absolutely no fear of the apparatus of the state. He knew that dealing with someone like himself would consume resources in a county already stretched thin.

Things have changed, Fletcher thought, since 1978 – when Terry Swilter was thrown over a fence onto a substation, or when Shane Gaffy was doused in petrol and set on fire. Or the other kid, the third kid, stretched out on the frosty slabs, maybe feeling the little doll placed inside his boiler suit before he died.

Fletcher said, 'You catch much from here?'

'Some I do. Nice and quiet.' The boy grinned and winked. 'What, you meeting someone? Meeting a girl?'

Fletcher put the album under his arm.

'I think I just have.'

The Nissan chugged away in the late-afternoon heat. Thirty-five degrees, the fans just blasting warm air around the cabin. Fletcher felt suspicions driving a turbine inside his own mind.

The official records had told a story full of omissions and inconsistencies. The so-called Doomsday Book had told him more, connecting the little corn doll to the deaths of the Lovely Brigade, without explaining who had placed the dolls or what the symbolism was. Once that was known, the critical question of how the Russian engineer had died might be clearer.

Where could he go to find the real truth?

There was just one place, he realised. Somewhere people would remember the Lovely Brigade, and have their own doubts about what had happened to them, and who was responsible.

He could go to Lovely Street.

He took the Airwave handset from the glovebox. In half a minute he was connected to the network of encrypted radio masts, accessing the databases available to any copper on the beat: who lived where, for how long, what contact they had with the state. The kind of Doomsday Book the Normans would have loved. Problem was, when he searched for Swilter or Gaffy, he found nothing on that surname in the county. No electoral roll, no council tax payments, no PNC entry, nothing. Did the families move away? Out of grief, or out of fear?

He looked at that third photo, the handsome kid with the hooped earings lying dead on the stone slabs. He changed the handset to phone mode.

'I've only just got out of the airport, Fletcher. I'm trying to find my car.' The rest was drowned out by a jet going overhead. 'Could have sworn it was row D.'

'Sal, when we were talking about the Lovely Brigade, there were three names, three ringleaders. There was Swilter and Gaffy and there was someone else, a third one.'

'I can't hear a thing. There it is, row E. What are you asking?'

'There was a third boy in your plastic files. After Swilter and Gaffy, there was a number three in the Lovely Brigade. Some kind of Irish name.'

'This is hotter than Portugal.' Then Sal's phone hushed as if she'd just shut herself in the car, and an ignition turned on. 'That was Paddy Legsey. Legsey with one g.'

Fletcher checked the databases again. This time he found the surname, exactly where he wanted it to be.

A minute later, he moved up out of the meadow into

a late sun boiling above the roofs of Grantchester, thin bands of cloud sending rivers of corrupted light down onto the horizon beyond.

It was early evening when he met her at a services near Ely. Modern families were taking their kids into Burger King and Little Chef, filling up with unleaded and diesel, sweating but well behaved.

Sal's hair was loose and her skin looked slightly damp. She was sitting at a picnic table, drinking a bottle of water, watching the cathedral towering above the suburbs. She raised an eyebrow.

'Hungry?'

'My body says *feed*. After Lovely Street.'

Out there, he thought they might confirm the theories he was starting to have on two very simple questions.

First, why exactly the corn dolls appeared on the bodies of teenage burglars *and* a Russian engineer.

And second, who placed them there.

Friday Night

'And there they are. The Wittris Teeth.' Sal aimed the Vectra towards the yellow blocks rearing up beyond the fields, their windows reflecting the fading sunset, and she accelerated towards them.

The databases showed just one Legsey. An entry for Daniel 'Dad' Legsey, Lovely Street, Wittris. Convictions for assault and handling stolen goods dating from the 1950s to the 1970s. And the right age now – sixty-seven – to make him Paddy Legsey's father in the days of the Lovely Brigade.

The Legsey phone number was continually engaged – but Fletcher had nothing else to work with, nowhere else to go. Mauve shadows were folding in across the fields on both sides, sweeping across the sheen of the roadside drainage channels, like the covers of a book closing shut. Sal put the headlights on.

The last time Fletcher had been to Wittris, he'd gone to the smarter end of town where Teversham had lived. Tonight he turned the other way, skirting the margins, the headlights brushing across the scrappy verges. It was still hot, and the open window let in a tang of vegetation and smoke: the unashamed body scent of a fenland town.

At one point he recognised the outline of the Hereward Pool Hall, its gable window shining on a mist seeping up from the fields. Then the Wittris Teeth loomed up right ahead, and Sal's Satnav told them to take the next turning on the right. A small council estate appeared on either side: squat 1960s' housing behind chainlink fences, some doorways sealed with plywood, others bearing carriage lamps or statuettes. A gang of big-jawed kids watched them pass, leaning on street-racing hatchbacks. Then Sal slowed and the Satnav said *that* was Lovely Street: the gap in the houses leading a Tarmac lane into the dark. They stopped and found the name bolted on the chainlinks.

It was a cul-de-sac, containing eight square houses with narrow windows, a postwar architect's fantasy. The street that had unleashed such mayhem on the surrounding countryside in 1978 was unremarkable tonight. Only one of the four houses even seemed occupied – with a door lamp attracting midges, and a glow behind some downstairs curtains. That was the house they wanted.

They walked along a rutted path, through a gate in a dusty hedge. The front door, though, was freshly painted and finished with a brass knocker which echoed out along the street and across the marshland beyond.

They waited. Fletcher could feel the bugs against his face, and hear an animal yelping in the fields.

'Difficult conversation,' Sal predicted. 'Might help if we talk like locals. Get him on our side.'

'Good point. Once we get in the house.'

The door opened on a chain. A voice said, 'You are?'

The man was still a threat: old muscle in his neck, plus a combative scowl, lips moving as the small eyes flashed over the warrant cards held out to the space in the doorframe.

Fletcher said, 'Mr Daniel Legsey?'

The eyes flicked up, opal in the door lamp. 'What you wanting?'

'I'm wanting Daniel Legsey, because I think he's the father of Paddy Legsey.'

'What you want to know about Paddy?'

Sal leaned to the door, her hair falling forward. 'We want to know what happened to him. Before these frigging midges eat us alive.'

The man thought for a while, rubbing his lips with the bluebird tattooed on his thumb. Then he came to a decision. The door slammed, then opened wide.

'Me,' he said, 'I'm Dad Legsey.'

He grinned: Wittris Teeth.

Dad Legsey showed them into a murky downstairs room with a big window to the back, where a garden was slashed luminous by floodlights. He pointed to some easy chairs.

'Tried to phone,' Fletcher said. 'Engaged.'

'Millionaire. Been trying to get on there for years.'

'Dad Legsey, need to talk about the past.'

'You fucking patronising me? I talk like that, not you.'

There was a pause while Dad Legsey sat down.

The chairs and the television were the only furniture

in the room. From somewhere, Dad Legsey produced a tin of tobacco and rolled up in two fingers, making a lighter appear from his pockets.

'Say about the past, boy?'

'Yes, Dad Legsey. 1978.'

Dad Legsey stopped, with the lighter throwing jagged shadows on his face, and looked straight at Fletcher, then at Sal. Then he lit up, the tobacco shreds splintering.

He said, 'You want tea?'

'No thanks—'

'Come on, boy. Not PG Tip. I mean *blue* tea. In the old day before the draining we brew her up from poppies, keep the aches out. That old recipe still going around. No law against it, they say. I got some boiling in the kitchen there, help you sleep. Look like you need it.'

'Police officers tend not to consume opiates, Dad Legsey. But I'm too busy to look in your kitchen.'

Dad Legsey shrugged. 'Suit yourself. So what you—'

'Wanting? 1978. It was a cold winter.'

'Keep warm, me. Don't go out.'

'There was a crime wave back then.'

'Was there?'

'People were hurt.'

'People *got* hurt.'

'OK,' Fletcher agreed. 'People got hurt. House-holders, some criminals too. I'm talking about the Lovely Brigade.'

Dad Legsey flicked some ash and ran his eyes around the room. There was a light in them that was partly the floodlamp and probably the blue tea as well. The light swelled and suddenly two big childish tears ran down his face.

'They was boys,' he said. 'The Brigade was boys, nothing more. They was fated.'

'Your boy among them, Dad Legsey. Your boy named Paddy Legsey.'

The man said nothing.

'Named Paddy Legsey,' Sal repeated. There was a slight echo.

'Got nice voice,' Dad Legsey said. 'Say his name again.'

'Say—?'

'Say my boy's name.'

'Paddy. Paddy Legsey.'

Dad Legsey closed his eyes for a while.

'Only once I heard a girl say his name. A young *woman*, I mean. He were fifteen, she came to the door there. She had her hair combed across, wet. She said, *It's Paddy I'm wanting.* I thought, I'll hear that again.' Dad Legsey's eyes glowed, studying his cigarette. 'What you know of my Paddy?'

'He was sixteen, but he was in with the Brigade,' said Fletcher. 'The records say he was as bad as Swilter or Gaffy.'

Dad Legsey looked up. 'Swilter and Gaffy was mad, they was fated. From kids they was fated. We all knew the way they finish.'

'Was Paddy very different? I've seen his record. He burgled houses, used a cosh.'

'That's a lie.'

'Is it? The autumn of 1978, things were haywire between here and Thinbeach. You families from Lovely Street were burgling whole villages, ransacking farmhouses—'

'It's Normans hold the farms. They get what comes.'

'—and fencing the stuff in Wittris. Your boy Paddy Legsey was part of it all, using his cosh—'

'He never used a cosh.'

'—to subdue honest householders. You know what subdue means?'

'You know what honest means?'

Sal said, 'Dad Legsey, what was Paddy like?'

'Paddy? My Paddy was a prince of a boy. Handsome, and clever with it. He joined the library at fourteen. I seen him use the little card to open sash windows, talking to himself with things from the books he read. Villain's not the word. He was a young prince.'

'But what happened to him? There's nothing in the records. Was it after Gaffy and Swilter died?'

Dad Legsey nodded. 'He kept going. That December, bit before Christmas, he fell from a window he were trying to slit.'

'Where?'

Dad Legsey's voice changed.

'Norman house. In Thinbeach.'

Of course it was Thinbeach, Fletcher thought.

'Which house?'

'Big house at the end of the street, looks like a blockhouse.'

'You mean, The Blindy House?'

'That's the name. Right on the mound there, by the

Pool. I walked past after he fell, a lot of times, looking at it with Paddy's eyes. I could see why he took a fancy to it, my Paddy. It's tempting. Looks like a little castle from the front, but you slip round the back and there's a porch for the bloody servants. You get a footing on the porch and you're up there. Top windows are wide.' Dad Legsey was living it all again, showing them with his hands. 'Slip a card under the frame, no fancy locks to worry a boy.'

'You saw all that from walking past?'

'After. My Paddy must have got up there, got his hands under the sash. Full moon to see by that night.'

Fletcher saw the teenage cat burglar, frozen forever with his feet on the porch, his moonlit breath fuming the glass.

'And then?' Sal's voice was gentle.

'Paddy fell. Fell bad, caught the porch roof and she flip him on his back. Landed my Paddy on his head.'

'And the last of the crime wave stopped,' Fletcher said. 'Terry Swilter, Shane Gaffy, then Paddy Legsey. Calm was restored.'

Dad Legsey's eyes flashed again. 'Happy? The old police were, they come to tell me he fallen, grins on their faces.'

'Was anything said about the circumstances of the fall?'

'Eight feet, onto stone.'

'I mean, was anything said about the owner of The Blindy House? You ever heard of someone named Alain de Minching?'

'Norman? Sounds it. But no, wasn't nobody in the

house when Paddy climbed up there. He was clever, I told you that.'

'You do believe he died accidentally?'

Dad Legsey turned his face to the wall.

He said, 'He never.'

'You mean, he didn't die accidentally?'

'No. It *was* an accident. But he never died.'

'But he landed on his head.'

'The Legsey got thick heads. My Paddy's still here.'

Dad Legsey began to move his fingers over the empty wall, tracing whatever he was seeing.

Fletcher said, 'Here? Where?'

'Where you think? He's my son.'

'You mean he's here, *in this house?*'

'Where else would he be? He's my son.'

'He's not on the electoral roll.'

'He don't fucking vote.'

Fletcher watched the patterns the fingers were making in the gloom.

The Doomsday Book said *She got him then, that girl of eels*, and he'd assumed Paddy Legsey died on the flagstones of The Blindy House. But the old copper had snapped an unconscious body, not a dead body. Maybe a body The Wake assumed was dying, like Shane Gaffy, and tucked a corn doll in his pocket. But the Legsey got thick heads. Paddy survived, and still disappeared from the records. Alive but—

'Is he damaged?' asked Sal.

Dad Legsey took his fingers off the wall. Then he flexed his palms, stood up with his thumbs in his belt. The old fenland scrapper, afraid of nobody.

'Is it really important?'

'It's crucial,' she said. 'Believe me.'

He thought for a while. 'I suppose visitors might be good for him.' He glanced at Sal. 'He won't tell you nothing, mind. He never speaks.'

Paddy Legsey, aged forty-four, heard the creak of the stairs, then another creak outside his door. More creaks than there should be. He kept his eyes on the wall.

He had to, because he lived in the wallpaper. The wallpaper he'd had since his eighth birthday, never changed. It had a pattern: seven different types of boats. He spent hours, whole days sometimes, looking at the boats, sailing them in his mind.

It had always been like this. Just him, the boats, the window with the view of the fields. Sometimes the headaches that made him shiver, now and then the times that everything went dark and he woke up with bloody lips and a plastic spoon in his mouth that Dad said stopped him swallowing his tongue.

On those days, as he lay on the floor trembling, Dad would bring him a jug of tea. It was sour, but it calmed him, and those were the nights he took the longest journeys on his boats.

Things were changing, though, in Paddy's world. The wallpaper was fading now, and the boats at chest-height were rubbed away completely. Elsewhere, his fingers had left marks like storm clouds.

The door opened and three people came in – he could tell by the sound of their feet. He'd never had this many visitors before, but he kept his eyes on his boats.

The his life changed.

He felt someone touch him on his cheek – not the rough fingers of his father washing him, but new fingers, and there was a fragrance that made him turn his face.

She was beautiful, looking at him with her brown eyes, frowning slightly. Maybe she was worried about the boats too. He thought for a while, and decided on the one she might like. He found it for her: the yacht with the portholes. She liked it.

He heard her say, 'You were in The Blindy House, Paddy. It was a cold night, a long time ago. What happened?'

Paddy shivered. He didn't like to think about the other room in his life. Those three men grabbing him, heaving him back to the window. His scream echoing in the cold air.

'Paddy? Can you tell us?'

Paddy looked up into her face, and felt the first shocks. He opened his mouth to speak, but he had no voice. Another pulse went through him, and he screwed his eyes shut. He felt spit run down his chin. He turned to the yacht, and he smiled, despite the convulsion, because he wasn't alone any more.

They climbed the ladder together, onto the deck where the red sail was snapping in the breeze. She began pointing to the dolphins and the flying fish. He slipped the ropes, catching her eye as the sail filled out. He knew the fit was going to hit him, but then it would all blow clear – and after that she would always be with him on the boats, and he would take her anywhere. Anywhere she wanted to go.

'Coppers don't listen. I told you he never speaks. You brought on a fit, for nothing.'

They were downstairs again. Fletcher was still trying to make the final connection in his mind. Was he any further forward now? He didn't feel it.

'I'm sorry,' Sal said. 'We really thought he could tell us something. Is he receiving medical care?'

Dad Legsey was stirring a saucepan of his technically legal poppy-based tea. 'Doctors don't help. Only this helps. The way it always has round here.'

The stuff smelled like dug earth. Fletcher watched it turning in the pan – blue and full of seeds – without really seeing it.

He had maybe twelve hours left. Problem was – it still didn't work. OK, he could see how the Wittris lads fell victim to The Wake. What he still couldn't see was the last link: why The Wake wanted to drown a Russian tractor engineer as well. Why would they? It made no sense at all.

'Dad Legsey, was anything found on Paddy after he fell?'

'Like?'

'Like a little doll made of corn.'

Dad Legsey stopped stirring. 'His stuff was just his clothes, his hoops, a ring I give him. But there was something, later.'

'What was there?'

Dad Legsey swivelled his head suddenly and fixed

his luminous eyes on Fletcher, then Sal. 'I were the
only one. The only one of the three.'

'The only one who—?'

'Stayed. The Swilter and the Gaffy, they gone up
north. They left quick after the deaths. Some said they
were afraid of something, some said they been paid
money to leave, given roads to go down. I say what I
know. A little time after Paddy fell, New Year it was, a
man came to this door. Said he was a charity for the
epileptic. Said he could ease my burden. Wanted to take
Paddy away and put him in a home. Where they could
look after him, he said. *Look after him.* My Paddy.'

Fletcher could imagine how Paddy would have been
looked after – a living witness who might recover his
memory and his speech.

'What did you say to him?'

'Nothing. I had tea on the stove here, big pot for the
whole street, boiling hot. It went all over him.'

'You scalded him?'

Dad Legsey laughed. 'It was the winter of discontent. Ambulance didn't come for two hours. He rolled
around in the garden there, pushing his face in the
snow. But few days after, something came through the
post. A little box, first class. Inside was what you say: a
dolly, made of corn. Some piece of folky tat. Scratched
me when I unwrapped it. I burned it in the garden.'

Fletcher stared into the steaming brew. The final link
was starting to form. It was worse than he'd ever
imagined. Far worse.

'This would have been, what, first week of January?'

'Yeah. January '79.'

Fletcher caught Sal's eye. He asked, 'How old were you, Dad Legsey?'

'Me? I was forty. Younger than Paddy is now.'

Fletcher nodded, looking the man up and down. 'Thank you, Dad Legsey. You've answered the last question I had. And also the most important.'

The fields snapped past on the outskirts of Wittris. Lovely Street and its chainlink fences were soon a long way behind, the moon beginning to glint on the drainage channels beside the road.

Sal was driving. Fletcher said nothing, watching the horizon ahead. He saw the lights of the few other cars, the floodlamps of a harvester working by night, its husks rising against the moon. A fox ran across the road with a rabbit trailing from its jaws. In a while, Ely Cathedral rose on the horizon. Fletcher turned to Sal.

'I can see it all now. What the doll means. The link between the Lovely Brigade and the Russian.'

'I think I can too.'

'Hungry?'

She glanced across and nodded.

He said, 'I'll cook for you.'

She took a while to think about it, then nodded again.

'Not eel, though, Fletcher.'

A long-legged fly clumped along the dash. The clock read 10.28 p.m.

*

Tom Fletcher came out onto the fire escape. It was dark and cold, the moon beyond the rooftops pierced by televi-

sion aerials and garden conifers. The steel tread of the platform was slippery with frost.

'You could fall easily, couldn't you?'

He turned, startled. She was standing behind the door, against the brickwork, looking at him. Light from the window of another building showed her pallor, the coppery hair twisted into a knot on one side of her face, the other side in darkness. She was wearing the old raincoat, and a scarf.

He said, 'Where does Edmund go when he walks around at night?'

The vapour from his words drifted away. She looked back at him.

He said, 'Why don't you leave?'

She closed her eyes for a moment. 'It's too late.'

★

The windows of Fletcher's apartment were open on the heart of Cambridge, where the battlements of the colleges were tinted amber by the streetlamps and the moon. There was a cloud cover, and the air was still. The brickwork of Green Street harboured the day's heat like a grudge.

Fletcher had rummaged in the fridge and come up with sea bass, steamed in lime juice and thyme, some mashed sweet potato. Sal looked impressed.

Now they sat facing each other on the big window sill, looking down at the few remaining lights, the air scented with the decaying moss of the rooftops. A bottle of chilled water stood between them, catching the glow from the street. The Belize sax was unwinding long and low from a turntable hi-fi, the vinyl chiming in with its crackle and hiss. Sal had her legs stretched out, her calves smooth in the streetlight, a sandal swinging from one toe, keeping rhythm.

It was well past midnight now – the day of the Wedding itself – and Fletcher realised their silence had gone on for a while, and that neither of them were in a hurry to break it. In the end, he said, 'So what do we know?'

Sal kept looking down into the street, her hair falling across her eyes. She said, 'Start with what we don't know. We don't really know how The Wake got started.'

Fletcher refilled their glasses with water. He watched Sal take a long drink, her throat moving gently.

He said, 'I think they really did start as a village history society, some time in the mid seventies. I think Billy Breakman and Thomas Denton did dress up in chainmail at village fêtes – and Peter Charter really was just the driver, taking them around in his van. Then, some time in the later seventies, things changed.'

Sal nodded. 'The kids born in Wittris when the new town was created began to come of age and look around at their lives, and they didn't like what they saw. They imagined themselves dispossessed, the victims of this ancient rivalry, and that helped to give life some meaning, some glamour. They weren't just burglars, they were fighting the old enemy. They probably found the little Norman parishes were easy targets at first. The ringleaders saw the Red Brigades on the TV news – an armed gang attacking the privileged. The

Wittris boys fancied that, and came up with the Lovely Brigade. They liked seeing it in print when rumours began to spread. On the old police records, you can see the attacks stepping up a gear in the autumn, houses being ransacked at the rate of two or three a week – and even when Shane Gaffy or Terry Swilter or Paddy Legsey were picked up, they had alibis to fall back on. In Thinbeach, the villagers must have seen this Anglo-Saxon crime wave rolling towards them and wondered how to protect themselves. Who do you think had the idea?'

Down in the street, a restaurant light turned off, and Fletcher watched the light change on Sal's face, one cheekbone suddenly dark, her hair still falling across it.

'Fletcher?'

'It was Alain de Minching. He was aged around thirty, and he saw the situation as the latest phase in the old war, himself as the Norman lord who could defend his community. He knew the police were over-stretched, with the winter of discontent brewing up, and the village was exposed. There were a couple of attacks in Thinbeach itself, people being tied up and pissed on, I think he told me. That was a declaration of war. Maybe he had a long night of thinking, alone there in The Blindy House with his corn dolls. In the end, he decided to learn from Hereward the Wake, and lie in watch for the enemy. He put his idea to Billy Breakman and Thomas Denton, two men he despised, but with the muscle and the discipline to carry it through. They signed on.'

'And Peter Charter?'

Fletcher shrugged. 'We'll never know. For sure, they still used him as their driver. He must have wondered why he was driving around late at night, but I think in his case it was a feudal instinct, the need to serve his superiors. The first place he drove them to was Ulsingham Hall, wasn't it?'

'Ulsingham Hall, with its little substation. They found a way of luring the boys into places like that, maybe passing them messages saying the houses were undefended. Terry Swilter couldn't resist it, the stable block giving that easy climb up to the first floor. Did he ever make it up there?'

Fletcher tried to picture the struggle: Denton, Breakman and Alain de Minching appearing out of the night, breaking Swilter's arm and leg, and heaving him over the substation wall onto the cables. The flash and explosion must have been sizeable, and then the sparks racking Swilter's body. They must have stayed listening to the screams, until the heat died down. Then they flipped the little corn doll over the wall onto him and slipped away, back to the van on the main road.

He said, 'The corn doll was important to Alain – his sense of history, the spirit of Thinbeach overcoming the marauders. Also, probably, as a prearranged signal to the investigators that this one shouldn't be investigated too deeply. You see, Alain's talent is staging scenes. No – not staging them, but *falsifying* them, trying to change what really happened. His version of Agincourt has the French knights trampling the English archers. The scene he created at Ulsingham Hall was almost perfect, except that the moss on the stable block roof was completely intact. In the end, that didn't matter, did it?'

'No,' Sal said. 'Because Alain had prepared more than the scene itself. The photos showing the corn doll and the stable roof disappeared from the records, though they made their way into the Doomsday Book for the amusement of junior policemen.' She raised her eyes to Fletcher's. 'What exactly are we saying about the extent of police involvement?'

'We're saying that Teversham, or someone like him, was first on the scene. We're saying the investigation of the case was strangely superficial, both circumstantially and at the inquest. The Wake had sympathisers in the police and elsewhere.'

'Like Lord Ruddick? Back then he was Jonathan Ruddick-Spencer, hereditary owner of Ulsingham Hall. Did he *know* about the trap?'

'We'll have to come back to that, after the Wedding.'

But he felt she was right to highlight the point. People grow and change. An ambitious barrister becomes Lord Ruddick. A case detective becomes an Assistant Chief Constable. A coroner becomes a college chancellor. But in November 1978, the detective and the coroner were involved in another case: Shane Gaffy.

'Gaffy was a harder one to hit, maybe,' he said. 'The Lovely Brigade took a knock with the death of Terry Swilter, but the Wittris kids kept on burgling. The Wake set another trap. Alain, Billy and Thomas got Gaffy in that culvert and doused him with petrol, flicked a match and stood clear. They waited till the flames stopped before throwing the corn doll on the body. That means they *watched*. Billy Breakman began to be affected by it, to feel guilt. He went back to each scene, staring at what he'd done. What did he say to you yesterday? *They were kids?* But PC Teversham was there again, tidying up. Paddy Legsey was next on the list, but that one was different. They thought they'd killed him too, but he survived, and Dad Legsey refused to give him up. The Wake's parting shot was to send him a corn doll in the post. Which brings us to the Russian.'

Sal glanced up at him suddenly and held the glass of water against her neck. 'It's going to be stifling tomorrow, can you feel it?'

Fletcher *could* feel it: the air unmoving inside or out. From down in the town someone began shouting, the noise receding into the distance. Sal's foot was next to his on the window sill, not touching.

She said, 'Maybe there's some truth in Alain de Minching's version. The freezing weather, the Russian engineer arriving late, the car skidding on the main road. Dusk coming down, this big man going from house to house, shouting something the villagers couldn't understand. People saying, it's a wrecker, an outsider. The doors staying shut.'

He noticed Sal wrap her arms around her knees, perched up high in the warm fug of a Cambridge night.

He said, 'That much may be true, but the ending was very different. De Minching said the Russian wandered up onto the mound and staggered into the river. I think it began with phone calls inside Thinbeach, people telling Alain that this outsider was making his way down the Shamblings. By then the Russian was probably desperate, kicking at doors and shouting, people in the houses just glimpsing this figure from behind their curtains. Not a teenager like the rest of the Wittris burglars, but a middle-aged man. Alain jumped to a conclusion. What middle-aged man would want to challenge Thinbeach, shouting furiously?'

Fletcher emptied the bottle and went to the fridge for another. When he got back, Sal was still sitting like that, her eyes distant.

She said, 'Dad Legsey. Alain thought it was Dad Legsey. He thought Legsey had figured things out and come to confront him about Paddy. Alain had to think fast. He phoned Billy Breakman and Thomas Denton. Not Charter – he never knew anything about this, even afterwards. They assembled in the dark, watching the stranger lurching down the street. Maybe they threw something over his head, pinned his arms behind him. They must have marched him up over the mound.'

'Whatever state he was in, he must have struggled,' Fletcher added. 'They must have got him down to the water somewhere away from the village and held his head under. He must have been twisting around, trying to get his face clear. When it's as cold as that, it's like a clamp around your throat. Maybe he called out, but the noise would have been lost in the snow. Their arms must have been shaking with cold by the time he went still. I suppose they tipped him in, but the water was so slow-moving that the body stayed by the bank, collecting ice around it. And who do you think tucked the corn doll in the dead man's pocket?'

'Alain,' she said. 'Alain wearing a stylish winter coat, something with epaulettes. Maybe he got the sleeves wet. Then stood there getting his breath back while the other two looked to him for guidance. Big clouds of breath. I can imagine Alain taking his men back to The Blindy House, stoking up a fireplace, thawing out with something from the cellar. They thought they'd done it – eliminated the last of the Wittris threats. They must have thought the war was over at last. In a way they were right: everything went quiet. Even when they realised their mistake, it didn't really matter, because the authorities had already made the Russian body disappear for political reasons. The crime wave collapsed, the Lovely Brigade really was finished. The winter of discontent ended and the 1980s began. They got away with it.'

In the street outside, the remaining restaurant lights turned off, except one which stayed flickering and buzzing, sending a strobe effect around the walls. He watched the light flicker on Sal's face before it snapped off completely, and she was lit by the glow from the sky.

'It's late,' he said.

She nodded and sipped more water, leaving a trace of lipstick on the glass. The air felt warm in Fletcher's throat. He tried to imagine the lives of The Wake after 1979. Alain de Minching alone and unmarried in The Blindy House, investing carefully, breeding his wolf-hounds. Billy Breakman expanding his machinery business – a tough guy, but brooding over what he'd done, guilt growing inside him. Thomas Denton in his weird little kingdom, whatever grotesque relationship he had with his daughter. Peter Charter on his farm, unaware of the Russian's death, disowned by the others, becoming ever more paranoid. All of them thinking The Wake was a closed episode in their lives. None of them foresaw Ivan.

Fletcher said, 'I think I would have liked Ivan as a kid. When that corn doll came onto the kitchen table, he knew it signalled something very wrong about his father's death. Over the years it became an obsession, and his experience in the army, in the prison, only made it worse. When he left the military, he joined one of the mafias springing up under the Yeltsin regime, used his army training and developed his fascination with revenge. He became someone important, a businessman in the Russian sense. He had the resources to set up an operation like this, planting Olga here.'

'But Olga fell for Jake,' she said.

'And Alain de Minching tried to keep the lid on everything when Billy Breakman called him for help. Alain invited Jake to a meeting at the depot – maybe to hand over more cash. Jake turned the cameras off so they wouldn't be recorded. Alain thought it through – stunning Jake with a blow on the head, then dragging him by the arms into the shredder for the blades to obliterate the injury. Jake was a schemer, but I hope he was still unconscious when the engine started.'

'And I *told* you about Teversham, didn't I?' Sal said, leaning back against the window frame. 'We just didn't realise at the time. When Teversham found Jake's body, he grabbed the video tape because he wanted to see what the hell had happened. When he realised it was blank, he was puzzled, but he knew that Jake was meeting Alain that night. He went to Alain, told him he had a video of the death, tried the blackmail thing. Alain thought fast, calmed Teversham down, got him plastered. Followed him in the Citroën and nudged him off the curve. It worked fine, except Alain was worried that the video really existed. He had to search the maisonette to make sure. Remember what I said to you? Teversham hid it from someone who wouldn't notice something weird about the cistern float. That describes Alain pretty well – a man who's never looked inside a toilet cistern. Of course, none of this would ever stand a remote chance in a court of law. Alain's still the head of the community, still keeping the lid on everything. He'll still be at the Wedding.'

The Wedding. They'd already made a call to Webley, outlining their plans for Saturday in Thinbeach. Webley was uneasy, but in the end she signed on. Fletcher knew she would.

He said, 'We'll see if the lid stays on.'

It was quiet for a while. The record finished and began clicking in the groove. The noise was reassuring: measuring time, cutting the night into pieces while he thought about the day ahead. He looked up. Sal was watching him with her head on one side. She slipped off a sandal, letting it fall on the floor. She stretched out her leg and nudged his thigh with her toes. He felt them curl slowly. Then she moved her foot back.

'You'll damage the needle, Fletcher.'

He reached over and switched the turntable off at the wall. The speakers made a soft thump.

There was the smell of old wax. The door was still open on the hallway of his flat, the soft light spilling through. He saw her pause and look down into the stairwell. It was dark down there, a one a.m. summer dark. She turned, with the hall light on her face. She put her hand out suddenly and touched the side of his face and he felt her fingers brush against his stubble, making a rushing sound.

'What's your real worry, Fletcher? Apart from Ivan.'

'Since the Thinbeach thing started, someone's been following me.'

'Why would someone do that?'

'To find out about me.'

'To find out what?'

The door was still open.

*

Tom Fletcher heard the door open on the landing below. He waited for the floorboard to creak. He went out onto the landing and looked down. Edmund was standing there in the orange light, wearing an old tracksuit, fingering the wooden beads on his glasses, listening. Tom said, 'Hello, Edmund.'

Edmund jumped, tried to smile.

They went out onto the fire escape. The moon had risen above the aerials and was standing behind layers of white cloud. There was frost on the steel railing and the air glittered when the lights of a car on the main road brushed the building. Tom was fully dressed but he could feel the cold from the platform under his feet.

Edmund's hand rested on his shoulder. He could see Edmund's breath beside him, pluming into the air as he spoke.

'You mustn't worry, Tom. Everyone here is happy. My wife's happy. Cathleen's happy. At least, she tells me she is – and I believe her, she's honest. It's a rare gift, isn't it? Making people happy. I don't mean happy in a frivolous way, laughter and so on. I mean deeply happy, contented. It's a gift, to make people so happy they don't want to leave you, they can't leave you.' Tom felt Edmund's hand tremble on his shoulder. It was that cold: the air thin, sounds coming from the fields beyond the suburbs that would not normally be heard. An animal barking, voices, a machine rattling. Edmund exhaled in a long mist. 'The thing about you, Tom, is you could join us here. You don't have to go to your uncle. You can ask to stay in Blissey Avenue and we'll have you, of course we will. There'll be a weekly allowance. We'll put a TV in your room. And think of the happiness we'll bring to people. Not Cathleen, she'll have to leave soon. She's been careless. But there'll be another one in her room. Maybe two. Girls look at you, Tom, they like you, I can see that. We can work together. You don't have to decide now. Think about it a bit. Then let me know what you want.'

That animal barked again out in the fields.

*

DS Webley prepared to close her office. She adjusted the blinds and listened. The police station was hushed at this time of night, just the hum of the ventilators and fluorescent lights. She smiled, alone in the room. Someone once said to her that the station was a ship, and the trees outside were waves. Down in the cells, the singing of the drunks could sound like porpoises calling.

She reached for the switch of the desk lamp, but then stopped. She looked at the notes she'd made in her phone discussion with Fletcher and Sal Moresby tonight:

Thinbeach Wedding: 11 a.m. Saturday.

Q: What is Ivan Gorensky planning? 'Impossible to say.'

Can't cancel it. Can't use high-profile policing. DI Fletcher feels able to manage Gorensky alone -> DS Moresby concurs.

Q: How?

A: 'We know how his father died. He doesn't. Big advantage.'

Was it? Or did her boy want a second bravery medal?

Another page of notes covered the practical side: the concessions to public safety she forced them to accept.

But still:

OK -> no Glockenspiel.

And then:

Need full review -> events of 78/9. Potential major investigation. Allocate more staff? 'Investigate Alain de Minching.' Significant.

She finally tidied the notes away. She stretched her

arms: they were tired. They looked like the arms of a thirty-five year-old, she was sure – but maybe time to get a personal trainer, something at home? Her eyes were tired too.

One last thing on her desk: a manilla envelope. She'd found it in her postal mail on returning from that bloody seminar today. It had arrived anonymously: printed address label, yesterday's postmark from central Cambridge. No explanatory note, none at all. Inside were two sheets of paper.

She'd been puzzling over those sheets for a while.

They were photocopies of what appeared to be a confidential report by social services into events in a foster family in 1991. She went back and read the last paragraph again.

> *18th February 1991: Edmund Hartnell fell from the fire escape of 34, Blissey Avenue. He sustained multiple injuries including skull fracture, and died in Addenbrooke's Hospital on 19th February. An inquest in April 1991 returned the verdict of accidental death, noting the unsafe condition of the fire escape. In the light of this, no further action was taken regarding the various allegations against the Hartnell family.*

Webley had never heard of the Hartnells before, or even Blissey Avenue. She locked the sheet in her filing cabinet, then she put out the desk lamp and locked her office door. It could all wait until tomorrow.

Thomas Denton woke with a gasp, sprawled on a leather bench in Deep House, sweat between his shoulders. He shook his head and blinked. He reached for his cigar, couldn't find it.

He'd been dreaming again: something from the old days. Dreaming he was down by the Pool with Billy Breakman, holding a man's head under the water, ice on their hands. The man was a big bastard, and he fought back. Just once, he got his face free and shouted something. The words had stayed with Thomas because they came out so clearly, though at the time he thought it was some old fenland curse that Dad Legsey was putting on them: *U minya yest sane.*

Later, when they all realised what they'd done, Billy Breakman wrote the words out and deciphered them from a Russian dictionary. That's when it started going wrong for Billy, because he thought too much. For Thomas, the words only came back in dreams, when he heard them over the freezing wind across the Pool: *I've got a son.*

Thomas stood up. Sweat melted down his back. He found his cigar cold in the ashtray, an empty glass beside it. There was also a jewellery gift box: the necklace he'd bought for Judith as a peace offering. She hadn't opened it yet.

That dream. There was something else in that dream, but he didn't want to face it now, not tonight.

He called his daughter's name. The living space echoed it back. The marble reflected him as he went to the stairs, and again when he came down, his hands clenching and unclenching.

He went outside and stood on the rampway. The air was hot and close, moths fluttering in the door light. He heard something, out in the old fen: the sound of an engine throbbing and stopping and starting again.

He began to walk towards it. At the edge of the reed bank, he thought he caught a trace of Judith's perfume – and though he knew that was impossible, he speeded up, pushing aside the ferns until he stumbled on a pathway. The engine noise came again up ahead – and he saw a beam of light too, reaching out and shutting off.

He called her name. It sounded out across the water. He felt something swoop over him: a bat, circling its territory. With that swoop, he knew what was happening – but he couldn't accept it, couldn't believe she would do it to him. He ran forward on the path – an old causeway leading beside the tributary rivers of Thinbeach Pool. He accelerated, feeling branches cutting his arms, until he tripped on a root and sprawled headlong, the moss smearing his face.

Standing up, he saw the light ahead. It was on a boat – a speedboat – which was moving slowly along the tributary, avoiding the rushes and the overhead branches. Its engine was working slowly, leaving a blur of vapour. The light turned off again. He ran blindly towards it, calling her name, tearing at the undergrowth until he saw the stern of the boat – leaking steam, heading away from him.

'Judith,' he shouted, 'I'm sorry.'

He thought the boat was slowing for him, but it was only navigating a tangled overhang, and the engine soon revved again. He ran towards it along the bank, still calling her name. The other part of his dream came back to him: the woman detective's voice asking, *What's the worst he could do?*

Ivan had to use the searchlight when the branches grew too close to the boat. He could still hear the man shouting back there, but he could see clear water ahead – the dark of the open river. He glanced around and saw Judith looking over the stern, her hands gripping the rails. For a moment he thought she was going to jump off the boat. Then she clutched her hands to her ears and shook her head, and he held her with one arm while he steered with the other.

She said, 'Can't you hear it? He's calling for me.'

Behind him, he heard a great splash and he realised that Denton was in the water itself, thrashing around and still calling for Judith.

Suddenly the searchlight came on. Judith was using it, training it on the water behind the boat. He looked around again and saw Denton lit up. The man was plunging forward, half swimming and half reaching out to her, hands white in the powerful beam, his head going under and surfacing again and calling his daughter's name.

Ivan turned on the power, and the engine erupted under his feet as the boat surged out into the main river. He glanced back one last time and saw Denton swamped in heaving water, calling out and finally disappearing as the boat rounded the curve of the fen and entered the clean dark river itself.

Judith clicked the light off. He reduced the power.

It was quiet for a while, just the throb of the engine

and the hiss of the water going past while Ivan turned things over in his mind.

'Judith, I'm going to tell you about that woman you remind me of.' He wiped his face with his sleeve. 'Only, I think you could give her some lessons.'

Fletcher watched a late train moving away along the tracks beyond the steel gate at the end of the street. The air was so static that its fumes hung for a while, as the cables rocked themselves still. He watched the flashes tracing the last carriage towards the north. Then he let the curtain fall back against the window.

He stretched out on the sofa in Cathleen's downstairs room. She was upstairs, asleep, and so was Luke. He closed his eyes. There was sweat in his eyelids. He said, 'Cathleen.'

He knew she couldn't hear him.

Saturday Morning

Fletcher slept five hours, until the sun climbed over the rail yards between bronze and red clouds. He pulled the sheet over Cathleen's shoulders, stood looking at her a minute. He didn't wake her. Back at his flat, he took a shower and put on a blue cotton shirt, dark tie, then the best suit he had, plus a pair of rubber-soled shoes. He thought he was going straight to the Thinbeach Wedding.

The phone rang.

Eight-thirty saw Fletcher driving past the Breakman depot and through the massive fields stretching out on either side, where the crop was rippling away to the horizon. He could see one of the combine machines already at work on the harvest, cutting a swathe around the ruined church. Then, as the grain fields gave way to the polythene tunnels, he noticed the white plastic shivering in the sunlight, releasing a fine mist of condensation.

He turned off the main road and into Thinbeach Fen, the willow and ash tangling their shadows across the windscreen. At the end of the gravelled track, a uniformed officer held up a hand, then waved him through.

Sal's car was already there, and she herself was standing on the bank, outlined against the sky. Trainers, combat trousers, a thin jersey, her hair tied back. She looked over at Fletcher, then back at the river.

Two police divers were fastening their drysuits, preparing to lower themselves into the black water. Not a huge task for the divers, more of a live training exercise. Thomas Denton was almost within reach. He was tangled in the base of a willow that grew out into the channel. The tree roots were spidered over the surface, their kinked limbs pinning him onto the silt under the bank. The big, confident face was turned up to the light, the eyes filled with fen water.

Sal said, 'No sign of Judith. No answer from Deep House.'

Fletcher watched the frogmen slipping into the river. He said, 'Ivan got close to Thomas. Let's stop him getting close to Thinbeach.'

He took a last look at Thomas Denton as the divers slid their rubberised hands around him. The face tilted, and the water in his eye sockets drained away to join the North Sea.

Back on the main road, the polythene gave way to the fields around Thinbeach. Vehicles were already arriving in the rough meadow signposted *Wedding Visitors*, including a camper from which some Morris dancers were clambering – the fenland variety known as Molly dancers, their faces brightly painted.

Beyond that, well away from the other cars, was a white Transit with roof fans spinning in the heat. Fletcher parked beside Sal, then banged once on the van's rear door. It opened on a smell of sweat, creak of body armour, helmets and goggles, the sight of creased uniforms. Ten pairs of eyes waiting for action. Fletcher sincerely hoped they wouldn't see any. These uniformed officers were the minimum level of support Webley had insisted on in case it became necessary to subdue Ivan Gorensky and Berlitz. He or Sal could summon them with a single code from an Airwave handset, and in half a minute the men would be charging down the Shamblings. Fletcher knew it wouldn't be necessary. He could control Ivan now, defuse this whole situation, and then move on to Alain de Minching.

'Will we get a scrap?' a constable asked.

'You will if you're late,' Sal answered. The bored eyes glinted at each other. She shut the door on them. Beside the Transit was a dog-handler's van, a pair of jaws drooling behind the grille.

By now it was well after nine a.m. Fletcher and Sal checked their Airwave receivers, then tucked them into their clothes: Fletcher in his jacket, Sal in a combat pocket. They started walking into Thinbeach.

She said, 'You know, it's only just occurred to me.'

'What?'

'Where's the mast? There must be an Airwave transmission mast around here somewhere. But it's totally flat.'

'Can we worry about that later?'

They walked together along the Shamblings, past the Normandy twin-town sign. Through the traffic-calming, past the people beginning to gather in knots. The Fen Deli was bustling, customers milling on the pavements, sipping coffee. The kerbsides had been lined with traffic cones to prevent cars parking, and the few side alleys were cordoned off with yellow tape.

There was no sign of Alain de Minching among the groups of people on the narrow pavement, or the faces peering into the street from the windows. There was no sign of Ivan, either – the man coming to ask the critical question of his life, and expecting an answer. In the space between the buildings, the triangular bunting strung from wall to wall hardly moved, and the early burst of sunshine was giving way to humid warmth that tinted the air blue-grey.

Fletcher looked around at the crowd. There were a few people who looked like visitors from Cambridge – folky types, some curious students – but most were Thinbeach villagers: mature faces, damp with sweat, exchanging the expectant glances that said this was their special day. They were innocent, vulnerable to whatever torment Ivan had ready for them – yet Fletcher kept thinking of the Russian engineer's desperate journey along this street on a freezing night. How many of these people had refused to answer his knocking?

There was the sound of a violin starting to play, people clapping along in rhythm, tapping their feet. A woman began to sing the old ballad from Alain de Minching's book:

She was fine but she was faithless
That nameless eely girl
Faithless in the orchard
With every village churl . . .

They waited, watching the crowd assemble. As time went on, the sky began to glaze over with a sheen from the west. Fletcher's shirt spread damp against his back.

At ten twenty, they agreed to split up, and Fletcher walked further along the Shamblings towards The Blindy House. He came to the narrow funnel, where the timber buildings crowded close. People were three deep under the eaves, peering over each others' shoulders.

The ballad started again, then faded behind him –

But she will always rise again
Our faithless nameless girl of eels
Our faithless girl of eels

In the garden of The Bride, people were standing on benches to get a better view. Debbie was leaning in the doorway with the same look of expectation as everyone else. She saw Fletcher, and gave a slow wave.

Was this where Ivan would make his move, play whatever insane mind games he'd devised? Again, though, the kerbs were coned off, no cars were visible, and the narrow side streets were empty.

Fletcher turned to look across the road at The Blindy House. Behind its iron gates, under the cosmetic blur of wisteria, he could picture the little fortress that must have stood on the site a thousand years ago. But the blinds were drawn behind the slit windows and the door was shut inside its lintels, and Alain was still nowhere to be seen.

Fletcher waited, watching more people arrive. In the centre of the funnel, a few Molly men began dancing a jig under the bunting, sweat blurring their face paint as they called out a guttural chorus, shaking their sticks. The sounds echoed above the murmur of the villagers on the pavements.

He walked on, up the slope of the mound itself, the grass releasing a dust that itched in his nostrils. Above that came the smell of roasting, and at the top he found two village men tending a long bed dug into the earth, full of glowing coals. Chunks of meat were sizzling on iron spikes, spitting fat. The men were in their sixties, but their faces were like children's before a party, continually glancing down to the village below. The meat was releasing drifts of heavy smoke, and Fletcher walked further along the mound to get some clean air. Close below him was the glossy Pool, the surface broken only by fish ripples. The opposite bank was deserted – and beyond the fields, the cathedral shimmered in the haze.

Behind him, there was a shout. Fletcher turned and saw one of the villagers gesturing excitedly, pointing down along the Shamblings.

'I can see her. I can see the Bride.' The man slapped his friend on the back and winked at Fletcher. 'And she's a beauty. A beauty.'

Fletcher looked down into the village. He expected to see someone carrying one of the little corn dolls dressed in silk for the special day. He realised his eyes were tired and he pressed his lids together before looking again. Beyond the houses in the funnel, above the heads of the crowd, he could see something taking shape.

At the other end of the Shamblings, Sal was also expecting to see a corn doll appear by now. Instead, six men arrived, pushing a farm trailer – sweating as they manoeuvred the wheels into the centre of the street. There was something positioned on the trailer: an uneven object maybe three metres long, shrouded in a tarpaulin. The crowd stepped back to give it room, and their voices dropped. The fiddle stopped playing.

For a minute, the six men stood panting, looking around and smiling. Then one of them stepped forward and put his hands on the edge of the tarpaulin. Excitement ran through the crowd, everyone watching the wrapped shape. All except one person, a young man who—

She lost him, because the tarpaulin was pulled away and the crowd surged forward, blocking her view of the trailer. Sal could make out a lot of activity around the platform, the six men huffing and stooping to get their shoulders under something. Then the onlookers broke into applause, and Sal saw an object swaying into the air above their heads, rising almost as high as the eaves of the houses. Sal froze for a moment, although people were pushing around her. She couldn't believe what she was seeing.

It was a Thinbeach Bride, there was no doubt of

that. But this one was colossal, as if a little doll had mutated overnight. This Bride was three metres long, needing all the six men to lift her, the bearers gripping her flanks and each others' shoulders, holding the giant effigy still for everyone to admire.

She was woven from reeds and wheat stalks, the ends cut and split to create a fuzz, making her radiant in the humid light. She was in the voluptuous shape of a woman, long-limbed and full-breasted, reclining with one arm on her flank and the other behind her head, each of her hands finished with three curling fingers tipped with bunches of barley ears. Her face was tilted to one side, and a wide smile was woven onto it with parted lips of rags. She had no eyes, but as the six men began carrying her at a slow walk towards the Pool, the Bride seemed to be looking ahead along the Shamblings. The crowd jostled each other, moving slowly along the street to keep pace with the procession.

Sal saw that young guy again, the one who didn't seem to fit here, and didn't seem to hold the Bride in quite so much affection as the others. He was smirking, his smile visible under a dark baseball cap, and despite the heat he was wearing a puffa jacket zipped up. It wasn't Berlitz or Ivan, that was clear. As the man lifted his face, she saw him make a movement of the eyes across the street. She turned. On the opposite pavement was another man in a dark baseball cap and a puffa jacket, also watching the Bride pass.

Sal swallowed hard. She felt her heart pounding, and damp in her palms. She pushed her way along the Shamblings, behind the crowd surging forward onto

the kerb as the Bride approached. Sure enough, standing just ahead of her in the doorway of the first timber
building, there was another man wearing the same
model baseball cap – but with his jacket unzipped –
looking left and right. An earpiece ran on a wire down
inside his collar.

Sal felt sweat trickle down her neck. This wasn't
what they'd agreed – it was the *opposite*. She was
furious that nobody had briefed her. She was wondering what the hell to do now. She took the handset out
and dialled Fletcher. Fantastic – a guaranteed-perfect
network, and she couldn't even get through to him.

Someone in the crowd shouted, 'What a beauty.'

From the crest of the mound, Fletcher watched the
object materialise as it progressed towards him along
the Shamblings. He was thinking of something Alain
de Minching had said – *This Year's will be the best ever*.
He was wondering – watching the giant Bride come
into the funnel area, where people were leaning out of
the upper windows of the houses to watch – wondering
why Alain had decided to make this one so big. Was it a
gesture of defiance against the outsiders, the people
starting to uncover the past?

The Bride's leering face approached the end of the
street, swaying from side to side, always pointing
roughly ahead at the mound. A few more people were
already scrambling up the slope for a better view, some
of them gathering around the roasting pit, breathing in
the aroma, their eyes bright. Everyone was watching
the Bride move under the bunting strung between the

final buildings, then pass the pub and come level with The Blindy House. The six men paused, and the crowd stopped too and fell silent. The bearers were panting audibly as they caught their breath – but this was more than a rest stop. The front door of The Blindy House swung open.

The spectators' heads all craned towards it, but the interior was too dark to see anything. In a moment, the two wolfhounds appeared and sniffed at the air before padding down to the garden gate, the tendons flexing under their pelts. Then Alain de Minching himself stepped out, dressed in a tailored cotton suit with flap pockets, an open collar showing clean white skin below his neck. Freshly shaved.

He stood blinking in the light for a moment, then smiled, showing off his profile. He moved confidently along the garden path. Opening the gate, he stopped and surveyed the street, the dogs on each side with their tongues lolling. He looked up at the Bride. He looked around at the crowd, his eyebrows raised, as if considering. Then he curled his fingers to his lips and blew a kiss.

At that signal, the bearers began moving the Bride again, lurching forward to the beginning of the mound itself. The crowd followed close behind – Alain leading them, with his eyes fixed on the effigy.

Fletcher thought this was it. If Ivan was going to do something, surely it would be now. The crowd in the Shamblings surged between the buildings, with scores of people being pressed against the walls and the leaded windows, people squeezing past the iron railings of The Blindy House, a bottleneck of people jamming the funnel.

Fletcher scanned the crowd, trying to see into the side streets – expecting Ivan or Berlitz to appear. He felt sweat on the side of his face.

The Bride was carried a few steps up the incline of the mound, and then Alain led the villagers out into the open, the crowd spilling through the funnel and streaming happily onto the grass slope. In a minute, only a few stragglers were left behind in the street: a couple of Molly dancers, and a man in a baseball cap and puffa jacket who Fletcher realised was talking to Sal Moresby.

He tried to call her on Airwave – but his damn handset wouldn't connect. *Piece of junk.* He could see Sal's conversation becoming heated, as the man gestured at her to move away along the street.

Then Fletcher lost sight of them, because the whole crowd began arriving on the ridge of the mound, surrounding the Bride as she swayed up towards the high point: at least a hundred people, intent on seeing the effigy thrown into the water, speaking in hushed voices. The crackling of the meat on spikes was loud now, the embers smouldering under the overcast sky.

In a minute the Bride herself topped the ridge, outlined against the distorted shapes of grey and black clouds gathering in the distance. Her bearers stopped there, gathering their breath before the final descent on the other side, and Alain de Minching paused too, wiping his face with a handkerchief, the rest of the crowd leaving a little respectful distance around him in which his dogs dropped to their haunches. He was about thirty metres from Fletcher.

'So who else?'

Fletcher span round.

Ivan was standing just behind him, wearing his pinstriped suit over the army boots, an open shirt revealing the scar glinting with sweat. His almond-shaped eyes were watching the scene with interest: the bed of coals, the Bride beginning to move again, swaying down the slope, her bearers shouting instructions to each other to keep a foothold, the onlookers calling encouragement, Alain in his tailored safari suit leading the crowd that followed her down.

'Who else killed my father?'

'I know exactly what happened. There'll be an investigation, but it's complex. You need to calm down. It's going to take time.'

'We don't have time.'

Behind Ivan, Fletcher saw a movement among the tall rushes surrounding the Pool, where one of the tributary streams came into the main channel. It looked as if the wind were brushing them, but the air remained oppressively still and close.

'What's going on, Ivan?'

'You need to tell me who was involved, police. You really need to.'

Behind Ivan came the movement again, something happening fast behind the screen of reeds, approaching the Pool itself. For a few yards the reeds had a gap, and in the space Fletcher glimpsed a man's face, scowling in concentration, his leather jacket zipped up tight in the slipstream, the white polo neck cupping his chin.

Berlitz.

Fletcher looked back at the mound. The Bride was approaching the edge of the water, the bearers making one last effort to lift her even higher on their shoulders. They were getting ready to make a final run and hurl her in.

From out in the tributary came a growl as a powerful engine was revved and then throttled down. Fletcher saw a sleek white hull turning in a spray of water.

'What's he doing with that boat?'

Ivan hadn't even glanced at it. He was watching the scene on the bank, the bearers still trying to heave the Bride into the air. He said, 'They love her, don't they? She means everything to them. A thousand years of continuous history. Now I'm going to take her away.'

'How?'

'I'm going to kill her.'

'Kill the Bride? She's made of straw.'

Ivan just made a gesture. On the far side, the engine exploded into action with a noise that made everyone on the mound turn and stare. In a second, the boat came charging into the Pool. It was a serious power craft, not a pleasure boat but a professional racer – stolen, Fletcher guessed, from one of the marinas around Cambridge. It had a white body, a low super-structure, with a long tapering prow already beginning to lift into the air. At the stern, Berlitz was standing at the controls in an open cockpit, leaning over the side to give a line of sight towards the group on the waterside.

Fletcher felt sweat in the hollow of his neck. He could see the idea. The way the boat was accelerating, the prow would be high enough to mount the bank if it crashed onto the side of the Pool where the Bride was being readied for drowning. The whole craft would come tearing up out of the water and into the crowd. A fifteen-metre boat, weighing – what, two tonnes?

'What happened, police?'

'Don't do this. There's no need.'

'They won't get hurt. Not if they run.'

Down on the bank, things had stopped: everyone turning to watch the boat as it came roaring across the calm surface of the Pool towards the Bride, a plume of white water spreading behind it, the noise rolling out along the river. The bow lifted even higher, sending long beads of water spinning aside. In the few seconds remaining, the crowd began to run, people shoving and scrambling over each other to get clear, beginning to scream. Fletcher glimpsed Alain's dogs among them, but not Alain himself.

The men holding the effigy lasted a second longer, then dropped it and bolted too, leaving the Bride to thump down on the turf, the huge face looking up with its fixed smile, her barley fingers spread on the ground. In the last moment before the boat hit the shore, Fletcher saw Berlitz crouch down and grab the cockpit rails. Then the bow of the powerboat slammed into the bank.

There was an impact that echoed off the mound and went cracking out across the Pool. The whole underside of the boat reared up into the air, flailing water and river weed, the sharp keel glinting with sediment.

Things hung like that for a split second – until the hull tipped forward and smashed down onto the grass. The Thinbeach Bride disappeared under it – a limb already severed, whirling up into the air, trailing stalks. Then the boat's stern thrashed clear in a spray of weeds, the propellers screaming until they ripped into the ground, sending bits of metal and clods of peat hurtling left and right. Fletcher saw people hit by the debris, being flipped over on their backs. The boat kept going, its momentum taking it up the slope for twenty metres until it finally ploughed into the incline of the mound and stopped with its keel partly buried in the earth. The remnants of the propellers raced and then died, and oily smoke began spewing from the vents, collecting in a static cloud.

Berlitz himself jumped neatly over the rails and began to walk up the slope towards the village – an action so calm and immediate that he succeeded in blending in with the confused crowd.

Ivan turned to Fletcher. His eyes were dilated, exultant. 'Did you see? I killed her, police. I cut her stupid throat. She's dead – they all know it.'

Fletcher tried to send the Airwave code, guessing that Sal would have done it by now anyway. Around him, the crowd were in shock. The people hit by flying debris were being helped to their feet or tended where they lay. Others began clustering around the boat, peering at the pieces of the Bride trailing out from underneath it: a hand with the fingers wrenched off, a breast tangled with the weeds in the propellers. The head was nowhere in sight.

Alain de Minching reappeared, perfectly calm, studying the boat, his dogs poised behind him, their ears up. He stooped to pick up one of the stalks and rub it in his palms. Then he began walking up the mound back towards the village, the dogs following behind. Halfway, he looked across at the Russian, then ahead again. On the top of the ridge, he paused and looked again. Something passed between him and Ivan, clear even in all the turmoil and the drifting fumes of the powerboat engine. The Russian pointed.

'It was him. I know it was him.'

'How?'

'The look on his face. He just recognised me.'

'He's never seen you before.'

'No. But I look like my father now. You understand? Exactly like my father.' Ivan took a step forward.

'Stop, Gorensky.' Ivan paused and looked back at Fletcher. His face was impassive. Behind him, Alain was shrouded in fumes from the wrecked speedboat. 'This is England. I've got ten men arriving.'

That was a bloody mess, he told himself. *That was a mess, but it could have been far worse.*

He waited for the uniforms and the police dogs to appear on the slope. Ivan and Alain were waiting too, standing utterly still, the smoke trailing around them. Fletcher knew he'd got it right. Messy but right, with an element of luck, like most police work. Thank God it was over.

Just as he thought that, the sound of a gunshot came echoing between the funnel of buildings and up the slope.

Turning, he saw Berlitz down there, standing frozen outside The Blindy House, his hands stretched out empty, and two men poised in a semi-crouch in front of him: two men wearing puffa jackets and dark baseball caps, each training on him a pistol that Fletcher knew was a police-issue 9mm Glock. At this distance, the guns were just dark points in the men's pale hands.

No Glockenspiel.

Fletcher wasn't totally surprised that Webley had a reserve plan. What amazed him was that he hadn't been told.

Sal Moresby felt her ears ringing from the first gunshot, when the officer fired into the air because Berlitz ignored the shouted order to halt. She was only a few metres away from him, outside the pub garden. Behind her, one of the Molly dancers was watching too, his paint smeared with sweat.

The two marksmen and Berlitz formed a small triangle, its three points utterly still. The sky above The Blindy House was beginning to fill with silent clouds, each swollen with blue-black vapour – and in that light, the red dots of the Glock laser sights being trained on Berlitz's chest were the brightest thing in the world. Berlitz clearly knew it.

She saw him look over to the mound, where streams of people were beginning to come back over the ridge. She saw him stand up straight and take a deep breath, his chest filling out.

Sal called, 'Let me speak to him.'

By way of reply, one of the Glockenspiel men

adjusted his weight and shouted another warning that echoed back between the houses. She could see the fingers curled on the triggers, the built-in safety catches already released by the pressure. Berlitz glanced over at Sal and just smiled, raising his eyebrows. Then he took another long breath and lifted his hands slightly, and the officer yelled one final time.

When Berlitz sang his first note, the sound was so powerful that it filled the space between the buildings and flowed away along the Shamblings, lasting for long seconds where the marksman's shout had been a momentary spasm. He stopped and smiled again, looking up at the clouds. One of the officers glanced at the other in confusion. Then Berlitz put one hand on his chest, over his heart, because that was where he was singing from.

She'd never seen a shooting before. What shocked her was the way the bullets didn't stop – they hit Berlitz and went straight through him. Things came hammering out of his back: bits of clothing and body, lines of fluid streaking into the garden of The Blindy House, spattering the shrubs. Before the echoes had even stopped, Berlitz was twisted up against the iron gate, his face tilted up to the sky, the officers still crouching but edging closer. Behind her, the Molly dancer puked in the gutter, as more armed police began arriving around them.

She saw one officer step close to the body and keep his laser trained on Berlitz's head. Then the other came forward, reached carefully and lifted the edge of Berlitz's jacket.

Suddenly she found Webley standing next to her, wearing a waxed coat, jeans and boots, looking around at the scene.

'You OK, Moresby?'

Sal was trying to control her breathing. She kept her hands by her sides.

'That was totally unnecessary. And you didn't brief us. We agreed last night, no Glockenspiel.'

The marksman unzipped the jacket fully and brought out the old Margolin pistol, laying it on the pavement. There was so much blood leaking away from the body that it reflected the darkening clouds overhead.

Webley said, 'If you remember, we agreed on the firearms unit as a last resort. This *was* a last resort. At least they followed procedure. Very professional.'

Sal looked around.

Webley was walking away along the Shamblings to a black Range Rover studded with roof aerials.

Sal looked back at the gun, lying on the pavement near the dead man's hand.

Fletcher looked at Ivan and saw nothing on his face to suggest he'd ever known Berlitz. Ivan just stared down at the armed police starting to swarm around the funnel area, then glanced up as a helicopter rattled in the threatening sky. There was a wail of sirens from the main road, blue lights flashing across the buildings.

Then Ivan let out a single shout: an enraged bellow that hung in the static air. Down by The Blindy House, the police were starting to take an interest in the mound, pointing up at the ridge, but not coming closer.

Why don't they come up here? And where's my back-up, anyway?

He realised he wasn't the only person wondering about the police. Alain was watching the village too, eyes furrowed, turning something over in his mind. Ivan himself looked puzzled, tilting his head and watching the landscape as if expecting the enemy to come from all sides. Lines of smoke were entwining and blowing across the grass.

Ivan took a step through them, towards Alain.

Alain looked at him. He looked past him to the village, calculating, then seemed to change his mind. He whistled to his dogs and turned to walk quickly away back down the mound. He passed the boat, still leaking oily vapour. He ignored the few casualties stretched out on the ground, and stopped just once – to pick up another piece of straw. Then he and his dogs began moving along the Pool bank towards the polythene tunnels in the fields beyond. He finally broke into a jog where the rushes grew in clumps beside the bank, his hounds picking up speed and lumbering beside him into the reeds.

Fletcher called Webley's phone, but still had no connection, as if he'd dropped right off the Airwave network. His civilian phone had no signal at all. When he looked around, Ivan had gone.

He identified him by the pinstripe suit and boots, striding along the bank in the same direction as Alain, his reflection skimming the dark water beside him.

A single gap in the clouds opened up and shone off the river, then closed. A pair of swallows dipped away over the Pool, escaping the coming storm. Down in the village, the police were still holding back. Fletcher decided there was only one possible reason for that. It was Webley.

Webley knows I can do it. She wants me to finish the job.

He began running down the slope, towards the rushes where the two men had disappeared. The wounded villagers were climbing to their feet, and the turf was littered with straw and reeds, amber against the trampled grass. A long groan of thunder came shuddering across the fields.

Sal Moresby walked back along the Shamblings, past the black Range Rover. Its long aerials were flexing slightly, twitching like insect antennae. She walked past the timber houses, past the stone houses. People were standing in groups along the pavement, in the traffic-calming chicane, talking to each other in confusion. Two ambulances were turning into the street, shielded by uniformed police. Not the police from the white Transit.

She identified herself to a young constable, and asked to borrow his folding baton. She walked faster, then picked up speed and began to jog, with the baton in one hand. By the time she got to the meadow she was sprinting. She noticed that the Transit and the dog van had both gone. She snapped the baton and aimed straight for Fletcher's Nissan. She smashed the passenger window in a shower of crystal fragments. The alarm shrieked. She popped the locks and yanked the tailgate open.

A steel filing box was secured in a mesh carrier. She opened it and tipped out the plastic folders of notes on the death of Shane Gaffy – all the reports and press cuttings and photos. What she wanted wasn't there, but she kept looking.

When the officer whose baton she'd taken appeared behind her, she threatened to slam the tailgate on his neck. He backed off.

She opened the notes on Terry Swilter and rifled through until she found the photos from the so-called Doomsday Book, the ones kept out of the official report. The photo of the substation at Ulsingham Hall, various people standing around the scene.

She looked around at the constable behind her. A copper just trying to do the job.

In a minute, Fletcher was into the reed clumps along the margins of the Pool. He was running, and the humidity slicked the shirt against his back – but, after the fumes of the speedboat, he was glad to breathe the scent of the water. He saw lilies on the surface and weeds spiralling in the current. Then he left the Pool behind, following the path along a small river. At times he saw dog tracks in the moist earth, and elsewhere the print of an army boot crushing them.

The reeds creaked as he brushed between them, and something scurried off into the water – otherwise it was quiet, with the mayhem of Thinbeach blanked off by the distance and the clatter of the helicopter circling but coming no closer. The helicopter was something else he hadn't known about. He felt thirst collecting in his throat.

The path went on for half a mile, until the reed bank was broken by the wreck of a barge – its twisted planks bubbling with moss. From there, the track rose along the side of an embankment leading up to the open landscape. He climbed it, the peat sinking under his rubber soles.

At the top, he found he was at the point where the corn fields met the fields of polythene.

The plastic tunnels stood against the darkening sky like cocoons: their white skin stretched tight over metal ribs, glowing against the dark fen earth. Some stray poppies were leaning against the sheeting: red discs as bright and still as laser gun-sights.

There was no sign of the two men.

Fletcher walked up to the nearest tunnel. In the plastic wall, he found a slit torn roughly by hand, the jagged edges releasing mist from the interior.

He took a last look around. He took in the corn fields and the rushes and the tower of the old church, and the cathedral on the horizon – above everything, the storm clouds ranged across the county.

Then he stepped through the plastic, into the jungle.

Sal Moresby tried Fletcher's civilian phone again: unobtainable. She threw the filing box into the boot of the Vectra, and spent a minute listening to police transmissions on Airwave. There was a lot of dialogue between the control vehicle and the helicopter, the aircrew wanting to land before the storm broke. When she heard what she needed to hear, she took off across the meadow, the tyres whining on the grass, the whole car lifting off the ground as she crested a slight rise, then landing with an impact she felt in the back of her neck. She wrenched the car around onto an unsurfaced road that led through the farmland, aiming towards the place the helicopter had reported three targets disappearing from view.

In a minute, she saw the polythene tunnels ahead, an expanse of white under the sky. She began to drive on a rutted track that ran around the edge of them, looking for signs of activity. The track was deserted, just the old ruined church up ahead. Crashing out of one pothole, she heard the box in the back sliding around. It felt like a huge weight – the heaviest weight she would ever have to carry.

Saturday Afternoon

Inside the tunnel, Fletcher stopped and blinked in the heat. The atmosphere was so damp that things were blurred in haze: the ribbed ceiling stretching just over head height, the floor snaked with hoses leaking water and crammed with endless rows of strawberry plants, their pitted flesh gleaming inside trays of soil. He noticed that every twenty paces was a flap leading to the adjacent tunnel. From the nearest of these, he saw a movement.

When he reached the side flap he found a jumble of crates, tools, coiled hoses, and then the light of the next tunnel. Also two men, kneeling on the ground repairing a tap. The men turned and stared back at him: Chinese origin, barely in their twenties, damp fringes hanging into their eyes. When Fletcher began to speak, they frowned and spoke in what he guessed was Cantonese.

Illegals. Illegal labourers, here at the whim of gang masters who might pay a few pounds a day. One youth pointed with his spanner to the next tunnel, and Fletcher pushed through the flap.

In there, he found the same crop and the same vaporous heat, so close that he had to wipe his eyes.

Plus two more Chinese men, lifting and dividing the plants with long knives. The men studied him and looked at each other, the blades dangling in their hands. One of them glanced deliberately ahead, up the tunnel – then they stooped to their cutting again.

Fletcher walked along the tunnel. His clothes were soaked with sweat and the hot air was difficult to inhale. This went on for long minutes: the steel arcs passing overhead, the damp crops and the dribbling hoses, the haze, his own breathing. At one point, a lightning flash filled the space, making the vapour a sheer wall in front of him. When he had no idea any more where he was, just somewhere near the dead centre of the tunnel, he saw Ivan in the blur up ahead, looking left and right and then stepping through another of the side flaps.

Going in after him, he found the next tunnel more fully occupied: Chinese people shining with sweat, packing the strawberries into plastic crates. Following Ivan at a distance of twenty metres, Fletcher began to notice things along the route.

He passed a makeshift shrine, its incense colouring the air purple, and then a cart that doubled as a canteen, with a Chinese man staring glumly into a huge pot. As Fletcher came level, the cook glanced at him and held out a plastic beaker. It was cold water, and Fletcher felt it splashing his chin as he gulped it down. The man didn't look up when he thanked him.

At the next flap, there was a small crowd of the workers, peering over each others' shoulders into the adjoining tunnel. Fletcher pushed past them and found he was in a crossroads at the centre of the complex: a space without crops, the run of the tunnel more clearly visible to left and right. He noticed the light fading sharply: the outside air tensing as the storm gathered.

Ivan was already there. He was kneeling over the body of a Chinese man who had been slashed with one of the harvesting knives: a cut to his neck drenching his shirt with blood. The victim was still conscious, his eyes moving left and right, hands trembling while Ivan tried to press a wad of cloth against the wound. Ivan glanced up.

'You said this is England.'

Yes, it is. A Russian killer saving an illegal Chinese from a Belgian horse-butcher.

Then another worker took over, and Ivan stood. The scar on his own throat was more vivid than ever.

'You speak any Chinese? Nor me. But I guess he took the guy's knife.'

More of the workers were gathering now – among them some wide-eyed kids barely nine or ten years of age. Fletcher looked around at the crowd.

'Where is he now?'

Someone spat and said something, pointing into one of the tunnels. Someone else handed Ivan one of the harvesting knives – a battered curve half a metre long, stained with rust but sharp at the whet edge. Fletcher put out a hand to restrain him, but Ivan began to stride along the tunnel, the blade held loosely in one hand.

Fletcher was glad he hadn't stopped. He followed him out of the crossroads area and into more cultiva-

tion that made the air thick and damp again, the smell
of ripe vegetation almost a colour.

Sal dumped the Vectra when a tyre split apart coming
out of a pothole. The way ahead was blocked anyway,
by standing wheat growing almost up to the tunnel
walls. The helicopter had gone now, and the sky held
only the electric clouds.

She began running along the narrow space between
the wheat and the plastic. She came past the old
church, its square tower covered with ivy and moss,
one wall long since fallen away.

She stopped for a second.

Inside the Norman tower, concealed from view, a
grey metal structure had been installed, crowned with a
ring of high-performance aerials aiming out across the
landscape. It was buzzing and clicking with static from
the approaching storm. The Airwave mast.

She kept on running. She was telling herself this
wasn't her fault. The remark that had stuck in her
unconscious mind – the thing that didn't fit – nobody
could have picked that up. All she could do now was
find the place where the three men were going to come
out of the tunnels. If they came out.

There were fewer workers along this final tunnel.
Those who were here just lifted their heads from the
work and nodded on, towards the end. Fletcher kept
Ivan in view through the haze, the pinstripe jacket dark
with sweat.

At that moment there was a noise from outside the

tunnels that made the polythene roof ripple even in the still air – a rhythmic pounding that then faded and receded.

Fletcher heard a movement behind him, and turned to find one of the Chinese kids trying to follow, clutching a home-made kite. The boy pointed to the picture painted on it: a fire-breathing dragon. Fletcher put a hand on his shoulder and pushed him back down the tunnel, then walked on. The noise was still out there in the distance. It was another half a kilometre before the end wall of the tunnel reared up ahead: a blank sheet lit by the storm light outside.

There was no trace of Alain de Minching, but Ivan was outlined against the polythene, still holding that long knife, his head on one side.

As Fletcher came up next to him, whatever he'd been listening for was drowned in the return of the noise from outside. The polythene overhead began to flap and crackle. Fletcher realised what it was.

They were at the edge of the tunnel system, where the polythene gave way to the wheat fields. The noise was one of the combine harvesters labouring past – one of the house-sized machines that made electrical dust of the pulverised husks in its wake. The Chinese kid had been right – it really did sound like a dragon.

Ivan turned to Fletcher and put a hand on his chest – the hand that wasn't holding a razor-sharp farm knife. It wasn't a threat – he was just saying, *Wait*.

It went on for a long half-minute, Ivan with his hand on Fletcher's chest, the fingers totally still through the cloth. Another lightning flash exploded right overhead.

As the machine grew closer, the plastic ceiling began to buckle in long waves – even the steam in the air rippled visibly.

Ivan took his hand off Fletcher and pointed.

Where the sides of the tunnel met the end wall, the plastic was wrapped and folded around the last of the metal ribs. In one of these folds, something moved. There was a nudging at knee height, a shape pressing itself against the plastic – then, as it lost patience, a snout and teeth began tearing at the skin and one of Alain's hounds muscled through, saliva trailing from its jaw. The other dog followed, beads of spit glimmering in the grey light, and then the plastic behind them began to lift and bulge and disclose the contour of a man beneath the polythene, the figure turning its head towards them, the nose and lips distorted by the film. The dogs panted and looked up at it.

Then a rusty blade slit the plastic from waist to shoulder, and Alain de Minching came through to meet them.

Alain's suit was soaked in sweat, his hair hanging in strands across his eyes, and he was breathing hard – but his eyes were bright, full of calculations. He glanced behind him to where the pulsing of the cutter was getting closer, then turned and faced Ivan.

He said, 'It was all a mistake. Understand? Now the police are coming. They're coming to help me.'

Ivan's eyes held Alain's.

'The police? Where are they?'

Fletcher reached out for Ivan's blade – and, to his surprise, Ivan gave it up: throwing it point-down into the soft ground where it sank in halfway. Fletcher gestured to Alain to do the same.

The dogs ran long tongues across their jaws, scattering drool. Alain looked around the tunnel, swallowing hard. Then he looked at Ivan again – and, despite his knife, there was fear in his eyes. He turned and slashed at the polythene and forced himself through, out into the fields, whistling for his dogs to follow.

Ivan ran forward and jumped through the opening too. Fletcher glanced at his phone: nothing. He climbed through the rip in the plastic.

Outside, it was dark and cold.

The tunnel gave onto a plateau of corn that reeked of dust and earth. A few heavy raindrops were streaking the air – one hitting Fletcher in the face, tasting of static.

The combine was twenty metres away, approaching at an angle, the noise deafening. Everything Crispin Breakman had said was true: the cutter was generating its own field of static, flashing with light, and the air was swirling with husks blasting out of the ejection pipe. In the tinted cab, the driver was lit by his TV monitor, working up to the last minute before the storm broke.

Alain de Minching was standing in the uncut wheat, turning to the combine thrashing its way towards him, turning back to Ivan, still making his calculations. With the angle the machine was taking, he had a chance of running past it and away on the other side. Alain turned one last time and looked around the field – maybe searching for the police who were going to save him, because even prosecution would be better than facing Ivan. Then he dropped the knife and bolted out into the crop, still out of view of the driver's camera, aiming to go past the cutter, forcing the wheat apart around his knees, the wolfhounds' ears streaming back as they ran on either side of him.

Fletcher put out a hand and felt the stalks. They were still dry, but heavy and close-growing, hard to move.

Alain was almost through – his stained safari jacket swerving through the crop – when he stumbled, going down so his head vanished, then clambering to his feet again and trying to run on. The spiked cutter reared behind him, sparking and tearing.

When it hit him, Alain threw up an arm to protect himself, but the spikes snapped it back against his body. Alain fell headlong, partly under the cutter and partly under the massive tyre of the combine, causing the whole machine to lift fractionally as it ran him over. Then it came to a halt, the drum slowing down and stopping, a cloud of husks and stalks enveloping it for a few seconds before drifting away. A door in the cab opened and the driver clambered down, horribly pale, and began crouching in the stubble to peer under the wheel.

The rain started crashing down.

When Fletcher got there, Alain was still conscious, lying face up. One leg was still wedged under the tyre, crushed into the stubble, and the safari jacket was ripped open, exposing his newly-shaved body punctured by the spikes. His chest was rising in short spasms, but blood was spreading across it, the skin becoming darker even as Fletcher knelt beside him with the rain pouring around them.

The driver was standing in shock, his hands clasped on his head. 'I didn't see him. I just wanted to finish—'

'Got a radio? Then get an ambulance, for God's sake.'

The man scrambled back up into the cab.

Fletcher's basic medical training was irrelevant to this. Alain's eyes were still open, blinking, trying to focus on something behind him. Fletcher looked around. Alain's dogs were unharmed, and were standing quite still in the untouched wheat, panting, their eyes fixed on their master.

There was the sound of rain drumming on the tunnels, bursting against the combine's sides, and the hiss as water touched hot metal, the clang of the engine starting to cool. Thunder from the west rolled towards them over the polythene.

Ivan materialised in the corn, and the dogs looked at him in curiosity. The driver gawped down at him from the cab: the Russian's soaked shirt half open, revealing weird tattoos across his chest, his face completely impassive.

Fletcher put a hand out to restrain him, fearing what he was going to do to the dying man, but Ivan simply stood and stared, his face dripping with rain in the light of the storm. The water coursed through his hair and down his slabbed cheeks, and he parted his lips for a second, letting some run into his mouth. He reached into his shirt pocket and pulled out the little corn doll. The twisted thing stared upward. Ivan held it in his hand for a moment, letting the rain have it. Then he tossed it onto the stubble, where it landed in the hacked-off stalks.

Fletcher looked back down at Alain. Water was pounding on the exposed body, sluicing the blood down into the earth. Alain's eyes closed for a second and then opened, still trying to focus. Fletcher glanced around again.

Ivan had gone.

Fletcher could only see the furious sky, the air grey with streaks of rain moving across the field, a fork of lightning that stayed on his retina. The wall of uncut wheat was bucking under the downpour. In front of that, Alain's two hounds were still watching, their eyes bright and their ears up, their fur slick with water. One of them took a step forward, sniffing the air.

Sal rounded the corner of the polythene tunnels and pushed the wet hair out of her eyes. She saw what she dreaded: two black Range Rovers with roof aerials, bumping over the stubble from the direction of Thinbeach, their headlights burning through the rain. Even worse, she saw Fletcher appear from behind a combine harvester that seemed to be stalled in the wheat close to the tunnels. As she watched, he began walking towards the approaching vehicles: a single tall figure against the drenched blur of the field. She closed her eyes for a moment. The rain was running over her eyelids and down onto her lips. She parted her mouth and tasted it. It tasted clean. She didn't want to open her eyes.

★   ★   ★

Ivan got to where he wanted to be: a point on rising ground away from the tunnels and the combine, where the remains of an old hedgerow hadn't been completely ripped out. There were some stunted hawthorn trees growing close to the ground, and he managed to get underneath them before the Range Rovers came to a halt beside the British policeman who was flagging them down.

Ivan grunted and pulled the Margolin out of his waistband and racked the mechanism. It was a good piece – quiet and accurate at close range – but it was nothing against the Glocks those police had, the men in puffa jackets and baseball caps clambering from one of the Range Rovers now and clustering around the combine harvester. Still, there was something about this situation that made him think he may not even need to use his gun.

Something began happening down by the combine: the police were grabbing those big dogs, trying to get them by the collars, pulling them away from something. The dogs were twisting and trying to bite, wanting to keep hold of whatever they had on the ground. Ivan realised what it was, and smiled. He didn't even know the man's name. He hadn't had time to discover his worst nightmare, but this must be close to it.

He saw the door of the other Range Rover open and a woman climb out: a woman in her forties, maybe, fit-looking, in a waxed coat, putting on a baseball cap against the rain, adjusting the peak low over her eyes.

He saw Fletcher walking over to her with his arms

open, and for a moment Ivan thought the two were going to embrace. But she reached out and held his cheek with her hand, gently. They looked at each other for a second. Ivan thought that Fletcher was speaking, explaining something.

Then something happened that amazed him. He saw the woman raise her other hand and strike Fletcher once across the face.

Fletcher shook his head. He could feel blood mingling with the rainwater on his lips. He saw Webley looking back at him, her eyes catching the lightning overhead. Behind her, he saw Sal walking over from the edge of the tunnels, her hair spread wet across her shoulders. He refocused on Webley.

He said, 'But I've done what you wanted.'

He noticed one of the Glockenspiel turn away and spit into the stubble. Two others were struggling with the dogs, wrenching their collars to keep the teeth away. The dogs' muzzles were slick with Alain's blood, and their heads were twisting furiously. Fletcher was trying to keep his own thoughts under control.

He said, 'We need a full investigation into 1978.'

Webley held his stare. Rain flickered across her face, water shining in the lines around her eyes. Her skin was pale against the grey sky, her lips parted. Whatever was going through her mind was hidden, her eyes showing nothing.

She said, 'You'll forget 1978. The things people do when they're young – they happen, and they get left in the past.'

Fletcher heard himself saying, 'Ivan Gorensky's here. He must be somewhere in the field.'

Webley shook her head.

'There was only one Russian. He's been eliminated. That's what the record will show. If by some fluke there's another one out there, we've sent him a signal he'll understand. He knows what'll happen to him, if he ever has the audacity to come back. But no, the Russian's been eliminated. If you think about it, so has The Wake.' She adjusted the peak of her cap. Some drops of water fell over her eyes. She smiled. 'Did I hurt you?' He didn't answer. 'Then I'm sorry. I was so proud of you.' She reached out and held his face, but he twisted it away. Then he looked back into her eyes.

One of the officers cursed as a wolfhound bit him on the arm. The man put his boot on the animal's neck and forced it onto the earth, then drew his pistol.

Webley didn't take her eyes off Fletcher's.

Ivan couldn't hear the shots above the rain noise, but he saw the Glocks being lowered against each dog in turn, and two small puffs of blood that vanished immediately. The men stood up and holstered their guns and began to move back to the Range Rovers. Ivan rested the Margolin's oily fin on his arm. He expected them to come across the field towards him, or bring in their own sniffer dogs, but in a few minutes they climbed back into the vehicles. The woman in the waxed coat joined them and the cars began to crawl away back towards Thinbeach. They left policeman Fletcher standing in the field with someone Ivan recognised as the young policewoman – the two of them standing alone in the rain.

Ivan rolled onto his back, thinking. He looked up through the leaves, to the clouds twisting across the sky. A last flash of lightning lit up the whole canopy.

Ivan was trying to calculate it all. Why did they leave him here, when they could easily have captured or killed him – the way they killed Berlitz?

They were trying to scare him away, but he would make them pay for Berlitz. The roof man. The singer. It might be ten or twenty years, or it might be when his own son could come back here. Such things, they wait a long time.

Right now, why am I still free?

He closed his eyes and breathed in the damp air. He opened his eyes. The rain was slackening, and the grey sky overhead was tinted with blue.

There was only one way to explain it. His critical work wasn't finished yet. Charter, Denton and this man with the dogs – they were down, but Billy Breakman was still out there.

Ivan wanted to finish his work. Now he realised that the Cambridge police wanted him to finish it too.

All along, maybe.

All along, since that stupid kid died in the shredder and the police realised the Russians were here, digging up the past.

All along, they wanted me to kill The Wake.

The plastic tunnels were beginning to steam slightly, even before the last rain had fallen. Sal had water in her hair, on her neck, her back, in her shoes. She watched the combine driver waving to the ambulance trying to make its way across the field. But she'd seen Alain de Minching's body, felt for vital signs, seen what the dogs had done.

'When did you know?' Fletcher asked her. His eyes reflected the vaporous light as he watched the ambulance.

'Just now, in the Shamblings. They were making it seem as if Berlitz had drawn his gun, when he hadn't. Webley said, *Very professional*.'

Fletcher wiped rain off his face. 'So?'

Sal went on, 'You remember what she said on Wednesday morning, in her office? When we played her Teversham's cassette? She said, *Not exactly professional*. We thought she meant the recording – that it was amateurish, the knackered old tape. But it stuck in my mind. In fact, I think she was talking to herself. She was criticising the men on the tape. She knew they were coppers. She was saying it wasn't professional for them to be discussing The Wake. She thought they should have known better, been more discreet.'

The ambulance was drawing up. Fletcher said, 'But she wasn't even *in* the Cambridge force back then. She started in Essex, everyone knows that. She told us herself.'

'Yes, she told us that.' Sal took a few breaths. 'Last night, I was dead beat when you showed me the photos from the Doomsday Book. It didn't mean anything to me until now. It didn't mean anything to you, either. Maybe it should. The photo of Ulsingham Hall with people standing around. There's an officer with her back to the camera. *Her* back, Fletcher. It's a woman constable, probably a young probationer. Maybe just transferred in from Essex. Doing what she's told. A few years later, she was smart enough to have her name torn out of the records. An officer was first on the scenes of death, yes. But I don't think it was Ron Teversham.'

Fletcher's eyes had that blue swimming-pool look. He was watching the ambulance crew staring at the situation around the combine harvester, wondering what the hell they'd found. He looked at his Airwave set and held it out to show her: perfect connection again.

He said, 'Where are the files?'

'In my car.'

'You want to keep this all covered up?'

'No. I don't think so.'

'OK, Sal. Let's leave separately.'

'Why not together?'

'In case we meet with an accident.'

Fletcher stepped back through the ripped wall, into the heat of the polythene tunnel. He felt the warmth and the scent of strawberries wrapping around him again. A few of the Chinese were still nearby, but the wounded man had gone. He walked past the hoses and the plants, back to the crossroads, and found the meal cart. The cook held out another beaker of water.

Fletcher took his time drinking this one, swirling it around in the cup, watching his own reflection. Just the outline of a man against a white background, the face invisible. Thinking back.

Sal was right: it must have been Wednesday. In the afternoon, when Webley phoned him from her office, catching him by Thinbeach Pool with the grasshoppers chirping over the bad reception. She was all for calling Fletcher off, sending in the Glockenspiel to deal with the Russians. But someone else was in the room with her, putting another point of view. Fletcher could guess what point of view it was.

Solve the whole problem.

Because the real problem was The Wake itself. The Wake was a risk getting worse as each year passed. The management said they were giving Fletcher a job to do. Fact is, they were just giving Ivan time to do his work. Giving Ivan time enough to wipe out The Wake, wipe out the only weak link going back to 1978. Who *were* the management, anyway? Commanders, Assistant Chief Constables, Vice Chancellors. Who else? Maybe Fletcher was wrong about Alain de Minching. Maybe the original idea didn't come entirely from him. Maybe it came from Jonathan Ruddick-Spenser at Ulsingham Hall.

Something Webley said: *It's important for a modern police service to be in tune with the Home Office.*

Something else: *The police are your family.*

He finished the water. He thanked the cook again, and the cook still didn't look up.

Fletcher was going to show the police family they couldn't keep this quiet. He was going to use the old files, the photos from the Doomsday Book. Everything. He had a real family now. He had Cathleen and Luke.

Cathleen.

He began running.

While Sal Moresby was changing her wheel, the sun came out in a torrent of hot light. The ground began to steam. She looked back just once, and the old church tower was pulsing with vapour. By the time she got moving she was driving in a haze, the landscape smoking against the still-dark horizon to the south.

Back at the flat, she threw clothes into a suitcase and dragged it into the hallway, parked it next to the steel box containing the files. She didn't know where she was going, but never back here. Not this flat, not this city, this job.

She went out onto the balcony for a last look. Below her, Midsummer Common was drifting with mist, and beyond the trees she could see a massive rainbow taking shape in the blue-grey sky.

The phone rang.

Steam was rising from Cambridge, blurring the glass domes of the science park, drifting off the Tarmac and the pavements of Milton Road. The sunshine on the river under Elizabeth Bridge reflected an oily spectrum of blue and green. To Fletcher, glancing out through the smashed window of the Nissan, the rainbow looked the most solid thing in the city. As he ploughed through planes of water along Mill Road, it filled the windscreen, seeming to be planted on earth down on Electric Mile.

A car had stalled in another flood beyond the railway bridge, and Fletcher left the Nissan behind. Steam was rising from the electric cables, from the steel rails he could see through the slatted gate as he ran into the alley.

He stopped.

Parked in front of the gate, out of sight of the house, was a dark blue Omega. There was damage to the bonnet and a headlamp was smashed, taped over with plastic. A man was standing beside it, looking through the gate onto the tracks. He was wearing chinos and a pressed denim shirt, smart but totally anonymous. He turned to look at Fletcher. He was in his fifties, grey hair brushed back from a lined face, alert eyes flicking around. The sky behind him was full of the rainbow, heavy blocks of colour.

'Fletcher. Take it easy.'

The man's voice was local, old-fashioned and wary.

Something was pulling at Fletcher's mind. This was the man he'd seen in the driver's seat of the Omega that night on Magdalene Bridge, but something else about him was familiar. Was there a smell, some kind of oil or tobacco?

He said, 'Who are you?'

The man shrugged. 'I'm the same as you, boy.'

Fletcher took three steps and pushed the man up against the gate, the thin steel clanging with the impact, water splashing down from the spiked top onto the man's head.

The man laughed, panting, blinking the water out of his eyes, looking up at Fletcher. 'You can do what you want, boy. Others come to take my place. Let me go now and I talk to you.'

Fletcher kept him there, looking at him, not speaking. In the man's silvery hair, the water was glistening like – what? He'd seen something recently, shiny stuff in someone's grey hair. A man about this age. Glass fragments. Glass in a man's hair, a dead man crumpled over the bonnet of a red Ford.

'Teversham. You were speaking on Teversham's recording. You were the first voice, the one who knew—'

'I told you we're the same. I'm an ex-copper and so are you now. If you had any sense, boy, you'd have left it alone when you heard the tape.'

'Webley knows you. She's using you.'

'The police are your family, Fletcher boy. You dig up family secrets, you ask for trouble. Webley's fond of you, but she knows what loyalty means. She knew there was something about you, something not right. You wouldn't tell her, but it didn't take us long to find out. Tom Fletcher's little secret.'

Fletcher pulled the man forwards and slammed his head down on the boot of the car. It echoed along the street, and the man grunted, his cheek pressed against the wet metal.

Fletcher said, 'You haven't been into this house.'

The man tried to laugh, speaking with difficulty. 'I won't need to, boy. As long as Tom Fletcher keeps the family secret, right? The day you start talking is the day we tell the kid the truth. Where he came from. Who his daddy was and what Tom Fletcher did to him.'

Fletcher looked around. He wondered for a second what Ivan would do now. Over the wet rails the train cables began to sway and flash, and above that he saw the rainbow starting to break up, the columns bleeding apart.

The man laughed again, twisting his head free. 'I told you. We're the same.'

Sal Moresby put the phone down. A twelve-minute call, the noise of trains in the background. Fletcher asking her to do something that didn't make any sense at all, until he told her why.

She picked up the file box. She went into the kitchen and found some white spirit. She went out to the balcony. Boats were out on the river again, rowers sculling, people jogging on the towpath.

She opened the box and stood looking into it: the coroner's reports, the press cuttings, the Doomsday Book. She put the album on top, standing open. The word *Memories* in gold script on the cover.

She crumpled the papers underneath, then soaked them with white spirit. She dropped in a match. The flames were blue at first, then red and yellow. The old photos made an ugly black smoke, drifting around the balcony and away in tendrils along the river. After a few minutes, the spine of the album loosened, and a few pages lifted up and broke apart, the ashes rising in grey flakes into the air.

One Month Later

In late summer, when the traffic was light in the mornings, Tom Fletcher sometimes took his car and drove out to the two hills south of Cambridge. He usually ran for an hour. He liked being on the only high ground for miles around, being able to see the city, and he liked the names the hills had: Gog and Magog.

One morning, he asked Sal Moresby to meet him up there.

They parked where the cornfields were studded with bales, the ends spiralled into fingerprints. There were still some poppies along the path. It was a clear day, with a few high clouds.

They ran without talking. He liked the sound of her breathing and the way she clenched her hands as she ran. They jogged up to the high ground where the fields were all grass, and they stopped and looked at the view. There were a few figures moving on the golf course to the west, there was a train going into Cambridge in the distance, a plane rising from the airport, the hospital chimney, and the edge of the suburbs glinting in the sun.

The other way, looking east, was an older landscape: the plateau of stubble, the long straight cutting of the

Roman road, the shine of the river, then the ancient earth mounds called Fleam Dyke and Devil's Dyke rising from the plain. The modern roads looked cheap and fragile. He could smell the scent of her hair.

She said, 'It means something, doesn't it? Gog and Magog.'

'They were two angels. They fell to earth.'

'Angels are clumsy. I'll miss you.'

'It's a great opportunity,' he said. 'Detective Inspector in Lincoln. Nice place to live.'

'I've been promoted away from trouble. They say it's a long tradition in the police.'

'You deserve it.'

She picked up a flint and threw it out across the stubble. She said, 'I've sold out, haven't I?'

'No. You've joined the family.'

'And how do *you* feel?'

He smiled. 'It's a new feeling, being on my own, out of the job. But it's not a bad feeling. I'm starting to like it.'

'What are you actually going to do? In practical terms.'

'Come back to the car. I'll show you.'

Sal studied the business card he handed her from a carton in his glovebox. It was embossed and professional-looking – she just couldn't believe what it said.

'Are you serious?'

'Completely.'

She looked at it again. *Green Street Investigation*.

'A private detective? Is that really what you want to do with your life?'

She felt angry with him, but his eyes had the old blue calm.

He said, 'I'm going to give it six months. I've turned the hallway of my flat into an office – it's big enough. It's got a desk and a floor lamp and so on. I've put in a leather sofa for clients.'

'You'll be working on shop theft and divorces. Following someone's spouse around, taking photos. I can't see you doing that.'

'Nor can I.' He smiled. 'I wasn't sure about this until I came up here to think about it. It's the view.'

'The view?'

'Think what we've just seen. There's modern Cambridge, all the colleges and research labs and development, all the rest of it. Then you look the other way, and there's the stuff that never changes.'

She looked into his eyes and felt her fingers move a millimetre.

'Explain, Fletcher.'

'What do people *really* want, Sal? Whether they're individuals or organisations? What they want is to understand their past. They're trying to escape it – or they're trying to stay loyal to it, and that's even harder. That's where I come in, when people or groups of people want to understand their history. I think there'll be a high demand for my services. Keep the card.'

It was eight a.m., and she had to go. He kissed her, the way men kiss when they're saying goodbye. She took his face in her hands and kissed him so he'd remember it all his life. Then she tried to smile.

'Just don't ever go back to Thinbeach.'

'I won't need to, Sal. There'll never be another Wedding, not without Alain. In a strange way, Ivan Gorensky's right. He thinks he's killed the Thinbeach Bride.'

'Killed the Bride? After a thousand years? Billy Breakman says she'll live for ever. You don't think *he's* right?'

Sal looked back just once as she drove away, saw her wheels kicking up earth dust. Her mirror showed Fletcher standing there by his car, staring out over the fields of stubble named after a dead angel. A man with a set of business cards and eyes the colour of chlorine.

In Portugal that summer, the sun was cruel in the afternoons. Most people who weren't British chose to stay indoors until the shadows lengthened a little, and the breeze from the Atlantic ruffled the palm trees and dusted a little sand out of the golf bunkers.

Parque da Pinta had golf. It also had two pools and a well-stocked residents' bar, a social secretary for bridge evenings, and lawns kept freshly watered by a helpful manager who spoke perfect English.

Once the sprinklers were hissing in the late afternoon, the manager had little to do except watch the sky through the smoke of his Marlboro and the slats of the office blind, the sun getting bigger and redder until it touched the horizon in a sweep of purple cloud.

A knock on the door startled him. He opened it to

find two English guys with golfing shirts and pink faces, and a gentle slipstream of sherry.

When they were all seated, one of them said, 'Look, I'm sorry,' – so the manager knew they were here to complain.

'But it's about Billy Breakman,' the other one continued. 'It's the smell from his apartment. I'm sorry, but it's completely unacceptable.'

The manager flicked some ash, and thought back.

After that neat English policewoman, old Billy had no further visitors until three days ago, when two people came to see him. They were a couple.

The woman was amazing: built like an athlete, with a face like an angel. The man looked the sort who would take on a woman like that: silent, some kind of foreign *bandido* with a scar under his chin only partly hidden by his collar.

The manager was observant, and he noticed they each wore shiny new wedding rings. The young woman was clearly proud of hers, the way she kept glancing down at her hands. Anything to do with Billy Breakman interested him, so he asked the couple if congratulations were in order.

'Are you in Portugal on honeymoon, perhaps?'

The *bandido* didn't reply.

The girl said, 'We have a delivery for Billy Breakman.'

'I can take it up myself, later on.'

'No. It's overdue already.'

After twenty minutes, they came back down and walked straight out. He watched through the blind as they drove away in a standard airport rental car.

Now the manager sighed and asked the Englishmen to wait. He unhooked Breakman's key from its peg and went up to the third floor. The smell was noticeable even from the lift, and outside his door it was simply disgusting – not the usual reek, but something rotten.

Inside the apartment, the heat and the smell formed a physical presence. The sunset was spread in bars across the chaos of junk and unwashed plates, bottles and scattered books. The manager looked around the place. Billy wasn't in the main room, nor out on the balcony or in the squalid kitchen or the bedrooms, among the discarded clothes and the drifts of dust. For a moment the manager wondered if Billy had finally left – slipped away without paying his maintenance fees.

Then he realised the smell was coming from behind the bathroom door. He screwed up his face and knocked. In answer he heard only the dripping of a tap. He pushed the door open. The red sun poured in and mixed with the strip light flickering above the sink. The manager felt his stomach heave, and tried not to retch. It wasn't just the smell now. It was Billy.

He was in the bath, fully clothed, in a pool of cloudy water beginning to spill out over the edge as his corpse expanded in the heat. He was on his back. His head was being tipped under by the rise of his swollen stomach – but his face was visible just below the surface.

The manager crossed himself. He stepped forward and peered down at the dead face. Billy's expression was hard to place. It wasn't terror, or even fear. The manager tried not to breathe, and looked closer. He decided it was almost *recognition* – as if something Billy had expected for a long time had finally come to meet him.

Outside the apartment, the manager closed the door, reached for the crucifix around his neck and kissed it. He walked back to the lift. His legs were unsteady. He looked in the mirror, and he was shaking.

He asked himself, *Como? No nome de deus, como?*

As the lift moved, he began to realise what had happened. Billy Breakman hadn't fallen in accidentally. No – *they drowned him*, that couple. One of them held Billy's face under until he died, maybe even looking into his eyes.

The manager asked himself which of them had done it.

It must have been the man. It must have been. He couldn't believe it was the girl – not with her hair falling across her face, and those long arms, and those slender fingers with the wedding ring, the last thing Billy saw on earth.

He couldn't believe it was the bride.

Acknowledgements

With thanks to my agent, Lucie Whitehouse, for some serious support, and to my editor, Nick Sayers, for some serious editing. Thanks also to the people in both Britain and Russia who gave their time to advise on different aspects of the book, and to everyone at the library in Henley. Most of all – thanks to my wife, Ruth, for everything.